Gorethria was a bizarre and beautiful country which had spawned an equally strange people. They were tall, slim, graceful, and deep purple-brown of skin; their hair was black and worn long; they dressed ornately and were beardless; and their eyes were many-coloured and brooding. They loved beauty and brilliance; they were intelligent and creative, strong willed, loyal to their country – but they were an arrogant and pitiless race.

For over a thousand years they had subjugated the entire continent once known as Vardrav, now called the Gorethrian Empire. Their almost aesthetic delight in war and bloodshed had meant that stronger but less finely-honed civilizations than theirs had fallen before their cruel armies. Their inborn ruthlessness and power of invention had kept those countries under Gorethria's dark control ever since.

A Blackbird in Silver

FREDA WARRINGTON

NEW ENGLISH LIBRARY

This book is lovingly dedicated to Mum and Dad, Mic, Lucy and Keren . . . who believed.

A New English Library Original Publication, 1985

First NEL Paperback Edition January 1986

NEL Books are published by
New English Library,
Mill Road, Dunton Green,
Sevenoaks, Kent.
Editorial office: 47 Bedford Square, London WC1B 3DP

Typeset by Rowland Phototypesetting Ltd,
Bury St Edmunds, Suffolk

Printed and bound by
Richard Clay (The Chaucer Press) Ltd, Bungay, Suffolk

British Library C.I.P.
Warrington, Freda
  A blackbird in silver.
  Bk. 1 : The quest of the serpent.
  I. Title
  823'.914[F]   PR6073.A74/

ISBN 0-450-05849-2

Contents

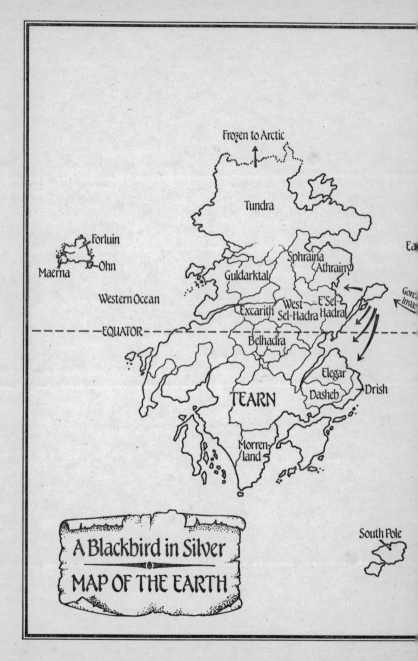

Frozen to Arctic

Tundra

Forluin
Ohn
Maerna

Sphraina
Athrainy

Guldarktal

Western Ocean

Excarith
West
Sel-Hadra

E'Sel-
Hadra

Gore
Invas

EQUATOR

Belhadra

Elegar

Dasheb

Drish

TEARN

Morren-
land

South Pole

A Blackbird in Silver

MAP OF THE EARTH

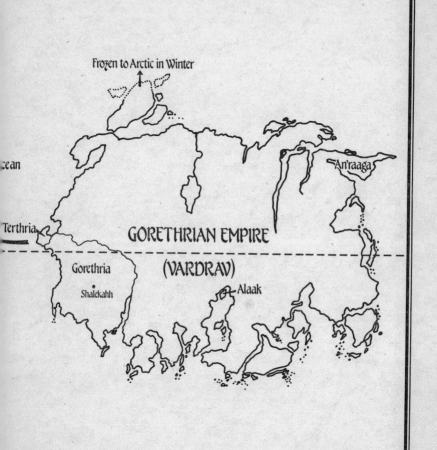

Frozen to Arctic in Winter

ean

Terthria

An'raaga

GORETHRIAN EMPIRE

(VARDRAV)

Gorethria

Shalekahh

Alaak

1

The House of Rede

In a different universe from this there is a spherical world through which circle three flat planes. The world is quite unlike ours; not so much in the nature of the two vast continents that lie on its crust, nor in the great slate-blue oceans that foam ceaselessly around their edges, nor in the two white moons that arc like twin, perfect opals across the night sky; but in the existence of the three strange planes. Each is flat and infinite, existing in its own dimension but circling round and through the Earth on its silent, mystical orbit. The White Plane Hrannekh Ol, the Black Plane Hrunnesh, the Blue Plane H'tebhmella. They are an intrinsic part of Earth and yet apart from it; they can only be reached through 'Entrance Points', invisible gates to other dimensions. But as the Planes circle, so do the Entrance Points shift and change. They are elusive, almost impossible to track and find. At the same time, as they move on their blind impassive course, they may swallow creatures unawares, trapping them in the arid White Plane or lightless Hrunnesh, with no chance of finding an equally elusive Exit Point back to Earth.

But most know little of the Planes, and nor do they care. Only the occasional traveller might glance at sun-silvered clouds blowing tattered across a crystal-blue sky, and thrill with a vague longing to find an Entrance Point to the exquisite Blue Plane H'tebhmella. Part of the Earth, untouchable as the sky. The traveller sighs and goes on.

And should our traveller be free to choose not to wend his way home, but to skim at speed above the Earth's surface, he would see spread below him the great Western continent of Tearn. There landscapes of hills and rivers, forests and cities lie in rich profusion, a chaotic tapestry of brown, green, grey and silver. The countries there are anarchic and disunited, containing a great diversity of peoples and many wonders of nature.

Leaving Tearn and speeding across the Western Ocean, the traveller perhaps glimpses isolated green islands to the North: Forluin, Maerna and Ohn, where there lives a gentle, fair race. But the isles are small and insignificant, quickly forgotten as the coast of the Eastern continent approaches. Its name is Vardrav, though it is more usually called the Gorethrian Empire. It is a vast, exotic land of purple mountains fringed by lush emerald jungles; deserts of burning gold and torrential white rivers; vistas of black volcanoes edged with red fire. Many races live there, proud, fierce and warlike yet all unable to break free from subjugation by one powerful nation. This terrible country on the Western coast of Vardrav is Gorethria, shimmering like a black opal under torn violet and orange skies.

Turning North, the traveller arcs towards the frozen ocean on the roof of the world. The North Pole is a merciless domain of snowfields, glaciers, biting storms and avalanches. Yet unexpected forests spring up there, unexpected creatures erupt from the ground, crawl on the snow for a while, and burrow again. Weird fires and lights hover on the horizon. Few venture there. That anything inhabits the North Pole is only a myth, our traveller knows; but still nothing would induce him to pause and verify what he may have glimpsed. Faster than ever he continues his swift circuit of the Earth towards the South Pole.

The tiny Antarctic continent is mountainous and barren, a cold, harsh land where the dull terrain is streaked with snow and darkness falls for six months at a time. The traveller would not guess that anyone lives in this unwelcoming land, still less that they receive a steady trickle of visitors from all parts of the world throughout the year. But at the Pole a small valley drops unexpectedly between brown bluffs of rock with granite buttresses leaping up from them into massive hills. A spring runs from a rock near the top of the concealed valley, becoming a flat silver stream that bubbles into little cataracts of white foam where it hits a rock here, an inlet there. Some hardy trees fringe the water, their bronzes and browns melting into a faint mist that persists around the stream and the dark rocks. And on the bank a shadowy shape can be seen, something so old that it seems to have fused with the rocks, or even grown out of them. Cupped in the valley, at the very South Pole, stands an ancient house. It is built of stone and it is square and unadorned; it is two-storeyed, with a sloping slate roof and many windows. In the light season, people sit round its door and on the stream's bank, while others come and go on foot or on horseback. In the dark season, its windows flicker eternally with gold and yellow and red firelight, welcoming guests from the icy hills. If our imaginary traveller could choose to stay here, he would.

It is a house where the weary come for rest, where wise men come to argue philosophy and science, where the uncertain come for advice, and where champions come to find companions in their causes. Its keeper is reputedly the oldest man on Earth; his name is Eldor.

He has never given his house a name, but it has come to be called the House of Rede.

On the night on which the Quest of the Serpent was begun, the light season was drawing to its close. A greyish twilight was on the hills, turning the snow patches to splashes of luminous white, while the valley deepened to shades of slate-grey, agate, dark silver and black. The square shadow that was the House melted back into the bluffs, but its windows shone as squares of gold. A solitary horseman cloaked in black heard the clatter of a mounted party echoing on the hills behind him and spurred his horse to a canter to avoid having to ride with company.

He rode down a narrow pass between steep rock walls, until at length he was crossing the valley floor. He dismounted, tethering his horse where the groom would find and attend to it. At the heavy oak door he paused, fingering a chain of fine steel that hung round his neck. He drew the black hood of his cloak over his strangely-fashioned helm, placed one long-fingered dark hand on his sword hilt, and entered.

Within the large stone porch, a woman greeted him. She was silver-haired but unbowed by age, her tall form clad in a long grey robe with a sleeveless tabard of white wool over it. She was Dritha, Eldor's wife.

'Welcome to our house. It is cold on the hills, but you will find it warm in the hall. Can I take your cloak?' she asked.

'No, thank you,' the man replied shortly. He looked around the porch at the torches flickering on the walls, drawing a soft glow from the dull grey stone. 'I hope I shall not be staying long.'

'Have you come a long way?' Dritha asked, her keen, ancient

eyes giving the feeling that she knew everything about him. He was tall and thin, but his face was hidden by the hood.

'Aye, a very long way,' he said grimly. 'Is Eldor here? Can I see him?'

'He is at table, but if you go in, he will come to you as soon as he sees you.' The thin warrior did not reply, but continued to stare at her. 'If you would prefer to wait in private—' she began, but at that moment the mounted party rode talking and laughing past the door.

'No. It doesn't matter,' he said, making for the great wooden door of the hall. The riders were nothing to do with him and he did not wish to have even the slightest contact with them. Turning abruptly away from Dritha he entered the hall where he could become anonymous among the other guests.

With a bitter smile he reflected that anonymity was something he had forfeited long ago. That was a price paid for being feared and loathed the world over.

The dining hall was a large room, brightly lit by two great fires and many torches and candles. Its centre was dominated by a long table at which a disorganised meal was taking place. About thirty people were seated along the benches, though there was room for many more. The warrior did not join them but seated himself in a dark corner next to one of the great fireplaces. From there he studied the assembled guests.

At the head of the table sat Eldor himself, discussing various metaphysical matters with the four sages gathered around him. There were always scholars of some description at the House of Rede. Then there were about fifteen or so sailors, big, pale men typical of Morrenland in Southern Tearn, their blue leggings, tunics and short cloaks bleached almost white by salt. They were jovial and rowdy, frequently calling out for more bread, beer and wine. Two women and a young man were waiting at table, their long robes showing that they were members of Eldor's household.

Further down the table, to the warrior's surprise, were five Forluinish people, three men and two women. He had never seen anyone from Forluin before – they were reputed to leave their land very rarely – but even by word of mouth they were unmistakeable. They had an aura, an extreme beauty and a gentle grace of movement that set them apart. They spoke little but sat very close together, as if they were one person, not five.

12

At the very end of the table, nearest to the warrior, was a woman sitting alone. She was white-faced and black-haired, her small and slender form clad in travel-worn riding clothes of dark grey. There was an air of isolation and misery about her, and her expression was very grim.

A servant came by and offered the warrior a goblet of wine. No one else seemed to have noticed him. He sat quietly, twisting the goblet between his fingers. It was of a curious design. The stem was the body of a serpent carved in silver, with a gaping mouth; and in its fangs it held the cup, which was in the form of a human head, with face twisted into such fearful agony that it was impossible to tell whether it was male or female. A serpent swallowing a human head. Very pleasant, thought the warrior, and drained the wine at one gulp.

He was beginning to doubt the wisdom of coming into the hall, and wished he had waited in private as Dritha had suggested. He was exhausted, world-weary . . . why had he come here at all? He watched as one of the Forluinish women, a silver-fair girl, leaned forward and addressed a few words to the solitary black-haired woman. Her attempt at friendliness was ignored. The warrior's depression deepened; the Forluinish had a reputation as the gentlest, most joyful and laughter-loving race on Earth, but there was an air of despondency about them that seemed to cloak the whole room. They disturbed him; the woman disturbed him. He began to think that the best idea was to return to the hired ship that had brought him here, and set sail at once.

Then Eldor noticed him, and gave a nod and a small sign of greeting. But he made no move to come over to the warrior, because a loud discussion had broken out among the Morrenish sailors and this now commanded his attention.

'—so, Master Eldor, we tacked about and came straight here,' one of the sailors was saying, raising his voice above the argument of the others.

'It was a stupid impulse. The Captain panicked. These things happen,' said another sourly.

'These things do not just happen! Ships do not just vanish!' the first exclaimed, but Eldor stood up and raised a hand to quiet them. He was a tall and solidly-built man, the contours of his massive frame softened by a long, shapeless white robe tied in with a cord at the waist. His old face, with its high forehead and broad nose, had a weather-beaten, dauntless look like a sky that remains untroubled by any number of storms. It was framed by dishevelled white hair and a beard, and his grey eyes had the same shrewd and kindly expression as his wife's. When he spoke, everyone listened.

'So, you say that you were accompanying a merchant ship around the coast of Morrenland – and that ship vanished before your eyes, and could not have sunk?'

'It might have sunk. It was a long way ahead of our vessel,' said the second sailor morosely.

'It did not sink!' insisted the first.

'All the same, I say it was a complete waste of time coming to the House of Rede—' the argument began again, but Eldor silenced them.

'Please. You are both right; these things do happen, and ships may be lost without sinking. What happened is that the ship encountered an Entrance Point, and passed through to one of the Planes. It is a tragedy, but there is absolutely nothing you or I can do about it; that is all I can tell you. So, perhaps you have wasted your time in coming here.'

'Not at all. Your hospitality has made the journey well worth it,' one of the other sailors put in, and the rest laughed.

'Is that all you can say, Master Eldor?' the first persisted. 'Well, I still say there's more to it. Everyone insists that the Serpent M'gulfn does not exist, but in Morrenland we have a different tradition.'

'Oh, shut up, can't you. Have some more wine,' muttered one of the other sailors, but the man continued more determinedly.

'We know it does exist, thanks to a monarch of several hundred years ago who had the arrogance to try and slay it. There's a nautical belief that the Serpent causes adverse weather conditions. It's treated more as a joke in these days; but I think there's truth behind it. Couldn't the Serpent have had something to do with that ship's disappearance?'

The warrior sat forward, eagerly awaiting the answer. One of the Forluinishmen had put his head in his hands, and the silver-haired woman was doing her best to comfort him. But Eldor hesitated, looked apologetic, and said lamely, 'On that I cannot comment. It's very unlikely – most unlikely.'

The warrior sat back, angered. Was this all the great, wise Eldor had to offer? Disgusted, he cast the empty goblet aside and made his way to the door.

14

Immediately Eldor pushed back his chair and strode past the long table to intercept him.

'Prince Ashurek,' said the sage, staying his hand from the latch. 'Forgive that unfortunate interruption; please, do not leave until we have had a chance to talk.'

The warrior stared at him. 'Is my identity so obvious?'

'I have been expecting you. Won't you come and sit down again?'

Sighing, Ashurek returned to his place near the hearth, and Eldor sat beside him. Noticing that they were now receiving uneasy glances from the other guests, the warrior said, 'Listen, if you would rather I did not stay, I will leave at once. I was told to come here for advice, but it does not matter; I do not want there to be any trouble.'

'I know there are those who will object to your presence, but all are welcome in my house. You have some necessary business to conduct, and until it is finished I'll see you are left in peace – as my guest,' the sage replied cheerfully.

'My thanks, Master Eldor.'

'And when you say your need for advice "doesn't matter", I fear that, in fact, what I said a moment since has convinced you that I am unable to give you advice of any kind whatsoever.'

'Yes, that is so,' said the warrior with a grin. 'It's because of the damned Serpent that I am here. So you understand, if you "cannot comment" upon the Worm, Eldor, I might as well be on my way. The sooner I begin the better.'

'Because you are determined to destroy the Serpent,' Eldor stated. Ashurek looked at him with surprise.

'You were expecting me – and you also know that? Then it's true that you are the all-seeing, all-knowing sage?' he said sardonically.

'Not exactly,' the old man chuckled. 'Sometimes events have a certain inevitability. You will have to fill in the details of your story for me.'

Ashurek hesitated, then proceeded to relate, very briefly, the reasons for his visit. When he had finished, Eldor paused a few moments to take in what he had said. Then he nodded gravely.

'You were right to come to me, Ashurek; your journey has not been wasted. There are two others here who also wish to slay the Worm. They will be your companions on the Quest. I'll introduce you shortly, and then we shall talk of the Serpent and the need for its death.'

This pronouncement so astonished Ashurek that he was speechless for several seconds.

'Silvren was right. How could I have doubted her?' he muttered at last. At that moment the mounted party who had followed him to the House entered, having stabled their horses. There were four of them, not newcomers but other members of the Morrenish crew, who had been back to the ship on an errand. Now they were no longer laughing, but decidedly agitated.

A rough-looking, abrupt man who appeared to be the Captain cried out over the murmur of voices, 'Did anyone know that there's a Gorethrian horse in the stable?'

There was silence, then a few faint exclamations of disbelief from his sailors.

'A vicious-looking beast, looks as if it's made of gold metal – it's unmistakable. Go and look if ye don't believe me!' The Captain looked round the room. 'Where is its rider?' His eyes alighted on the warrior who remained sitting, legs stretched out, appearing quite relaxed. 'What is this – is this continent now part of the Gorethrian Empire?'

The warrior put back his hood, revealing a helm of black metal, fashioned into the shape of a creature with outstretched wings and a hawk's head. The face beneath it was thin, with high cheekbones, long nose, and a grimly-set mouth. The skin was a sheeny purple-brown, and the eyes were of a moody, glaring green. He stared coldly at the sea-captain until the man became disconcerted; for however much they might despise all Gorethrians, even fighting men held them in a certain amount of terror.

'I don't wish there to be any trouble. I'll leave, sooner than let my presence upset you,' the warrior said at last. There was a murmuring from all the guests.

'All of us against one Gorethrian! Why do you hesitate to kill him? Are you a coward?' shouted one of the sailors, made brave by too much wine.

The Captain was breathing heavily, his mouth twisted with anger and indecision. His hand was on his sword hilt.

'If you wish to fight, please go outside,' came Eldor's authoritative voice. 'But the Gorethrian is my guest, and as such, I'd thank you to treat him politely.'

'Damn it,' the Captain expostulated. 'My crewman is right. It is coward's work to attack, so many against one. Perhaps later – outside.'

'There will be no fight,' Ashurek stated coldly. Finally, quite disconcerted by him, the Captain and the other three men turned away and went to sit with their fellows at the table. The atmosphere was heavy with their fear and frustrated anger.

Eldor sighed.

'Perhaps it is best that you meet your companions now, before another such scene ensues,' he said.

'It is only to be expected; it means nothing to me,' said Ashurek with a somewhat bitter smile. 'However, I am in some haste to glean whatever knowledge and help I can here, so I put myself at your command.'

'Good,' said the sage cheerfully. 'We'll go to the kitchen; we can be private there, and warm. Dritha will show you the way, while I fetch the others.'

Ashurek left the hall and Dritha led him to a square room with a heavy oak table in the middle. The air was warm and steamy from the preparation of food.

Dritha left, taking the four kitchen maids with her. Now alone, Ashurek sat down at the table and removed the metal helm from his unkempt black hair. He reflected on the easy familiarity with which she and Eldor treated him, even though they were complete strangers. There was an odd kind of comfort in it; since the loss of his family there was only one who had not approached him with aggression, fear, subservience, or a combination of those. Now she was lost also . . .

After a few minutes Eldor entered with the five Forluinish folk. They all had long shining hair, and their clothes, though simple and of drab blues, greys and browns, took on the graceful, flowing lines of their slender forms. The aura of beauty and sorrow about them was tangible, and utterly alien to Ashurek.

Behind them came the dark-haired woman, automatically keeping her distance, her face as expressionless as white stone.

'Do sit down,' Eldor said to them. 'Are there enough chairs? Good. Perhaps I can persuade you all to take a glass of warm mead . . .' No one spoke. The lone woman seated herself next to Ashurek. Facing them were the silver-haired Forluinish girl and a dark-haired man. At the bottom of the table a woman with chestnut hair sat with her fair-headed male companion; and at the top a brown-haired man sat next to Eldor's empty chair. The sage, meanwhile, was busying himself at the long fire hearth with goblets and a stoneware jug, apparently oblivious to the uneasy silence of his guests. In his cheerful, unhurried way he served them each a vessel of mead, and provided a plate of honeyed cakes which remained untouched.

Then, at last, he sat down to talk to them.

Who Eldor was, or where he came from, no one seemed to know. There were various theories, the least outrageous of which was that he was the first man on Earth, and had fled to the South Pole to escape the growing madness of mankind. There, all-knowing, he gave freely of his wisdom to help men as best he could. As little was known of Dritha, who had always been with him. Yet no one, least of all Eldor, would provide a true history; and so he had become a living legend. The most ancient books preserved mentioned him. But of himself he would not speak, and it was an unwritten rule that no one should question him. His domain was neutral, inviolable, a place of refuge, and all accepted that.

'Now,' the sage began, pulling back the loose sleeves of his robe and resting his arms on the table, 'you have all come here with the same purpose in mind, though perhaps for very different reasons. I am here not to investigate your motives, but to give what help and advice I am able. You have embarked upon a very grave and serious mission, to destroy the Serpent M'gulfn.'

Ashurek saw the distracted glance the young silver-haired Forluinish woman gave to the dark-haired man at her side. He took her hand. The white-faced woman was staring fixedly at a knot in the table as if she were wishing herself somewhere, anywhere, else.

'Now the Worm is, according to legend, the source and channel of many evils in this world; you are taking a great task upon yourselves to destroy evil—'

'Will our efforts be wasted?' the dark-haired man broke in, a beseeching note in his voice. 'At every turn we are told the Serpent cannot be destroyed, so – what use is it?'

Eldor paused as if pondering how to phrase a complicated answer in clear terms.

'The Worm is a power that holds sway over our Earth. Can such a thing be destroyed? I do not know. Perhaps you will fail. But I do know that your Quest must take place, for there are vaster powers beyond the Serpent—' The young Forluinishman looked lost, and Eldor stopped, shaking his grey head. 'Even if I told you it was useless, would it discourage you from going? No; and even I cannot swear that there is no hope at all. Be assured there is some, however little. But to begin,' he went on gravely, 'would one of you recount, as you did to me, what has happened in Forluin? Falin?'

The Forluinishman next to him, possessed of a fine-boned, gentle face and curling brown hair, looked bleakly across at the warrior and the grim-faced woman. He was the one who had been distressed when the Morrenish sailor mentioned the Serpent.

'The Serpent attacked Forluin,' he said abruptly. Drawing a breath he continued, 'You do not know our land, I imagine—'

'No, but its pastoral gentility is much envied throughout the world,' said the Gorethrian with a touch of irony.

'Envied, oh,' the man muttered, lowering his head and shuddering. 'For no reason we can comprehend, several months ago the Worm left its home in the Arctic snows and flew South to Forluin. It came like a whirlwind of death upon us, flying low and slavering a searing grey fluid which burnt our farmlands and laid low our forests. It settled its long body, which was a loathsome, indescribable colour, on our land, spreading disease; and then it took to the air again, seizing many people and animals in its maw, chewing them and drooling the blood of our friends and families down upon those of us that it left. Eventually it flew North once more, though the stench of it hung over our land in a foul cloud for many days. Much of Forluin is smoking, diseased ash; few escaped without losing parents, or children, or loved ones. I watched it seize my mother—' tears choked him, and he said, 'Arlena, please finish for me.'

'When those of us that were left gathered together,' said the girl with the bright silver hair, 'a Lady of the Blue Plane responded to our sorrow – she came through an Entrance Point, weeping when she saw what the Worm had done. We were all for forming an army – this after thousands of years of peace – and going North to destroy it. But she said we must send a party to the House of Rede for help, and select just one Forluinishman to go with the companions he would find here. And that the H'tebhmellians would provide a small ship to take them to the Blue Plane, where they would be given help in the Quest . . .' her voice was very even as she finished, although tears coursed down her face. 'But it has taken us months aboard an ordinary ship to sail here and we do not know what is happening in Forluin. Perhaps with our herbal arts, all the diseases have been cured, and there is green growing through the ashes; or perhaps where Maerna and Forluin and the islands were, there is nothing.'

A strangling coldness crept over Ashurek as he listened. For the Serpent to him had always been remote, only a symbol of evil. Now, even though he had purposed to destroy it, to hear of its actual existence and the horrible physical reality of it was an unexpected shock. But his face betrayed nothing; neither he nor the solitary woman spoke or reacted at all to this news.

'Well,' said the third man, who had sea-bleached fair hair, 'now you know about us; what of you?'

'I was sent upon this Quest on behalf of one who cannot fulfil it herself . . .' Ashurek answered vaguely. The fact that the Forluinish seemed to have no idea who he was disconcerted him; the hatred of the Morrenish was easier to deal with. But Forluin was so cut off from world affairs, it was only to be expected. 'Which of you has been assigned to this Quest?'

'By mutual agreement, it is I who am going,' the dark-haired man who had voiced doubts about the expedition replied. 'My name is Estarinel.' His face was clear-featured, beautiful, fair of skin and dark of eye. His black hair was long and curly and he was clad in a tunic and breeches of dark blue linen, with a white muslin shirt.

'And I am Ashurek of Gorethria,' said the warrior.

There was a silence. The five Forluinish stared at him; Arlena went white and muttered, 'Oh ye gods.' The dark-haired woman continued to stare at the table as if this horrific revelation meant nothing to her. Eldor merely maintained a serene expression, determined not to influence the proceedings.

Brother of the Emperor Meshurek, High Commander of the Gorethrian armies and navies, murderer, ravager of countries, loathed miscreant, and – so some thought – demon incarnate was Ashurek, Prince of Gorethria. Even the isolated Forluinish knew who he was, all his evil misdeeds. Unexpectedly confronted by the most feared and hated man in the world, it was impossible to find anything to say.

Eventually Ashurek spoke.

'I would only say that I no longer have any connection with Gorethria. I do this for myself, and one other. I understand how

20

you feel; it may well be the best for all of us if I pursue the Quest alone.' His green eyes shone very bright and cold in his dark face.

Falin, Arlena, and the other two – the fair man and the chestnut-haired woman – looked at Estarinel with a sort of stunned relief. But Estarinel continued staring at the Gorethrian. His brown eyes were thoughtful rather than full of fear.

'Wait,' he said. 'We've been told that we must go to the Blue Plane before we even consider setting out after the Serpent. Without the H'tebhmellian ship you'll stand little chance of getting there.'

'I know,' said Ashurek, looking levelly back at him. 'I have been trying to reach the Blue Plane for years. Eldor was my last hope. But it is entirely up to you.'

'We had better go together, then,' the Forluinishman said quietly.

'E'rinel, you can't!' exclaimed Arlena, clutching his hand.

But he replied, 'I can't judge you on hearsay. The H'tebhmellians sent us here to find companions, and since it is you we have met, fate must bind us together. I trust the H'tebhmellians and I trust Eldor. We share an enemy in the Serpent, do we not?' He sounded hopeful rather than confident.

'Yes,' agreed Ashurek. 'That is very true.'

'What Estarinel says makes perfect sense,' Eldor put in to reassure the stricken Forluinish. 'If, Ashurek, you would explain to them what you told me earlier, they might view things in a different light.'

'I doubt it, Eldor,' he sighed. 'I will explain, but only to Estarinel. Not his companions.' And he reached across the table and shook hands, unsmilingly, with the Forluinishman.

'Good,' said Eldor. 'And now, my dear, will you introduce yourself?' He indicated the small, slim woman who so far had not uttered a word. Now she looked up at last. She was young and yet it seemed she had experienced suffering far beyond her years. Her long, ebony-coloured hair accentuated the extreme paleness of her face, and there was something in her large, dark grey eyes that no one could look into them for long.

'My Quest is also to destroy the Serpent M'gulfn, and I must seek a way to the Blue Plane,' she said in a quiet, toneless voice. Estarinel reached out to shake her hand and her fingers were like ice. 'I am Medrian – of Alaak.'

Estarinel had never heard of Alaak, but Ashurek knew it only too well. It was a small island belonging to the Gorethrian Empire, and the Alaakians were Gorethria's bitterest enemies.

He looked round at her and said sharply, 'Might we know your reason for wanting to set out upon this Quest?'

'I have just told you,' she said in the same flat voice, not meeting his gaze.

'You've told us nothing,' he said harshly.

'Please,' Eldor intervened. 'There is time enough for the three of you to resolve your differences. Now, listen to me: your meeting here may have led you to think that the Quest of the Serpent was in some way pre-ordained, but it is not so. There is no such thing as pre-ordination; it is merely that the time for the Quest is now ripe. It has become inevitable. Remember that you share an enemy, not just with each other but with all mankind; even the world itself.'

'You make it sound very simple, Eldor,' said Ashurek. 'I am sure there is far more to it . . .'

'There is a simple and a complex way of viewing most things,' Eldor said with a rueful smile. 'I have discovered the simplest view to be the wisest, in most cases. Begin with that, and it will continue to guide you through the heaviest onslaught of complexities.'

'I find you very ambiguous,' said the Gorethrian, glaring at him.

'Whichever way you wish to take it,' said the sage with a good-humoured shrug of his great shoulders. 'Now, to practical matters. The H'tebhmellian ship should arrive in some twelve hours' time. I suggest that the three of you now be left alone to become better acquainted. Then you must take as much rest as you can before commencing your journey.'

Refusing to be drawn into any further discussion, Eldor rose and motioned Estarinel's four friends to follow him from the room. They all looked at Estarinel anxiously as they left, and he continued to stare uneasily at the door after Eldor had shut it behind them. Now the three were alone at the table.

Ashurek stared broodingly across the kitchen. He was still not sure that he had been right to come to the House of Rede. There was the H'tebhmellian ship, it was true . . . but Eldor had said so little, and he was disconcerted by the two people he was expected to travel with. Instinctively he felt he would be stronger alone. Estarinel at least had a genuine motive for wanting to destroy the

Serpent; but the Forluinish were a gentle, peaceful people with little knowledge of travel, and none at all of war. No amount of fervency could make up for inexperience and cowardice, he thought. As for Medrian, no one could have more reason for loathing him than an Alaakian, yet she gave every appearance of not caring who he was. He did not trust her. His only recourse was to confront her.

He turned to her and said, 'How can you, an Alaakian, consider going on a Quest with any Gorethrian, let alone me?'

She looked up, her shadowy eyes meeting his. He had to resist an impulse to avoid her gaze.

'It was a long time ago,' she said thinly. 'Eight years; nearer nine.'

'So time excuses patriotism?' he demanded sharply.

'Apparently.' The merest hint of a cold smile touched her face.

Ashurek let out a slow breath.

'Well, as I said, the Gorethrians are now my enemies also.' The sardonic note in his voice had been replaced by regret. 'I just want to be sure that we can ignore enmities between our countries for the duration of the Quest.'

'Then be assured. I no longer care about Gorethria . . . I don't care about anything, except this Quest,' Medrian said in the same faint, icy tone.

Estarinel witnessed this exchange with increasing foreboding. He did not know what he had expected to find at the House of Rede; certainly he had not expected these two cold strangers, who apparently hated each other on sight. He longed for the warm companionship of his friends. He was acutely aware that in some twelve hours' time he would be truly severed from them, perhaps never to see them again. Had he been rash in agreeing to travel with Ashurek? Perhaps his Forluinish instinct to trust and befriend strangers had betrayed him already. He began to feel less and less fitted for the Quest, more and more uncertain of himself.

'Listen,' he began. 'We three are now committed to undertake a journey together. We must learn something of each other, understand each other's motives so that . . .' he trailed off as he saw the dangerous narrowing of Ashurek's eyes and the even bleaker cold of Medrian's.

'Very well,' said the Gorethrian. 'You are right, of course. I said I would explain myself to you. But tell us of Forluin first; then I will relate my story, and then it will be Medrian's turn . . .'

So Estarinel repeated the sad story in full to the two, who had previously heard of his country only as a distant and perhaps fabulous green land, of no importance in world affairs. And as he spoke he saw not the dark and the pale faces before him, or the recesses of Eldor's kitchen, but the land he had recently left and perhaps lost forever.

2

The Coming of the Worm

Forluin, Maerna and Ohn were lands of legend, half-forgotten by the rest of the world. Few foreigners ever went there, and those who did tended not to return. For Forluin was indeed a place of beauty and peace, and so remote from any other land that even the voracious Gorethrians had never made the long sea-voyage to conquer it. Tearnians tended to regard it with a faint awe and longing, whereas those of the Gorethrian Empire dismissed it as a country of cowardly farmers and peasants, barely worth invasion. Yet there was more, which none would admit: that Forluin and its neighbours were somehow protected by enchantment. Their very names seemed to induce a dream-like apathy which washed away any idea of making war upon the lands, or even visiting them. And this, it was whispered, was because of their enigmatic connections with the Blue Plane H'tebhmella.

The Forluinish themselves rarely ventured from their country, except for the occasional horse-trading expedition to An'raaga, the nearest tip of the Gorethrian continent, or visits to the more hospitable parts of Tearn. Those that met the Forluinish spoke warmly of their beauty and gentleness of character, too warmly the listeners might think. So it was that these gentle people were regarded with a mixture of jealousy, awe, fear and scorn by the rest of the world. Of these opinions the Forluinish knew nothing, which was as well, for all were misplaced.

So Estarinel, as he recounted the dreadful day of the Serpent, was quite innocent of what preconceived ideas Medrian and Ashurek might have of him. He was thinking only of the long green curve of the hill on which he had sat, watching the distant river that led to the sea, on the morning of that day.

Before him, miles of green fell away; fields, woods, hills and vales, until at last there was a thin streak of silver that was the river. Behind him, the hill sloped gently into a flower-filled meadow on which horses grazed, and which was fringed by trees in the fresh, green raiment of summer. A few yards away his own horse, Shaell, grazed. He was a heavy, powerful stallion, whose coat looked grey in some lights and rich brown in others; but in the early sunlight that flooded everything, he shone a cobweb silver.

A young man with long, brown hair, also dressed in a white linen shirt and blue breeches, walked up the hill to where Estarinel sat.

'Morning, E'rinel. We thought we'd have some breakfast and then ride home.' The previous day a party of four of them had brought a herd of some twenty young horses to this farm, half a day's ride West of their own lands. 'What are you looking at?'

'The river. Don't you know there's a ship due from An'raaga any day?'

'Yes, I do,' said the man, Falin, 'and if you can see it from here you must have the eyes of an eagle!'

'Just a vivid imagination! I had half a mind to ride down and wait for it . . . we asked them to bring us a Gorethrian war-horse, if they could.'

'Oh I see,' said Falin. He lay down on his stomach, propping his head in his hands, and commented on the beauty of the view.

Perhaps once a year a Forluinish crew would make the long voyage to An'raaga, a small country semi-independent of Gorethria, and exchange some of their indigenous heavy-horses for other breeds. Many disapproved of this practice, saying that even such a tenuous connection with Gorethria was dangerous. Others were afraid that their great, gentle silver-brown animals would be used in battle in the Empire. But the trading went on; apart from the farming of sheep and crops necessary for survival, horse-breeding was one of their main loves.

'We could eat breakfast up here,' Falin suggested. 'Do you think they really will bring a Gorethrian horse? It'll be the first one . . .'

'I wondered if there might be some prejudice against them, as if they were not innocent of the actions of their masters,' Estarinel grinned. 'Mother really needs a pair, she's got ideas of breeding them.' He rolled up his sleeves as the sun grew warmer. 'I dreamed we had one last night but it was *blue* with a gold mane and tail!' They both laughed. Estarinel closed his eyes, trying to remember the dream. 'I also dreamed about a woman . . .'

'Dreaming about them! That sounds serious! What was she like?'

'Not Forluinish . . . what nationality have very pale faces and jet black hair?'

'I don't know. You could look it up in a book, along with where blue horses come from.' Falin suddenly ceased teasing and said, 'I don't trust your dreams – remember you dreamed that your mother bred a *black* heavy-horse, and that spring one was born?'

'Don't remind me – the one I had last night was more a nightmare and I wish I hadn't thought of it! I wonder what Farmer Taer'nel puts in his wine?'

Falin grinned, shaking his head. He plucked aimlessly at a few blades of grass and after a minute said quietly, 'When's your sister going to agree to marry me?'

Estarinel looked round at him.

'Which one?' he said.

'Oh, very funny. The one who wants to gallivant off to Ohn to learn book-binding. Arlena, remember her?'

'I really think you'd better ask her, not me,' Estarinel said, laughing.

'Yes, but – sometimes I can't be sure how she really feels. I thought perhaps she might confide in you . . .'

'Well, if you want to know the truth . . .' he paused and Falin began to look anxious. 'She is far more fond of you than you realise. She loves you, but she hides her feelings. She won't admit she's afraid you'll find someone else while she's away.'

'I wouldn't, but she might,' he groaned. 'If only I could go with her!'

'Why don't you? If you both continue to be so reticent, you've only yourselves to blame.' Estarinel grinned. 'Falin, ask her. She'd like nothing better, I know.' Falin's eyes brightened.

'If only my parents can spare me on the farm for a few months.'

'That can be arranged – I can always help them out.'

Delighted, Falin thanked his friend profusely.

'I can't say I see the attraction of book-binding to someone who prefers to spend most of her time careering about on horseback,' he added with a wry smile.

'Oh, Arlena's always loved books. She has a plan to start a library in the village – I think it's an excellent idea. She says she is sure to receive loose manuscripts, or ancient books falling out of their covers – so all good librarians must know how to bind.'

'I suppose she'll make me learn as well! But I think I'll stick to farming . . . and horse-breeding for you, eh?'

'It seems to be what I'm best at,' Estarinel agreed.

'Do you think you'll continue your mother's tradition of experimenting with other breeds?'

'Oh, I don't know,' he said, looking across at his fine stallion, Shaell. 'The Forest ponies and the idea of Gorethrian horses are all very well . . . but I'll always like the heavies best of all.'

'You'll need someone to help you,' said Falin cryptically.

'What's this – a hint that I should be getting married as well?'

'You and Lilithea seem very close; I only wondered . . .'

'Oh, nonsense! We've been like that since childhood – just like brother and sister, really.'

'She's very fond of you—' Falin began, then abruptly thought better of what he had been about to say. If Estarinel knew that Lilithea saw him as rather more than a brother – well, he did not want to be responsible for the sudden shattering of her hopes. 'Here comes breakfast,' he said, pointing to three figures approaching them up the hill.

Estarinel laughed.

'Good. By the way, about your trip with Arlena – while you're there you might bring us one of those bay Forest ponies the Ohnians have. Mother needs a good, sound mare.'

'Of course,' Falin answered cheerfully. 'What else are friends for?'

Estarinel remembered every detail of the morning, the last normal morning there had been. He could not have conceived that Arlena would never go to Ohn to learn a craft, or that she and Falin would never marry; or that his other sister Lothwyn, 'the little dark one' as people called her, would never teach her weaving skills to the village children, as she had planned; that his mother would never raise another crop of foals, nor his father lambs.

The two women who made up their party – Falin's sister, Sinmiel, and Lilithea, who was Estarinel's neighbour – and Farmer Taer'nel who had traded some fifty sheep for the horses, joined them on the flower-laden hill. There they sat until the sun was high in the sky – no clock ruled them – eating a leisurely breakfast and appreciating the beauty of the land, and the good and bad points of the horses they had brought.

At mid-day the party of four riders bade farewell to the farmer and wound their way home through the beautiful fields of Forluin, herding some fifty sheep before them. By mid-afternoon they came in sight of the farm of Estarinel's parents.

Set in a bowl-shaped green valley, the farmhouse was built of ancient grey stone, so encrusted with climbing plants it appeared to have grown from the earth on which it stood. Vegetable gardens surrounded it, and then meadows in which mares grazed, tails flicking lazily.

He saw his father – a dark-haired man who looked not much older than Estarinel himself – look up from his cabbage-hoeing and wave to them. He returned the greeting. As they rode up to the house, his mother came out to meet them.

She was a beautiful woman, fair hair tied loosely in a long skein, and amber eyes full of warm delight at seeing them. She wore a rough muslin shirt over brown riding breeches – Forluinish clothes being always practical and unpretentious.

'You can leave the sheep in the home paddock for now, my dears,' she said. 'Will you not all stay for supper?'

'It's very kind, Filmorwen,' smiled Falin's fair-haired sister, Sinmiel, 'but we did promise father we'd take our share of the sheep home as soon as we got back.'

'Oh, doesn't he trust you?' Filmorwen laughed.

'No. He's a very wise man,' said Falin. 'But look – why don't you all come to our house, say an hour before sunset? Arlena and Lothwyn too?'

They agreed to this, the sheep were shared out, and Falin and Sinmiel set off along the long wooded path to their own farm.

'I also must go home,' said their neighbour, Lilithea, 'a man from the village is bringing me some seedlings and I am afraid I will miss him.'

'I'll walk up with you,' said Estarinel. Lilithea lived in a tiny cottage on the rim of the valley, where she had a vast herb garden. She was a quiet and sweet-natured girl, small, pretty and slim with an abundance of long, rich bronze-brown hair. She had lived there since she was about six; four years ago her parents had moved to the South of Forluin but she had stayed on alone, having become the village's most valued and dearly-loved healer. She had a secretive quality about her that Estarinel thought was almost mystical, as if no one could ever really say they knew her well. Still, as he had said to Falin, she was like a sister to him.

As they walked up the valley – both on foot, she leading her horse – Estarinel's sister, Arlena, came cantering down towards them on her brown cob.

Seeing them, she called out a greeting. She jumped off her

mount, her bright silver hair flying, and embraced them both. 'The strangest thing happened today – I was in the village, and a messenger dove came from the North. It said they've seen something in the sky.'

The other two looked blank.

'What do you mean by "something"?' Estarinel asked.

'Well, I don't know. I didn't see the message myself, there were too many other people trying to read it. It sounds as if it was just a big bird – why they sent a message about it I can't understand!' She shook her head, laughing. 'We think it must have been a message to the bird-spotters that an unusual eagle has been sighted, but the dove went astray.'

They reached the cottage at the top of the valley and got their breath back. As they stood there, Lilithea looked to the North, shielding her eyes from the bright sky.

'You won't believe this,' she said, 'but I can see something too.' The others looked; a little above the horizon was a grey speck, hardly seeming to move. They were on high ground and had a clear view for many miles.

'It is coming this way,' said Estarinel, 'but it must be miles away – and if we can see it from this distance, it must be huge.'

'How fascinating,' exclaimed Arlena. 'Oh, it's disappeared – has it landed?'

'I have a Book of Creatures,' said Lilithea. 'Shall I fetch it, so we can find out what it is?'

While she fetched the book, Estarinel and his sister continued to watch with all the patient curiosity of those looking out with interest for a wild bird or animal. Presently it reappeared, but closer now; it seemed to be a large grey eagle, and it made a faint whirring noise as it flew.

'I cannot see any bird as big as that in here.' Lilithea had put the heavy tome on the ground and was flicking through the pages. 'Nor any flying reptile. Some of these creatures only existed in the author's imagination, I think.' She turned to a page on which a hideous dragon was portrayed, undoubtedly stylised and inaccurate, but horribly realistic for all that. It was headed 'Ye Serpente Mugulf'. Lilithea left the book open at that page and stood up to look.

Quite unexpectedly, a flock of little blue-grey dunnocks – the sort that hopped around Estarinel's father's feet looking for insects as he dug – flew overhead, shrieking alarm calls. More followed, then other birds, calling loudly. All around them a barely perceptible rustling began – the panic of small, wild animals.

'Oh!' Arlena gasped, 'whatever is the matter with them?'

'They're afraid,' muttered Lilithea, who had an instinctive sympathy with all plant and animal life.

The flying thing disappeared from sight once more. This time it was out of sight for many minutes. Where it had landed, thin trails of vapour began to rise against the sky.

'Smoke – can you see it?' Estarinel asked. 'Do you think something's on fire?' Behind them, the man bringing the seedlings came up to see what they were looking at.

'By the Lady,' he said, 'is that a forest fire? There's not been one of those for many a year.' They could see no flames; only the heavy grey fumes hanging over the distant treetops. Suddenly, sending the vapour swirling, the grey object rose into the air again and flew on. Still they could see no details of it, only a basic shape. There was a long body and the tiny wings sticking out from it seemed hardly able to support its weight.

Now they realised that it was flying very fast. Threads of some stuff that caught the sunlight fell from its head, and more wisps of vapour rose in their wake. It was less than a mile from them when it twisted and began a ponderous circling.

'Oh ye gods,' moaned Lilithea, as if she heard the noises a split-second before they became audible: thousands of animals, in sheer panic, rushing towards them. Sheep, horses, deer, gazelles, cats, foxes and all the rest; their stampeding feet and fear-stricken cries formed one swelling sound, through which they seemed to hear human screams.

The creature's circling brought it closer, and they could see it more clearly: a long, thick body tapering to a tail, a misshapen, heavy head. The small wings were a blur as they kept it airborne. As they watched, it made a swoop and plucked a tree from the ground, then dropped it. It fell, grey and smoking, all its foliage shrivelled to nothing. The first of the terrified animals burst from the trees, and they watched, absolutely incredulous, as the ghastly Worm dipped and caught several in its huge jaws.

The four ran along the valley rim to see better. And they saw half a sheep fall from the Serpent's careless mouth, strings of blood and saliva whipping after it. They could hear the awful droning whirr of its wings, and a dreadful stench reached them. The atmosphere suddenly seemed warped by a mocking, diabolic evil.

In Forluin there was no crime, no murder, or even dangerous animals to prevent the night being a joyous, star-filled time. Hatred, vengeance, cruelty, ambition had no place there; war was unknown, illness rare but skilfully cured by herbal arts. They were truly a people with everything to live for and nothing to fear; they were innocent, open-hearted and in total symbiosis with their beautiful land. And, indeed, there had been contact with the Blue Plane H'tebhmella, which they believed had bestowed a kind of blessing on the land. Thus they were very slow to realise what was happening, and even slower to believe it; and fear, rising in each of them for the first time, felt like a suffocating death.

'Oh, it really is that thing,' whispered Lilithea, pushing the book with her foot. 'It's killing our animals!' she cried, hanging onto Arlena's arm. They saw it drop like a stone behind a clump of trees.

'That's Falin's farm,' Estarinel said. And he felt knowledge and terror flood through him, and he was shouting, 'We've got to help! Arlena – get down to the farm and warn our parents. Oh ye gods, where's Lothwyn? Go on, hurry!' And she was on her cob and galloping down the valley. The man had dropped his seedling tray and was running, running, as if in a nightmare, back towards the village.

Estarinel remembered running across the valley and down towards his friends' farm only as struggling through a heavy grey sea. Whether it was the noxious exhalations of the Worm, or his own terror that made the journey so slow and painful he did not know. Lilithea was behind him, trapped in her own cell of agony and fear; how the world could be so normal, so full of sun and joy one moment, and so drowned in grey horror the next was more incomprehensible than the worst nightmare.

'Why us? Why send this thing to us?' she kept gasping, the words escaping her lips like soundless screams of pain.

Estarinel ran through the trees and gained the farm. Many images flashed before his eyes, but he did not take them in, for the Worm was before him and he saw nothing else.

It was lying on what had been Falin's house; like a beached whale, a gross immovable slug it lay on the ruins, blood running from its fissured lips. The colour of its shapeless form was indescribable, overlaid by a colourless, filmy skin. In its ugly, heavy head two tiny blue eyes glinted malignly, while in a third, empty, eye socket, muscles twitched.

All this Estarinel took in in a split-second, for immediately the thing leapt into the air with impossible speed for its bulk, and Estarinel threw himself to the ground with a scream. Over his head the Worm took off with a deafening, groaning, continuous roar and its body seemed to pass endlessly over him as he looked up; an infinite tube of wrinkled, sickening, evil flesh.

A stream of searing fluid fell from its mouth, striking the ground only a few feet from him. He lay for a long time without moving, until he felt Lilithea's hand on his arm, and heard her voice crying urgently.

'E'rinel! E'rinel!'

He stood up, and saw the devastation around them. The trees through which they had just run were now blackened ash; the fields and plants all around were scorched and smoking. Pools of the steaming grey fluid lay everywhere, vile odours rising from them. And the farm where Falin's family had lived was rubble, with pieces of broken timber sticking out of it. A terrible grey horror flooded Estarinel and Lilithea, and they stood clinging to each other. But even as they watched, they saw Falin and Sinmiel emerge from the ruins, weeping.

'Our parents, our parents,' Falin cried when he saw Estarinel and Lilithea. 'My mother went outside – to frighten it off, she said—' he began laughing with hysterical despair, '—it just seized her, like a doll—' He trailed unintelligibly into tears.

Lilithea stretched out her hand as Falin and his sister began to stumble towards their friends. But Sinmiel missed her footing and stepped into one of the fluid pools. They watched, helpless and lost in disbelief, as she screamed in agony and collapsed. They all ran to help, but she was already dying, gasping convulsively as the acid consumed her.

Between them they held her, speechless with grief as she died in their arms; the same four who had that morning ridden joking and laughing through sunlight.

'Oh – our farm, the village!' Estarinel said hoarsely.

'What can we do? We who are powerless to save even one life—' Falin buried his head against Sinmiel's hair.

The village had been spared, but many others had been seared and burnt, the blood of the people slavered on the streets.

Over all Northern and Central Forluin the Serpent spread doom and decay. It could not have happened to a people more disattuned to horror. Many survivors suffered Estarinel's experience, of seeing

33

loved ones murdered and looking into M'gulfn's dreadful eyes. They survived, but not unscathed.

When he, Falin and Lilithea ran back to the Bowl Valley, they found the farm untouched. Estarinel's sisters Arlena and Lothwyn were both there with his parents; the horses had been stabled before they had bolted. They sat, close together and silent with dread, for many hours before they knew the Serpent had finished its evil work and gone.

People came from Maerna, Ohn and all the untouched parts of Forluin, to gather together the survivors and give them comfort. In some ways those whom the Worm had left alone were even more horrified by the devastation than those who had suffered it. Surely the Serpent was only an ancient myth with its superstitious origins in Tearn or Gorethria? That such a thing could happen was beyond reality.

Forluin had no government, but the oldest and most respected men and women now formed a Council of Elders. In the dim and terrible days after the Serpent, they called all survivors to a meeting in the Vale of Motha, many miles North-East of where Estarinel lived.

His parents and Lothwyn would not go, because there were animals to tend, and his father had developed a cough and fever from the ash the Worm had left behind. But Estarinel, with Falin, Arlena and Lilithea, set forth on horseback across their desolate land. They rode swiftly and in silence, the cause of their grief too obvious all around them to need any expression in words. It took them three days to reach the Vale, and in that time they missed the coming of the H'tebhmellian Lady.

The Vale was still whole, only the edges having been scorched by M'gulfn. There was a small cluster of cottages in the Vale, with a vast green stretching in front of them. Here the council was held, many people seated on the grass around the Elders. Estarinel and the others greeted many friends, but heard of the death of many others. And although the sun shone, there was a greyness in the air, and the stench of the Worm still hung over them. Many were falling sick with an unknown fever, and a terrible sense of doom filled them, made far more terrible because they had never experienced such a thing in all the island's history.

'We have no resources to draw upon,' the oldest of the Elders, Englirion, was saying. 'We cannot ask how our ancestors faced this situation, or any other; for they knew only peace, as we have . . .'

the Elders did not look physically older than the rest, except that most of them had white hair; only there was a quietness and grace about them. 'So it would seem we have no guidance but our own instinct and judgment. Now there are two foolish lines we might follow. One is to remain drowning in sorrow, wailing with grief and regret that the Worm ever came, and to dream of how sweet life would have been if it had not come. The other, which has been suggested to me by many people, is to form an army and chase the Serpent, in mad anger, back to the Arctic. Where, I tell you, we would all perish and the Worm would live – if you can call its miserable existence "life".

'Now, we must all accept that an appalling, senseless, dreadful attack has taken place on our home. That cannot be changed, it is already history. And to undertake a suicidal journey to the North Pole to destroy what is reputed to be an invincible monster would be useless. It is easy to forge off on a journey fired by a desire for revenge – but when that desire evaporates amid freezing snows and ice-storms, and you die in greater despair than ever, how will that have helped your countrymen?' There was a murmuring of agreement. 'In truth there is only one course we can take. Our priorities must be to restore our country to its former perfect state, eradicating all traces of the unspeakable Worm; to cure the disease it has left behind; and to prevent it attacking us, or any other country, ever again . . .' Englirion paused, and Estarinel looked at Falin, wondering if his friend knew what the last statement meant. But Falin looked equally puzzled.

Englirion made to continue, but suffered a fit of coughing, and a woman with long silver-white hair went on in his place.

'Most of you know, for most of you saw her, that a Lady of the Blue Plane came to us.' At this there was a murmur of wonder from the fringes of the crowd. 'Not *the* Lady, but her name was Filitha. However, I know some of you only arrived today, and I sorrow that you missed her. She said many things, I can only tell you a few of them. If you want to know it all, a scribe has written it down . . .' Estarinel felt, rather than heard, Lilithea sigh beside him. 'She came because of the Worm, and the sorrow and despair we are in. She grieved for us . . . and she said that although the H'tebhmellians have never been able to help the world directly, they can offer us advice, and this we accept with the love and trust there has always been between us.

'There *will* be a party to try to destroy the Worm. But only one of us will go, and he or she must first sail South to the House of Rede, there to find the rest of the party. It will be a long voyage, but necessary, the Lady said, to distance the one chosen from the immediate horror of the Worm.

'For it must be understood, she said, that others in this world know of the Worm and wish it dead also, and a great circle of powers moves according to whether it lives or dies. Therefore we cannot go selfishly North alone, but must go to the House of Rede for the help and companionship that we will find there. And then the H'tebhmellians will provide a ship to take the travellers to the Blue Plane, where they will be told what they must do.'

Englirion finished a long draught of water and stood up again, saying, 'So we are not without guidance after all. This is what must be done. One person will sail South, with a few companions to man the ship. The rest of us will stay here and wait, doing what we can to repair the damage.'

Suddenly Falin jumped to his feet and cried out, 'Surely one should go who has lost all his family, and has no one left to grieve should he not return?'

'Please sit down, my dear child,' Englirion replied gravely and sadly, and as Falin did so, Arlena held his arm and bowed her head against his shoulder. The Elder continued. 'There will be no volunteering. I have the job of choosing who will go. For this purpose the Lady Filitha gave me a device, a lodestone which will point to the one who must go. You must therefore all form a great circle, so I can set up the device in its centre; anyone who truly does not wish to go may stay outside the circle.'

'We all want to go, and we are all afraid to,' said someone.

But as the circle was formed, the only ones outside it were children. The device was a small, slender gold tripod, with a pointed blue stone hanging under its apex by a thread. Englirion positioned it carefully, then set the stone spinning. It seemed an age before it came to rest, and then the Elder moved round the edge of the circle and peered through a sighting glass for several seconds before nodding solemnly and walking towards Estarinel and his friends.

Estarinel hardly realised he had been chosen until Arlena exclaimed 'Oh E'rinel!' and Englirion was there in front of him, saying, 'The lodestone pointed to you – it was a totally arbitrary choice. Are you willing to go?'

'Yes,' he said blankly. And he thought of it all – the malignant

36

evil that the Worm had brought and left behind, Falin's mother trying to 'frighten it away' as if it were a crow, his father's fever, Sinmiel – and he knew that he had to take action, that he could not remain behind waiting, waiting, waiting for the Worm to decide Forluin's fate. 'Yes; I am afraid to go, but I will . . .'

Preparations were made. The ship from An'raaga had returned, and this was the ship they took. It was built to hold ten horses, and was small and seaworthy. But the only horse it carried on this journey was Estarinel's stallion Shaell.

Englirion spoke much to him in private, telling him of Filitha's words, and of Eldor – for he had met the sage. He explained that Forluin would see him as their sole hope; and that it was a perilous and grave journey upon which he embarked. Estarinel by now felt only numb, for he had already felt too much. He knew the grief his family would suffer if he should go and not return; and he knew he was stepping from the terrifying known into the terrifying unknown.

He was to take four companions with him to the House of Rede. Falin and Arlena went gladly; but when he asked Lilithea, tears came to her eyes.

'I cannot go; I can't bear you to leave without me, but I am a herbalist, and people are sick, and I must try to cure them.' She hung her head, fighting tears for a few seconds, then said shortly, 'I hope you come back, E'rinel,' and walked away.

Lothwyn wished to stay with their parents, for their father was now very ill. Eventually Estarinel took two of the crew who had been to An'raaga, for they were so distressed at the state of Forluin that they wished to be away again, and they knew how the ship handled. They were a fair-haired man, Edrien, and a chestnut-haired woman, Luatha. He had met them because, in spite of the Serpent, they had gone to his mother to apologise that there was no Gorethrian horse for her.

A sword had to be fashioned for Estarinel, for there were no weapons on Forluin except for fencing foils. They were given travelling clothes and provisions; and as they set sail there were blessings and tears from all. And they had just heard that Englirion had died of the Serpent-fever.

The Worm's attack was a few weeks ago now. Yet the grey gloom and its stench had not lifted; no new growth had appeared on the devastated land. Many people were in the grip of a fatal fever, others in danger of starvation because of the ruined crops.

This was the country that Estarinel watched slipping over the rim of the horizon; his home, which had always been green and its people loving and joyful. He might not see it again, either in its present state or in its old, true one. And his misery was so great that it seemed to be outside him, so he thought he felt nothing.

As Estarinel finished the tale he was shaken to see how little the Gorethrian Prince and the Alaakian woman reacted; they hardly seemed moved by what was to him a monstrous tragedy. And these are to be my companions, he thought, these people who do not care . . .

Then Ashurek spoke.

'I shall not comment on your story, because I do not expect comments on mine. Make of it what you will; it is a wild and evil tale, but true in every word.'

So Estarinel and Medrian heard a history that no one, not even Eldor, knew in full; and that was the story of Ashurek, Prince of Gorethria.

3

The Egg-Stone's Bearer

Gorethria was a bizarre and beautiful country which had spawned an equally strange people. They were tall, slim, graceful, and deep purple-brown of skin; their hair was black and worn long; they dressed ornately and were beardless; and their eyes were many-coloured and brooding. They loved beauty and brilliance; they were intelligent and creative, strong willed, loyal to their country – but they were an arrogant and pitiless race.

For over a thousand years they had subjugated the entire continent once known as Vardrav, now called the Gorethrian Empire. Their almost aesthetic delight in war and bloodshed and the fanatical precision of their strategy had meant that stronger but less finely-honed civilizations than theirs had fallen before their cruel armies. Their inborn ruthlessness and power of invention had kept those countries under Gorethria's dark control ever since.

Ashurek's father, Ordek XIV, had been Emperor of this vast, darkly shining realm. He was an extraordinary man, Ashurek remembered, as brilliant, fierce and unapproachable as a leopard, yet also wise and fair, and a loving father to his children. He had ruled the Empire well, consolidating many tentative conquests without causing much unnecessary bloodshed, and improving communications across the continent. Under him the Empire was stable.

Ashurek could not think of his father without bitter sadness. Ordek, the last Gorethrian worthy of admiration and respect. Then the vultures had come, in the form of his own children, to tear everything he had built up into bloody pieces.

Ashurek also remembered his mother, the Empress Melkish, with love and sorrow. True, she had been in some ways eccentric and cruel – was she not a Gorethrian? – but it was a loving, gracious woman that he remembered.

She and Ordek had three children. Ashurek and Meshurek were

twins, but Meshurek, being the first-born, was heir to the throne. Their younger sister was named Orkesh.

How innocent can a Gorethrian be? Only in so far as he is ignorant of his own guilt – of the part his inborn sense of superiority and cleverness has played, or will play, in the cruel subjugation of other races. Yet Ashurek could remember a time – it had seemed infinite, stretching from horizon to horizon – when he had been, or at least had felt, innocent.

His earliest memories were of colour and brilliance. Courtiers moving through the marble halls of the palace, their dark skins like satin and perfumed with sandalwood and amber, dressed in reds and greens and golds, as jewel-like as tropical fish. The porcelain-white spires of the palace glittering under the burning sun as endless processions marched past – war-horses dancing like living fire in their purple, white and gold trappings. Soldiers, seeming to Ashurek alive with some dark, invincible strength, whose jet armour was as full of scintillating colour as black opal. Banners of coloured silk, the cheering of dazzlingly-dressed crowds, and above all the majesty of his parents, who seemed brighter than the sun on such occasions.

Growing up amid the excitement and beauty of life in Gorethria's greatest city, Shalekahh, and being trained from birth to fit naturally into his role as one of the country's foremost statesmen, the palace lifestyle seemed to Ashurek as easy and invigorating as breathing. The army represented something desirable, wondrous in its mystery. If someone had sat down and explained to him the reality of their work – the fear, pain and misery they inflicted – it would have meant nothing to him. He had seen pain. It was a royal pastime to hunt a human – say an insubordinate slave – through the woods like a fox, and as soon as he and his brother and sister were old enough to ride, they were allowed to follow the chase. Pain was something to be inflicted on lesser beings to make them understand Gorethria's supremacy.

And his parents – his mother, she who had personally stabbed a bringer of bad news and caused the floor to be inlaid with gold where his blood had fallen, and his father, he who had brought the 'King' of a distant country, who had politely begged for independence, back to Shalekahh and had him tortured to death in public – they were to be emulated, not feared. It was for lesser mortals to fear them. Their splendour – Gorethria's splendour – eclipsed all else, justified every act.

40

Ashurek remembered being happy. He was certainly not un-aware, as he reached adolescence, of how lucky he was to have been born into a life so full of glory, excitement and power. He recalled feeling actual pleasure when his father found time to speak to him. He remembered the dark elegance of his mother, the secret smiles she kept only for him, and how he used to talk and laugh with his sister, Orkesh, as they strolled through the vast palace gardens. What did we find to smile and laugh about? he sometimes thought bitterly. How clever we were, or how unthinkingly cruel? No, he thought. I can't remember, except that sometimes it was about Meshurek. There's no expression of emotion black enough for me to mourn him – to mourn all of them. Even weeping would seem like laughter.

His twin brother Meshurek, heir to Ordek's throne, was the only being that in any way marred Ashurek's childhood and ado-lescence. Some twist in Meshurek's personality made him a jealous and insecure child. He lacked the confident, extrovert nature of Ashurek and Orkesh, and he suffered dark moods in which no one could reach him. He did not have Ashurek's skill at sport, riding and weaponry, and he knew, though they tried not to show it, that his parents preferred Ashurek. Slowly his envy became obsessive. Frantic to prove to the Emperor and Empress that he was as good as Ashurek, he would challenge him to races or fights which he then tried to win by trickery. Ashurek took it all in good humour, often saw through the deception, and usually won anyway. Meshurek would be left feeling foolish and angry as his brother walked away with what appeared to be a mocking smile.

Ashurek did not mean to mock his brother. In fact, he loved him, and found his envy incomprehensible. There was no point in letting Meshurek think he could win; better to make a joke of it, and perhaps one day Meshurek would laugh too.

But to Meshurek it was no joke. He had no sense of humour; only paranoia, and a painful awareness of his own failings. He was a tongue-tied, physically awkward boy, and although the courtiers only said it in whispers behind the unfortunate Prince Meshurek's back, it was no surprise to him when he eventually overheard that they, and the general populace, thought he was an unfit heir to the throne and a shame that Prince Ashurek had not been born first.

Meshurek sank deeper into his fears. He became obsessed with the idea that his parents would oust him, even murder him, and make Ashurek heir. He convinced himself that Ashurek hated him. Paranoia ate at him like insatiable hunger.

But he was wrong. None of his family hated him, although they hesitated to show him love because he often reacted with hostile resentment. The laws of succession were strict, and in fact Ordek believed Meshurek would make an adequate Emperor, being of above-average intelligence and a well-read boy. He had other plans for Ashurek than having him take a throne to which he was not entitled.

Even if the Emperor had explained this to Meshurek, he would not have believed it. His obsession had gone too far; his imagined fears had become real to him and by the time he was thirteen he was convinced there was a plot to remove him.

But he was a Gorethrian. Though he was lacking in some ways, he had all the royal Gorethrian traits of cleverness, determination and desire for power. As he matured he realised that fighting Ashurek openly was pointless. He had to seek his own way to victory, and this he did by immersing himself in the things he did excel at: reading and learning. He spent all his spare hours in the palace library. His awkwardness was replaced by a kind of malicious charm, which, once perfected, he knew would make him far more acceptable in court and in public. And he sought for himself some sort of weapon, against the day when he would have to fight for the throne.

Ashurek was relieved when Meshurek apparently found his feet at last. He was a changed youth; he had found his own interests, and showed all the brotherly affection Ashurek could hope for. Ashurek did not bother to look any deeper, because he had other, more exciting things to think of and was simply glad not to worry about his brother's problems any longer.

The Emperor Ordek had had Ashurek well trained in all the arts of soldiery, and the young Prince showed more skill, enthusiasm and inspiration than his father could have hoped for. His plan was for Ashurek to become, eventually, High Commander of the Gorethrian army; that way, true power would be in Ashurek's obviously capable hands and his insight, coupled with Meshurek's knowledge, would make them an excellent team. The Empire would be safe for years to come; and that was Ordek XIV's true purpose, not just to rule well while he was alive.

At the age of sixteen Ashurek went away with the army for the first time, under the wing of an experienced, loyal General from

Ordek's personal guard. Army life was everything he had dreamed of, and more; and most importantly, he discovered that the subjects of the Empire were far from meek or abject. There was still a challenge, and work for the army to do.

Ordek and Melkish were delighted with the way he had taken to army life. He went on many forays and missions and was made an officer at the age of eighteen. Long tours of the Empire meant he did not see Meshurek or Orkesh for many months at a time, but they still heard of his exploits as the praises of the young, brilliant Prince Ashurek were sung in Shalekahh.

And Meshurek's jealousy grew darker. Even when Ashurek was not there, Meshurek must suffer to hear how wonderful and how much better than him his brother was. Perceiving that he would spend a lifetime being eclipsed by Ashurek's achievements, even when he was Emperor, he spent many weeks pondering upon the knowledge he had found, how to gain his weapon and how he would use it. At last he made his decision, and set to work.

And from that moment, the Empire was doomed.

Ashurek was only twenty-one when Ordek deemed he was ready to be made High Commander. He was very young, true; but it was not unusual for an Emperor's son to be given such a high position of responsibility so early. He was well prepared and more than able to do the job; and most important, he was very popular. The people, and the army, loved him. Even Ordek sometimes mused that Ashurek would have made an excellent Emperor.

So Ashurek rode back into the shining, porcelain-delicate city of Shalekahh beside the retiring Commander, a white-haired man who had given many years of stolid service. They headed a column of cavalry mounted on those copper-and-fire horses he had so longed for as a child. Crowds lining the streets gave them such a rapturous welcome that, by the time Ashurek reached the white gates of the palace, he was almost moved to tears. Involuntarily, he thought of Meshurek and began to comprehend his jealousy. He never received but a token cheer in public; and this adulation was good, was worth having. Suddenly aggravated, almost embarrassed by the adoring shouts which he surely no more deserved than Meshurek did, he left his lathered horse with a groom and went brusquely into the palace alone.

He was exhausted from the long ride. He knew his family were

43

awaiting him in the throne room, but he could not face them yet. He sent a servant to apologise for him, and went alone to his room to strip off the dusty war-gear and bathe; and then he sought out his sister, Orkesh, and took her out into the palace gardens. They walked in silence along the avenues between pale fountains and lush sanguine flowers for a long time.

Eventually Orkesh said, 'Aren't you happy?'

'Why do you say that?'

'You're quiet – depressed. Most unlike you – and why didn't you want to see mother and father?'

'I'm tired. There's time enough for that later. I need to be on my own for a while.'

'I'm with you!' said Orkesh with mock indignation.

'You're different. You soothe me.' She shone a white smile at him and he grinned back, grateful for her gentle presence, her slim, dark, graceful form and the shared secrets in her brilliant green eyes.

'So – how have things been while I was away?' Ashurek asked. He noticed a brief hesitation before she replied light-heartedly,

'Oh – as always. They are building a new castle on the coast of Terthria – mother has been supervising that. I've been sent to preside at several dreary banquets for visiting nobles. I think they're trying to marry me off, but I'm happy as I am, except when you're away.'

'And how is Meshurek?'

Again a hesitation.

'Mother and father think he is making excellent progress. They're too busy to look underneath. He seems to have changed for the better – you know, he is confident and full of ideas – the new castle was one of his – but something is not right with him.'

'He's always been strange,' said Ashurek. 'Do you mean he is worse, ill perhaps?'

'Not ill,' Orkesh replied thoughtfully. 'On the contrary, he's never seemed better; quite articulate and charming, like me. It's the way other people react to him. Servants, courtiers, messengers, even the various cousins and uncles who know him well – they don't like him. No one likes him, and believe me, it is no secret that everyone wishes he was not going to be their Emperor one day.'

'I don't believe that,' Ashurek said with unexpected sharpness. 'Anyway, they have no choice – and no right to speak against him.'

'Oh, you're as bad as father!' Orkesh hated talking about things that worried her, and began to tease her brother. 'Can you honestly say you would not like to be Emperor? Ah – but what an Empress *I'd* make. It's time Gorethria had an Empress again. We could easily dispose of Meshurek – ah, but then I'd have to murder you, too, to achieve my ambition—'

'Be quiet,' Ashurek laughed, 'I think you're only half-joking. Meshurek has grown up at last, and people find it hard to accept, that's all.'

Orkesh turned to face him, her green eyes shining very bright with that strange combination of humour and sincerity that was unique to her.

'No, you're wrong,' she said. 'People are frightened of him. And so am I. There's something in him that terrifies me. But if you can look at him and tell me it's my imagination, I'll not say another word about it – agreed?'

'Yes, Your Highness,' Ashurek grinned. 'Now we had better go in and ready ourselves for yet another dreary banquet.'

Innocence. Talking and laughing with his sister, thinking the palace garden was the loveliest place in the world. Greeting the rest of his family with joy, knowing that in only a few hours he would receive the high office that he had worked so hard for. It would be the beginning of a wonderful life – the beloved army at his command and the freedom to wander the Empire like a hawk. Ashurek looked forward with almost boyish eagerness to a life of glory and high adventure fighting for Gorethria. He was aware of his vast responsibility; but to him responsibility was a joy, a way of serving his father and country. And it was not power he longed for; he was simply in love with army life, the smell of horses and leather, sweat and dust; the long treks across changing landscapes; the fascination of planning strategy, arguing long into the night as he and his fellow officers pored over maps by the light of a single lamp. The skills of battle and weaponry were an art in themselves to him, and the deaths they caused just a by-product, stones on Gorethria's path to ultimate supremacy.

Ashurek was indeed innocent as he walked into the dazzling opulence of the banquet being held in his honour. He did not dream he was only a few hours from doubt, and a few months from dreadful knowledge.

There were many people to speak to, and not much chance to talk to Meshurek, but in the few moments Ashurek found to observe his brother's behaviour, he seemed cheerful and self-assured. Slightly shorter and more broadly built than Ashurek, he seemed in the best of health and looked a suitably regal figure in a robe of ornately quilted green, purple and gold satin. Eventually Ashurek saw him talking to the Emperor and Empress, and moved across to join them. He found Orkesh on his arm as he said, 'I hear you've initiated the building of a new castle at Terthria, Meshurek. How is it progressing?'

Meshurek turned round, smiled, and said, 'I think you mean, why am I building it? Terthria is a region of rare beauty and an ideal Northern outpost.'

'It is all black ash and volcanoes,' said the Empress Melkish. 'Some might find it beautiful, but I cannot abide the starkness of it.'

'An outpost?' said Ashurek. 'What for? There is nothing there.'

'There is the ocean,' said Meshurek cryptically.

'What he means,' said Orkesh, 'is the ocean between Gorethria and Tearn. It is at its narrowest there.'

Ashurek heard his mother give a faint sigh as if anticipating a familiar argument. But the argument was new to him, and he listened, fascinated, as Meshurek said, 'You look surprised, my brother. Father and I have had long discussions on what I believe to be Gorethria's only future. We need to establish posts along Gorethria's coasts with a view to the invasion of Tearn.'

'Discussions!' the Emperor Ordek snorted. 'I have explained to Meshurek in exquisite detail why it is impossible to subjugate Tearn. The—'

'Wait, father,' Meshurek said politely. 'Let us hear Ashurek's opinion.'

'Tearn is another continent, not just another country. The army is at full stretch keeping control of the Empire. The strength of arms we would need to consider taking even a small part of Tearn would leave the Empire weakened, maybe in chaos.'

'Exactly,' confirmed Ordek. 'I have shown Meshurek the logic of it, and he is unable to reply with an equally logical argument. Yet he will not let the matter drop.'

'The Empire is stagnant,' Meshurek went on, apparently unperturbed by his father's fierce adamance. 'What is there left for us to do, but conquer the other half of the world?'

The last remark was typical of the arrogant, dry humour

sometimes heard in the royal court, but no one smiled. Ashurek felt chilled by Meshurek's words, for no reason he could pinpoint.

'The Empire, my son, is stable,' Ordek contradicted. 'We have everything we have worked for. Tearn is no threat to us – so why risk all we have, for the sake of greed?'

'Gorethria has always taken risks,' Meshurek replied smoothly. 'That is why we are great.'

Ashurek was beginning to believe Orkesh. His brother did seem different. They had always been respectful, even a little nervous, with their father before; but now he got the impression that Meshurek was teasing Ordek, tantalising him with what seemed a foolish argument, while underneath there was some great and terrible meaning that Ordek did not suspect.

'If you think, as I do, that invading Tearn is impossible, why has the building of the castle gone ahead?' Ashurek said, looking into his father's hawk-keen eyes. But Ordek did not reply.

Meshurek said, 'Oh, it is just mother indulging my whims. As I said, I like it there.'

'It is an Emperor-to-be's privilege to have a personal retreat,' Melkish added.

'I can go there to dream,' Meshurek smiled, 'of my brother sailing across the sea to even greater glory.'

Ashurek felt disturbed for the rest of the evening. Even the company of his mother and sister could do nothing to dispel his mood, and when he noticed that Meshurek, having grown increasingly restless, had left the banquet early, he decided to follow him. They would have a long talk which would finally solve the differences between them.

There were no footmen on duty in the darkened corridor leading to Meshurek's suite of rooms, although Ashurek could hear him talking to someone. The ornate gold door to his bedchamber was ajar, so Ashurek looked into the room and called, 'Meshurek.'

Darkness lay in the large room like a crouching wolf. He could just make out the figure of his brother, with his back to him, outlined by a faint incandescence that seemed to glow from everywhere and nowhere at the same time. Meshurek appeared not to have heard him, and went on talking. Ashurek realised he was talking to himself, or uttering a chant; the words were running together in an inhuman drone.

As he listened, Ashurek began to feel cold and sick. The language Meshurek was muttering was a form of ancient Gorethrian; the exact sense of it escaped Ashurek, but it seemed full of implications of horror, like a nightmare which cannot quite be remembered except for a sensation of terrible dread.

Meshurek was summoning something.

Ashurek was transfixed, fascinated and horrified, at the door; he could find no power to speak or move. His head felt like lead. He did not understand what was happening, had no power to alter or stop it. For the first time in his life, he felt fear.

In front of his brother, silver light flared and a figure appeared as if from another dimension. It had a perfectly symmetrical human body which shone with a dazzling argent light; but the light was not beautiful. It burned Ashurek's eyes like acid, and through the glare he saw his brother ducking and edging back like a cowed servant waiting to be struck.

The room – or was it his head? – was filled with a thrumming like an iron bell vibrating in response to distant thunder. Ashurek felt his skull would surely crack open with the strain. My brother – he thought – what have you done?

Then the being spoke.

Its voice sounded like metal and cobwebs. A voice that could make a word into a real object, a poisoned needle that would slide into the listener's skin and pin him to some dreadful fate. And it was also hypnotic, and persuasive.

'You have called me again, Prince Meshurek. How can I help you?'

'Meheg-Ba,' the Prince gasped as if in physical distress, 'I want – I want assurances. Did you hear them earlier?'

'Hear what, O Meshurek? Calm yourself – explain,' said the being. Its broad silver face was stretched in a smile, or leer, and the mouth gleamed red as if full of blood.

'The people – cheering Ashurek my brother. Tomorrow he is to be made High Commander. How much louder they will cheer then . . . I . . .'

'Meshurek, now that you have called me to your service, I can see or hear anything you want me to. Once summoned, I can wander freely on Earth to do your bidding. What assurance can I give you?'

'I want them to cheer me, not him!' Meshurek almost shouted, his voice ravaged by both fear and greed. 'The people should love and worship me, I am to be their Emperor – not Ashurek!'

The silver being let out a hiss like an echo of laughter.

'One thing I cannot do, my Prince, is make people like you.

Only you can do that. But listen, I can give you all the power you desire – you know that, for that is the true reason you first summoned me.'

The creature stretched out magnesium-white hands and placed them on Meshurek's shoulders. 'You and I together shall be invincible. With such power, I promise you will not care that you are not loved!'

Meshurek's shoulders shook, as though he was laughing.

'Yes, Meheg-Ba. I trust you. I can make them worship me on a whim!'

'It was a happy day when you thought to summon me. Now you are destined to be the world's most powerful man – and the bargain was so simple. All I require in return is the loyalty of you and your family, and to be unleashed upon the world – in your service, of course.'

Ashurek reeled back from the door involuntarily. In panic – made twice as terrible because he had never felt panic before – he stumbled and lurched down the corridor as if blind drunk until, somehow, he gained the safety of his own rooms. A minute later the thrumming in his head subsided and he knew the creature had returned to wherever Meshurek had called it from.

Shaking, so weak with dread and terror he could no longer stand, he lay upon the bejewelled and brocaded cover of his bed. He did not understand what he had seen, but it was obvious that Meshurek had ensnared himself in some terrible evil.

Why? He cried to himself. For power? But you are going to be Emperor anyway, by birthright. No – he could not conveniently ignore the truth any longer. Orkesh was right – their brother was not better. He believed that everyone hated him, and had summoned the supernatural being to jealously guard that which he was sure was going to be taken from him.

Ashurek wept for a while. He still loved his brother, as he had always done. Now he was shattered to realise the truth, furious at his own foolishness in imagining that Meshurek had solved his problems. What did the being mean, the loyalty of you *and your family*?

Eventually, when he had calmed himself, he left his room. The banquet was long over, the palace in silence and darkness. He said to a guard, 'I cannot sleep. I am going to the library to read for a while.' And once in the vast library, he searched until the first light of dawn for whatever fell knowledge Meshurek had found there.

49

The being he had seen, he soon learned, was one of the Shana – a supernatural race which inhabited a region removed from Earth. They were evil and powerful and they were 'of the Serpent', the ancient book said – though whether this meant they were its servants, or that it had created them, Ashurek could not tell. They lusted for power over Earth, although Earth was protected from them in that they could only come there when summoned by a human, and the first summoning was arduous and dreadful. There was no 'sorcery' on the Earth, the potential energy for it did not exist. So anyone who desired power that could only be achieved through necromancy had to resort to calling upon the Shana. In return for performing whatever tasks the summoner wanted, a Shanin would take control of the unfortunate human and extract whatever payment it desired. And if the human fell short in fulfilling his side of the bargain, it was easy enough for the Shanin to drag him down to the Dark Regions and make him regret it for eternity.

Not surprisingly, man called the Shana 'demons'.

Ashurek could find nothing on the actual ritual of summoning. No doubt Meshurek had concealed that information in his own room. But there were hints of the terrible difficulty and danger of breaking through to the Dark Regions to call a demon into the world. Ashurek could imagine how his brother's cleverness had overcome the problems of understanding the ritual and putting it into practice.

Once the bargain was made, subsequent summonings were simple. The demon could even come without being summoned. As he read on, the cold, archaic language of the old book and the implications of the appalling, apocalyptic danger of demon-summoning left Ashurek sickened. Had Meshurek any real conception of what he had instigated? If so, did he care?

The next day, including the ceremony at which Ashurek received the office of High Commander, passed like a dream. Externally he went through all the correct motions; internally he was totally distracted by what he had learned. He could not meet Meshurek's eyes. Whenever he looked at the rest of his family – all sparkling like hummingbirds as they happily greeted an endless stream of courtiers, relations and officials – he felt fear for them.

They don't know, he thought. They have not the slightest suspicion that Meshurek . . . They were in terrible danger.

Ashurek had no idea what he should do. If he told his father

50

and mother, they would be furious and confront Meshurek. Then Meshurek's worst fears – that his family meant to oust him from the throne – would be realised, and there was no telling just how powerful the demon, Meheg-Ba, was. He did not doubt it had the power to destroy anyone who challenged Meshurek. That was exactly why he had summoned it.

Ashurek could not even confide in Orkesh. She was too outspoken, she would be outraged and would challenge Meshurek with the accusation. He could not be sure he could stop her, for she had the same degree of spirit as did he.

Least of all could he speak to Meshurek. Already eaten by paranoia, now in the grip of a supernatural being – even if he could make him see reason, what strength did Meshurek have to dismiss the powerful, greedy Shanin? None – less than me, Ashurek realised.

It was strange to look at his mother and father – the great hawk-fierce Emperor Ordek XIV – and realise that they were as ignorant and helpless as children.

The burden was on Ashurek's shoulders. There was no one he could tell, no one in the entire world who could possibly help. Strangely, he came up with the only solution immediately – he should trick his brother, take him away alone somewhere, and murder him. Then the demon's contact with the world would be broken, his family would be safe. He gasped with pain at the thought.

'How can I murder Meshurek? My own brother, whom I love. It would be the realisation of his fear that I planned to take the throne from him. Then his fear would not have been misplaced all these years – indeed, it could have been a premonition,' he thought despairingly. 'There must be another answer.'

In fact, there was not.

He dreaded leaving his family behind with Meshurek when he went away into the Empire again.

'It would be useful,' he told his father – the only man in the Empire to whom he was now answerable – 'if I could spend a few weeks more in Shalekahh. There is much to discuss with other army leaders.'

But Ordek answered, 'Discussion must always take second place to action. There is a full-scale rebellion in the North of the Empire which I want you to deal with personally. And there is similar trouble in Alaak. These must be your first duties.'

There was no question of arguing with Ordek, so when Ashurek heard that Meshurek was going alone to supervise the completion of his castle at Terthria, he felt that his family would be safe for a while, at least. Perhaps in that time he could find an answer.

To begin with, all went well. There was so much to be planned, discussed and done that there was no time to think of Meshurek; eventually the scene he had witnessed in his brother's room seemed no more than a distant nightmare. The rebellion was a challenge and it took all Ashurek's ingenuity to subdue it, so it was easiest just to forget other distractions. The loyal enthusiasm of the army for their new leader was a real joy to him, and he could not have wished to be anywhere but roaming the Empire with them, except that he sometimes missed Orkesh.

One day his second-in-command, Karadrek, said confidentially to him, 'What an Emperor you would make, your Highness! No disrespect to your brother, of course – but, well, you know as well as everyone that he is unpopular. A word to the army and you could take the throne easily, when the time comes.'

'I will take that as a joke, Karadrek,' replied Ashurek, 'as I am sure you meant it.'

'Naturally,' said Karadrek with a shrug, 'but it nevertheless would be the fulfilment of the people's wishes, and for the good of the country, if . . .'

'I doubt it,' Ashurek silenced him sharply. 'There are more traditionalists than you think, who would support Meshurek in his absolute right to the throne. There would be civil war. And why should I want to be Emperor – chain myself to Shalekahh and its responsibilities when I can be wandering the Empire as free as a hawk?' The second-in-command, realising Ashurek was sincere, fell into uneasy silence.

Then the letter came from Orkesh. It was short, for her, and he could read some distress underneath her cool, light style. She mentioned that their father was unwell, and could he consider coming home, just for a few days. At once, Ashurek left the army under Karadrek's command and rode home, with just a personal guard. When he reached Shalekahh he was aware that a full two months had passed since Orkesh had written the letter. He could almost see and feel the pall of gloom over the city, and knew that bad news awaited him.

Guardsmen of the royal household stood ready to greet him, but

Orkesh broke through them and ran towards him, her face wet with tears.

'Was it so difficult to get here just a day earlier?' she shrieked at him. Two of her maidservants stepped forward to restrain her. 'Father died this morning!'

Ordek XIV had not been an old man. He should have ruled for many more years. Ashurek, confused and anguished, could get no straight answers from any of his family. Orkesh could do nothing but weep, and their mother, dry-eyed but in obvious shock, said she could not discuss it and just wished to be left alone. Only Meshurek would look him in the eye and say, 'He had a terrible fever. The physicians did all they could for him, but to no avail. We have suffered an appalling loss.' So Ashurek quizzed the royal physicians, who all confirmed that Ordek had contracted a lung infection which their skills could not cure.

The palace without the Emperor's fiery presence seemed an empty, superficial place, as if only his fierce brilliance had breathed life into it. Ashurek could hardly believe he had grown up here; the familiar rooms and halls seemed totally alien, every corner filled with dark mourning.

And Meshurek was now Emperor.

The funeral came and was over, and Ashurek felt so distant from the remaining members of his family that the lowest slave in Gorethria might have felt closer to them. He seemed to have lost all power to comfort his sister and mother or even to communicate with them, and he continually felt that Meshurek was watching him and smiling at him, although he knew that this was not actually so. Tortured and enraged, without anyone to turn to for help, he retreated to his own rooms and paced about in the darkness, struggling with his thoughts.

Father! I should have told you about Meshurek – perhaps you did know a way to deal with the demon, and you would have been saved. Yes, it is my fault. I alone knew what Meshurek had done, and I ran away and hid the knowledge. And now you are dead. Is there anything I can do now to salvage what is left?

As he cursed himself in his anguish, the door opened and his mother and sister glided into the room, dressed in mourning grey like distant stone figures in an unreal landscape.

'What do you want?' he exclaimed, sounding angrier than he had intended to.

'I know you are distraught, as we all are,' said his mother in a low voice. 'Orkesh and I have decided that we cannot remain silent. We three must stay together and help each other, now that Ordek is gone.'

'Father should have ruled for another twenty years, at least,' Orkesh broke in, 'but twenty years was too long for Meshurek!'

'Meshurek murdered your father,' Melkish concluded drily.

Ashurek, suddenly having his fears confirmed, felt emotion running through him like fire. He felt like screaming, I know! I am the one who left you in this terrible danger, and now you ask me for help, unaware of how I've betrayed you?

But he said nothing.

'Meshurek is insane,' Melkish went on, her voice trembling. 'It is unbearable to me to suggest this but – he must be killed, or at least removed – imprisoned at Terthria, perhaps. He cannot rule. You must take the throne.'

'No, mother,' Ashurek spat out the words. 'Don't you understand – that is exactly what he has always feared. That is why he is insane. That is why he murdered father.'

'What?' Melkish cried. 'But he deserves it! Curse the day I gave birth to him! You can't be saying that if we do not remove him, he will become sane and wise and Ordek will return to life? Ashurek – don't make me think you are both fools!'

'Nevertheless,' he said heavily, 'if we try to kill or imprison him, we will all die. He has supernatural help. You must know that, or you would've been happy to believe that father died of a lung infection.'

'We know there is something,' Orkesh whispered, her eyes bright with tears. 'Didn't I tell you? There's something wrong with him. He frightens people.'

'I know. Meshurek has called to his aid a demon, a lustful, evil being of vast power. It has him totally under its control. It can do anything it likes. Our only hope is to lie low and pretend we are ignorant of it, and try to find an answer.'

In a tone of cold rage, his mother replied, 'Lie low? That is not a Gorethrian of the royal house I hear speaking. Meshurek shall be brought to justice, and I, as Empress and as your mother, command you to help me. *Do you understand?* I am a woman whose right arm has been severed, but my left can still hold a sword.'

'Mother, Orkesh,' Ashurek said as calmly as he could, 'please leave. I will deal with Meshurek myself – for my sake, you must keep yourselves safe.'

54

'Very well,' Melkish said, 'but if you fail . . . you must not fail. I could not bear to lose you too. What would become of Gorethria then?'

He kissed them and they left as quietly as they had come. Fired by rage – both at Meshurek and at himself – he felt dangerous, even invincible. He would force Meshurek to see sense, banish the demon, rule sensibly. It was the least Meshurek could do to atone for his father's murder.

He found Meshurek in a side room of the darkened library.

'My brother,' he began softly, 'I have come to tell you that your foolishness has gone too far. It must end. I know that you murdered father, with the help of a demon – or most likely at its instigation.'

Meshurek looked up and smiled blandly, without surprise or defensiveness but with the faintest trace of excitement.

'I'm glad you know. It saves me all the trouble of explaining.'

Ashurek felt himself shaking with anger and grief. Meshurek was indeed insane.

'Explaining? You were planning to explain your crimes to me?'

'Father had to be killed. I was sorry, of course, but there wasn't time to wait for him to die of old age. Now the Empire can expand, as it should.'

'Meshurek, why did you call that demon? I don't want the throne – I never have – I am no danger to you!'

'Are you not? Haven't you come here now, believing me unfit to rule, to try to murder me? You've always hated me – I had to take precautions. You believe you were cheated of the throne at birth. I would have felt the same in your position.'

Ashurek felt the dangerous emotion fading into a helpless despair as he realised nothing he could say or do would ever convince Meshurek that he had never wanted to be Emperor, in fact despised the idea. His brother had not the perception to comprehend feelings other than his own.

'The demon is using you, you fool!' he exclaimed. 'How can you believe otherwise? You must – you will – get rid of it!'

And Meshurek started laughing. And Ashurek, in his furious despair, flung himself forward and closed his hands on Meshurek's throat. Meshurek stretched his arms out and silver light began to incandesce around his fingers.

Ashurek felt an impossible pressure in his skull. His hands slid from his brother's neck; he lost all strength and crumpled to the floor. Then Meshurek looked down at him with a smile.

'Is the time ripe?' he asked.

And Ashurek heard a voice, like acid etching metal, reply, 'It is ripe.'

Ashurek was not easily frightened. He had been through many terrible and bloody battles without losing the cool detachment necessary for planning strategy. He had had nightmares and been able to laugh at them on waking. He had met many subjects of the Empire who hated him, yet he had never felt the need to look over his shoulder to see whether his guard was there, or an enemy with knife in hand.

But the demon, Meheg-Ba, took him by the hand and led him to the Dark Regions where he was systematically taught Fear.

A black door in the atmosphere closed and he was trapped, stumbling in darkness across a surface of living flesh where the only light was the searing, sick glow of the Shanin. When at last his eyes adjusted and he found his feet, he saw, stretching in every direction, a bleak landscape mottled with sick browns and blacks. Unnameable shapes rose here and there. Malformed birds, like bags of skin, uttered dreadful metallic shrieks as they flapped across a black sky that was as low and claustrophobic as a roof. The smell and texture and atmosphere of the Shana's region were in themselves enough to induce utter misery and despair even before the Shana began their tortures.

'Welcome to the Dark Regions,' said Meheg-Ba with a red grin. 'It was fortunate that your brother summoned me, for he is now the most powerful man in the world – how lucky the Shana have control of him. Now you are to be forged as the instrument of his power.'

Fighting down the panic induced by the Shanin's terrible presence, Ashurek growled, 'If you think to make me an instrument, think again.'

'So – you are a wilful one, as Meshurek said. No matter – fight me if you like. It will make the process longer and more painful for you, but no less effective.'

Ashurek did fight, mentally and physically. But in the endless black labyrinths of the Dark Regions, the cells of rotting flesh and the evil, infinite swamps, nightmares were made real and inescapable. Demons and other, more primeval creatures tortured him in body and mind until fear itself, fear of dark corners behind his back and of the sinister, laughing malice of the Shana, became the thing he dreaded most. And behind all he continually sensed the presence of another being, as vast and indestructible as the universe, formed not of the self-delighted evil of the Shana, but of absolute, ashen desolation. The Serpent M'gulfn.

He fought long and desperately until even Meheg-Ba was surprised at his endurance. He was fighting for Meshurek's release as much as his own sanity. But the struggle tired him as greatly as did the torment, and at last, exhausted and half-mad with the terror that the dark sky would be torn aside and the Serpent revealed to him, his will broke.

He begged Meheg-Ba to set him free.

The demon mocked him for a while, but eventually said, 'You know there is a price to pay for your freedom.'

'I had guessed,' said Ashurek with what sarcasm he could muster.

'Don't worry – it is a very simple task. I am going to deliver you to another dimension where you will fetch a small jewel known as the Egg-Stone. Then I will send you home.'

'Why can't you fetch the thing yourself?'

'Because no creature of the Serpent can enter the dimension,' the demon answered. 'And the stone is guarded by a creature who could destroy a Shanin with the merest touch. But it offers no danger to humans, you need not fear.'

'Fear,' Ashurek echoed bitterly. 'What if I refuse?'

'Fetch it, or keep us company here for eternity!'

'Very well. But if you are so eager for the stone, you can do something else in return. Swear that my mother and sister will be left out of your plan, and unharmed.'

The demon grinned with red delight.

'Of course! I swear it. But the bargain will also work in reverse. If you fail, your mother and sister will be brought here and used in any way it pleases me.'

The demon released Ashurek into a dimension of shifting grey rock which seemed to be a region between worlds, like the area where two great continental plates move uneasily against each other beneath the ocean. He crossed this strange, neutral landscape with a grim briskness, putting from his mind speculation as to what the Egg-Stone might be. He had no choice but to seek the artefact. At last he came to a grey mountain, sailing in the mist like a vast ship of stone.

When he set foot on the mountain he was still, in the Gorethrian way, innocent. But soon the final tearing away of ignorance was

57

to come, to be followed by agony and the destruction of all he knew.

A bird flitted across the rocks in front of him as he climbed. He started, because surely Meheg-Ba had implied there was no living creature in this dimension except the Egg-Stone's guard? He shook his head and went doggedly on. But the bird wheeled round and began fluttering alongside him, hopping from rock to rock.

He ignored it – until it spoke.

'Where, oh where, are you going?' it sang in a melodious, lilting, unhuman voice.

Ashurek stared at it. It looked like a large female blackbird; its tawny feathers shimmered with gold, and its small form contained more beauty and liquid grace than any living creature on Earth, human or animal. He could not look at its eyes, though. Shining black and sad, they were the most beautiful eyes, the only honest eyes, he had ever seen.

'I seek the Egg-Stone,' he said, and climbed on. The bird followed.

'If, only if, you can find it,' she sang. 'If you can find it, then you can take it.'

'Who are you?' he asked gruffly.

'You should know who I am, Prince Ashurek of Gorethria. No one should come here who does not know,' the blackbird sang, her voice gentle and sad as tears.

'How do you know my name?' he gasped, feeling ever more deeply disturbed by the strange creature.

'I know everyone,' she replied. 'Anyone can know a name. Mine is Miril. But do you know who I am?'

'You are the Guardian of the Egg-Stone.'

'I am. You know that and you know my name, but you do not know me. Alas, Ashurek – will you ever know me?'

'I know not and I care not,' he muttered, climbing faster. But something inside him was trembling, awakening. Worse than the grief for his father, fear for his family and all the torments of the Shana, he felt a terrible stirring within, like a chick struggling to break from its shell. He should care. He did care, but he fought the feeling as though it was killing him.

'No demon can touch me,' Miril sighed, like wind ruffling water. 'No human can look at me but they turn back the way they came, weeping for mankind. So should you, Ashurek, except that you will not let yourself care until it is too late, too late.'

58

'Let me be!' he cried. 'I have to find the Egg-Stone.'

Above, he saw a sort of eyrie with a small nest built upon it. He struggled up the sharp rocks and at last, breathless and bleeding, he gained the shelf of rock and looked into the nest. There he saw an object as small as a sparrow's egg, silver-speckled blue.

Forces welled within him. The shell of innocence became more fragile. There was a thunderous gathering of dark promise, terrible bloodthirsty lust, and it emanated from the Egg-Stone.

Miril had flown ahead and perched on the other side of her nest, facing him.

'I cannot fight one who does not know me,' she sang, her voice more strident and appealing than all the dawn choruses the world has heard. 'So it has always been. I sing and they close their ears, I fly into their gardens and they throw stones at me. I have kept the world safe from the Egg-Stone for so long, but now the Worm's time has come. Take it!'

And Ashurek reached into the nest and took the Egg-Stone. It was as heavy as lead and it transfixed him, seeming to whisper to him. He felt the throbbing of its dreadful, dark power and knew that, even if he changed his mind, he would be unable to put it back.

The bird's lovely body shuddered and sagged, as if racked by terrible pain.

'I know it for the evil it is,' she said softly, 'for it was given into my keeping, that the Earth be protected from it. Even so, it was as a child to me, the beloved egg that would never hatch. My pain on parting from it is unspeakable. And so will yours be.'

Then Ashurek did look into her eyes; and amid the lead-dark, irresistible pull of the tiny gelatinous Stone, the shell of his innocence shattered. He knew who she was.

'You look at me, Ashurek, too late,' Miril sang, her voice unbearably sweet. 'Am I not lovelier than the most beautiful creature or garden or flower you have ever seen? Am I not the longing of sunset and the joy of dawn? I am the Hope of the world.'

And in her eyes he saw his guilt. There, in the quicksilver shining depths of those black orbs was the misery and injustice, the blood and pain and hunger and utter wrong of Gorethria's atrocities, and those of every other race like them throughout space and time. There was a child crying in hunger because its parents had died in battle, and that battle had not made the conquerors more glorious, but less than the rat scuffling in the straw at the child's feet . . .

'Miril,' Ashurek said, his voice a rasp of pain, 'help me.'

'How can there be help without Hope? The world's Hope was I, and you have destroyed me. I will fade, and hide myself in darkness to mourn, and wait. And you, as soon as I am gone, will begin to seek me; and unless you find me again, your world will be doomed. No more can I say.'

Then Ashurek knew he had committed a more terrible act than Meshurek. The Egg-Stone was burning into his palm like molten metal as he was carried down into the dark spiral of his fate. Speechless, he watched Miril's lovely form fade.

'Oh, Ashurek, I think no wrong of you,' she sang before she disappeared, and the words pierced him like arrows of mercy he did not deserve.

When Meheg-Ba retrieved Ashurek from the dimension and stood before him again, the demon seemed an insipid figure, hardly to be feared. Ashurek was ready to fight the Shanin for the Egg-Stone, because its dark power had utterly possessed him. But the Shanin did not attempt to take the Stone. Meheg-Ba wanted it to remain in the High Commander's hands, for there it was most useful.

Ashurek was returned to the palace, to find that only a few hours had passed. Still dazed, feeling hollow and emotionless, he wandered in the corridors until Orkesh found him and seized him by the arms, her green eyes searching his face.

'Where have you been?' she cried. 'What happened – did you find Meshurek?'

He said nothing and Orkesh backed away from him, reading the terrible Serpent-power in his eyes. Filled with dismay and horror – and a dark desire she did not understand – she turned and ran, sobbing as she went.

He mouthed her name, only half understanding the misery he felt as she retreated. Then he went to his room and made a small leather pouch for the Egg-Stone, and he hung it on a chain about his neck. He was oblivious of Meshurek's presence, although his brother sat in full view, staring with greed and longing at the evil artefact.

It was not in Meheg-Ba's plan, but Meshurek was determined to take the Egg-Stone for himself.

Now began the most terrible phase of Ashurek's life and Gorethria's history. The Egg-Stone's black power made him invincible, flowing from him into his soldiers until they became one terrible, bloody entity that could scythe through the strongest resistance. Ashurek took one division with him to subdue the rebellion in Alaak. And although the white-faced, fierce, hard-disciplined Alaakian army greatly outnumbered the Gorethrians, they were nevertheless ruthlessly slaughtered in what came to be called the Massacre of Alaak.

And Ashurek discovered that with the fierce joy of bloodshed and victory came grief, guilt and self-loathing. But there was nothing he could do to resist the Egg-Stone's power over him. He was an instrument to extend the Empire over which Meshurek and Meheg-Ba ruled.

Now Meshurek's dream began to come true. As he had predicted, ships carrying his brother and over half Gorethria's armies sailed across the ocean to the continent of Tearn. There they ravaged their way through the countries of the East coast, and all, weak or strong, fell before Prince Ashurek's terrible might.

Tearn was thrown into a turmoil of fear as the months and years passed and more and more countries came under Gorethria's rule. Ashurek rightfully earned his reputation as despoiler, murderer and necromancer. He swiftly became the most loathed and feared man in the world; he was called child-slayer, devil, Grimhawk, Serpent in human form. As with all legends, eventually the colourful tales about him outstripped the reality. Those Tearnians who actually met him found a quietly-spoken, morose and troubled man rather than the grinning, wild demon of the stories.

He was troubled indeed. The more the Egg-Stone drove him on to cruel and violent deeds, the more he saw Miril's eyes in his dreams and became racked with despair. And as he fully realised the hopelessness of war, the Egg-Stone forced him like a puppet through battle after bloody battle, while he became ever more bitter and cynical.

Several times he tried to destroy it, but failed. He needed it like a drug; he was becoming a skeleton, held together and motivated only by the Egg-Stone's power. Yet somewhere inside, as though Miril had left a feather-barb in him, part of him was finding strength to rebel. It was some four years since the invasion of Tearn, a lifetime away from Shalekahh and his previous happy life, an eternity in the possession of the cursed Stone. He knew that if he spent much longer going through these appalling motions, the plaything of the Shana, insanity and self-destruction were imminent. Though the life he had enjoyed as a Gorethrian Prince was

61

lost for ever, he knew that unless he found the strength to resist the Egg-Stone, he, and the rest of mankind, were doomed.

About this time, after the invasion of Drish, General Karadrek betrayed him, attempting to disgrace him because he had shown mercy to the Drishians. Karadrek was punished, but Ashurek, bitter and dispirited, left the encampment and made for his main headquarters further to the North. His mood was black, near madness.

When he arrived at the small palace that the battalion had taken over, he found Orkesh and Meshurek waiting for him. He stared at them with surprise for a minute, then said, 'I did not expect you. No one sent a message.'

'We have only just arrived,' said Meshurek, sitting languidly back in his chair and smiling. But Orkesh was tense, her eyes glittering. And she was again dressed in grey.

'My brother,' she said, standing up to kiss Ashurek formally on the cheek. 'How good to see you again.' She seemed utterly unlike herself; her gestures were slow and plastic, and there was an awful look in her eyes, as though she had fallen in love with something that had previously revolted her, and was ashamed of her surrender to her dark lust.

'Is not mother with you?' Ashurek asked sharply. The room, suddenly small, dark and escapeless, began to spin slowly on its axis.

'No,' Meshurek answered with the bland look of a lizard. 'This is what we have come to tell you. She attempted to thwart me, and had to be stopped. Tell him, Orkesh, what happened.'

The voice of his beloved sister sounded like a jagged knife slicing the air. The heavy power of the Egg-Stone seemed to throb in sympathy with his painful surge of emotions as she said, 'Mother told you not to fail, Ashurek, but you did. Did you think, knowing that she was a strong-willed and determined woman, that she would not take action on her own? She sought out those who supported you, and made them into an army to take the throne from Meshurek. I would have no part of it. She did not believe me when I said you were in the demon's power as well. So, angry, I went to Meshurek and confronted him. But he calmed me down and made me see how foolish I had been, and that mother was wicked and must be punished. The rebellious supporters were crushed, and I sought out mother, and slew her.'

Dark and dangerous emotion filled Ashurek, growing larger than himself until it filled the whole room with black, swirling anger. Through it the figures of his brother and sister looked tiny and unreal.

'Now we are free of those who seek to hold us back,' Orkesh went on. 'The three of us will become great, the most powerful beings the world has known, more than human—'

'Orkesh!' Ashurek cried, voice rough with torment, 'I warned you not to confront Meshurek – you saw what happened to me – and still you did not take heed!'

'It's all right,' she replied calmly. 'I was willing. What Meheg-Ba offered, I found I wanted.'

Then Ashurek's anger and grief, magnified by the evil of the Egg-Stone, focused in his arm. In one swift movement he had drawn his sword and plunged it up through his sister's stomach into her heart. The shock and sorrow in her eyes turned them, momentarily, to Miril's eyes, and as the blood welled from her body onto the floor, his black fury bled into nothingness with it.

The room seemed pale then, expansive, as though he could walk across it forever and never reach the door. Meshurek had risen to his feet and the fleeting grimace on his face showed all the sorrow he was capable of feeling. Looking at Ashurek, shaking convulsively as he stared at the blood-soaked sword, Meshurek said, 'Don't weep, brother. It matters not. She was only biding her time, waiting to seize power from both of us. It would have had to have been done eventually.'

'You live in another world, Meshurek,' Ashurek said bitterly, biting back tears. 'Power – what is that? You have caused the deaths of father and mother, made a slave of your sister, turned me into a mass murderer – for what? The sake of the Empire? No – you are destroying the Empire. You have undone all father's work, and surely now it deserves to be destroyed. For your own personal power, then? You fool – Meheg-Ba is gaining the power, not you.'

'You are wrong! I will have my own power!' cried Meshurek, coming forward to face his brother. In despair, Ashurek knew that nothing he said was getting through to the demon-possessed Emperor.

'It doesn't matter to you, does it,' he cried, 'that thousands of people die every day for the sake of the Shana's lust? That your own family have been destroyed, the only beings in the world that should have meant something to you? Once I thought you a victim of an affliction, a paranoia which was not your own fault. Now I know – my eyes have been opened – we are all victims of the Serpent, but you and I are conscious, willing ones. We are guilty, you and I – as guilty as the Serpent itself. Don't tell me not to weep!'

But Meshurek was not listening. He was staring at Ashurek's throat, reaching out to it – and Ashurek realised Meshurek had sailed the ocean not to see him and tell him of their mother's death, but to steal the Egg-Stone.

That he could not permit.

With a howl that might have made the Serpent itself shudder, he struck Meshurek down with the flat of his sword and fled.

He ran from the palace, seized a horse and forced it at a punishing gallop away from the battalion, his insane brother and his beloved, dead, sister. He rode, fighting the evil pull of the Egg-Stone at every stride, until at last he was lost among the forests and mountains of Tearn, far beyond – so he thought for a while – pursuit or retaliation.

It was a strange time, those years spent wandering alone in Tearn. Ashurek tried to avoid all humans, and those he did meet responded to him with a fear and hatred with which they might have greeted the Serpent itself. He became an utter outcast.

Meshurek was in a torment of fury, made worse when the demon punished him for attempting to steal the Egg-Stone. But the punishment over, Meheg-Ba forgave him and together they plotted the recovery of Ashurek and the Stone.

Ashurek then found himself continually pursued by agents of the Serpent – misshapen creatures, or disturbances of wind and weather, or sometimes actual demons. But with skill and fierce determination Ashurek fought them, and remained free. The Egg-Stone was a paradoxical element in this, because although it darkened him and tried to bend him to its evil will, he also found he could use its power against the very creatures it was in league with. And because it gave him more power than a demon, Meheg-Ba could not catch him.

Meshurek ruled uneasily in Shalekahh. Rumours ran wild about Melkish's plot against him, her death, and the disappearance of Prince Ashurek and his sister. Always unenthusiastic about the Emperor, now the people of Gorethria were openly hostile to him.

Only Meheg-Ba's power kept him in control of the throne, crushed his enemies with malicious cruelty and bent his soldiers to his will. But without the Egg-Stone's force to hold it together, the Empire was crumbling. Meshurek realised he had been a fool. He knew how much Ashurek cared for Orkesh, yet it had not entered his mind to manipulate him by threatening her. And now there was no one left for whom Ashurek cared; Meshurek had no hold over him at all.

The Emperor became stooped and darkened in mind and body, hunched like a spider over his misery and lust for power. And the demon, Meheg-Ba, merely laughed at his plight.

Ashurek desired to die, or at least escape into madness. But he remained sane, and dared not risk what might happen to the world if he killed himself and the Egg-Stone fell into other hands. Besides, it was all that kept him alive.

But the black loneliness of his existence was growing beyond endurance. Wandering in a Northern country of Tearn – it might have been West Sel-Hadra – he found his way to a tavern in a small village and sat, sardonically heedless of the fearful stares of the folk there, drinking alone in a corner.

At length a woman came through the tavern door. She looked around, then saw Ashurek and stared at him intensely for several seconds. Then she retreated through the door and was gone as swiftly as she had come.

Ashurek's mood changed like lightning. He could not say how he felt different, except that part of his consciousness was now turned outwards instead of inwards. After a minute he rose and left the tavern also.

For he thought he had seen Miril in human form.

Outside, in the cold misty night, there was no sign of her. His mood reverted and he trudged across the thin village road and into the trees beyond, sighing bitterly as he went. All was darkness, escapeless and full of malicious laughter. He left the trees and found himself climbing the stony slope of a hill. Fog confronted him like a solid wall, lit eerily from within, and his hand went to his sword hilt as he realised that it was not natural. Something was moving towards him through the mist. He waited to see what would emerge; and out of the vapour came the woman he had seen at the tavern.

She was small and slender, dressed in white, with eyes, skin and luxuriant hair different shades of deep gold. She was beautiful indeed, exquisite; but there was something like pain or extreme weariness in her face. Her eyes were very wide as if with fear or intense concentration. She walked straight past Ashurek as though she had not seen him.

Behind her, as though enmeshed in the trails of light that drifted from her half-raised arms, stumbled a great, grey, misformed beast of the Serpent. As it came out of the fog, the vapour dispersed.

Ashurek drew his sword and followed swiftly; yet the creature did not seem about to attack her, and she was not running from it. Rather she held it in thrall by sorcery and was leading it purposefully down the hillside. She glanced round as if to satisfy herself that the fog was gone; then she stretched out her arms, stiffly, as though resisting a massive weight. She cried three words and a hole rent the earth in front of her; it was still widening as she made a desperate leap across it. Behind her the Serpent-beast tumbled into the blackness, uttering a frustrated shriek as the crack slammed shut above its head.

The woman sagged with relief and her light faded. Now Ashurek could barely see her, so he went straight to her side before she disappeared again.

'I cannot believe what I have just seen,' he said. 'How—'

'I'm glad you were there,' she said, breathless. 'I would have needed your sword, had my sorcery failed.'

'You claim,' Ashurek said, mystified but sceptical, 'to be a sorceress?'

'I don't claim to be one,' she answered with a faint smile in her voice. 'I know what you think. There is no sorcery on this Earth, no power but that of the Serpent and its Shana; no magic that can be learnt or drawn upon. Nevertheless, I am a sorceress. My name is Silvren, of Athrainy in the North.'

'I am Ashurek of Gorethria,' he responded with a slight bow.

'Prince Ashurek, yes I know,' she said faintly, drawing back from him.

'You recognised me in the tavern,' he stated with some bitterness.

'Yes, but – I was not afraid of you. I meant to speak to you but – it was a shock. I was afraid of the Stone around your neck.'

Ashurek felt cold astonishment flood him.

'No one knows about that,' he whispered.

'I told you, I am a sorceress. I can see it and – don't ask – I know what it is and what it has done.'

'Then you were right to run from me. And I should not have followed you.'

'Oh, but I am glad you did!' Silvren answered, a light like joy in her eyes. 'Are you not someone who knows how it feels to carry a burden of appalling power? You and I have much to talk about, and I am cold . . .' He followed her without argument back to the tavern where the landlord showed them to a small, lamp-lit room.

'The creature that was following you,' Ashurek said as he seated himself on a chair, 'do you know what it was – why it was there?' He half-feared that the beast had been searching for him and found her instead. But her reply, as with almost everything she said, was totally unexpected.

'When I left the tavern,' she began, sitting cross-legged on the floor, 'I just walked, trying to think what I should do. The beast concealed itself in a mist and attacked me on the hillside, so I mastered it with sorcery. There was no danger really; well, not much. Many such creatures have been sent after me.'

'Why? You have not been foolish enough to summon a demon?'

'No, not I! Someone else summoned it—' a wince of pain or regret crossed her face '—and sent it after me. Diheg-El is its accursed name.'

'They pursue you – because of your sorcerous powers?' Ashurek asked, leaning forward.

'Yes, but also because I have turned my magic against them. It is a long story. I cannot explain my powers, I was born with them – I certainly did not want them! Somehow I was born out of my place and time – I am the only being on Earth or the three Planes with these powers. I knew they could be dangerous, so I have travelled and learned how to use them properly. And I learned much else besides . . . have you not noticed how the world seems to be stagnating, growing ever darker and crueller?'

'Aye,' he laughed bitterly, 'you are right.'

'It is because of the Serpent M'gulfn . . . that hideous Worm that is no myth, but a physical vessel of evil. It is the channel by which the Shana can maintain contact with the world; it is the force that shapes cruel empires like Gorethria's; it emanates an aura that creeps round the world like a choking poison, and it has many minions to do its work and protect it. Its wormish body inhabits the North Pole, though once in a thousand years it might fly South to feed on flesh. But they say it also inhabits a human body, as protection against death – can you imagine locating that one human amongst the millions on Earth? And even if that one human were discovered and killed, M'gulfn would not be destroyed, for it inhabits both bodies simultaneously. Its wormish body is said to be impossible to destroy.

'But I am determined that it must be killed.'

'As you say, that would be impossible!' Ashurek exclaimed, amazed and fascinated by this strange Tearnian woman.

'Probably . . . but I must try, for it is now mustering its forces to dominate the world totally and for ever. This world has a bright and vigorous future with sorcery, not the sick power of the Serpent, holding sway – if only the thing can be destroyed. If not, the Earth has no future at all.' She gazed clearly into his eyes, and he knew she spoke absolute truth. 'I am the only one that knows this – unless Eldor knows. Not that I haven't tried telling others – people I thought I could trust – but they laughed, and called me deranged.'

'Not I,' he said. 'Go on.'

'I believe that on the Blue Plane they know a way that the Serpent might be killed. It is knowledge that can never come to Earth, lest M'gulfn find out. But every time I have neared an Entrance Point, the Shana have prevented me from entering. So that would seem to prove me right.'

When he did not at first reply, she said, 'Ashurek? Do you believe me?'

'Oh, yes,' he answered. 'I know that the Shana and Serpent are evil. And Gorethria is not the glorious entity I once thought it, but a ghoulish puppet of M'gulfn . . .'

She looked at him enquiringly, and he found himself telling her his own story.

'I have exchanged no more than a few words with anyone for years,' he concluded. 'I don't know why I trust you – except that your sorcery, although not evil, seems as much a burden as the wretched Egg-Stone.'

'You must get rid of that Stone,' Silvren said, her golden eyes still fixed on his. 'It's no good just fighting that and Meheg-Ba. The evil needs to be torn out at the roots – the Worm itself! Listen. I have strength to resist the Shana – but I am growing so tired, I know I cannot hold out much longer. I need to reach H'tebhmella. I need help – and so do you.'

Ashurek sat back, looking away from her.

'I cannot help you, Silvren. I can't dispose of the Stone, any more than I can tear my own heart out. You must see how dangerous that makes me to you. I would betray you eventually. I murdered my own sister . . .'

'But that is not the whole story! You are fighting the Shana already. If we separate, we are both lost. But together, we might find hope.'

Hope! Miril's eyes, burning into his. '*As soon as I am gone, you will begin to seek me . . .*'

'Silvren, I don't think you understand what I have just said to you,' he persisted bitterly. 'I am no fit company for you – I have become vengeful, bloodthirsty. I may destroy you.'

'No, you don't understand,' the sorceress said softly. 'I don't care. The truth is – I cannot stand to be alone any longer. I can't stand it. Can you?'

'No,' he admitted. And as she reached out to him, and he pulled her into his arms, he found she was trembling. He was already in love with her. And although he felt the fury of the Egg-Stone at this, his soul cried in relief.

What Silvren had said proved to be true. They were stronger together. Even the Egg-Stone became quiescent as if subdued by his determination never to harm her. And their love for each other in itself made life bearable, worth living and continuing the fight.

Ashurek had never met anyone like Silvren before; she made even his beloved sister and mother seem dark, snake-like, even sinister in character. She brought light to everything she touched or looked at, and that included his soul. She was basically a joyful person, and even through extremes of danger, weariness or despair her joy would eventually surface, just as an air bubble, besilvered by sunlight, cannot be restrained at the bottom of a dark pool.

She wove a web of sorcery to conceal them, for a while at least, from the Shana; and for nearly two years they had a time of calm, solitude and love. But in that time, despite all their efforts, they still did not find a way to the Blue Plane. And one day Ashurek, out hunting alone, was captured by a monstrous eagle-like creature and carried to a hideous castle. There Gastada, an insane minion of the Serpent, imprisoned and tortured him. Because the power of the Egg-Stone was dormant, it did nothing to help him; but Silvren forced her way into the impenetrable edifice and rescued him with her bright sorcery, nearly expending her life with the effort.

Gastada was deeply involved with the Shana (though he was also jealous and resentful of them), and so Diheg-El and Meheg-Ba found out that the Egg-Stone's bearer and the hated sorceress were together.

'Why has it taken you so long to find out?' Meshurek hissed at Meheg-Ba. 'Why can't you catch him, with all your wondrous powers?'

'I told you, dear Emperor,' the Shanin replied with a bland smile, 'he used the power of the Egg-Stone. Now the unnatural magic of the wretched sorceress protects both of them. But we can plan carefully and overcome this setback, if you have faith in me.'

'Faith!' Meshurek shrieked. 'I had faith in you! Where has it led me? I am the most deeply loathed Emperor Gorethria has ever had! The Empire is crumbling – my Tearnian conquests lost! And you cannot even catch my own damned brother!'

'Nevertheless,' Meheg-Ba said, staring at Meshurek with its dreadful argent eyes until he shrank back in fear, 'you have no choice but to continue to help me. Think; we have a two-pronged weapon against him now.'

'What do you mean?'

'There is the sorceress. He loves her more than ever he loved even Orkesh. And there is you – contrary to what you believe, he has always held you in deep affection. With this in mind, I have a simple plan which is bound to work.'

'All right. Tell me. We must do something.'

'Do not fear. We will soon recover the Egg-Stone and find other, more reliable hands to wield it – though, alas, not yours,' Meheg-Ba said with a mocking grin.

Meshurek snarled softly to himself, but dared say nothing.

So it was that Ashurek dreamed that his brother, hunched and pathetic with desperation, appeared before him and implored: 'My brother – I have never before asked your help. But now I need it – it shames me to admit it – but you were right. The demon is a noose around my neck . . . it is destroying me, and Gorethria. I have been a fool, and I am afraid – terrified. Only you in all the world can do anything to save me now. I know I do not deserve your mercy, brother – but please, please help me.'

Ashurek awoke, shaking and sweating. He roused Silvren and told her the dream.

'I must go back to Gorethria,' he said.

70

'But Meheg-Ba must have sent the dream! It's a trap,' Silvren cried, distressed.

'I know it's a trap. But my brother was not acting. Those words came from his heart, whether he realises it or not,' Ashurek answered heavily. 'Silvren, I am as guilty as he. Apart from all my other crimes, I have run away from him, not once but twice. Perhaps if I had stayed, things would have been no different, but I would not take the risk. That makes me a worse fool and coward than Meshurek. Now I must begin to repay, by going back and helping him.'

'You judge yourself too harshly,' Silvren half-sobbed. 'I will come with you.'

She expected him to argue; but he looked at her thoughtfully.

'With your strength and that of the Egg-Stone, if I can control it, we should be more than a match for any demon. Perhaps the trap can be sprung the other way.'

At this Silvren let out a breath of both relief and fear, and embraced him as though he was going to be torn from her that very minute. She was not afraid for herself, for she was confident of her powers; but the thought of Meshurek and Meheg-Ba waiting, like twin ghouls, to re-enslave him, wrenched her stomach and made her feel she was choking on ice.

They took a small sailing ship, manned by a crew of rough Tearnians who asked no questions, and started on their dreary journey. The ocean was unnaturally calm and a too-friendly wind billowed the sail and sped them straight as an arrow to Terthria. The voyage was days shorter than it should have been. Looking uneasily at each other, not needing to voice their thoughts, Ashurek and Silvren stepped onto the black ashen shore.

A cold, mist-filled wind caught at their cloaks as they made their way across the rough terrain. Meshurek had been right; the land did have an eerie, stark beauty, like a faceted piece of jet whose sloping and interlocking planes shone with hints of fiery colour. To the North, a mountain range reared up like black teeth savaging the sky. Smoke plumed from several of the peaks and the ground vibrated as though some vast creature were slumbering uneasily beneath the crust.

They had walked Northwards for several hours when a party of six Gorethrian horsemen approached and hailed them.

'Prince Ashurek and the Lady Silvren,' the leader called. 'The Emperor Meshurek awaits your arrival at his castle; we have been sent to ensure your safe passage across the mountains and into the Emperor's presence.'

Ashurek looked from one to the other, but he recognised none of the men. They all looked similar, expressionless and apathetic; Meheg-Ba's influence. With a bitter sigh, he took Silvren's hand and they walked on in the midst of the horsemen.

Silvren felt tired, disorientated and fearful. She tried to use her sorcerous vision to see the truth of the situation, when and how the trap might be sprung, but each time she glimpsed something the ground shifted beneath her feet and fog clouded her eyes. Her head ached with the strain of trying to see. The horses looked translucent to her; with a gasp she turned to look at Ashurek, but he appeared and felt quite substantial.

'I feel cold,' she said. 'I can't see properly.' He wrapped the edge of his cloak around her and pulled her to his side. It was unlike her to sound so afraid and unsure of herself.

'The easiest route is along the edge of this volcano, Your Highness,' the leader called. 'There is no danger, but it will be very hot.'

Ashurek felt Silvren shudder as the man spoke; his voice sounded unreal, full of sinister echoes. They completed the long climb up the trembling side of the volcano and were led through a cleft in the rock wall. They found themselves in the vast, circular crater at the volcano's peak.

Then the men pulled their horses to a halt. Silvren stared at them and rubbed her eyes; but the horsemen had become quite transparent. As she and Ashurek watched, astonished, they dissolved into mist and were blown away on the wind.

'It's not the castle. It's here,' Silvren whispered. 'Ashurek, I've lost—'

She broke off, because Meshurek had appeared as if from nowhere and was standing in front of them. He stooped as though weighed down by his brocade robes, and his eyes flickered ceaselessly to and fro, glittering with a mad light.

At the sight of him, painful emotions and memories swirled in Ashurek's mind. His brother was foolish, destructive, evil; but he was also a victim and slave to Meheg-Ba's cruelty. In one way he despised Meshurek and could never forgive him for the deaths of Ordek, Melkish and Orkesh. But in another he still loved him, felt he would sell his soul to save his brother from this torment.

'Meheg-Ba spoke truth!' said Meshurek. 'I did not believe you

72

could be naive enough to respond to such an obvious trick. Yet here you are, my brother, with your lovely sorceress.' He opened his arms in a mocking gesture of greeting.

'Ready yourself,' Ashurek whispered to Silvren, and began cautiously to summon the power of the Egg-Stone. Inside the rim of rock on which they stood, a pit of white-hot lava swelled and boiled sluggishly. The heat was already becoming uncomfortable.

'Meshurek,' he said, trying to keep his voice steady, 'the trick was obvious indeed. But so was your real need for my help.'

'What?' Meshurek sniggered uneasily. 'You are more of an idiot than I thought you. The last thing I have ever needed is your "help". You are expendable. All we need is the Egg-Stone.'

'You delude yourself. You know the words you spoke in the "dream" were true. Meheg-Ba has not increased your power; in fact you are now so feeble that you can only rule with the Shana's necromantic help. You are the weakest Emperor Gorethria has ever had.'

'You lie!' Meshurek shouted. 'I don't need Meheg-Ba – he serves me!'

'You serve him. But he has bled you dry – sucked all your intelligence, determination and judgment from you. And how has he increased Gorethria's power? The Empire is falling into anarchy, all our father's work undone. Even Gorethria herself is held together only by strands of evil magic. And that is because whatever the Shana might think they can do, in the end they can only fulfil the function for which they were made: to inflict the Serpent's destruction on the world. What is the use of power if it cannot be used to create – only destroy?'

'Well, if we are weakened,' Meshurek said, folding his arms, 'it is your fault. You deserted me. You took the Egg-Stone.'

'Can't you see beyond your personal lust for the accursed Stone? Yes, it is my fault – I should never have fetched the thing in the first place,' Ashurek said with bitter anger. 'Those who bargain with demons are witless fools. The demon swore to me that if I fetched the Stone, mother and Orkesh would be unharmed.'

Meshurek hung his head and shuddered. But he persisted, 'We must have the Egg-Stone back, Ashurek. Then Gorethria can be strong again. You want that, don't you?'

'Gorethria deserves to slide into hell! I don't care about her damned strength or lack of it. I came back, as I said, only to help you. Meshurek, listen to me for once. The demon will never let you wield the Egg-Stone. You're not strong enough. Meheg-Ba has reduced you to a husk and soon he will discard you altogether.' Meshurek said nothing, but began to tremble and looked nervously over his shoulder. 'Come here and stand with us. When Meheg-Ba deigns to arrive, Silvren and I will combine our powers to banish him.'

'Ashurek, this place—' Silvren said faintly. 'Look.' She pointed to the far side of the crater where a section of the rock was becoming translucent, like smoky crystal. Through it were blending two silver figures: Meheg-Ba and the Shanin who had been pursuing Silvren, Diheg-El.

Both glided forward and positioned themselves on either side of Meshurek.

'Diheg-El,' Silvren gasped. 'Ashurek, there's some strange force or magnetism here. Maybe the lava, I don't know. It neutralises my power, I can't do anything. They must have known . . .'

That was why Meheg-Ba had wanted them here, not at the castle. Ashurek felt terror slide icily down his throat. Silvren helpless. He felt the Egg-Stone throbbing sluggishly and knew it would only work against him.

'Greetings, Prince Ashurek,' hissed Meheg-Ba. 'You are most unfair to me. I did not harm your mother or sister; they chose their paths of their own free will. And now you try to turn my ally Meshurek against me.'

Ashurek said nothing. Arguing with the demon was even more pointless than trying to reason with Meshurek.

'Now that the Emperor Meshurek has finished prevaricating,' the Shanin grinned, 'it is time for us to conclude our business.'

Ashurek and Silvren glanced at each other; a glance that confirmed there was no chance of planning an escape. He could have cried out with savage misery at the horror in Silvren's eyes as she realised her imminent fate. Then there was a blaze of silver fire, faster than thought, and Ashurek crashed backwards into the rock wall. He lost consciousness for a second. When he recovered and pulled himself to his feet, he saw Silvren standing rigidly in Diheg-El's grasp. She did not cry out; but she was white-faced and shuddering, her body tensed with revulsion at the demon's touch.

'In the name of the Serpent, let her go!' Ashurek screamed.

'That's better,' said Meheg-Ba. 'Now we can negotiate. Give me the Egg-Stone, and we will release Silvren.'

Ashurek paused, glowering. He knew that he would feel

appalling pain when he relinquished the Egg-Stone. For Silvren's sake he was prepared to go through that fire; but he had to be sure Meheg-Ba would keep the bargain.

'Don't hesitate too long,' the demon leered. 'Would you prefer to deliver yourself into my service again?'

'Never,' Ashurek growled. 'How can I be sure you won't betray me?'

'Diheg-El will loose the sorceress. As you give me the Egg-Stone, she will walk back to your side. Then you will both be allowed to go unharmed. But only if—' the silver figure turned to look at Silvren, 'you both swear never to fight us or the Serpent again.'

Ashurek saw the cry of protest forming in Silvren's eyes and quickly interjected, 'Very well, so be it. Let her go!'

Then Diheg-El relaxed its grasp on Silvren. She came forward a few paces and stopped as if her body were totally under the demon's control. Ashurek, his eyes fixed on her, took the Egg-Stone off the chain which hung round his neck, and held it out towards Meheg-Ba.

Meshurek was between them in a flash, moving with incredible speed to intercept the Egg-Stone. Before even Meheg-Ba could react he tore it from his brother's grasp, stumbled a few paces and turned, clutching it to his breast and laughing.

Instantly, Ashurek was stricken by a sensation worse than pain, leaden veins of agony throbbing sickly through his body. And a ghastly emotion, like that which a demon might feel at the loss of its cruel, bloody power, seared his brain. But he did not forget Silvren. Through his blackened vision he could just see her being dragged by Diheg-El into the smoky crystal entrance to the Dark Regions. Crying out, he stumbled after them; but although he could still see Silvren's figure, faintly, as it melted through the translucent rock layers, to him the wall was impenetrable.

'Meheg-Ba!' he screamed, anger, pain and grief battling in him. He stumbled along the rim of rock and confronted the Shanin, oblivious to the blood dripping from his hands where he had pounded the rock.

'Don't speak to me,' said the demon, keeping its argent eyes fixed on Meshurek. 'I did not break the bargain. Diheg-El wanted the wretched woman, not I; and he made no agreement with you.'

Ashurek froze then. The pain from the loss of the Egg-Stone and Silvren were so intolerable that his mind seemed to be drifting above them, like a solitary, calm, evil eye. The scene continued;

75

but in slow motion, and as though he knew everything that was going to happen next.

'Meshurek, give me the Stone,' said the demon. 'I will take it from you eventually. You are not strong enough to keep it.'

'Not strong enough?' the Emperor panted, wild-eyed as a trapped animal. 'What happened to all the strength you promised me? Ashurek was right. I was a fool to summon you. Now leave – I have no more use for you, you betrayer!'

'Meshurek.' The demon was glowing brighter and brighter, gathering power with which to retake the Stone. 'You cannot make me leave. There is only one way I can be banished, and you are hardly about to take your own life, are you? Remember – only my power now holds the Empire together. You do not know how to use the Stone. If I go, Gorethria will collapse.'

At this, Ashurek's mouth spread in a slow, humourless grin. All this time he had been drawing his sword from its sheath. Now he swung it towards Meshurek's neck; it glittered as it caught reflected fires from the volcano. The movement seemed to take a thousand years; yet only at the last instant did Meheg-Ba and Meshurek remember he was there and react with astonished protests. Ashurek found time to pause and laugh at their sudden confusion. Then the swing continued, and the sword cleaved through Meshurek's neck.

The blow knocked both Emperor and Egg-Stone over the rim of the crater and into the broiling, white-hot lava below. A crust bore Meshurek's body for a second; then it broke, and the molten heat swallowed him.

Meheg-Ba uttered a roar and turned upon Ashurek like a dreadful basilisk of blood and acid. But the Summoner was dead. Even as the demon turned it vanished, returned by supernatural law to the Dark Regions. Ashurek was alone at the edge of the searing volcano, alone with the mourning, smoke- and mist-filled wind.

Slowly he returned to himself. He was dizzy, the crater seemed to be tipping crazily from side to side. Putting a hand out to the rock wall to steady himself, he began to comprehend what had just happened. 'I have killed my brother. First Orkesh, now him!' He found himself trembling convulsively, though far beyond tears.

Surely it is justice, he thought, that the royal house of Gorethria has come to grief and ruin in this way; it is retribution for her centuries of tyranny. Of all my family, my crimes have been by far the worst. I, too, must die to complete the payment . . .

He lifted his sword and stared grimly at its bloodied edge. And a voice cried, 'Ashurek! Don't!'

His eyes refocused on the far side of the crater and he saw Silvren standing there. But he realised at once that the image was not real; he could see straight through her slender form to the rock wall beyond.

'Silvren?' he said, lowering the blade. 'What has happened?'

'I haven't escaped,' she answered sadly. 'This is only a mental projection of myself; I mustered enough power to create it and speak with you, but my sorcery is weakened and damaged. It may mend . . . but not here in the Dark Regions. I can never escape.'

'I have been in that cursed hell-hole – I know—'

'Ashurek – beloved – don't despair. I came not to discuss my own agony, but to say that something good has come out of all this.'

'Has it?' he exclaimed bitterly. 'I have murdered my own brother, whom I swore I would never harm. And now I have even lost you.'

'But think – Meheg-Ba is banished from Earth, and the Egg-Stone gone as well. And Meshurek,' she added gently, 'in a way you have saved him. Normal life and freedom were lost to him. If you had not killed him, eventually Meheg-Ba would have dragged him down here to exist in misery forever. It was for the best. Now you must not give up; you must continue the fight.'

'Is it worth it?' he half-sobbed. 'You and I together could not even reach the Blue Plane.'

'For my sake, you must!' she cried, struggling to hide her distress. The sight of her, and the impossibility of helping or even touching her wrenched his heart.

'It's all right, Silvren – be calm,' he responded. 'For your sake, the fight against the Serpent will continue. What must I do?'

'I don't know – let me think.' Her form was shimmering and fading as though the effort of maintaining the projection was becoming too great. She turned her head slightly to one side and gazed at the ground, as she often did when thinking hard. He had hardly noticed the gesture before; now it seemed achingly familiar. She looked up at him again, her golden eyes wide and intense. 'Yes – you must go to Eldor. Tell him you have decided to destroy the Serpent. Ask his advice.'

To destroy the Serpent; a vast and impossible task, like destroying all evil or slaying the world itself. Yet the undauntable bravery

77

in her voice, issuing so faintly from her fragile, insubstantial form, encompassed the possibility that the task might be achieved; not by unrealistic hope, but by uncompromising determination.

Her courage and love shamed him. She had borne the leaden burden of her sorcery and learned to wield it – and risked being dragged down to hell by the enemies she made – because she felt the Earth was worth loving, worth saving.

And he knew he would set out upon the Quest with all the wrong motives: bitter hatred, desire for revenge against the Shana and Gorethria and even the world itself, and self-loathing. Silvren seemed to be voicing his thoughts as she spoke again.

'Try not to seek revenge. Keep your thoughts on the Quest, not too much upon me. Remember, the Serpent is the essential root of all this evil. When it is dead, the Dark Regions will cease to exist, and I will be freed.'

Freed? he thought. Not destroyed in that cataclysm? And what if, in spite of your trust and bravery, the Serpent really is indestructible? Silvren – only you matter to me now. I care not about the Earth or the cursed Worm. If I can find a way to rescue you, and escape this damned world . . .

But he did not speak his chaotic, miserable thoughts. He fought and subdued them; then he said, 'For you I will go to Eldor, and seek his help in this Quest.' Still she looked at him, her eyes wide and anxious. 'Not just for you, beloved,' he added. 'For myself as well.'

At this she relaxed, almost smiled, held out her hands towards him.

'Remember I love you,' she said. Then a white shimmer coruscated along her form, and she was gone.

For a while panic and grief took Ashurek again; he ran to the part of the crater where the entrance to the Dark Regions had been and clawed at the opaque, blind rock. He called Silvren's name without heed to the lonely, echoing walls. He sat down on a rock, barely noticing its scorching heat and, with his long, dark fingers entwined in his hair, he wept.

I am now the Emperor of Gorethria, he thought. But I do not want the throne; let those left in Shalekahh ponder upon the mystery of what became of Meshurek and myself, and squabble like vultures over a carcass about how Gorethria shall be ruled. It is better so. Let them discover the hard, bitter way that only the Serpent truly rules; and that only men who are impossibly brave,

78

or foolish, or desperate, set themselves up as challengers to the Worm's supremacy.

He grinned to himself, like a skull, at this thought. Here am I, O M'gulfn, a mad and desperate man seeking to kill you. Are you afraid? Or will you crush me like a tiny, unnoticed insect?

He got to his feet and strode away from the crater's heat and down the grumbling side of the volcano. The ache of the Egg-Stone's loss was still in him, but no worse than the other conflicting miseries that made up his dark psyche. In a few hours he gained the shore and hailed the Tearnian ship, which had waited for him . . . and Silvren.

Swiftly the vessel set sail for the South Pole and the House of Rede where he might find help in the Quest. And he spent much of the long, turbulent journey at the helm, staring into the distance as though seeking a reflection of hope in the waves or the sky. But all he saw was a dark wolf racing to its death, sometimes looking round, without success, for a glimpse of a blackbird's eyes; then racing on again.

4

The Star of Filmoriel

Ashurek ended his narrative standing with his back to them, his tall, cloaked figure silhouetted against the waning fire. Estarinel drew in a slow breath as if to speak, but the Gorethrian turned and silenced him with an icy glare.

Estarinel was not even sure what he had been going to say. The truth about Ashurek was worse than he had imagined; but at the same time he felt a sympathy for him so strong that it was like a cold pain in all his limbs. The 'terrifying unknown' was taking on its first faint shape as he perceived the reality of the grim, dark world outside Forluin. But to Ashurek, Estarinel's expression was more explicit than any words; there was horror in his clear brown eyes, but also understanding, even compassion. Bitterly, he reflected that if he had had any capacity for trust or fellow-feeling left, he might have felt some for the Forluinishman. But events had eradicated most of his humanity.

Ashurek turned his gaze to Medrian. By contrast her face was as cold and expressionless as it had been when they had first entered Eldor's kitchen.

'Well, Medrian,' he said, breaking the uneasy silence. 'What have you to tell us?'

She had been staring at the shadows cast on the stone walls by the red flickering of the fire, but now her eyes slowly refocused on him.

'Nothing,' she said.

'What do you mean?' Ashurek asked. His tone was polite but his green eyes were suddenly sharp and malevolent.

'I cannot tell you anything. Surely it is not compulsory,' she replied shortly.

'Estarinel and I have recounted our stories when we both would have preferred to remain silent. Is it too much to ask that you do the same?'

80

'You don't understand. I have no choice.' She pushed a few strands of her black hair out of her eyes. Her voice was so quiet and flat that it was hard to hear what she was saying.

'Could it be,' Ashurek persisted, 'that you are not totally committed to this Quest? How are we to know, unless you explain yourself?'

'I have no choice,' she repeated. 'I can't. But no one could be more committed than I; please take me at my word.'

Ashurek continued to stare at her. Estarinel felt the force of his will, and he sensed Medrian's distress like a taut cord that was stretching and stretching under the Gorethrian's insistent gaze.

'There's no need to tell us anything if you don't want to,' Estarinel interjected. 'It can't matter that much.'

'But it does,' said Ashurek. He came forward and leaned on the table next to Estarinel, glaring intently at Medrian. 'Why do you want to go on this Quest?'

The silent tension deepened like the shadows in the recesses of the room. Estarinel fought a desire to make for the door. Surely the cord of pain within Medrian would stretch to infinity before it ever broke and gave her relief. But at the same time Ashurek's force of personality seemed to make no real impression on her; she remained cold, self-contained, unmoved.

Eventually she said, 'You know what happened to Alaak, Ashurek. For some reason I survived. There is nothing left for me to do but try to destroy the ultimate evil of this world.' Her words were like ice crystals forming in the air.

Unexpectedly, Ashurek seemed to find this explanation acceptable.

'Obviously that will have to suffice for now,' he said, his black cloak falling in folds round him as he sat next to Estarinel. 'If that is your true reason, nothing could be more ironic, could it?'

She returned a small, icy smile; to Estarinel it seemed that she was laughing at some different, inward joke that was too horrible to be voiced. He noticed that what little colour there had been in her face had drained away completely; even in the red firelight she looked grey. He had an impression of someone who was in such chronic pain that she had learned long ago never to let her face betray it.

'Now, Estarinel, what do you know of this ship?' Ashurek was asking.

'Er – you know as much as I,' the Forluinishman replied

diffidently, not expecting this sudden turn in the conversation. 'It will find an Entrance Point and take us to the Blue Plane.'

'How long will that take?'

'I do not know – perhaps a few days.'

'Then what?' Ashurek's green eyes were glittering again, and he seemed dangerously restless.

'What do you mean?'

The Gorethrian rose and paced round the room.

'Then,' he said grimly, 'armed with what little help the H'tebhmellians can give us, we face ice and snow and storms, and at last the Serpent.'

'I know,' Estarinel said quietly.

'Do you? I have spent most of my life travelling and fighting . . . nor does Medrian seem inexperienced. But you would appear ill prepared for such a journey . . .' he sighed, suddenly feeling exhausted. 'Still, I expected nothing of Eldor. I have not been disappointed.'

Estarinel felt faintly annoyed at this. He wanted to ask what the Gorethrian would have preferred, why he doubted the H'tebhmellians' word that a great army was unnecessary, even useless against the Serpent M'gulfn; and if he considered the H'tebhmellian ship to be 'nothing'. But he felt too unsure of himself to speak. Eldor had brought the three of them together, and if he could not put faith in the sage, then all was lost before he had even begun. Perhaps he should not take Ashurek's sour words so much to heart. He looked across at Medrian, but could still detect no trace of fellow-feeling in her blank eyes.

'We will all be ill prepared if we do not get some sleep before the ship arrives,' she said drily. Without exchanging a further word or glance with either of them she stood up and walked briskly to the door, her travel-dusty grey cloak swinging in a slight draught as she left the room.

The fire flared up momentarily, catching purple lights on the Gorethrian's dark face.

'Well, she's right,' he said with a touch of sarcasm. 'Talk was ever a waste of energy.' He strode to the door, leaving Estarinel feeling bereft of any hope of achieving some communication with either of the two strangers. The kitchen, once so bright and welcoming, now seemed full of black, dancing spectres. All he felt was dread. But the Gorethrian paused in the doorway and said, in a slightly less menacing tone, 'I believe you're as exhausted as me.

Go to bed; brooding is an even greater waste of strength. I should know, though it's a damnably hard lesson to learn.'

Eldor stretched his feet out in front of the fire and smiled, with some sadness, at his wife. Dritha drew a curtain and went to sit at the other side of the fireplace. They were alone in their room.

'I wish I could tell them it all,' he sighed.

'That would not help,' his wife answered. The firelight caught silver glints in her hair and eyes. 'They would be caused bitterness . . . make wrong choices.'

'Oh, I know . . . Their motives are so painful and personal that they are all convinced they act for themselves. They would not believe that outside forces could so manipulate their actions. And while we are involved in that manipulation, we are just as much victims of it ourselves.' Eldor gazed steadily into Dritha's clear grey eyes. 'So it begins, the Quest of the Serpent. The flow of powers in the universe has been going the Serpent's way through the billions of years since the world's creation. Now at last it is time for the balance to be righted, before it tips completely in the Worm's favour . . .'

'We know that the balance must be righted, and assume that it will be,' said Dritha, 'but I believe you sometimes fear – as I do – that the Serpent will win, after all.'

'It's unthinkable,' Eldor replied rapidly. This doubt was rarely voiced between them. 'But yes, I sometimes think of what could happen . . . the chaos it would cause throughout the universe. And this world would be left floating in a timeless nightmare, adrift in an evil membrane through which the benign powers could never again penetrate.'

'That's what M'gulfn wants,' his wife stated. 'The odds are all in its favour, and more energy flows to it every day. Oh, Eldor, I wish it was over.' She leaned forward and touched his knee; he closed his large, craggy hand around her fingers. Perfect and sorrowful understanding passed between them.

'We, alone of all of them, elected to remain in human form when the others chose to depart. Now we must see through to the end what we have begun,' the sage said.

Dritha sat back, sadly turning her eyes away.

'What we have begun,' Eldor repeated softly, 'albeit inadvertently, and with the best intentions.'

'So be it, but it saddens me that three humans must suffer so much in the process – just three of them to be pushed this way and that by the struggling forces of the universe. Is there nothing we can do?'

Eldor looked as deeply troubled as his wife.

'We are doing what we can, though I agree it barely suffices. Only the H'tebhmellians can help them now. What knowledge they have is forbidden to us on Earth, lest the Serpent discover it.'

'That is a price the Guardians have delighted in extracting from us,' Dritha sighed.

'Indeed,' he nodded. 'But it is understandable. You and I are supposed to be neutral, concerned only with the balance; but by remaining in this form and among humans we have abandoned neutrality. We have developed conscience, become aware of the cruelty of manipulation and our helplessness to avert it. I know how you feel, Dritha; that the saving of this world is surely more important than the redistribution of distant, mindless powers. And I agree.'

'Yes,' she affirmed with feeling. 'The Guardians must eventually atone for what they – what we – have set in motion; therein lies Earth's only hope.'

'They would say that it is easier not to hope, or even to think, but to be mindless, if only that were possible,' Eldor said with a trace of humour. But Dritha shivered, as if the fire's yellow flames were ice cold. 'But Medrian, Estarinel and Ashurek are human; they must find hope. I give as much as I can without the lie of false optimism.'

'Oh, I fear for them,' Dritha exclaimed. 'When they find hope – if they are so fortunate – will they even then realise that it is more than hope they must seek?'

For once the great sage had no answer. He looked up at the wall above the hearth where there hung a small, beautifully-worked tapestry depicting a stylised bird. It was in shadow, hard to discern.

'It's only a tapestry, only an image,' said Dritha. 'The reality they must learn and recognise for themselves.'

It was dark outside, and there was a distinct chill in the air, though the Forluinish seemed unaware of it as they sat on a large, smooth boulder on the bank of the stream. Next to them a gnarled tree leaned out over the water, half its roots exposed by the erosion of the earth beneath it. The stream bubbled past, clear, calm, oblivious to the feelings of the five humans staring disconsolately down at it. It was the following morning – heralded by the merest hint of twilight – and in a few minutes Estarinel must leave to join the H'tebhmellian ship.

'There seems to be no colour at all here,' said his sister, Arlena. 'The valley's all brown and rust and grey . . . so different to Forluin. Yet it has a kind of beauty . . . peace. I feel as if I could see into the clefts of rock over which the stream runs, into the hidden secrets of the Earth . . . even through to the other side. So different . . .' her voice trailed off. Estarinel looked at her slender hands, white against the dark rock.

'What are they like, your companions?' Falin asked quietly. Estarinel hesitated, not wanting to say anything that would make them worry even more.

'Unhappy and desperate, like us,' he said at last. 'But as deter-mined . . . and stronger than me, I think. Yes, they are strong.'

'But to be trusted?' Arlena needed to know.

'Yes. I have faith in Eldor,' he answered.

'And I,' Edrien affirmed. 'Heaven knows, we must have faith in something.'

'He did not seem able to offer those poor Morrenish sailors much help,' said Luatha. 'I heard a couple of them muttering beside me that a time is coming when the Serpent will take over the whole Earth, and Prince Ashurek's presence here proves it.' Arlena looked at her, alarmed.

'But it was just gossip; the Morrenish are superstitious, aren't they?' she said. Then she clutched her brother's arm. 'Oh, E'rinel I wish you did not have to go with that man! He terrifies me.' He and Falin both put comforting arms round her.

'Arlena, there's no need to fear for me. He is the Serpent's enemy, I am in no doubt of that. That's what is important,' said Estarinel, trying to sound as reassuring as he could. His sister straightened and pushed back her silver hair, recovering her com-posure with a courageous smile.

'We must trust Eldor,' said Luatha, reaching out to take her hand. They all nodded in agreement, exchanging looks of love and hope that were as wretched as they were brave. Each was wrestling against private despair, the misery of parting, the feeling that the Serpent had already won and the Quest was just a pretence of hope.

'E'rinel, there is some good news,' Falin said as brightly as he could. 'We were talking to Dritha last night, after you'd gone with Eldor, saying – well, that the voyage back to Forluin would be a long and dreary one. She gave us something – I got the impression she did not part with it lightly, only because she was so concerned for us.' He produced a small, pointed grey stone. 'It is a sort of lodestone, which will enable us to return to Forluin within a month.'

'That's good. I'm glad,' said Estarinel, grateful that his friends would return home quickly, but not daring to wonder what they would find when they got there.

They sat without speaking for a time, the only noise that of the running stream; just as if they were sitting in some calm glade in Forluin before the coming of the Worm. Arlena jumped like a startled gazelle before the others even heard the sound of grooms bringing horses to the front of the House of Rede.

'E'rinel,' Falin said, 'you had better go.'

Ashurek watched, from a distance, as Estarinel said goodbye to his friends. They all embraced him – Falin, Edrien, Luatha, and last of all his sister, Arlena. She clung to him, weeping openly.

'Try not to worry about me, it won't help,' he told them, completely at a loss for what he should say. 'You must return to Forluin safely; that's all that matters now.'

Arlena let him go and stood close to Falin, who was almost as pale with sorrow as she. Estarinel mounted his horse and rode to where Ashurek, Eldor and Medrian waited. It was as if his four countrymen's distress at his departure had absorbed all his own capacity for sadness at that moment. He felt calm enough to produce a convincing smile and a wave as the four riders began to wind their way through the mountain passes that led to the shores of the Southern Ocean.

Eldor went first, on a sturdy, pale grey heavy-horse, with Estarinel riding beside him. His great silver-brown stallion, Shaell, moved at a high-stepping prance which was his normal walk. Following him came Ashurek, eyes fixed ahead of him but not really taking in what they saw. His mare, Vixata, was a finely-built, ethereal-looking beast, gleaming gold and copper and silvery-white with a light of her own. She went with her delicate head high, her eyes pools of liquid jet, fire dripping from her mane. Medrian tailed at the back, speaking to no one. She rode a long, low beast, black as a beetle, and with a sullen manner as if there was some dark power about it.

The mountains were bulks of shadow in the darkness. It was only a few hours' ride to the coast, where the H'tebhmellian ship awaited them. The hired vessel on which Medrian had arrived had already departed, and a message was to be taken to Ashurek's Tearnian crew that he no longer needed their ship.

Estarinel and Eldor rode in silence for a time. Then Eldor said, 'So the plan is for you to sail the ship until it takes you to the Blue Plane and find help there. It should take only a few days. Then you will go North to destroy the Serpent.'

'If nothing goes wrong,' Estarinel replied quietly, as new doubts and worries assailed him.

'Well, I must warn you that the Serpent will not remain in ignorance for long about the attack you plan.'

'But how could it know?' Estarinel asked, dismayed.

'If it could not see almost everything it wants to, it would be far less trouble to the world. It cannot read minds – as a rule – but it will know. Perhaps it knows of your coming already.' Seeing the expression on the young Forluinishman's face, Eldor continued, 'Estarinel, I am not trying to frighten you, just warn you of what you will have to face. There is much more to it than its hideous physical being.'

Estarinel looked at Eldor, perplexed.

'Please, give me some advice. How can Ashurek and Medrian be so certain of their purpose? To me this journey is like stepping into an abyss with closed eyes.'

'They are not certain of themselves; it is like that for them too, but need has made them push doubt from their minds. I know you are demoralised and confused by the attack on Forluin, and at every turn you are told you are trying to destroy something inde-structible. But you must put these difficulties behind you, because the Quest must take place.

'The journey won't be easy, and you may have to depend on those whom you think cannot really be trusted, so you must always have your wits about you. Never take anything for granted, but at the same time be aware that action is often more appropriate than analysis . . .'

Estarinel grimaced. 'If only the H'tebhmellians could have sent a mighty warrior – not me!' But Eldor laughed.

'You Forluinish have a charming unworldliness,' he said. 'You also have a great deal of common sense.' He paused. 'I may be wrong, but – it seems to me that the Serpent attacked you physically because it cannot attack you mentally. That may be your greatest weapon.' He did not add that it might be a weapon easily torn away in a violent world.

'My thanks for the encouragement, Eldor,' the fledgling knight smiled.

Eldor thought, I wish I could tell you, Estarinel – but it would help not at all, and it would make no difference, except to make things worse. He shook his head in sadness.

The cold Southern mountains reared around them, grey, bleak and impassive. Presently Eldor pulled up his horse and indicated a track climbing up the rocks to their left.

'Your way to the coast will be quickest if you go by that track. You can't miss the ship. It's best that I leave you here, my old horse is not as fit as he was . . .' He shook hands with the three, bidding them farewell and good luck. He turned his steed, but hesitated, and touched Medrian gently on the arm, saying, 'Fare you well, brave child.' Then he rode away, a grey figure receding into shadow, and Estarinel felt that he had said too little, departed too suddenly. It seemed that the very last vestige of friendship and safety was dwindling to nothing with Eldor, leaving only the cold unknown to welcome them now.

He glanced at his companions and was struck by the intensity of their gaze; Ashurek's eyes were bitter and piercing, Medrian's expressionless and dark. Yet for some reason it was the woman's eyes that chilled him to the heart.

'Well, come on then,' said Ashurek, nudging the warm flanks of his mare. They began the ascent of the steep side-pass.

After several hours' ride, they were guiding their mounts down slippery, black paths to the beach. The dark cliff dropped sheer to the water's edge, separated from it only by a narrow, gritty beach which gleamed with a faint radiance in the dim twilight. The horses slithered gratefully from the treacherous paths to solid ground. The sea was grey and sullen, but calm. The whole day had an atmosphere of foreboding, which probably suited the mood of Ashurek and Medrian very well; but Estarinel, of a laughing and light-loving race, felt increasingly oppressed by it.

Then they saw the ship.

She was moored beneath the shelter of a great bluff, only fifty or so yards away. She was clean-lined, slender and beautiful, of an ancient, simple design, built of pale, smooth wood. Her figurehead was tall and thin-necked with a mythical beast's head; at her stern was a slim, fluted tail. Her decks were smooth and shone with a glistening radiance that fell from her three tall, graceful masts. At the top of each a white light sparkled; but they had no sails. Nor were there holes for oars.

'Very pretty,' said Ashurek, 'but how does she move?'

They cantered towards her, Medrian hanging back slightly on her dark, skeletal steed. Clouds of the horses' breath floated on the crisp air and the crunch of their hooves seemed muffled by the rushing of the sea.

The ship was rocking gently in the grey waves, lovely as the moon. Her name was etched delicately on her bows: *The Star of Filmoriel*.

They sat and stared at her for a long time.

At last Ashurek nudged his ethereal mare forward. This made the others start, and see that a wide gang-plank has been lowered into the shallow waves, although none of them had noticed it being let down.

They dismounted, wading into the tide and leading the snorting, shying horses to the gang-plank. Estarinel went first, leading his courageous brown stallion who went calmly, ears flickering. Medrian's strange beast fought a little, teeth bared as it strained against the bit. She spoke a few words in its ear and it came reluctantly, showing the whites of its eyes. Estarinel felt an instinctive revulsion for the creature as strong as his fascination for Medrian; yet the bond between woman and horse was obvious. Ashurek came last. His delicate mare was half wild with fear, rearing and snorting, kicking up a foam on the water and nearly causing Ashurek to loose her. He managed to guide her to the gang-plank and she suddenly shot up sideways like a crab to stand trembling and dripping on the deck.

Another plank led down into the hold, where they found quarters for the horses, complete with straw and fodder. They settled the beasts, then investigated the vessel.

There were four small cabins, two fore and two aft, simple but comfortable. There was an ample supply of provisions and water. But there were no sails, no oars, no wheel. Furthermore, although the ship was behaving as if she was moored, she had no anchor. There were certainly no one aboard her; but when they returned to the deck the gang-plank had been drawn up.

Ashurek commented on the strangeness of this but added that even so, he felt the ship was to be trusted, an honest and well-meaning entity. At any rate, the horses were settling down in her very quickly.

'I did not really expect there to be a crew aboard. The H'tebhmellians are a strange people – our lands have close contact with them, but they are not human,' Estarinel said, leaning on the rail and gazing into the water.

'Is it true, then, that there is an Entrance Point to the Blue Plane in Forluin?' asked Ashurek.

'No, but the particular orbits of the Entrance Points bring them across Forluin quite often. So it is that we have had more contact with them than the rest of the world has. And they say the H'tebhmellians can use magnetism to deflect the Entrance Points, and make them appear where they want them.'

'Can they indeed? Silvren and I wasted much time and effort trying to get there – and yet you can walk freely in and out?'

'No, we cannot. It is rare that anyone visits the Blue Plane, and rare for a H'tebhmellian to walk in Forluin. I have never been there, nor seen an inhabitant,' he said, with a note of deep regret in his voice.

'Well, in a few days, so you say, we will be there.'

Estarinel glanced at the tall Gorethrian, then stared at the sea once more.

'I wish it had been in happier circumstances,' he muttered. 'First things first, though; how do we get this ship to move?'

At that moment there was a cry from Medrian, who had climbed up to the fo'c'sle deck: 'Look!'

They ran up the steps to the deck to find Medrian staring down into the waves, one white hand on the figurehead's neck.

'Look,' she repeated.

Harnessed to the prow of the ship were two horses, half-submerged in the grey water. They were strong, well-muscled beasts, with powerful, curving necks and broad backs. In the half-light they glistened grey, blue and green, as if formed from ancient, sea-washed rock. Below the water their legs graduated into great fins, and their heads were long and thin, like the heads of sea-horses – indeed, they were a kind of sea-horse. From their small mouths, plaited leather reins ran up and were loosely knotted round the rail.

Ashurek's verdant eyes came alive in his dark face. He unknotted the reins and made contact with the horses' sensitive mouths. They responded instantly.

'Ho! Forward then!' he called, and they began to swim forward, slowly at first, but gathering speed. *The Star of Filmoriel* cut smoothly through the waves. Estarinel turned to speak to Medrian, but she suddenly walked away and went down onto the main deck and thence down into the hold. Her face was white and expressionless and she looked almost ill.

'If only her hatred of me was open, I'd understand her,' muttered Ashurek, glaring after her.

'Why are you so sure that she must hate you?' Estarinel asked. That two people should dislike each other on such slight acquaintance was an anathema to him. He wanted to understand as well. But Ashurek only shook his head, grimacing.

'How little you must know of world events. Still, the invasion of Alaak was nine years ago . . . I dare say you were hardly out of childhood then.'

'I am twenty-three,' Estarinel informed him, 'and I believe Medrian is no more than two, three years older than me at most.'

'Ye gods,' said Ashurek very softly, leaning back against the rail. 'I was only twenty-three when Alaak . . . I believe she's a Serpent-sent reminder. You, also, must have every reason to despise me. I knew I should have embarked on this mission alone . . .'

'Listen,' Estarinel said, his gentle eyes becoming purposeful, 'I believe you've told me the truth about yourself, and I know that we are linked by a common purpose: to destroy the Serpent M'gulfn. I really don't care about anything else; I only care that the Worm is stopped from slaughtering innocent people. Whatever our feelings about each other, we must have a working relationship.'

Ashurek looked surprised, and smiled suddenly.

'Nobly spoken, indeed! For your philanthropic attitude, my friend, I have every respect.'

Estarinel shrugged. 'I have no personal grudge against you. But you believe Medrian does?'

'Put it this way: I don't see how she could fail to. So why does she deny it? If I knew the truth I'd feel easier, that is all; but it doesn't really matter. Only the Worm matters – as you so rightly say.'

The ship was sailing surprisingly fast as the horses swam strongly, shoulders heaving. Ashurek loosely wrapped the reins round the figurehead's neck and called, 'Come on, come on!' and the horses responded to his encouragement, swimming on without guidance from the reins. As they swam they dipped their slender muzzles into the waves, grazing continually on krill to sustain their energy. In fact the whole ship was a kind of lodestone, moving as sure as an arrow towards the Entrance Point, while at the same time drawing the Point towards itself.

The cliffs of the cold Southern continent slid below the horizon. The darkness grew. The open ocean was all around them. The slim figure that was Estarinel and the tall one that was Ashurek stood motionless for a long time. After a while Medrian returned, quiet as a cat, to join them, and they all stared at the waves, lost in thought.

Estarinel soon realised that he was unlikely to be able to draw his companions' minds from their dark labyrinths to dwell on more practical matters. In a way, also, the ship and the sailing to the Blue Plane were his responsibility. He decided to busy himself with plans for the journey rather than let his mind dwell on things he would rather forget.

He arranged a system by which they took it in turns to keep watch, eat, sleep and tend to the horses. The 'spirit' which had raised and lowered the gang-plank made no further appearances except to keep the lights on the mast-tops perpetually burning; it was as if the ship itself were sentient, and Estarinel found this reassuring rather than unnerving.

He hoped they would not be at sea for long, because there was so little space to exercise the horses. On reflection it seemed almost cruel to have brought them, but Eldor, in his noncommittal way, had hinted that it was a wise plan; they might be needed on the first part of the journey when they left the Blue Plane. Besides, concern for his horse Shaell at least kept him in tenuous contact with normality.

And so the Quest of the Serpent began. Estarinel found his companions morose and unfriendly; he had imagined they would perhaps be fearless and vigorous warriors, not these cold, introverted strangers. They were so unlike the warm and outgoing Forluinish, and in his own depressed and fearful state he did not feel inclined to offer them his own friendship. But while battling inwardly with dread and homesickness, outwardly he managed to remain calm and practical. And already – as was Forluinish nature – he was coming to feel concern for his companions.

Ashurek at least was fairly talkative, although he was obviously a deeply bitter and cynical man, and Estarinel preferred not to think about the terrible life he had led. But, although he felt drawn to Medrian, she remained silent and cold. Any attempt at conversation was met with short, icy replies, and she would even walk away in mid-sentence, as if it pained her to talk. She obviously preferred her own company, but the sight of her – a slender, dark figure staring out to sea – moved him in a way he did not comprehend.

On their third day afloat he joined her at the rail on the fo'c'sle and said, 'The horses are bearing up well – I think it will be no more than three or four days before the ship finds the Entrance Point.'

Instead of her usual terse reply, Medrian looked round at him, her face half in darkness.

'Why did no one question the wisdom of us bringing horses?' she asked, very quietly. 'There's little use in taking horses on a ship to the Blue Plane – and they cannot come to the Arctic with us.'

'I suppose we all thought we might need them,' he answered, slightly surprised.

'Yes, we will need them,' she said, and he noticed her hands tightening on the rail until they were white, 'because we cannot keep secrets from the Serpent, and it will not let us go to the Blue Plane.'

Estarinel stared at her.

'It will not—'

'Do you think it wants to commit suicide?' she said angrily; then she muttered, 'Perhaps it does . . .'

'Eldor warned me that it would know,' Estarinel said, trembling suddenly. 'So if it should stop us reaching the Blue Plane, what will happen?' Medrian shook her head, her dark hair falling across her face. 'Oh Medrian, look, we are aboard a H'tebhmellian ship. It cannot go astray, and surely the Serpent has no power over it?' he reasoned.

'No power over it, exactly, but power over the elements . . .' she bowed her head and clasped her arms around herself. 'I'm trying to warn you in the only way I can—' she bit her lower lip, turned away from him, and walked towards her cabin.

93

He made to go after her, but stopped himself. Was she mad? he wondered. Perhaps she was just very frightened. He went to the prow and looked down at the sea-horses, who seemed totally calm as they swam on strongly.

Estarinel had the utmost faith in the H'tebhmellians, but the premonitions of disaster that Medrian had instilled did not diminish.

Ashurek, in his cabin, woke violently from a nightmare. He had been dreaming about his sister, Orkesh; she was shouting at him, from a very great distance, tearing at her long hair with emaciated fingers.

'Why did you kill me? You could have saved me – if you had stopped, thought – not behaved as the automaton that Meshurek and the demon had set in motion. If you'd only had the courage to defy them, Ashurek. Oh, how I loved you, relied on you, my brother – my salvation – but do you know where I am now? Do you know? Do you know? Do you—'

She seemed to turn into Silvren, or she was both women at once – a woman with dark skin and golden hair, who was at the same time his daughter.

He sat up on his bunk, angrily forcing his mind to reason. He had no daughter, and Orkesh was dead. Perhaps she was right, he could have found a way to rescue her from Meheg-Ba – for killing his own sister he was certainly damned forever, damned by his own guilt and self-loathing. He shook his head to clear the nightmare.

He lay back, thinking of Silvren. He remembered how she had rescued him from the castle of Gastada, and that ghastly place came into his memory as he lay with the ship rocking gently beneath him. Against his will, he once again saw Gastada before him, and heard the thick, muffled voice of the hideous little man.

'Ah, Ashurek,' Gastada had whispered, 'I believe only the Serpent itself could break your will . . . all my most refined and exquisite tortures I have used on you, yet you still resist me.'

'Well, if I knew what you wanted, perhaps I could help,' Ashurek had replied with malicious sarcasm, in spite of being prostrate and in agony from Gastada's hospitality.

'Isn't it obvious? Surrender yourself to the Serpent – surrender to the Shana, and to me . . .' Gastada had been Duke of Guldarktal, a once-noble Tearnian country, but was now a minion of the Serpent, made insane by concourse with demons. 'It is so ridiculous – you possess the Egg-Stone, that ultimate instrument of the Serpent

M'gulfn, yet you oppose the Serpent! And the wonderful irony is that you cannot live without the Egg-Stone, although you so loathe it!' He waved a hand at the tiny squalid cell in which Ashurek was imprisoned. 'Ah well, you will be pleased to know that you cannot escape from my home. The one door is held shut by demonic power – that is, if you should ever unshackle yourself and kill all my guards, and so reach it!' Gastada chuckled madly at Ashurek, who was chained to a wall and helpless with fever and pain.

The Egg-Stone had not helped him; it seemed the Serpent had withdrawn its power while trying to control Ashurek. He remembered the terrible darkness as he had neared death, and then the equally terrible brightness as Silvren had forced her way into the castle to save him.

He remembered it as a vivid, unforgettable dream: Silvren, seeming to be bathed in a white light, unleashing to the full her sorcerous power. The chains falling from him, Gastada's guards dying, lightning flaring – the hideous castle trembling to its foundations. He saw again the dreadful pointed black door opening, straining against Silvren's will, and then there had been the terrifying descent of the rock face on which the castle sat, until they were both lying, exhausted, at its foot.

The memory was so clear that it seemed Silvren was indeed there beside him – pushing her golden hair back from her golden face with shaking hands. Neither of them had spoken for a long time, until Ashurek saw that she was weeping.

'Why are you crying?' he had asked. She clasped his hands and looked across the desolate heaps of ash that surrounded Gastada's castle.

'I knew this country,' she said, 'before Gastada became involved with the Serpent. It was beautiful, and many people lived here. Now there is desolation. This is what the Worm wants – desolation!' She shook with tears and he held her while she cried.

Eventually he said drily, 'I have caused such destruction also. Perhaps Gastada did this while the soldiers who might have prevented it were in the East, fighting the Gorethrian armies.'

She looked angrily up at him.

'Why say that? Do you want to make me hate you, to help assuage a guilty conscience?'

'I have no conscience,' he said.

'Say what you like!' Silvren exclaimed. 'I still love you.'

'You risked your life to save mine,' he said, more gently. 'I had no idea your powers were so great . . .'

'I was not sure, either.' She half-smiled, but she looked ashen. Suddenly he realised that she was in pain.

'Silvren, are you well enough to carry on? You seem ill.'

'Neither of us is very fit, are we?' She smiled up into his dark face. 'Ashurek . . . sorcery is not just a terrible drain on my strength. It actually hurts. It is not like the children's stories where the wizard just waves a hand. It is more like – giving birth.' She did not tell him this for sympathy; she seemed to have almost no thought for herself at all, except for an occasional amused bitterness at her lot. 'When the Serpent is gone, there will be more like me. I hope it will not be as difficult for them. At present, even for the smallest spell the power has to be dragged screaming into this world.

'I don't know whether my sorcerous power was a terrible mistake, or necessary for the evolution of the Earth. I think not knowing is the worst thing of all.'

He realised then how terribly alone she was. He had thought himself alone, sundered from his people by fate and circumstance. But Silvren was alienated from the whole of humanity by powers she did not want, and the awful burden of having to use them.

He remembered the warmth of her body and the softness of her hair on his hands as they lay below Gastada's castle, comforting each other while they gathered strength to go on. And just a few weeks later, the demons Meheg-Ba and Diheg-El, with the help of his brother Meshurek, tore them apart and sent Silvren to the Dark Regions . . .

Ashurek cursed and leapt from the bunk. There was nothing to be done – he was already doing what he could, which was to try to kill the Serpent. And as well as the grief at the loss of Silvren, which never lessened, there was also the burning hole that had been left when he parted with the evil Egg-Stone.

Estarinel saw him stride up to the prow and furiously urge the sea-horses to greater efforts, his dark face grim with anger and his whole frame alive with dangerous energy.

'I wish this voyage was over,' Estarinel thought, and went down into the hold to attend to his horse, who was apparently the only sane being on board.

For two more days they made a straight, smooth course North. The twilight deepened to a permanent night. Sky and sea were clear, calm, cold. The lights on *The Star of Filmoriel*'s masts cast a pure glow about the ship. The powerful sea-horses never tired or faltered.

It was on their fifth day afloat that dark clouds began to stream across the sky, obscuring the stars. The atmosphere seemed thick and stuffy; it was difficult to draw breath and the air felt clammy on their skin. The waves were rising gradually higher and higher, dragging the ship slowly up to each crest then sending her plummeting down with sickening speed. Salt spray flew, stinging their faces and crusting on their skin. Then the rain began, falling in great oily drops which had a bitter taste. Horribly, there was no wind, but powerful currents beneath the waves dragged the ship faster and faster Northwards.

There was nothing fresh and wild about this storm. It was sullen, sluggish and menacing. There was no thunder, no lightning; it was an unhealthy storm.

The three stood at the rearing and plunging prow, gripping the rail.

'Perhaps the Serpent does know we're coming,' said Estarinel faintly. Medrian shot him an unfathomable sideways look and Ashurek smiled with grim humour.

'Probably,' he replied.

The ship cut the top of a wave and they gasped as a sharp wall of spray hit them. The small ship pitched and rolled, careered down one black wave and was heaved to the top of another. The sea-horses were cruising with the current, not having to make any effort to pull the ship; but they were very uneasy. In the hold, too, the three horses were restlessly moving about their stalls.

'Nothing we can do about this weather except wait until it dies down. At least its carrying us in roughly the right direction,' said Ashurek.

The ship was tossed from side to side as wall after wall of sea water washed over them. The Forluinishman – hanging onto the rail as he made his way to the hold – went below to quiet the horses. When he returned to the fo'c'sle there was a strange heat in the air. Ashurek was pointing out to sea. It was difficult to see anything through the dark, bitter rain and with the spray half-blinding them; but they could just make out a faint pink glow stretching across the horizon.

'What is it? Surely not sunrise?' asked Estarinel, squinting through the storm. Ashurek pulled his hood over his helm.

97

'No . . . I believe it is what they call the "Roseate Fire". Some sort of natural phenomenon – a ring of fire on the water.' They looked to the South and found that the glow encircled them along the whole horizon.

'Natural, indeed?' said Estarinel. 'There is nothing natural about this storm.' The bitter rain grew heavier. 'Can we sail through it?'

'I know not, we can only try,' Ashurek replied with a humourless grin.

Medrian's dark eyes were very wide and, as she stood rigidly by the figurehead, her lips moved slowly as if she was whispering to herself. She seemed oblivious of the other two. She was staring at something on the horizon, or perhaps at something within herself.

Pitching and tossing, *The Star of Filmoriel* rushed towards the rosy glow. She rolled onto her side and righted herself, leaving the three clinging wildly to the rail, gasping with the force of the oily waves. The light from the masts seemed muffled by the brownish clouds that boiled low in the sky. The waves were carrying them forward at a sickening rate and the heat in the North was growing fiercer.

Ashurek stumbled, cursed, and dragged himself back onto his feet. The Roseate Fire was ahead of them, a thick, transparent wall that coloured the sea behind it pink. There were no flames to it, but they could feel its heat scorching their faces. The rain that hit it turned to steam.

Ashurek seized the sea-horses' reins and shouted to Estarinel, 'Find something to throw into the Fire – I'm ready to turn the ship if it burns!'

Estarinel found a short length of rope on deck and hurled it into the pink aura. There was a spurt of flame and a sprinkle of black ash floated down where the rope had been.

'There's your answer, Estarinel – we cannot sail through it.' They shouted to the horses to turn West, while the Gorethrian hauled on the reins.

The horses began to fight the swelling waves, which were keeping them almost continually submerged. They were powerful beasts; the strength of the current was still pushing them towards the fire, but gradually they were forcing their way Westwards.

Meanwhile, Medrian, feet spread to balance herself, was divesting herself of cloak, boots and sword. A thin streak of darkness, she suddenly dived off the side of the ship into the pitiless waves below.

'The fool! What's she doing?' cried Ashurek. They leant over the rail. Medrian, tossed by the waves, was clinging to one of the horses, fumbling with a strap. She was unharnessing the beasts from the ship.

'Stop!' Ashurek shouted over the noise of the storm. 'Don't unharness them!'

Medrian's voice was faint as she upturned her pale, spray-soaked face. 'They'll be swept into the fire!'

'They won't! They're pulling us clear!' Medrian ignored him. She unharnessed the horses and they swam free of the ship, but stayed closed to her as if reluctant to leave her to drown. The ship, without the help of the horses, was now being swept straight into the fire.

Estarinel, meanwhile, had thrown Medrian a rope.

'Help me pull her up,' he told Ashurek. Even as he spoke, the heat grew unbearable. The figurehead entered the pink aura and caught fire. Medrian could not reach the rope, but was suddenly swallowed by a great wave which hurtled, steaming, into the glow.

'We'd better jump!' cried Ashurek, leaping off the side of the ship. Estarinel followed. He thought of their horses as he fell towards the dark waves, feeling flames catching at his cloak.

5

Hrannekh Ol

Estarinel landed, to his surprise, in four feet of fine white ash. It caved in on top of him, filling his nostrils, mouth, eyes. He struggled to regain his feet, floundering and coughing, unable to breathe because of the dust. At last he was standing waist deep in the ash which floated in a cloud around him. He stood still, waiting for it to settle. He looked about him. On his left was *The Star of Filmoriel*, half-submerged in the dry ash, her figurehead badly scorched. Medrian was leaning against her bows, her back to him and an arm across her face. There was a sound of coughing and Ashurek emerged from the ash.

They were standing on a white plain which stretched endlessly in all directions. The sky, too, was white as a bleached bone. The air was as dry as the dust. It was not hot, but their water-sodden clothes were already drying out as if the air were greedily sucking the moisture from them.

'Is everyone all right?' asked Estarinel.

'It seems so,' said Ashurek. 'This must be the White Plane Hrannekh Ol; when we entered the Roseate Fire we must have gone straight through an Entrance Point. I suppose neither of you have been here before.'

'No,' both replied.

'Nor I,' he said. 'I have no idea what to expect of it; I have never made a study of the Planes.'

Medrian was still leaning against the ship, facing them now, with her eyes closed. A faint crust of salt was forming on her dark grey tunic and breeches. Estarinel went up to her.

'Are you sure you are well?' he asked.

'Perfectly,' she answered shortly. Her sharp-featured face always looked pale and ill, so it was impossible to judge by looking at her. 'Our being here is my fault. I misjudged the horses' strength. They could have pulled us clear.' Ashurek looked doubtfully at her, but whatever thoughts he had he kept to himself.

'Come on,' he said. 'Let us sort ourselves out.'

The horses were uneasy, noticing the lack of motion and the change in the air. They settled them as best they could and went on deck. As Medrian pulled her boots back on and retrieved her sword and cloak, they decided to climb a small hillock nearby. It was unlikely that there was any life on this moistureless, desolate place, but they must somehow find an Exit Point back to Earth.

They took water with them on their short walk to the hillock. Their mouths were dry and a cold sweat was on their skin, evaporating rapidly. They struggled through the four feet of fine ash, every move sending up a puff of choking dust which caught in their throats, making them cough continually.

It was a strange place. There was nothing menacing, nothing cruel about it. It was absolutely impassive. There was no sun and the light never changed. It was like a white cocoon that stretched infinitely in all directions. Such was the White Plane Hrannekh Ol.

They waded through the ash to the top of the low hill and discovered, as they had suspected, that there was nothing to see in the whole featureless terrain. Whether the Plane had been any different in the past they did not know, but it was like the inside of a perfect egg-shell that had never contained the promise of life. They stood looking about them, sipping enough water to moisten their mouths. Their ship lay in the ash like a dead swan.

'Poor *Star*,' said Estarinel, sounding distraught. 'How can I ever make amends to the H'tebhmellians? Perhaps it's lucky you unharnessed the sea-horses or they'd be trapped here as well.'

'I don't know,' Medrian muttered, handing the flask of water to Ashurek. Estarinel could not forget how strangely she had behaved during the storm, nor could he understand it. Whatever the reason, she was her normal quiet self now.

They kept their eyes on the ship, for it was the only relief from the depressing, monotonous whiteness.

In such a dead place, they could not have suspected that four figures were creeping silently up the hill behind them. Sensing their presence too late, Ashurek spun round, drawing his sword with one swift movement, but the four had long white spears at the ready, and quickly surrounded them. There were a few moments of absolute stillness. The four strangers were tall, pale-skinned men, clad in a transparent cellulose membrane that covered every inch of their bodies, even their faces. Beneath the strange membrane they were naked. They wore no armour.

'There is no need to threaten us,' said Estarinel calmly. 'We mean you no harm.' He glanced at Ashurek glowering over the point of his keen sword and grimaced at the nonsense this made of his statement.

With a sudden flick of his spear tip, one of the men caught Ashurek's sword and sent it flying; they were obviously skilled with weapons. Ashurek did not react openly, but his whole body became dangerously alert.

'Come with us,' one said, poking Estarinel sharply in the back. 'We've waited a long time for this.'

'Wait – all we want is to find an Exit Point back to Earth,' said Estarinel, his heart sinking as he realised the uselessness of Forluinish reason against the white warriors.

'Ah, sweet Earth! Don't we all!' the man spat.

'You have nothing to fear from us,' Estarinel persisted.

'Nothing to fear, but plenty to gain,' growled another of them. 'Your ship – how much water is aboard?'

'Water?' Estarinel looked at the man's face and saw it was wrinkled like a dried fruit. He felt breathless and weak as if he was rapidly dehydrating. 'Are you taking us prisoner?'

'It seems so. Stop talking, it wastes moisture.' Without warning Ashurek spun about, wresting the spear from the man behind him. Medrian and Estarinel drew their swords. The men swung their spears and they blocked the blows easily; but the fourth man struck at Medrian's legs from behind, so violently that she fell over. He sprang to her side and held her down with a spear at her back.

'Cease resisting,' he shouted, 'or I will kill her.' His spear tip had already torn her tunic. There was a desperate, animal-like streak in the four men which, judging by the dryness of the place, could easily be a maniacal desire for water. Meanwhile Estarinel had received a wound on the shoulder. Ashurek emerged coughing from the ash, but his opponent was now lying buried in the dust, not moving. He found a spear on either side of him. Estarinel, sword in hand, looked at the man who was threatening Medrian.

'Drop the sword,' the man commanded. Estarinel gave in and the man let Medrian rise. Then they saw that a further five men had come up the hill. One, who seemed to be in charge, grinned almost with greed.

'Well, ye've made a find that'll save your own skins for a week or two,' he addressed the first three men. He looked down at the dead man lying in the ash. 'Oh well. One less mouth to feed. Bring

102

the body along with the prisoners. Quickly now, before they start to dry out,' he said, as if talking about lumps of meat.

They were prodded down through the thick, dry ash. In the side of the hillock was a round hole like a man-made tunnel, with the dust swept away from it. The three prisoners were pushed inside. It was a round tunnel carved out of a glistening white stone like rock salt. It led down a long way into a labyrinth of tunnels and caverns. Whether they were man-made or natural was impossible to determine. There were no lamps or torches of any kind anywhere in the tunnels, but they were lit by the same diffuse, shadowless white light as outside. It made everything look flat and made it difficult to judge distance.

Presently they reached the end of the tunnel. Their cloaks and scabbards were forcibly removed and thrown in a careless heap.

Several of the men took their spears and inserted them into cracks in the rock. A section of it slid back towards them, revealing the entrance to a large white cavern about twenty feet high. But the entrance was nearer the roof of the cavern than the floor.

'Right,' said the leader, 'in with them.' The men prodded Estarinel first, towards the hole.

'It's a ten-foot drop to the ground!' he protested.

'And how will you get us out?' Ashurek enquired.

'We'll pull you up on a rope,' said the man, with a hard, joyless laugh. 'I once worked in a slaughterhouse, back on dear Earth!'

'How did you come to be here?' Estarinel asked quickly, but the warriors had no wish for civil conversation.

'Jump!' snarled the leader, poking him so hard that the spear drew blood. They had no choice. One by one they jumped down as gently as they could, sustaining several bruises but no broken bones.

Above them the rock was pushed back into place, sealing them in the white cavern. All three were feeling thirsty and faint. Estarinel rubbed the back of his hand, which felt dry and hot.

'This waterless place is going to take every drop of water in our bodies before long,' he said. 'That strange membrane they wore – it must be to prevent evaporation.'

'That "strange membrane", as you so delicately put it,' said Ashurek, 'looks remarkably like – ah, never mind. This is a sound prison. We could have fought better – if we'd been more alert.'

'Who would have expected there to be life on this place?' Estarinel asked. Ashurek scratched the wall with a fingernail but the rock was as hard as quartz. He was both surprised and relieved to see how calmly Estarinel was reacting. He had feared the Forluinishman might panic at the first crisis. However, that did not help their immediate situation.

'There must be a way out,' Ashurek muttered.

'Those people,' mused Estarinel, 'obviously Tearnians.'

'Morrenish, at a guess.'

They looked at each other.

'The Morrenish at the House of Rede? Their companion ship suffered a fate like ours. I wonder how long they've been here?'

'Two or three months, perhaps. They're obviously a very resourceful people. Even Gorethrians could never be so terrifyingly self-sufficient.' Ashurek grinned like a wolf and winked at Estarinel.

'I can't understand how they've managed to survive here,' continued the Forluinishman innocently. 'What on earth do they do for food?'

Medrian and Ashurek stared at him. Ashurek raised his eyebrows and looked round their prison. 'What do *you* think?' he said.

They were silent for a time. Their thirst grew unbearable. Their skin was beginning to shrivel.

Above them, the rock slid back and two pale, membrane-clad faces peered over greedily.

'Here are the prisoners, Captain,' one said. 'We've got three horses and plenty of water, too.'

'Excellent,' said the Captain, running a dry tongue over his lips. 'They fell through an Entrance Point, did they? They look a little better than those skinny Peradnians, eh! Make the preparations. Bring them out in half an hour's time.' The faces retreated and the rock slid back.

'How do they measure half an hour, without the sun?' said Estarinel, shuddering.

'We may have a chance to escape when they take us out of here,' Ashurek speculated. 'There are many things that can be done with a rope, if we take our chance.' But he felt he could rely only on himself to make an escape. Estarinel's gentle, fair face and dark eyes were troubled; and the Forluinish were not noted for their courage, Ashurek recalled. 'This is no time for diplomacy,' he added.

104

'Yes, that's obvious,' Estarinel said with a half-grin. Then he frowned. 'The Quest cannot end so suddenly, like this . . . can it?' Medrian stared at him, her eyes even blacker than her dark, salt-encrusted hair.

'As Ashurek said, we must take our chance,' she said, her voice as dry as the air.

They sat on the floor of the cavern, watching their prison 'door'. Estarinel struggled to turn his mind from thoughts of Forluin, and from the knowledge that the Worm could so effortlessly turn them aside from their mission and trap them in a white cell. And even if they should escape the clutches of these doomed cannibals, how would they ever find a way back to Earth? He sighed and buried a hand in his long, dust-filled hair.

About twenty minutes had passed when there was a grating sound of rock sliding over rock. They looked towards the entrance but the rock was not moving. The sound was coming from the ground. A round section of the floor sank slowly and a hole in the stone was revealed. After a moment a head poked up through the hole; the bony, white head of an old man. His face was round and small-featured, and he looked pleased to see them.

'Oh good,' he said in an aged, gentle voice. 'I've found you before they took you away. Come on, follow me quickly.'

'Who are you?' asked Estarinel.

'Er – a rescuer,' the old man said. 'Call me Hranna. I'll explain when we get to the other side.'

'Come on,' urged Ashurek. 'Never mind the questions.'

The old man climbed delicately out of the hole which was a good seven feet across. He was only about four feet high and he was thin and wizened with milk-white skin and no hair; but he moved with a fine grace and nimbleness. He was clothed in a robe of soft, glittering gossamer which was of dazzling whiteness and confused the eye if looked at for very long.

'Down the hole with you. I'll follow. Quickly, now!'

Ashurek lowered himself into the hole. To his astonishment he was struck by a swimming dizziness and for a few moments was completely disorientated. It was as if the centre of gravity had suddenly shifted beneath his feet. The shaft had dropped vertically into the ground but now he was walking along it horizontally. The others experienced the same.

The old man, Hranna, slid the section of rock back into place and followed them.

The tunnel must have been a good twelve miles long, for they walked for about three hours. At last Ashurek saw a round disc of whiteness ahead. It was the end of the tunnel. When he reached it, he looked out and saw that it appeared to be set in a sheer, vertical plane. He hesitated.

'Climb out,' urged Hranna behind him. 'It's perfectly all right.'

Ashurek began cautiously to lower himself over the lip of the tunnel-mouth. He was struck again by the dizziness, a feeling of the ground rocking beneath his feet, and was suddenly standing on flat ground looking into a vertical shaft.

When the others had climbed out and regained their orientation, they began to relax and look about them.

It was a flat, white landscape of hard, salty rock, but very different from the ash-submerged place they had just come from. Everywhere were crystalline formations like snow-covered trees, raising their branches to the white sky in delicate, glittering webs. It was like a vast forest after a thick fall of snow; ground, trees and sky all glittering white. It was beautiful. But after a time the endless whiteness became tiring to the eye; there was no escape from it.

The air was quite still. There was not a drop of moisture on the entire Plane. They felt dizzy and breathless from thirst, and Estarinel's wounds on back and shoulder were aching sharply.

Hranna made a strange, quick gesture with his skeletal hand.

'Follow me,' he said, starting to walk. They followed slowly, winding through the crystalline trees in silence.

Presently Estarinel began to wonder why he was accepting all that was happening without a word, and stirred himself to ask, 'Where are we?'

The old man was ready to talk and answer questions openly.

'On the other side of the White Plane, as you call it. It is flat, therefore it has two sides. I believe you term it Hrannekh Ol, but we also call it "Peradnia".'

'I see . . . but I don't quite understand – do you know who those people are? And how did you come to be rescuing us?'

The old man looked thoughtful.

'Those people, we believe, were the crew of a – what do you call it – a merchant ship that fell through an Entrance Point, about three months ago by Earth reckoning – we measure our time by Earth, of course. There are about twelve of them, living in those caves and tunnels. There were more, but their numbers grow fewer as they prey upon each other.

'There are other shafts, like the one down which I brought you, connecting the two sides of the Plane. When we first calculated the humans' arrival, some of my colleagues went through another shaft to help them – only to be attacked, and all, but two, murdered. They are obviously savages with whom it is impossible to make intelligent contact, so we cannot help them regain Earth. They have made two forays down the shaft and seized more of my people – and they keep the opening guarded, so we cannot seal it against them. It is – well – difficult to work in such an atmosphere.'

'How many are there of you?' asked Ashurek.

'Three thousand, four hundred and twenty-three,' the man answered automatically.

'And only twelve of them? Why do you not fight them?'

'We cannot fight. We have never fought, we would not know how. Our bodies are but feeble vehicles for our minds. Our whole existence is devoted to the study of mathematics; we have senses only in order that we may communicate knowledge from one to the other. Our bodies shatter like brittle bones when attacked.

'You see, we are entirely self-sufficient; we do not take in sustenance, nor do we excrete; we were not born, nor shall we die. We have only the physical strength to exist, not to fight for survival.'

Hranna gave them a thoughtful look, then frowned. He waved a greeting to another small, wizened man who sat against a tree, scratching writing on a thin white slate.

At length they saw a dome of filigreed white stone with an arched entrance, like a cobweb frozen in ice.

'Here we are,' said Hranna, ushering them through the door. Inside was another of the ancient, pale people, clad in the strange gossamer.

'Ah, Hranna,' said the man, 'you've got them, have you?'

'Yes, Lenarg – it all went to absolute perfection,' Hranna said.

'Well, naturally,' the second old man smiled, as he left the dome. 'I'll go and set up the – er – thing.'

'Do sit down,' Hranna said, indicating a circular stone ridge in the floor which served as a bench. They sat gratefully, all feeling light-headed and out of breath. 'Tell me how you came to Hrannekh Ol.'

'There's not much to tell,' said Estarinel. 'We were sailing across the ocean when a storm blew up and swept us through an Entrance Point. We had not been on the Plain of Ash long before we were

107

captured. Our ship and our three horses are stranded on the other side.'

'Never mind that,' Ashurek said sharply, looking at Hranna with narrowed green eyes. 'Did I hear you say you could help us regain Earth?'

'Patience, patience,' Hranna muttered with a quick movement of his hand. 'Our calculations are accurate, but they take time.'

'What calculations?' Ashurek asked.

'We are mathematicians – I thought we were well known on Earth—'

'Alas no, except to those who specifically research the matter of the Planes. Are we to understand that you knew of our arrival?'

'Of course!' the small man exclaimed. 'Look, let me show you.' He picked up a thin white slate and with a sharp stone hurriedly scratched a series of figures on it. He handed it to Ashurek who found he had to hold the slate carefully to the light to discern the faint numerals. They formed a long, complicated equation with many unfamiliar symbols. Hranna waited excitedly for their reaction.

'That means nothing to me,' Estarinel said.

'Goodness, but it is only a simple one!' Hranna exclaimed, amazed. 'Oh, oh – forgive my rudeness. You obviously do not realise what we do. Once a few basic calculations have been made, it is possible to work out, in pure mathematics, the entire history of the Universe.'

'Everything?' Medrian said.

'Well yes – down to the tiniest movement of the smallest particle. The past is easy, for theory is proved in fact, over and over again.'

'What of the future?' she asked, mouth dry.

'That is possible also – you have seen we calculated the merchant ship's arrival, and yours, which is how we were able to rescue you. This is our work – we have an ever increasing library of such computations as this.'

'So you could tell us what will happen to us?' Ashurek inquired, cynicism masking a note of pain in his voice.

'If you want, yes,' the little man said hesitantly. He seemed to flutter, like a white moth, then selected a number of the thin slates from a low shelf that lined the dome wall.

Each was covered in the faint, scratched writing, forming

equation after equation, which even a skilled Earth mathematician would have been unable to interpret.

'What does it mean?' Estarinel asked at last.

'Well – that,' said Hranna, pointing at the slates. Sensing the loss of communication with the three humans, he sighed. 'I cannot phrase it in any other way, except in arithmetical terms.'

'So you cannot actually tell us what will happen?' Ashurek said acidly.

'Only if you can understand our physics. I'm sorry,' the old man replied with regret.

'Thank goodness,' Medrian said quietly. 'I did not want to know.'

'Well, with Earth's future we have predicted the presence of a strong random factor; we have yet to identify it, so the alternative computations could run into thousands. It is a marvellous project!'

'I'm sure,' Ashurek said. 'Meanwhile, this talk is not helping us. Estarinel is wounded and we are all three weak with thirst. Have you no food or water?'

'I'm terribly sorry,' replied Hranna slowly and thoughtfully, 'but as I told you, we need neither food nor water to live. There is little free water on either side of the Plane; most is trapped in the crystalline structures—'

'I have no wish to threaten you,' the Gorethrian interrupted, 'but we will die if we stay here. We must return to Earth, very quickly. Do you understand?'

Hranna shrank back, looking dismayed.

'Er – er, yes, of course. I apologise if I seem a little abstracted, we find it difficult to adjust to non-theoretical matters. Lenarg is already making the calculations that will return you to Earth. I will see how he is doing.' And he fluttered hurriedly from the cobweb dome into the pale forest beyond.

How long it was before the Peradnians returned, Ashurek was not sure. It may have been one hour, or two. He wandered aimlessly round the dome. His tongue was dry and swollen and he felt ill from lack of water. Estarinel had gone white and had closed his eyes. He had lost a lot of blood from his shoulder. Medrian's dark eyes roved round the dome and an unhealthy colour had come to her cheeks, making her look feverish. Ashurek blinked. It was difficult even to keep his eyes open. The air kept drying them up. A few hours in this place was the equivalent of days in a desert. Ashurek sat down, closed his eyes, and tried to think.

Hranna eventually returned, with a train of ancient Peradnians curious to see the humans. The three stirred tiredly as he approached.

'We have worked with mathematical instruments and located an Exit Point back to Earth.' Medrian, Estarinel and Ashurek visibly brightened.

'However,' Hranna went on slowly, 'the Exit Point is unfortunately on the other side. We will direct you down the other shaft – not the one of your rescue, but the open shaft of which I told you.'

'Very well. Let us be on our way,' Ashurek said.

'Wait – ah – as you will be going that way, you could seal the shaft for us.' The Peradnians rolled forwards a thick disc of white rock. 'All you need to do is jam it in the tunnel at the correct point. It is so designed that the humans could never remove it from their side. And they will all be dead in a few Earth weeks, anyway.'

'At the moment they are very much alive,' said Ashurek. 'Presumably we will be attacked, as you were.'

'Yes, I expect you will,' Hranna considered. 'It is the only way we can help. You cannot go back into the cave, for that is a trap, and if you walk miles to the next shaft you will die before you reach it.'

Ashurek glowered at the man, but Estarinel said, 'Any hope is better than none.'

'I agree,' Medrian said with a faint laugh.

Then Hranna handed them a pointed white stone on a thread.

'When you reach the other side, suspend this from your hand. Whichever direction it points in, follow that path. The stone follows the axis along which the Exit Point is moving, like a magnet; let it guide you. Now we will take you to the shaft.'

Again they were led through the strange white forest, this time to the mouth of a smaller shaft. Before they set off down it, Hranna looked sadly at them.

'People of Earth have been here before. Some have died of dehydration, some have gone back. But it has always been the same; the lack of communication between us has stopped us helping each other. We cannot express what we know except in figures, and they cannot interpret our equations. Once, some Earth mathematicians worked with us to learn at last our algebra, but I presume that when they died, their work was abandoned. If only you, back on Earth, would initiate that work again!' His thin hands

110

danced. 'Perhaps then we would know why the Planes exist – why the Earth exists. Otherwise what is the White Plane but a wafer of crystal stretched across infinity?'

'Why not come back to Earth with us?' Estarinel asked, feeling a sudden warmth for the tiny, ancient mathematician.

'Oh no, far too wet,' Hranna chuckled. 'You must go now – so I will bid you farewell. I've so much work to do . . .' Even as they began to thank him, his small, pale figure was retreating through the crystal trees.

The dizziness struck them again as they entered the shaft, but this time it did not trouble them. They began the long walk back to the other side, Ashurek rolling the disc of stone which, although it came up to his shoulder, was eerily light for its size. Then came Estarinel with the lodestone, then Medrian.

Physically exhausted as they were, the walk took them four hours this time. But at last they came to a place in the tunnel, near the opening, where the disc wedged itself between floor and ceiling and would roll no further.

'This is the point,' Ashurek said. They slid past the disc and, together, slowly forced it round upon its axis until it filled the shaft. Ashurek flung himself against it, but it was solid.

'Good,' he said through clenched teeth. 'Now prepare yourselves, the tunnel mouth is ahead and we are unarmed.'

But when they stumbled to the end, there were none of the pale humans to be seen. The danger that Hranna had feared was non-existent. With relief they climbed out dizzily onto the choking ash.

'Now, Estarinel, the lodestone,' said the dark Gorethrian.

'The horses,' the Forluinishman corrected him. 'First we rescue the horses.'

On the far side of the White Plane Hrannekh Ol, Lenarg scratched busily upon his slate. Hranna looked over his shoulder.

'They should reach the Exit point here—' he wrote an explanatory theorem, and Hranna nodded. 'And Earth here—'

'I see,' Hranna said. Lenarg's hand moved rapidly on, but he suddenly paused, crossed out his previous calculation, and wrote more feverishly than before.

'Of course, of course!' he cried; then 'Oh no . . .' The slate fell from his hand and smashed to the ground.

'What is it? I missed that last bit,' Hranna said.

'I never even thought – their ship was from the Blue Plane. They

111

should have returned to it – they should have stayed with it all along – oh dear—'

'Is it too late to tell them? Yes, of course it is.' Hranna sat down on a rock. 'So we have set them on the wrong course. We are only supposed to work out the Earth's fate, not influence it. How embarrassing.'

'Perhaps *we* are the random factor,' Lenarg mused. 'It would make our predictions much easier if we were . . .'

'Do not rely on speculation of that sort,' Hranna warned him. 'There is no place for egotism in physics!'

6

Whither the Lodestone Pointed

They were near the low hill that they had seen when they first came
to Hrannekh Ol, but now they were on the other side of it. They
ran – as best they could through the thick ash – to its summit.

What met their eyes was several of the men clambering about
on *The Star of Filmoriel*'s decks like white ants. As they watched,
five men came up from the hold, carrying various objects. One
man, supervising the rest, stood arrogantly on the poop deck,
prodding at the planks with his white spear. Then he shouted a
command. His voice did not carry far in the dusty atmosphere but
they could just make out the words: 'When we've sorted out all
the goods we'll dismantle the ship. The wood will come in useful.'

Estarinel felt sick at heart at these words.

'So,' said Ashurek, 'the shaft is unguarded because they are all
down there looting the ship. We would be best to find the horses
as quickly as we can, while they're still busy.'

'Wait,' Medrian said, laying a hand on Estarinel's arm.
'Estarinel, hold up the lodestone.' He did so. It pivoted on its
thread and came to rest pointing on a line straight past the ship.
'That's the end of our luck; we can't walk past the ship unseen.'

'First things first,' replied Estarinel. 'Let's find the animals.'

They went back down the hill and entered, for a second time,
the tunnel in its side. They walked a long way down the main
tunnel, and made their way at last to the entrance to their former
prison to retrieve their weapons.

Their belongings had gone.

They walked on deeper into the maze of round white passages,
until they reached a junction of three tunnels.

'Suppose we separate,' Ashurek said, 'and meet there . . .' he
indicated a shallow recess a few yards away, where they could
conceal themselves. The others assented, and each went on alone.

As Estarinel walked he caught glimpses of caverns that were

used as living quarters. He kept an eye out for weapons, and listened keenly for any sound of the horses. Presently he saw a cavern that appeared to be a storeroom, and cautiously entered it.

It was a curious place. A small, high-roofed cave, it was littered with the soft white robes and strange sparrow-like bones of the Peradnians; crumpled heaps of parchment; scattered wooden crates; a pile of translucent membranes reminiscent of human skin. It seemed a place filled with rubbish of all kinds which they were desperately hanging onto in the vain hope of squeezing some use out of it.

But at last Estarinel saw something that was useful; a short steel knife with a padded handle of blue velvet. The blue was a spark of colour so unusual in the endless whiteness that it shone out like a star. Estarinel could hardly take his eyes off it. He picked it up.

Then he heard voices. Swiftly, he dived down behind a pile of boxes, and waited.

Three men came in, laden with the ship's provisions, which they dumped unceremoniously in the middle of the cavern.

'Now,' said one imperiously, 'fetch those iron bars. We're going to rip the ship apart. And you—' he commanded one of the men '—go and see to those horses. They can't be left much longer, they'll dry up.'

Estarinel's eyes widened at this. The man who was to tend the horses had already gone, but the other two seemed to take forever rummaging in the piles of junk. At last they too left.

Estarinel, making no sound, crept inch by inch to the cave entrance. He started off down the tunnel quickly and lightly. At last he had the man in sight, and he tailed him for about five minutes, pressed close to the tunnel wall. He thought he saw the opening to a cave ahead.

Suddenly he heard the clop of hooves echoing through the passages, and Medrian emerged from the cave, leading the three horses. She came out cautiously but the man had seen her, and jumped her in an instant. He wrapped one arm tightly about her throat, his other hand twisting her arm behind her back. She struggled, and he grunted as her elbow stabbed into his stomach, but held her tight.

Estarinel ran down the corridor, gripping the knife. He dealt the man one sharp stab in the neck and he died almost instantly. He collapsed to the floor in a loose heap, dragging Medrian with him, a thin pulsing trickle of scarlet running down his spine.

114

She extricated herself from the corpse and hurriedly recaptured the horses who were shying back into the cave. She looked at Estarinel with a mixture of relief and irony in her black eyes. But he was staring at the knife in his hand, blank-faced and seeming shaken to the core.

'Oh gods, what have I done?' he muttered.

'Saved my life, I think,' Medrian smiled, slightly puzzled. But as he turned to look at her, she was taken aback by the horror in his eyes.

'I know it feels bad, but don't worry,' she said brightly, pushing Shaell's rope into his hand.

'But what right had I to end his life?' Estarinel exclaimed, as they began to lead the horses back towards the meeting place. 'Those men are not evil – just sailors, who no more deserve to be here than we do.'

'Destiny is a strange thing . . . if someone had told that man, "you will die at the hand of a Forluinishman", he would have laughed in their face.' Medrian grinned with icy humour.

'How did you become so cold – callous?' Estarinel said thinly. Medrian sighed.

'Look, if he were not dead, I would be. Would that not make you guilty of my murder?'

'I know I had no choice, and I'd kill a thousand times over to save a friend,' he said unhappily. 'But I still think it is wrong. The deed can't be undone, which makes me forever—'

'A murderer, or murdered. That's always the choice,' Medrian said briskly. 'Oh gods, are you always like this? This wild and lawless world has no use for gentleness or conscience.'

'Well, perhaps it should,' he replied quietly.

And Medrian, though she would not admit it even to herself, agreed with him. She said more gently, 'Just remember why you came on this Quest – if you keep that alone in your mind, it will help.'

They reached the recess and backed the animals into it. The three were listless and afraid, but became calm under the touch of Medrian and Estarinel. Only Vixata fought, snapping at Medrian's hands.

Estarinel stared down at the floor, trying to clear his mind. To be single-minded, and not to care – he began to see why his companions were as they were.

Medrian watched him. He did not seem strong – yet he had

115

saved her, without hesitating. Better to be tortured by doubt after a deed than before . . . an unexpected tenderness stole into her unguarded mind. But as it did so, a hole seemed to yawn open in her brain, a subterranean tunnel that led down into a mole-black cavern, from which another tunnel led to another lightless cave – on and on through the centre of the Earth, like jet beads strung on an infinite thread. From that black pit issued a rank wind, chill and burning at the same time. Agony – not pain, something worse. She gasped, clutching at her horse's back to steady herself.

Another second and she had forced the hole closed, sealed it with iron; she pulled herself upright, drawing a long, shuddering breath of relief. By the time Estarinel looked up at her, she had composed her face into its usual pale mask.

He is a danger to me, she thought.

Ashurek appeared at last, a grin gleaming very white on his dark face as he saw them.

'You have a knife,' was the first thing he said to Estarinel. He outstretched a thin, dark hand. 'May I?'

'Certainly,' said Estarinel, quickly handing the knife to him.

The Gorethrian looked at the rust-red stain now congealing upon it, with some surprise.

'Always clean your blade . . . one of the first laws of soldiering,' was all he said.

Ashurek leading, knife in hand, and Medrian coming last, often glancing behind, they progressed through the passages. When they finally came out onto the Plain of Ash for the third time there was no sign of life. They ploughed through the ash to the top of the hillock, dust catching in their throats. They could stifle their own coughs but not those of the horses, who snorted and jibbed as they came. If the men were still on the ship they must have heard them by now.

But when they reached the peak a strange sight met their eyes.

Aboard *The Star of Filmoriel* and around her bows stood eight or so men, frozen motionless like statues. Some were caught in an attitude of striking out at the ship. The figures seemed to ripple, as if they were becoming translucent, as white and dry and crystalline as the Plane itself.

Wits dulled by thirst and the beginnings of fever, the three took a long time to take in the significance of the scene. Then Estarinel laughed uneasily.

'I should have known – *The Star* has her own means of defending herself!' He held up the lodestone and it swung to point their course.

'This is our path,' he said, pointing with a long, white finger.

The horses were too weak from lack of water to be ridden. The humans found it difficult to keep their own feet for the same reason; the dust and the salt-rock and the air seemed to wrap them in a suffocating blanket that drew all vitality from them. They spoke little, for their voices came hoarsely from their parched, swollen throats; they felt hot and feverish, although the faces of Estarinel and Medrian were pale as death.

They instinctively gave the ship a wide berth. Frozen though the men were, their pale eyes rolled malevolently in their heads, disconcerting the three. Vixata, hyper-sensitive to the aura generated by the men, collected enough energy to crab-walk past as fast as she could, head in the air, mouth foaming.

Estarinel held up the lodestone for as long as his arm could bear it. Eventually his hand dropped limply to his side.

They walked, walked, walked for hours. They walked until they could walk no more, and then they crawled, staggered, stumbled until the dryness had sucked every drop of energy from their bodies and they felt sick and giddy with fever; and still they moved on. Estarinel was not sure that they were going in the right direction and eventually he no longer cared. Their limbs dragged like lead and their heads throbbed with the whiteness and they could not breathe for the ash. Their horses limped and stumbled, fell to their knees, rose and struggled on.

Estarinel began to hallucinate. He was back on the other side of the White Plane, on Peradnia, and he was strolling at ease through the forests that were like cobwebs of glistening ice. Hranna was with him. *The White Plane is infinite*, he said, *and for eternity we will traverse it, nomads of infinity*. They were standing on the edge of an endless lake; but it was a solid lake of white rock, glittering with a million tiny crystals. Hranna put his hand on Estarinel's shoulder and pointed across the lake. Estarinel was swamped by a nameless fear, and he looked down and saw, not Hranna, but the emaciated figure of a girl with flowing golden hair; and as he watched she changed and became a tall, vibrant warrior woman, bronze-limbed, chestnut-haired, with proud laughing head and grave eyes. She, too, was pointing. And the lake was not white rock at all, but an expanse of snow. And the woman at his side became Medrian. She stared at him with dark, terrifying eyes and he knew he loved her. And she was holding a needle-thin staff at his throat as if to slit it, but then it seemed she was offering him the staff; she opened her mouth and it was not her voice that spoke, but another's; and it said *kill me*.

And then he thought he was in Forluin, wandering down a cool valley alone, then laughing with his friends; but he opened his eyes suddenly and saw only the depressing eternity of white ash ahead. He could not see Medrian, or Ashurek, or the horses; a greyness came over his eyes, then blackness. He thought he felt great cold drops of water raining exquisitely on his back, and smiled to himself at the realism of this last hallucination.

Dark shapes seemed to loom in the blackness. Grass was beneath his feet. Suddenly he was lying face downwards on rain-sodden turf, and he realised that he was in truth back on Earth! It was a wet, black night. He had passed through the Exit Point back to the world, but he knew not where on Earth he was.

'Medrian? Ashurek?' he called out. There was no sound but the rain, rushing in the distance and pattering onto leaves and rocks nearby. He climbed to his feet. He thought he saw a square of light ahead.

Then something touched him on the arm. He started violently, then turned to find it was his horse, nudging him with his soft brown nose. Placing one hand on the beast's firm neck he turned slowly this way and that, peering hard through the walls of dark rain. He had become 'snow-blind' to a degree on Hrannekh Ol, and could not now adjust his eyes to darkness.

But suddenly he saw Vixata, and he saw her clearly, for the golden mare shone with a light of her own. And near her was Ashurek, and gradually his eyes focused on a shape that was Medrian, and her strange horse that he and Ashurek called 'Nameless'.

The three stood motionless, staring at each other; and those few moments were like a dream. Then, as one, they all sat down on the soaking ground, almost laughing with relief. The horses were already munching the wet grass. Gratefully they let the rain pour down on them, soaking their dry skin and hair, running in rivulets down their faces. They sat there for many minutes before they revived sufficiently to consider their situation.

They were at the bottom of a hill. At its peak a lighted window shone yellow, and dark bulks that were buildings rose against the skyline.

'We'd be well advised to stay clear of human habitation,' warned Ashurek.

'It looks only to be a farm,' answered Estarinel, one hand pressed over the wound on his shoulder.

'In the darkness, the castle of Gastada looked only to be a farm, but that was a most vile—' Ashurek stopped short, then continued, 'We do not know where in Tearn or the Empire we are. We cannot risk approaching the place.'

'But we must find food and water; and what of clothes, and weapons?'

Ashurek shook his dark head dubiously.

'Estarinel is wounded,' pointed out Medrian. 'We must go up to the building. Let just Estarinel and I go, for he has an innocent face, and they will not suspect a woman.'

Ashurek grinned at this.

'Very well. See what you can gain by it. I will wait in the shadows among the trees.'

They climbed the hill, leading their beasts. A small stone farmhouse surrounded by barns and sheds loomed up in the rain-veiled night. There was a door by the lighted window, and Estarinel knocked gently.

It opened a crack, letting out a sliver of yellow light. The head of a middle-aged, grey-haired woman peered out; her face was careworn.

'Yes?' she said, and her eyes widened as she saw Estarinel with his long black hair dripping around his white face. 'What do you want?' Her accent was mid-Tearnian.

'I am sorry to disturb you. We are only travellers, seeking food and water for us and for our horses.'

'Just a minute,' the woman said, and closed the door in their faces. After a minute it opened again.

'Where do you come from?'

'Forluin, originally . . .'

A new voice intruded, the arrogant voice of a young man.

'Those of Forluin are harmless enough, mother,' it said, from within the house.

'Who is with you?' the woman insisted suspiciously. From her attitude it was quite obvious she had no intention of letting them in. Estarinel felt desperate. They might have to walk miles before they came upon another source of provisions, and they were all exhausted and unwell.

But before he could speak, Medrian suddenly fainted theatrically against the door. The woman jumped back and Medrian collapsed across the threshold.

'Goodness! A girl! Oh dear—' The woman glanced back into the interior of the room.

'Let them in, mother,' the arrogant voice said.

'Come in then,' said the woman agitatedly.

Estarinel picked up Medrian's rain-soaked frame and carried her into the room. As he did so she opened one eye and winked at him.

It was a large, bare stone room that served as both kitchen and living room. A vast fireplace cast a warm yellow glow against the cold stone walls and plain furniture. The woman was dressed in the rough brown smock of a farming woman. But by the fireside sat a boy, only about eighteen, dressed most unlike his mother, in ornate robes of brocaded purple and blue. His face was rosy and handsome, his brown eyes bold, insolent, and bright as a fox's; his straight brown hair was cut short. He was sitting lazily with his feet stretched out, looking most unlike a farmer's son. His grey-haired mother seemed almost afraid of him.

He gestured Estarinel to lay Medrian down on a bench by the wall.

'Now,' said the youth, 'what do you want here? You are strangely garbed for travellers – no cloaks or provisions?'

'We fell into misfortune, and have been without food and water for days.' Estarinel disliked the boy's insolent manner and deliberately addressed his mother.

'Without water? It's been pouring with rain here for weeks,' the boy interrupted.

'To be honest, we are quite lost. We need food, clothing, and maps. Medrian is ill and I have a wound that needs dressing. Would it be possible for you to help us? Truly, we offer you no harm.'

'If you really are of Forluin, I am sure you do not,' the boy said with a note of scorn that antagonised the normally peaceful Estarinel. 'Is she your wife?'

'No; we are simply travelling companions.'

'And to where are you travelling?' enquired the boy with blatant curiosity.

'Not much further, if we cannot obtain help.' Estarinel stood shivering with cold from his wet clothes while the boy rested his chin in his hand with an affected gesture.

'How many are there of you?' he asked suddenly.

'We have horses . . .' said Estarinel evasively.

'Mother,' the boy said, beckoning to her. They conferred in a corner near Medrian.

'Very well . . .' the boy began after a minute or two, but the woman interrupted sharply.

'Have you means of paying us?'

'We have no money but we could give you a horse . . .'

'No! We will provide your needs, but there is no need to worry about payment as yet,' the boy said quickly.

'I don't wish to be in your debt,' argued Estarinel.

'You won't, you won't. Mother, prepare food. I'll find some clothes for you.'

Medrian made a pretence of coming round from her well-timed 'swoon'. They were re-clothed in rough brown tunics and leggings, then given food and drink.

As they ate, they concealed what food they could – some bread and sour cheese – for Ashurek, but Estarinel wondered if the boy had noticed this.

The woman dressed his wound. Then the boy said, 'I'm sorry we cannot offer you beds; but you can sleep in the stable.'

They followed him outside, and by the light of an oil lamp he showed them to a dark wooden building.

'You can feed your horses here. There is the water pump, and steps up to the hayloft; you'll find it quite comfortable. Where are your horses?' He swung the lamp around, and raindrops danced like fireflies in its glow.

'Er . . . tied up, a few yards away . . .' Estarinel muttered uncomfortably.

'I take your word for it,' said the boy with a patronising smile. He handed them the lamp and said, 'Good night. Sleep well.'

Estarinel waited until he had walked languidly back to the house, then whispered, 'What do you make of him?'

'Something fairly unpleasant,' Medrian answered. 'I think Ashurek was right, we should not have come here.'

They found Ashurek sheltering beneath the trees just to the right of the stables, holding the horses who grazed peacefully.

'You took long enough,' he said, grimacing.

They settled and fed the horses in the stable, then climbed a wooden ladder to the hayloft. It was a warm-smelling, musty place, with soft mounds of hay glowing beige under the swinging disc of light from the oil lamp. It was paradise after Hrannekh Ol.

They settled themselves on the hay and gave Ashurek the food they had secreted for him. As he ate, they related what had happened.

'It's a strange situation,' Medrian said. 'A small, poor farmhouse, and in it a lad with the clothes and manners of an arrogant young lord.'

'I expect he has found himself a position with some squire or lady, and is overcome with his own importance,' Ashurek said disinterestedly.

But Medrian went on darkly, 'You are more right than you know. He is certainly in someone's pay, but no mere squire. When they were whispering near me, his mother asked him what he was going to do with us! He replied that he was sure we were hiding someone.' She smiled coolly at Ashurek. 'The mother gave a sort of gasp of fear, but he told her not to be alarmed, and that "She To Whom We Pay Tribute" would be very interested in us.'

'What?' the Gorethrian said.

' "She To Whom We Pay Tribute",' Medrian repeated.

'A wordy title,' scoffed Ashurek. 'Some little game of power he is playing, I expect . . . but we have nothing to fear from a young boy and his ageing mother. We'll sleep a few hours and be gone before he knows it.'

He cast himself down on the hay and turned on his side. Estarinel turned down the lamp and lay staring at the dark.

At last sleep came to all of them, and they forgot Hrannekh Ol, and their doubts and pains; and even the spectre of the Serpent dissolved in the darkness for a while.

7

The Mirror of Soul's Loss

The boy stood in the half-darkness, staring down at Ashurek. The faint glow of the lamp caught the unmistakable features, the purple-brown colour of the skin, the handsome, cruel face. Black hair curled over his shoulders.

A Gorethrian. The boy was shaking; no wonder they had been so evasive. He looked across at the other two strangers, sleeping quietly on the hay. They all had black hair, he noticed, three vipers . . .

Fear and hatred of Gorethrians, always present in Tearn, had been made acute by the invasion of the Eastern coast in recent years. But there was something else that moved the boy's hand to the dagger in his belt, an hysterical loathing of something so far in his past he did not now remember what it was.

A Gorethrian! His careful plans were swept aside as he experienced a complete loss of will to blind panic; his fingers had seized the knife and his arm was moving independently, sweeping down towards the accursed being.

Ashurek, by some sixth sense, awoke to find a dagger flashing down towards his throat. Automatically he twisted to one side and the blade stuck quivering in the floor beneath the hay. He grabbed the wrist that had held it.

'What have we here?'

'What's the matter?' came Estarinel's voice as he stirred from sleep and turned up the lamp. The warm light flooded the loft, illuminating Ashurek holding the attacker's arm in a steel grip.

It was the arrogant boy from the farmhouse.

'Accursed Gorethrian—' he muttered through clenched teeth, struggling uselessly in Ashurek's grip. Ashurek jumped to his feet and twisted the boy's arm, forcing him to the floor. With one arm he held him, while with the other he reached and tugged the dagger from the floor.

He held the point at the boy's throat.

'Ah – a further extension of your hospitality, is this?' he growled, his eyes green flame. 'Would you die now, or after you have told us what you are doing?'

'Ashurek! He's only a child!' Estarinel exclaimed. There had been no fear in the boy's face, only malignant hatred. But the sound of Estarinel's voice seemed to break the spell, and he began to breathe quickly, suddenly limp with terror.

Ashurek pulled the youth violently to his feet, then threw him down onto a mound of hay. He handed the dagger back, and the boy took it, humiliated because they all knew he would not dare to use it again.

'I don't blame you for trying to kill me,' the Gorethrian Prince said. 'But you do understand my instinct to preserve my own life.'

The boy, now sulkily silent, sat up and began picking bits of hay from his clothes, trying to regain his dignity. Estarinel and Medrian looked curiously on as Ashurek sat beside him, and asked, 'Well? What is it you want?'

The young man, realising he was no longer in imminent danger of death, took on some of his arrogance again.

'I want to know what's going on.'

'A common human problem,' Ashurek said.

'You are no Belhadrians – coming out of the night, complaining of thirst in this rain, and hiding a Gorethrian among you . . .'

So, we're in Belhadra, Ashurek thought. He said, 'We are only three travellers, and I did not wish to startle you by my presence.'

'Three travellers? A Forluinishman and a Gorethrian travelling together, and through Belhadra? Come now!'

'It's easily explained,' Estarinel broke in. 'We were stranded on the White Plane, and when we got back to Earth, we were near your farm.'

'I see,' the boy said, his mind now working briskly. 'That still does not explain who you are or what—'

'But that is none of your business,' Ashurek said softly. The boy glanced nervously at his dark face, remembering the Forluinishman had called him 'Ashurek'. That was a royal name . . . the name, in fact, of the Emperor's notorious brother, who was reputed to be wandering alone across Tearn after his mysterious disappearance.

If I delivered *him*, Prince Ashurek, to Her – his cheeks reddened with excitement at the idea.

'When I came up here,' he continued, masking the tremor in his voice with an arrogant drawl, 'it was not with the intention of killing anyone, Prince Ashurek.'

'Ah, you know who I am suddenly.'

'An educated guess . . . but when I saw you, I let my emotions get the better of me. It was foolish of me and I apologise.'

Ashurek said nothing.

'Well, er – I came, in fact, to help you.'

'The only help we need from you is somewhere to sleep, and the chance, perhaps,' broke in Medrian curtly.

'Presumably you want to continue your journey,' the boy went on, 'and you will need provisions, maps, weapons, and so on.' He waited for an agreement, but they just stared at him, not reacting. Hate stirred again in him and his foxy eyes hardened. 'It would be my pleasure to escort you to Beldaega-Hal, the nearest town, there to show you to the finest merchants, so that you may travel on swiftly and fully equipped.'

'And how will you profit from this venture?' Ashurek enquired.

'I'm going there anyway, but perhaps it will make up in some degree for my foolishness,' he replied with what he hoped was impressive coolness.

'What a touching change of heart,' Ashurek grinned dangerously.

'Well, just let me know,' the youth said, affecting imperious indifference as he moved towards the hatch. 'I will be riding out first thing in the morning.'

'Very well. Now let us rest.' The young man began to descend the ladder. He felt he had, albeit clumsily, got them in his control, and dared not risk outstaying his welcome.

'I'll bid you good night then. Oh – my name is Skord,' he told them as he disappeared from view.

Ashurek closed the hatch.

'He was spying on us, that's for sure,' he said. 'We may as well ride to the town with him, though.'

'But he tried to kill you!' Estarinel remarked.

'That was unpremeditated, I'm sure – as he said, just a foolish loss of control. Not that I trust the devious wretch.'

'Why go with him, then?'

'We need weapons and maps for our journey. Think; how can we now reach the Blue Plane?'

'Return to Forluin, and ask for help again, I suppose,' Estarinel sighed, hanging his head.

'Exactly. So we need to find a river, and a ship, and sail for the open sea. The boy can help us in that; I will see to it. And if he has other plans for us, I'd be interested to know what they are.'

'Very well,' said Estarinel, extinguishing the lamp. 'I suppose you are right, he is probably harmless enough.'

Medrian knew Ashurek was wrong, but she felt cold and could not seem to speak.

The next morning, dawn came pale and misty, falling on a turfed hill crowned by a tangle of farm buildings, a copse falling away on its Western flank. Behind it, fields stretched away for miles to a grey horizon.

Estarinel's slim figure emerged from the block of stables and went to the door of the small farmhouse. He knocked. There was a long pause and the grey-haired woman answered, looking distraught.

'Excuse me,' began Estarinel, 'is your son in?'

The woman looked very upset and her watery eyes had dark circles beneath them.

'Skord? I've not seen him since midnight. Ridden out on one of his accursed errands, and his father returned with the sickness of Her anger upon him—'

'Are you in need of any help?' Estarinel asked concernedly.

'Help? No, no.' The woman collected herself, pushing back strands of hair from her tired face. 'Now, let me give you this warning: stay no longer in Belhadra, but make due East for the border. To work for Her or against Her is certain ruin. What treachery my husband worked I know not, but her plague is upon him.'

Estarinel was beginning to think the woman was mad. But he looked into her eyes and they seemed only slightly hysterical.

'Go,' she urged. 'Go before my son returns. He works for Her.'

'Who is "She"?'

'Do you not know? Then it's better you are not told—' She broke off and stared straight past him down the hill. He looked behind him and there was the arrogant boy in purple and blue, mounted on a prancing chestnut, riding up towards the farmhouse.

'Good morning!' he called. His mother pushed past Estarinel and ran to meet him.

'Skord!' she cried. 'Your father returned in the night – he is ill!'

The boy did not look particularly surprised. He jumped off his mount and pushed the reins at Estarinel.

'Hold her,' he said, and went into the house. Estarinel left the horse to graze and followed them.

They went across the living room and through an oak door to a small bedroom. It was furnished with just a low wooden bed. A man lay there, deathly faced, sweating, with jaundiced eyes. Sores were on his neck and arms.

'A fever, Skord—' the woman began, but he interrupted with no emotion in his voice.

'Mother, you know as well as I that it is *Her* plague. Do you think I didn't know of his treachery? Well, now her just punishment is upon him.'

His mother stared at him as if seeing a blinding truth for the first time.

'You betrayed him to Her! You! His very son!' She screamed. She staggered back against the wall, weeping.

'Someone else's son,' muttered Skord to himself, putting a hand over his forehead. Then he saw Estarinel. 'What are you doing?' he demanded.

'Perhaps I can help your father. I have some knowledge of herbs.'

Skord laughed humourlessly. 'No herbs will touch his affliction. The Dark Regions for him!' He put his face close to his mother's ear and whispered, 'That's the penalty, eh mother?'

She turned and tugged pathetically at his robes.

'Skord! Make Her leave him be! Don't let Her harm us,' she begged, weeping in desperation. For a moment there was a note of genuine regret in his voice.

'If only I could . . .' He glanced at Estarinel. 'Saddle your horses. We ride in half an hour's time.'

'You can't leave your parents in this state!' Estarinel exclaimed. 'Ye gods – what can you be thinking of?'

'It is no business of yours. Mother! Pull yourself together. Find some more riding clothes and prepare us provisions. And don't try to poison me again; I showed you mercy the first time, but don't expect it again.'

The woman stood up and walked wordlessly into the kitchen, scrubbing at her face in a desperate manner that was terrible to see.

127

'Come on,' said Skord to the Forluinishman, and followed her.

Estarinel bent down to the sick man. 'What is wrong with you? Who is this "She" they speak of?'

But the man just groaned and foam drooled from his lips. Estarinel sighed, wishing desperately that he knew what to do. 'Was it misfortune that brought us here, or the Worm itself?'

'It's unbelievable – the callousness of the boy to leave his mother in a state of hysteria and his father dying,' Estarinel told Ashurek and Medrian as they readied the horses. 'She seems to think the father's illness is Skord's fault as well – I can't believe it.'

'The truth is, everyone outside Forluin is mad,' said Ashurek, not altogether pleasantly. Estarinel glared at him, genuinely angry. 'Estarinel, let them be,' Ashurek said more gently. 'It's none of our business; they must sort out their own problems.'

'How can you say that? They need help.'

'There's nothing we can do! They are doomed – I know the Worm's work,' the Gorethrian said. Medrian glanced at him oddly, then busied herself with her horse's halter. 'These are but symptoms of an underlying disease . . .'

'But—' Estarinel persisted.

'We leave this place behind, forget it, and ride with Skord. Don't argue!' Ashurek said sharply but good-naturedly. Estarinel looked round at Medrian, but she seemed cold again, closed to him.

'We must go,' she said shortly.

'Very well.' Estarinel took a slow breath. 'I am forced to trust your judgment. I only hope you are right.'

Morning activity on the farm was growing. A herd of grey cows ambled past to be milked. The voices of farmhands could be heard raised in an argument about crop yield.

The door of the farmhouse was open and Estarinel, as he led out Shaell, saw several men and women entering. Skord, already mounted on his fine chestnut mare, appeared round the corner of the house and hailed him.

'Listen,' he said. 'I know that you, for some obscure reason, are worried about my parents. You think I'm irresponsibly leaving them? Well you need not worry; I'm leaving some peasant men and women to look after them. Does this satisfy you?' The half-mocking tone in Skord's voice antagonised Estarinel.

'You're a heartless child,' he replied in a low voice. 'No doubt your parents will be better off with you gone.' Skord seemed to ignore this remark as his mother came to the doorway. She appeared calm; her face was expressionless but her eyes were red and her mouth sagged.

'Here; a saddlebag with provisions for four,' she said, her voice trembling. 'Take it and get you gone. Go to Her, then; and if you wish you can tell Her that I condone your father's treachery. You need not come back here, for you are no son of ours.'

'No, that's true,' said Skord, strangely.

Anger flashed on his face as she turned to Estarinel and said, 'I tried to warn you, and I am truly sorry for you.'

'Mother—' Skord began, but Ashurek appeared and interrupted.

'There is no need to fear for us, madam, we can look after ourselves. And if there's a way to help you, we'll find it.'

'You don't understand—' the woman began, but then it dawned that a Gorethrian necromancer stood before her. As if this was the last blow, she uttered a low moan and fainted. One of the peasant women picked her up and, giving Skord a sour look, slammed the door in their faces.

The country of Belhadra was a large, pastoral land in central Tearn, situated on the Equator, which on that Earth was not unduly hot. Its cities were few, small and poor; most of its population were farmers and peasants. It was a hilly country of grass and swamps, forests and fields. It was wet, fertile, and deep in superstition and mystery, not entirely without cause. There was a mystical city of glass just North of the Equator, of which few knew and even fewer had found. It was concealed amid plains and forests, mountains and waterfalls, protected from man so that it could fulfil its delicate function. But, in this age of the Serpent, it seemed it was not protected well enough.

A sprinkle of fine rain fell through the light cool mist of the morning, a mist which turned everything to pale yellows, greens and greys. A faint harmony of birdsong filled the air, against which the clear notes of a blackbird rose and fell away. Watery sunlight, where the mist was thinner, turned the air pale gold.

The hooves of the four horses brushed the long, soaking grass, sending up sprays of dew as they went at a brisk walk down the far side of the hill, heading North and slightly West. The four riders rode down into the Beldaega-Vale, with its network of vast fields, its grey copses, its thin rivers and scattered clusters of buildings. First rode Skord, now in rich travelling gear of embroidered cloth in shades of lilac and blue. His mount was a superb-looking mare, proud and fiery, golden-chestnut in colour. The other three rode a little behind him, Estarinel on his noble, silver-brown stallion, Ashurek mounted on Vixata who went skittishly, shining with shifting metallic colours, then Medrian on the ill-looking, sullen black 'Nameless'.

Their saddles had been lost on the White Plane, so they rode bareback, with halters instead of bridles. They were unarmed, except that Ashurek had in his belt the short blue-hafted dagger that Estarinel had found on Hrannekh Ol. That dry place had left both them and their horses weak and still suffering from dehydration, so it was a slow ride through the pale, misty morning, and Skord would often drift ahead and then wait, impatiently, for them to catch up.

They stopped to drink at a shallow stream running glassily over mica, and rode on across the fields. The Vale seemed a paradise of scintillating colours, and the scent of moist earth a revelation, after the White Plane; though often their thoughts would intrude to mar it.

Sunlight was sparkling through the rain as they rode into a wood of grizzly trees. Young leaves clustered on the twisted branches, but the ground was thick with leaf mould, with brambles and all kinds of rampant wild flowers and creeping weeds. Skord led them along a stony track which wound round the brink of a chasm. Below they saw a small lake, lying still and stagnant with steep walls rising all around it; dregs in a granite cup. Skord rode dangerously close to the edge.

'It was a quarry,' he said, his voice sudden and strange in the stillness.

The trees gave way to pasture, and they rode for many miles until at last they came to the crest of a hill and entered a tall, charcoal-black forest. A squirrel ran before them in the twilight as they led their horses to a camping-place. It had been a fine day, but now there was something oppressive in the air, a black electricity crackling between the skeletal trees.

They lit a fire and ate the bread and meat Skord's mother had provided, then prepared to sleep.

'We'll take it in turns to keep watch,' said Ashurek.

'There are no wild animals to eat us alive,' replied Skord scoffingly.

'I was not thinking of wild animals,' Ashurek said icily. Skord glared at him with barely veiled hatred.

'Please yourselves. Keep watch between you,' he snapped with an arrogant wave of his hand. He turned over and went straight to sleep.

Estarinel, keeping the last watch, looked out over the embers of the waning fire. He thought of his sister, Arlena, and of Falin, Edrien and Luatha, who now must be alone on the cold sea, on their way home to Forluin. How many days would it take them? Perhaps the Serpent had sent a storm to swallow them also . . . but no, the image of them arriving home was stronger. He could see Arlena greeting their mother in the doorway: 'We took him there, and he boarded *The Star of Filmoriel* with two dark-haired strangers.'

The two women looked at each other, the two women he loved so dearly; and to his shock he heard his mother reply, 'Lothwyn is well, but your father died . . .'

Estarinel shook his head, trying to subdue his thoughts. 'It is only my imagination . . .' He tried to concentrate on his task, but exhaustion took him into an uneasy sleep, and for an hour he writhed under the pressure of nightmares, unable to wake himself.

Arrows of silver rain drove into his body, and he realised he was awake, and the nightmare was real. A violent storm had brewed. As he sat up he could hear Skord shouting.

'Wake up, all of you! Get up! I thought someone was keeping watch, damn it—' He had saddled his horse and was trying to mount as it danced.

'What's the matter?' Medrian shouted back. 'It's only a storm – why the panic?'

'This forest is not the place to be in a storm!' Skord said insistently. 'Come on – get on your horses. Don't stand staring! Quickly!'

There was nothing to do but humour him. A minute later they were mounted and following Skord at a brisk canter. It was a nightmare ride, swerving and twisting round tree trunks, while the forest reached out all its tendrils and gnarled, brittle fingers to hamper them. They chased Skord blindly, the horses stumbling in the undergrowth and blowing hard in fear. After what seemed an age, they left the forest; and as they came out from the cover of trees, the full force of the storm hit them.

A sheet of ice-cold water cut across them like a steel wall. The sky screamed and thrashed, spewing out a wind that tried to pin them to the tortured ground. Eyes screwed up against the rain, they ploughed forward. The ground was treacherous, running with branching rivulets of water. But now all was not pitch dark, for blood-red lightning was blazing along the leaden banks of cloud.

A foul discoloration flooded the atmosphere; and in that moment they all became part of a horrific vision. They were phantasms blown across the battleground of a cosmic war. A hole yawned open into the domain of the Serpent itself; and the grey, writhing sky was the Serpent, drowning the world in its sick power and ancient, impassive cruelty.

Estarinel felt they were puppets, who had been put a million times through this motion. He had always been there, this was where he belonged; a spectre running beneath the string of diseased flesh that hurtled overhead, leaving him behind but never ending. Then he saw that something fled before it.

It was something tiny, a small black bird, and it wept as it fled, tossed like a cinder on the Serpent-winds. Its cry rang across the world, and it seemed an ash of hope and bravery. But the Worm never quite caught up with it.

The Gorethrian, remotely, realised what the bird was. Medrian knew also, but her whole body felt like lifeless white crystal and she thought she would never come down from the sky.

Only when the horses began to prop and swerve did reality re-establish itself. They saw that they were at the brink of a drop down which the animals refused to go. The Gorethrian cursed and urged Vixata forward, but she stood on her hind legs, forehooves flailing at the red and silver rain, bright gold. And as Ashurek forced her over the drop, his black hair flying, he laughed wildly like some demon of darkest hell.

Skord's mare shied in terror and bolted down the drop. There was a sinister rumbling, and a great red fireball rolled along the underside of the sullen clouds. The other horses, in a panic, raced headlong after Skord.

It was a tall, steep face of stones and earth, with tough bushes and roots sticking out from it. In that breathless gallop down, it was a miracle that the horses kept their feet; their hooves were a blur barely touching the ground.

Then there was an ear-splitting, howling screech and from the fireball shot a barbed spear of white fire, bright as a magnesium flare. It struck the top of the drop, then leapt from top to bottom of the face in an arc of blinding light to stick as a blazing sword of electricity stretching from sky to earth, where the riders had been a second before. All the charge of the sky seemed to pour down it to earth.

Then it was suddenly gone; the wind still howled and the rain continued to pour, but the storm had drained itself, and the clouds were calmer, higher. The thunder and blood-red lightning had ceased. The ground tingled a little beneath the horses' hooves for a moment; there was a crack of distant thunder and a thin fork of pure white lightning. It was a normal storm.

Gradually the horses slowed down and allowed themselves to be stopped, though they were breathing fast with fear. The riders turned and looked behind them; and where the fire-spear had struck, the drop had crumbled and a great blackened, burnt-out crater was left. They stared, collecting their wits.

It was obvious from the dreadful look of horror in Skord's eyes that he had not been immune to the strange illusion in the storm. But the fear was swiftly replaced by amusement.

'I'm sorry,' he laughed. 'We have the most appalling weather in Belhadra at this time of year. That forest has been hit by lightning so many times I should have known better . . . you saw how blackened it was by fire. The lightning will strike anything tall, or better still, something moving. I do apologise.' He looked insolently round at the three, enjoying the disruption the storm had caused, although he had been far more frightened than they.

'So you thought it amusing to lead us into deliberate danger of being killed by lightning,' Ashurek said acidly. 'Don't apologise. Anyone who will risk his own life to play a joke has my utmost admiration.'

Skord gave an offhand shrug and rode on, smiling to himself. His memory of evil things was short.

The normal storm persisted for some time as they rode on towards Beldaega-Hal. Dawn melted through the clouds, leaving everything in a half-asleep, dull, silvery twilight. It was a weird light, deep and stormy although the worst onslaught was past.

Towards the afternoon they came upon the first straggling red buildings of the town, and later a paved road leading into the centre of Beldaega-Hal. They joined the road and as they jog-trotted down it they passed flat, unfenced fields and the occasional cluster of peasant dwellings. All were built of a garish red stone cut to blocks, all were squat and squarish in shape.

The buildings grew more numerous until they formed a ragged row on either side of the road. There was activity. Poorly dressed peasant children stared at the four riders. Peasant men and women looked with curiosity also. Carts were in the street, mangy horses stood half-asleep, thin dogs ran among the piles of rubbish that lay about the houses.

As they went further into the town, the oddness of the buildings struck them. They were like cube upon cube of red stone piled on top of each other, with rounded corners; scarred and pitted with age. All the buildings seemed crowded together, split by dingy white, paved streets barely wide enough to let a cart through. It was as if a child had thrown building blocks together at random. And as they drew closer to the town centre, a whisper of their coming preceded them. 'It is *Her* favourite . . . with three black-haired strangers . . . one a Gorethrian!'

Skord paused to attract the attention of a small boy. He pushed a small silver coin into his palm.

'Run to the shop of the merchant Mel Skara, tell him I am coming with three guests, and he is to display his best wares – clothing, weapons. Go on.'

The boy, with a look of delight, shot off down the street and vanished round a corner.

Meanwhile, people were greeting them with mixed feelings. Everyone seemed to know Skord, and saluted him, but there were grumblings of suspicion when they saw Ashurek. By now it seemed that the entire town knew of their arrival. '*Her* favourite . . . a plain, white-faced woman . . . a handsome knight . . . a Gorethrian . . . all riding bareback!'

All three, Ashurek especially, were now regretting coming to the town. They rode at a painfully slow walk, twisting and turning through the streets until they were sure they would never find their way out again. A variety of smells filled the air. Dogs barked. Children shouted. Babies wailed. It seemed over-crowded, claustrophobic; a town where no one could have any secrets.

Ashurek was reminded of the sad, terrified people he had seen

134

when the Gorethrian army had occupied parts of Tearn. Bitterness awoke at the memory of those days, when the Egg-Stone had moved him like an automaton to crush such cowering mobs. But he still felt no pity for them. Better the fierce, single-minded rebels of the Empire than these pathetic folk; at least the rebels had something in them he could recognise.

Up a twisting alley Skord led them. Then, at last, they reached a building with a square featureless entrance; the only decoration was a sign in a beautifully painted black-letter, saying, 'Mel Skara: Merchant'. They dismounted and tethered their horses in a small paved yard at the side.

'Here,' said Skord, 'we do our shopping here.'

'But—' Estarinel began.

'Before you say again that you have no money,' Skord interrupted in a confidential tone, 'I do not have to pay for my requirements in this town. I just ask, and it is given . . . if you understand my meaning.'

'No, I don't, and I don't think I want to.'

'Well, well,' said Skord. He beckoned with an affected gesture and, dubiously, they followed him into the shop.

Ashurek whispered to Medrian and Estarinel, 'Let us humour him for now, but be on your guard. His generosity is in a good cause.'

The merchant was waiting for them, like some bloated creature of prey, as they entered. He was a gross man, his brown hair and beard neatly oiled and groomed around his doughy face. He wore a richly brocaded robe of red and gold and green.

'Greetings, noble sir,' he welcomed Skord, in manner at once servile and sly. 'I have been expecting you. I sincerely hope I can have the pleasure of being of service to you.'

'I sincerely hope you can too, Mel Skara,' replied Skord. 'I have three companions who require travelling clothes, maps, good weapons; the *best* weapons, do you understand?'

'Yes, the best weapons in Belhadra – nay, in Tearn! – are to be found here—' The merchant broke off in mid-sentence, mouth hanging open as he took in Skord's fellow travellers.

'Ah yes,' said Skord, 'allow me to introduce my companions: Estarinel of Forluin; the Lady Medrian; and, ah, Prince Ashurek.'

Mel Skara swallowed nervously and cleared his throat.

135

'Er yes – the best weapons. Would you be so kind as to come through to the back?'

They let him lead the way, following slowly and looking about them. The shop was a large, square, dusky room, red-tiled with an exotic fringed carpet. The merchant's goods appeared unusual, expensive and select. Furniture of fine, dark wood; richly-bound books; tapestries and rugs of intricate design; ornaments of silver, gold and platinum. Yet, in this poor town, it seemed more like a museum than a much-used shop.

They were led through an archway to a smaller room, lined with red velvet curtains. Here was everything a traveller could need: strong riding clothes, saddles and bridles, swords and shields.

'Here, good sirs and lady, you may choose whatever goods please you,' said Mel Skara with an obsequious smile. 'As you will observe, all are of the finest quality—'

'Mel Skara,' interrupted Skord in his cool, arrogant tone, 'when my guests choose their clothes, allow them to use the mirror.'

An oily grin seeped over the plump face of the merchant. He bowed slightly.

'Certainly, sir,' he smiled.

Estarinel looked at Ashurek, who shrugged.

They were all uneasy in the shop, yet there seemed to be no plot to imprison them. A side door was opened so they could fit their horses with saddles and bridles. And Skord sat on a pile of material in a corner, watching them impassively as they chose weapons.

Ashurek noticed that although the weapons were fine and un-used, all lay under a layer of dust. No one had bought a weapon here for many months, even a few years. Belhadra no longer had an army then, and even knights and squires went unarmed. And a farmer's son rode through the streets, lording it over a cowed populace. What was his source of power?

They each chose a keen steel sword and a long knife, and Medrian in addition took a good bow and a quiver of arrows. They all took shields of bonded leather and steel.

'And now, my good lady and sirs,' said Mel Skara, 'I have clothing of the most excellent quality, fine brocades in the Goreth-rian style, tunics of silk, gazelle-skin boots . . .'

'So we see,' Ashurek remarked. 'We just need strong travelling gear.' He picked out a tunic of black linen, dark purple leggings, and boots of a soft black hide. The others chose equally undistinctive clothing; Estarinel a shirt, tunic and leggings of bronze-brown, with boots of russet leather, and Medrian similar garb in dark reds and greys. Then she and Ashurek chose full-length black coats with high collars; Estarinel took a similar one, slate-coloured.

'Perhaps you would do me the honour of stepping behind this curtain, where you will find cubicles in which to try on the fine clothes you have so wisely—'

'Spare us,' Ashurek grimaced. Mel Skara's face twitched nervously, but to his relief the three strangers made their way between the red velvet hangings. He looked across at Skord, who gave a small, purposeful nod; and he reached out a portly arm and grasped a cord of maroon silk.

As the three re-emerged, tying laces and tightening belts, the merchant smiled graciously and waved towards a rich velvet curtain.

'I will now reveal a mirror for your convenience,' he smirked, and his plump hand pulled the cord. The red curtain slid back soundlessly, and Estarinel found himself facing a large looking glass with a decorated rim; a still, silver lake waiting for their reflections to plumb its depths.

Then he stared at the mirror. For what he saw was not his own reflection. He did not at first realise it, nor did he notice it change; but he was looking at some other scene, something that should not have been in that mirror. He saw whiteness, like the White Plane, or like snow; he saw a scrawny bird of black; he saw an indistinct streak of silver, like a needle. And the nameless fear returned, and the words came to him, 'A loss beyond bearing'. He did not see them, nor did he hear them; but the words were there.

It was as if the glass had found the core of his soul and reflected it with cruel incandescence; and it was calling him, sucking him down into its sweet silver-and-green depths to meet a cheerless fate. From a great distance he heard Ashurek cry, 'Damn you!' and then 'Silvren!' and Medrian uttered an inhuman groan of despair.

But in an instant, everything they had seen was forgotten, even the mirror itself. Estarinel found himself staring at a velvet curtain, conscious of a slight headache. He felt faintly disorientated, but otherwise unaware that anything had happened.

'The clothes look magnificent!' the merchant exclaimed with feeling. Pearls of sweat stood on his face, but he knew he had served Skord well.

'Mel Skara,' the youth said, 'rest assured that you will receive full reward for your services today . . .'

Mel Skara almost prostrated himself with gratitude. He had had little trade in recent years, but his work for Her had more than recompensed him.

'You are well pleased?' Skord enquired of the three travellers.

'We're grateful,' Estarinel said quietly.

'Excellent!' the merchant exclaimed. 'And now I have maps, accurate and up-to-date, hand-drawn on finest linen . . .'

8

Nemen from the Abyss

It was night in that dusty, disease-ridden town when they entered the inn. Skord had insisted generously that they guest there at his expense, and although they felt that they should leave Beldaega-Hal as soon as possible, they gave in without argument. The awful dehydration of Hrannekh Ol had taken its toll, and after two days' riding they knew they must rest.

The inn was a dull, square, red building without even a sign outside to distinguish it. Within the dimly-lit public room there was a low murmur of voices which abruptly died as the four entered. Skord strode across to the wooden bar that was opposite the entrance, but the others stood still in the doorway and looked about them. Their gaze met pair after pair of sick, glazed, half-dead eyes, until their skin began to creep under the collective stare of the townspeople.

Almost every table in the inn was full, and every person there gazed unblinkingly at them; except for one woman who sat near the door, and she was weeping, slumped across the table with her head on her arms. She sat alone and the others ignored her.

'I want four rooms for the night,' Skord was saying to the landlord, a bulky, grey-haired man with a bitter face. The man paused in polishing a glass.

'And who are your guests, sir?'

'A knight, a lady, and a Prince,' replied Skord in a tone which warned him not to pry.

'A Gorethrian, sir?' The landlord's hairy, big-boned arms moved as he began to work at the glass again. He had the air of a servant trying to pluck up courage to rebel against a despotic master.

'Just ready the rooms and prepare us a meal, Skarred,' Skord insisted. The landlord stammered, as if he must have an answer although the consequence of asking the question might be disastrous.

'But the Gorethrians are our enemies, sir . . .' and his face hung as if his very last hope of life had been dragged from him.

'How can you have enemies, Skarred,' said Skord, smiling, 'when you have not a single friend?' And he put three gold coins on the bar.

'What do I want with your filthy money!' cried the landlord, not out of courage but because he had lost his temper. 'Our only enemy is *She*, She whom we worship as a goddess who is no better than the Worm! And She is *your* enemy too, whatever you tell yourself!'

Skord went white, as if Skarred had hit some truth.

'Another word and you will be removed to a Region which will make this place seem like the fields of Paradise,' he threatened, pale with anger.

'Do it then!' the landlord cried, losing all control. 'I would rather a million years in the Dark Regions than another minute looking at your wicked face, child! And word is your own father felt the same—' he was trembling violently, possessed by fury and fear. But as Skord made to reply, he was silenced by Ashurek's icy grip on his elbow.

'Skord,' the Gorethrian broke in, 'perhaps I had better explain to Skarred. The Gorethrians are my enemies too. I have rejected them and all I perpetrated for them. We are only innocent travellers pursuing a personal goal; you have nothing to fear from us . . .' he looked at Skord. 'And I fail to see why you all exist in living terror of this boy.' He glanced round the townspeople who had suddenly broken into a murmur of astonishment.

Skord began, 'Now I—'

'Be silent,' Ashurek commanded, and to the people's surprise, he was. 'Does he often carry out his frequent threats? By what power can he do this?'

'By *Her* power. She To Whom We Pay Tribute,' muttered the landlord. Skord folded his arms with a slight air of condescension.

'So,' said Ashurek, 'this country is in the power of some sorceress and you are her minion?' He stared unnervingly at Skord. 'You speak with light abandon of the Dark Regions, but you are playing with fire. One slip and you will be down there yourself!'

And Skord began to look afraid. He turned on his heel and made quickly for a flight of stairs, disappearing upstairs without another word.

At once there was a relaxing of the atmosphere, as if the

townspeople were silently celebrating Ashurek's humiliation of Skord. With a gloomy expression, his mouth turned down at the corners, Skarred showed the three to a table and brought them a meal of dry bread and cheese so sour that it stung their mouths like acid. They ate swiftly, anxious to be out of the townspeople's gaze.

'I will show you to your rooms,' the landlord said. They began to make their way to the stairs; but as Estarinel mounted the first step, Skarred took his arm. 'In the name of mercy,' he whispered, 'don't let your companion go on angering Skord. If he's humiliated before us now he'll bring all hell down on our heads later – and I've just signed my own death warrant for my loss of temper. We're all sick of his terrorising but defy him and disaster follows.'

'Do you know of a way we can stop him?'

'No. There is no way. Kill him and She will just send another – a worse. And if She were in league with Gorethria, it would be the end for us . . .'

'I don't think there's a chance of that,' Estarinel tried to reassure him. 'We are only three travellers – we know nothing of Skord or the purpose for which he has "befriended" us.'

The landlord's weary grey eyes widened. 'Then don't trust him – get away from him. He'd sell his own parents if the price was right.'

Estarinel nodded grimly, released himself from Skarred's grip, and bade him good night.

As they reached the doors to the cramped, dim rooms, Estarinel paused and looked round at Medrian.

'I feel lost,' he said wearily. 'What are we doing here? Thousands of miles from anywhere we know, and further than ever from even starting the Quest. Is this what the Worm can do?' Medrian turned the frozen, grey-and-black shadows of her eyes upon him, and he knew immediately that their tenuous contact on the White Plane was lost. There seemed to be a sighing waste of ice between them, and fear clawed at his throat – fear of her.

'Good night,' was all she said.

She waited, still as an icon, until the Forluinishman had gone tiredly into his room. Then she went to Ashurek's door and entered without knocking.

A lamp filled the chamber with an acid, lemony light. Ashurek, who had been peering out of the small window, looked sharply round at her.

'Did you see what was in the mirror?' she asked, and he noticed the cold metallic tone of her voice.

'What do you mean?'

'Mel Skara's mirror – reflected in the mercury.'

Ashurek's icy green eyes met her blank ones.

'Have you come in here to speak riddles?' he asked harshly.

'Just to say – you are wrong.'

'About what?'

'About this – this journey,' she almost gasped, and he realised with what difficulty she was finding her words, as if something struggled to silence her. Her face was sallow with hidden pain, but he only felt angered.

'Are you saying we should not have come with Skord?' She nodded. 'But tomorrow we go North to find a ship. It's the only thing we can do now, isn't it?'

'It's too late,' Medrian answered.

'Why?'

'Because of the mirror.'

'Well, what did you see?' he enquired, his tone vitriolic.

'I don't remember.'

'Convenient. Do you know something, or is this just a feeling?' She was silent, and suddenly there was a presence between them; she was the Alaakian rebel, and he the Gorethrian oppressor. Fury and bitterness shook Ashurek, and Medrian felt an old malevolence awake and focus upon them. Anger flamed white in her face, but was gone in a second.

'The Serpent can muster more hate for my race than Gorethria ever could,' she said quietly. 'But it's all gone now, it doesn't matter.'

'Go. Just go, Medrian,' Ashurek whispered, his hand straying involuntarily to his sword hilt. She turned slowly to the door.

'I'm sorry you wouldn't listen – sorry I could tell you nothing worth heeding anyway,' she said, her voice as quiet and sinister as a distant iron bell.

Morning was again pale with a light drizzle that darkened the paving stones before them as they rode. The peasants fell back in their wake as they had the day before, staring, whispering, coming from their houses to the litter-strewn streets to watch the travellers. They were now riding out of that miserable town. Skord had hardly said a word that morning, but the look in his cold, foxy eyes turned often to burning anger when he looked at the Gorethrian; an awful look of hatred which did not appear to disconcert Ashurek.

As they rode, Skord in his finery at the front, the other three a little further back, talking quietly, an hysterical girl ran out from an alley and threw herself at Skord's horse. Skord jerked his mare to a halt. The girl was shouting, barely coherently.

'. . . take my respect and treat me like filth . . . witch's bastard . . . you'd betray me for my just revenge . . . curse be on you as the curse She laid on me for you! . . . I spit on your damned soul . . .'

The girl's face, framed by tangled, flying dark hair, was sweat-streaked and crusted with black sores. She clutched at Skord's stirrup with emaciated hands. Skord looked away and dug his heels into his fretting mare's sides. The crowd of peasants did nothing as the mare, mouth foaming, started forward skittishly. The girl seized Skord's leg and began tugging at his cloak.

'. . . what revenge is there for me . . . oh, may your fall from Her favour be hard and terrible . . .'

Skord spurred his mare to a canter, but the girl still clung to him, and, losing her footing, was dragged along. Then there was a ring of metal as Skord drew his sword and dealt the girl a crunching blow on the head with the pommel. She fell, outstretching white, claw-like hands which tore at the boy's robes as she collapsed to the flagstones. And Skord, in a clatter of hooves, was gone.

Ashurek sent Vixata in a gallop after the boy. But Skord's mare seemed to have wings and, as they reached the edge of the town, he disappeared as if by sorcery. Ashurek cursed and turned his blowing mare back into Beldaega-Hal.

None of the peasants drew near to the little white heap that was the girl. Estarinel dismounted and lifted her weightless frame. Her head fell backwards, disclosing the lifeless, contorted face and staring eyes. Despair stirred in him, as he was suddenly and terribly reminded of Sinmiel, dying in Falin's arms.

'She is dead,' said Estarinel. He still held her up, looking round the faces of the townsfolk. And a woman came towards him, weeping.

'Give her to me,' she said shortly. Once with the girl's thin corpse in her arms, she vanished into the crowd; and within a few minutes they too had dispersed and withdrawn miserably into their own houses and dark alleys. The three travellers stood alone with the sheer, ugly red walls rising around them, rain pattering onto the pale flags from clouds through which the sun no longer shone.

Ashurek leaned forward and stroked Vixata's golden neck.

'The three of us alone again,' he said. 'The miscreant Skord has vanished. Do we interrogate the townsfolk, or continue on our original journey?'

They rode on at a walk.

'What if Skord wreaks some kind of revenge on them?' Estarinel asked. 'We must try to help, somehow . . .'

'No, we must go on. The Serpent comes before all else,' said Medrian.

'I've never met anyone like you!' Estarinel exclaimed. 'How can you be unmoved by events in this town? How can you watch murder and not turn a hair?'

'But she is right,' Ashurek answered. 'To stay here, fishing for an obscure and shallow source of evil, would be useless. The Worm is the root of this, and we must forge straight on to destroy it. Have you forgotten why you came?'

'Oh gods, no,' he whispered.

'Neither have I. I want Silvren back; I want M'gulfn to perish, and the demons; and if the world is turned upside down and Gorethria destroyed also, so be it.' The single-minded, obsessive purpose shone in his eyes and voice, and Estarinel knew that this man would destroy the world if it meant the Serpent's death. He shuddered, emptiness tearing at his stomach.

'I don't want revenge on it,' he said softly, as if to himself. 'I just want my country back.'

'That may be the same thing as revenge, in the end,' Medrian said, sounding strange and distant. 'But perhaps setting out to kill yourself is equally selfish . . . still, what does the motive matter?'

'The motive is everything,' said Ashurek, staring at her harshly. 'Perhaps Estarinel's is right and mine is wrong – but at least both are known. What of you? If you want to kill yourself, Medrian, there are quicker ways, if not surer ones.'

She half-opened her mouth as if to retort, but no sound emerged. Instead she became so pale, her expression so bleak, that Estarinel thought she was going to pass out. He felt angered by Ashurek's harsh words and distressed by Medrian's reaction. He wanted to shake both of them out of their unexplained hostility and coldness,

144

but realised, unhappily, that nothing he said was likely to help.

Briefly he remembered how, on the morning of the Serpent, he had related to Falin his dream of a woman with a pale face and dark hair. Had he had a premonition of meeting Medrian? If there was such a thing as precognition, why should he have dreamt of her, and not of the Serpent itself?

Medrian urged her black beast into a jog ahead of the others, forcing them to follow or lose her in the twisting streets.

'Oh, only let us find a doorway to H'tebhmella,' she said, as if there was one round the next corner.

But at that moment there was a sound of running footsteps behind them, and a voice shouting, 'Wait! Wait!'

It was the inn's landlord. They halted and turned in their saddles to watch him come gasping and red-faced to a stop. 'I wanted to give you all a warning.' He recovered his breath. 'I've just heard about the girl's death, her mother told me. You three seem innocent of what is happening here, so I felt I must explain. The girl, rest her soul, was Skord's betrothed – yes, well may you look surprised. But under the guidance of She To Whom We Pay Tribute, he played on her love and used her most cruelly; but she was no fool. When she realised that Skord was in Her pay, she rebelled openly and rejected him; so he had her struck with the plague.' Tears squeezed from the landlord's eyes, and a great sob wracked his body. 'That plague will come to us all in the end, all who still have some pride left.'

'Skarred, what has happened to Belhadra?' Ashurek asked.

'I don't think I can remember, only vaguely . . . there were no soldiers . . . just messengers, such as Skord, saying they had come from the Glass City. Well, the Glass City is only a fairy story, anyway. No one's ever been able to find it. But they said they had been sent by the Sorceress there, to tell us that she had come to rule and protect our country, and we were to pay her tribute in return . . . or die.' Skarred laughed. 'Yes, it sounded mad, but the mental and physical sickness they brought were real enough. Men of power and their soldiers lay down their arms, became witless, disappeared or died.'

'But what was the tribute she wanted?'

'Just our minds, I think,' Skarred said chillingly. 'And she has them. All sense of time has been lost; purpose, everything. We will all die of apathy; no one cares. Tomorrow I will have forgotten

145

all I tell you today. Tomorrow the plague may come upon me. It doesn't matter. But Skord – he hates Her as much as the rest of us. He was no victim of Her slow brainwashing, was never threatened with the plague that comes to all who defy Her. He has some vile bargain with her from which he must long to be free.' He looked at them, as if struggling with a puzzle he knew he would never solve.

'Have you ever seen Her?' Estarinel asked.

'Seen Her?' Skarred answered strangely. 'Her mirrors are everywhere. It is no longer possible to tell reflection from reality; is this town an ill reflection of a fair city, or is the truth far fouler? Does my real self still exist apart from this poor mirror-image? You see, one glimpse of Her looking glass destroys all sense of perspective. Somewhere, perhaps, Belhadra exists as it used to be; we live in a reflection. Oh gods, what am I talking about?' The landlord shook his head, and his eyes became clear. 'But look – this is what I meant to tell you. I can see why Skord picked on you three – you are spirited, and dangerous. If he can deliver you to Her, he will be well rewarded. Or perhaps he hopes to play you and Her against each other, hoping both sides will be destroyed.'

'You obviously know the lad well, but you do not know us,' Ashurek said. 'We are going our own way, not Skord's.'

'But he must have made you look in the mirror, in Mel Skara's shop—'

'I can't remember,' said Estarinel, frowning.

'No, you wouldn't. So you see, you are in Her power already; you can only go straight to Her.' There was a strained, cold silence as they all stared at the landlord.

'My curiosity is thoroughly roused,' Ashurek said, with an unfathomable gleam in his eye. 'Let us ride on, and see what awaits us.'

'Perhaps we can find some way – to help you,' Estarinel added uncertainly.

But Medrian exclaimed, 'You're wrong! Something awaits us that is better avoided. Darkness is there – I can see no escape.'

'So it has been for me, many times. So it is still,' Ashurek said more gently than before. He looked searchingly at her as if to discover the truth of her enigmatic words. 'The question is, have you the courage to endure it?'

146

'Yes. If it must be faced, it must,' she said, looking down at her horse's neck. 'Come on, let's waste no more time.'

They bade goodbye to the landlord who soon stood alone in the greyness of ever-falling rain. Presently he heard a distant cry: Ashurek's voice.

'Ho, Skarred – we ride to your salvation, straight into the unknown!'

Estarinel watched Ashurek shouting with exuberance on a leaping, plunging Vixata, and realised that the expression in his eyes was not unfathomable after all. It was a dangerous eagerness, and in that moment he glimpsed a key to all Gorethrians' eccentric and destructive behaviour. They enjoyed trouble.

For a week they rode North. And what Skarred had said of Mel Skara's mirror seemed to be true; it was a complex hypnotic device which was drawing them, irretrievably, to a certain point in the world. Their maps seemed to make no sense, and their horses were unusually spiritless as they plodded the unseen pathway.

For the first three days they passed through undulating farmlands, networks of grey hedges criss-crossing greenish fields, with narrow, crumbling paved roads running this way and that between them. There were straggling red villages here and there, some deserted; but they kept clear of them, camping in fields and hedgerows, living on their own provisions and on small game or crops pilfered from fields and orchards. Sometimes people saw them, but seemed afraid to stop them.

But in one village they did not seem afraid to state their opinion of Her. They came upon the villagers digging a mass grave for victims of the plague. As they rode past, even at a distance, they saw a man spit and heard him say, '*That* for She who took my children and my wife!' There were already feverish sores on his own face.

Gradually farmlands gave way to forests; scrubby greyish trees with dull green foliage, growing thick and choked with undergrowth. They were hilly with thin paths that always seemed to take the most difficult route, treacherous with loose shale. The tree-crusted hills were full of precipitous drops concealed by undergrowth or overhung by crumbling ledges; sudden deep bogs; dead ends which meant hours of retracing steps over untrustworthy ground.

147

On the sixth night, as they slept in a forest hollow, Ashurek saw a vision; at least, he was sure it was not a dream. He was not in the forest, but in a tiny chamber, all its walls shrouded in grey velvet curtains. A dusky glow highlighted the heavy folds, and the honey-gold hair of Silvren. She sat facing him, cross-legged. She was dressed in a milky-coloured garment, and she was smiling, but she seemed unutterably distant.

'I wanted to tell you something I noticed about the Dark Regions,' she said cheerfully. 'It's not black at all – it's blue. Did you ever notice that? Blue – navy blue, indigo blue, blue like bruised skin or like the egg of a small bird, washed by the rain and left to rot in a deserted nest . . .' She almost seemed to be singing a spell. He felt sure she would not hear him if he spoke.

'I also wanted to tell you that I'm going to try and watch you. You are diving into darkness. I feel it, even from here . . . it's not so bad, now pain has become a monotone dream. But I wish I could see what you are doing! Ashurek . . . and I wish you would remember why. It's for the world the Worm must die, not so you can have vengeance on all that has hurt you.'

The bitter truth of her rebuke impaled him, like a needle of pure gold turning in his heart.

'Well, there is my useless warning,' Silvren said. 'And oh, damn her, she was my friend!'

Like a faint light being extinguished, she was gone. Trees surrounded Ashurek, emanating a heavy malice. He had not been asleep, and Silvren had been there, in shades of gold and pearl, though what she had said was dream-like, if not incomprehensible. She had been there, and now she was gone.

At dawn they were glad to be out of the close, over-silent forest and on a wide, barren plain of wiry grass. After resting the horses they took off over it at full gallop for several hours; dwarfed by the vast dome of tattered grey above them, borne on a dry gale that swept the wind away to the North. They had seen no sign of Skord.

Later that day, still on the downs, they came in sight of strange ice-white hills that marked the Equator.

They rode, single file, into a pass between white cliffs that rose quite suddenly out of the plain. The path between the faces of glassy quartz was uneven and slippery and they had to dismount and lead the horses. At last the pass opened out into a wider terrain of crystal hills rising in steps and ledges to oddly shaped peaks.

Little glistening streams bubbled over rock here and there, running together to form small rivers and then wider ones.

They must have climbed and trekked about ten miles over the hills of white crystalline rock, following an ever-widening river, when they came to the peak of a final, high ridge, below which a sudden valley fell away – falling, falling into grey depths. There lay below their feet an abyss miles across, filled with the thunder and vapour of many plunging waterfalls. It seemed bottomless, but they could see the far rim of the chasm on the horizon. Shafts of late sunlight caught the water, turning it to spirals of golden glass, glinting on white peaks of quartz, illuminating the banks of vapour to translucent silver-blue. Ahead lay many more such valleys, separated by hills like great crystals clustered together.

They began to edge slowly along the ridge, eyes fixed on the depths where water like molten diamond leapt on downwards from ledge to ledge.

Medrian trotted on in front, hair and cloak streaming, to a viewpoint some yards ahead. They were now riding across a shallow dip patterned with rock pools, surrounded by a jagged, sunlit ridge. They saw her silhouetted against a golden sky as she turned Nameless and sent him trotting and slithering along the glassy ridge back towards them.

'Quick!' she was shouting. 'Back the way we came!' She cantered up to them. 'There are about thirty – er – swordsmen down there. Better not to wait and see if they're friendly.'

'We'll wait on the far ridge,' Ashurek said as they rode back. 'Then they'll have to get below us to get at us, and we'll have an advantage.'

As they waited, three mounted figures gilded by the sun's last shafts, Estarinel thought that perhaps if they approached the swordsmen peacefully, they would do them no harm. When the armed men actually appeared, it was obvious the three companions would be pitched straight into battle. The swordsmen came over the ridge and across the dip; they came behind the ridge, streaming round from both sides until Medrian, Estarinel and Ashurek were surrounded; and there were far more than thirty of them.

They were on foot, running lithely and strongly across the glassy rock. They had dark golden skin and hair, and were on average about seven feet high, almost naked but for straps about their thighs, waists, chests and arms, which seemed to be for carrying

149

weapons; their features were long and strange, neither male nor female; each had four arms, one pair below the other. And each held a sword, a shield, an axe, and a 'morning-star' – a spiked iron ball that they whirled on a chain.

Ashurek and Estarinel drew swords. Medrian set arrow to bow.

Then one of the creatures, apparently their captain, pointed at the three and cried, 'Take them!'

9

To Her Door

They were not taken without a battle. They had the advantage of being on the narrow ridge and mounted on horses; but there the advantage ended. The creatures advanced in silence but for a curious rushing sound that was the slap of many bare feet on wet rock. Before they reached the three, Medrian was already sending arrows skimming with accuracy into the creatures' ranks, picking off several of them.

Ashurek was the first to be assailed. It was difficult fighting several of the creatures at once, each handling four weapons with skill and ferocity. He lopped the head from the first creature and it fell back, knocking down one behind it. Vixata jumped sideways and a morning-star whistled close to his ear. A sword swung at him, and he turned so that it fell with a shuddering blow on his shield. He sliced two arms from one attacker, took another through the chest. His mare, a metallic streak of light, was rearing, kicking, dodging. She was a highly-trained war-horse and this was a Gorethrian technique of fighting. The horse was finely schooled to strike, bite and kick at all assailants of her own accord, and to obey the slightest command of her rider. The rider, too, used great skill in sitting firm on the plunging, fighting steed, and fighting swiftly and ferociously at the same time. It was spectacular to watch, and it terrified and demoralised enemies.

Ashurek, as he wielded his sword, cutting off a limb here, a head there, feeling the lithe, strong movements of his sweating mare beneath him, was taken over by a familiar blood-lust. He was in his element. He gave an unearthly howl of joy.

Estarinel, meanwhile, was having a hard time of it. It was the first battle he had ever experienced. The Forluinish learned the use of weapons as a sport, and skilful with the sword as he was, there was a world of difference between a fencing match and a life-or-death sword fight. But he had killed once, and the next time

151

was not so hard. The golden-skinned homonoids crowded in on him. He twisted, ducked, blocked blows with his shield, severed limbs, struck and parried. Shaell had no such skill as Vixata, but through sheer strength and bulk of body was able to push the men aside, push them over and off the ridge.

There seemed no end to the number of creatures. Their attack never faltered. Strong, bronze-limbed, expressionless, they had a kind of asexual beauty. As one was killed or wounded, another would take its place. Those not fighting would be waiting, manœuvring slowly to be in the right position. Their four arms moved with graceful co-ordination. They had so far dealt no fatal blows, but horses and riders were incurring many wounds, rents, bruises. Blood creamed with sweat on the horses' steaming coats and the animals were all growing distressed, breathing hard.

Medrian had to give up her arrow-firing and fight hand to hand. Ashurek, finding a second to draw breath and glance at her, recognised her Alaakian style of fighting, very fast and accurate; she favoured taking the attackers through the throat. Although her shield arm had taken a bad wound and blood was pouring down her wrist, dripping from her hand, she fought on. She manœuvred Nameless, using leg aids only to push the creatures over.

The sun sank. A grey, dim half-light shadowed the battle; mists fell. The roar of the falls was punctuated by the high, clear sounds of clashing weaponry.

Estarinel, attacked from both sides, turned one way to plunge his sword through a homonoid's chest. From the other side there was a low whirr of air and a morning-star caught him clean across the back. He cried out and half-fell from his stallion.

'Come on!' he heard Ashurek shouting. 'Gallop for it!'

Ashurek turned Vixata, rearing, knocking three assailants out of the way and jumping over their bodies. Medrian followed, Nameless going swift as a gliding crow in the dusk. Shaell galloped after at full speed with Estarinel hanging onto his mane. They sped up the ridge. This tactic surprised their enemy who were unable to stop them.

They careered down the outside of the ridge, forced their way round bluffs of white rock. Ashurek led them to the comparative safety of a barrier of several large rocks overhung by an unclimbable knoll.

'Now what?' said Medrian, as they hurriedly took the horses

behind the rocks. The homonoids ran surefootedly at an amazing speed and were quickly catching them up.

'Get your breath. They're following us . . . set arrow to bow!' Ashurek said, sliding down from his sweating, shaking mare.

They crouched behind the rocks – which were high enough to conceal even the horses – and waited.

'That was well timed,' Estarinel said.

'It's worked before,' replied Ashurek. 'Hold your ground, look for a thin patch, and then run like the devil . . . it's a way out of a hopeless battle that gives you a break to rest and form a plan.'

'Ho there!' A cry broke in from below. 'Surrender yourselves as prisoners – make no resistance.'

They glanced over the top of their rock barrier. Three of the golden-skinned creatures were approaching their refuge. Medrian released three arrows and felled them all.

'Only one arrow left,' she whispered.

A morning-star flew towards them and bounced violently off the rock about a foot from her face. She jumped backwards with a curse, crouching down again.

'This is the best we can do,' she said. 'We've killed about fifteen but there's still over forty of them. They're starting to surround us. We couldn't fight our way out – not with our horses exhausted and us pouring with blood!'

'Very well,' the clear voice continued. 'We will wait for you until you decide to come out.'

There was silence. But when they looked out again they were indeed surrounded.

'Let's make ourselves comfortable,' Ashurek suggested. 'We're here for the night now!'

Outside, the homonoids were making a camp, lighting torches, making small fires which reflected a flickering red glow on the rocky knoll above the three companions' heads.

Estarinel was tearing up a muslin shirt to make bandages. He wished his store of healing herbs had not been lost on Hrannekh Ol; there was nothing he could do for their various wounds except stop the bleeding.

'Medrian, will you roll up your sleeve please?' he asked.

'What for?' she said absently, still listening acutely for activity outside.

'So that I can bandage your arm.'

'Oh,' she murmured, holding her hand out. It was crusted with blood, and from the knife slash that had caught her wrist, blood still welled. Estarinel made a tourniquet and held her lower arm up to stop the dark red flow.

'Do you feel all right?' he asked. 'You must have lost a lot of blood.'

'Well, I expect I could bleed dry and still walk about,' she answered shortly. 'I feel better than usual.'

As he sat close to her, gently supporting her arm, he noticed that she did look less pale and ill than normal. It was as if whatever internal pain she felt was relieved, or at least numbed, by external danger.

Presently she looked at him, her face in shadow, and said, 'What did you feel about having to fight?'

'Frightened. And sickened,' he replied.

'And shocked that your instinct to live is greater than your horror of killing?'

He smiled, grimly, at her perceptiveness. 'Yes, I suppose so.'

'You'll get used to it.'

'Used to it! I don't want to get used to killing.' He shuddered.

'But when you do, the pain will be less, which will make it easier for you to fulfil the Quest,' she said, her voice distant and somehow ominous. And he knew that while Ashurek had felt wolfish joy in that battle, Medrian had felt nothing, nothing at all, and somehow that seemed much, much worse.

'Yes, but I came to kill a mindless beast, not human beings,' he said unhappily.

'But it is all part of the same thing. And even the Serpent has a mind, and when you kill it, it will feel, and know.' She uttered a grim laugh. 'Estarinel, don't be tortured by self-doubt; it will pass.'

'I don't understand you,' he said softly; and he did not understand how he could feel so drawn to someone so cold, strange, even callous.

'Nor I you,' she replied. 'How can you have suffered so much for Forluin, yet still be able to care what happens in Belhadra?'

'That's just the way we are – in Forluin, I mean. I can't help it. I care about you as well, Medrian.'

'Listen,' she said thinly. 'What are you going to do when it all gets too much? Emotion is pain . . . I'm not afraid of pain, but I can only function by not feeling anything.'

He stared at her; she appeared small and frail, hardly any older than himself, her shower of black hair falling around her pallid face. But the terrible darkness was still in her eyes, and she seemed as delicate and clear and indestructible as a diamond. He could not bring himself to ask her reasons for coming on the Quest.

'If you must care about so many things, Estarinel,' she continued, a strange cold note entering her voice, 'don't make the mistake of including me. I am not to be trusted. As my companion you can help me best by finding a way to the Blue Plane . . . and bearing with my silence. The bleeding has stopped now.'

She gently drew her arm from his hands. Her words had brought an unexpected pressure of distress to his throat, but before he could say any more to her, Ashurek interrupted.

'Nemen,' he said. 'That's what they are.'

'What?' Estarinel said.

'Our friends out there. Some of the races of Tearn have three sexes: men, women, nemen. The Northern countries, Athrainy and Sphraina . . .'

'Silvren came from Athrainy, didn't she?' Estarinel asked.

'Yes,' replied Ashurek, 'that is how I know. It is said they are neuter, and having no sexual purpose they are shunned by society. So, they wander from their homelands and take arms for the highest bidder. It's a life that makes them bitter and formidable adversaries . . . being an accident of nature without use. Like the whole damned earth!' He laughed cynically.

Estarinel shivered, looking up at the two alabaster moons gleaming benignly in the cobalt sky. He wished more than ever that he was at home, and that the Serpent M'gulfn did not exist.

They slept. The black globe of the sky pivoted above them.

They awoke again quite suddenly to find Skord kneeling on top of their rock barrier and looking down at them.

'Hello, what brings you to be hiding behind a rock like frightened rabbits?' he mocked. 'You three are fools. I send out an armed escort to look after you and what do you do? Attack them. Well, you've had it now! These nemen are no better than barbarians and they're not likely to forgive your behaviour, even if it was a mistake – ahh!' The last exclamation was drawn from him as Ashurek seized him and pulled him bodily from his perch to their refuge.

'What are you talking about this time?' Ashurek demanded, his eyes glinting dangerously. Skord sulkily nursed a bruised arm.

'*You* may not know where you're going, but—'

'To She To Whom You Pay Tribute? The Mirror of Mel Skara?'

'Oh. Well, you're not complete fools.' Skord grinned. 'I sent the nemen out as a sort of escort of honour – since you can't avoid going to Her now, you may as well be made to feel welcome – but you've obviously rubbed them up the wrong way.'

'Skord,' said Ashurek, 'what would you do if fifty or so four-armed warriors suddenly rushed you from all sides?'

'Well, it's just their way,' he said apologetically, still grinning slightly.

'I see. It's your idea of a joke to have us attacked and held to siege!'

'Now then! I—'

'Now you're here,' Ashurek interrupted, drawing out a knife that gleamed coldly in the darkness, 'it's time for some explanations.'

'What have I got to explain?' Skord said, a trace of uncertainty cutting across his arrogant tone.

'Tell us about your bargain with Her.'

'I have none – I work for Her of my own accord—'

'Do you not loathe Her?'

'We worship Her – we all worship Her.' Fear was beginning to show in his eyes. 'I have only to shout a command and a horde of nemen will descend on this place.'

'With you as our hostage?'

'They have no love for me,' Skord said, and it was probably the only honest statement he had ever made to them.

'In that case, you'll have no chance to shout,' and Ashurek put the knife to Skord's throat. It was not the knife that Skord feared, but the Gorethrian himself. 'What is your bargain with Her?'

'None – none!' Skord spat. 'She'll make you pay for this!'

'Why should I fear your threats or Her's? I who have defied demons and escaped the Dark Regions?'

'She has more power than a demon – no, no, I am not threatening you, I am warning you.' There was a note of hysteria in Skord's voice. 'I was only serving Her – I – oh no, no—' His fair, rosy face became contorted and purplish, his eyes glazed, and his breathing became quick and shallow like a small animal's.

Ashurek groaned slightly and sheathed the knife. He had tried to dismiss it from his mind, but he could no longer: Skord's erratic behaviour was similar to that of his own dead brother.

'Something stopped him speaking,' Ashurek said. 'He was going to tell us too much, so something blocked his tongue. Whether it was Her or some other power . . . the Worm is dogging our steps all the way.' He sighed and rested his dark head in his hands.

156

Estarinel broke hesitantly into the silence.

'I think I can make him speak. An old Forluinish technique – a kind of hypnotism – it's only supposed to be used for healing purposes.' He looked uncertainly at Ashurek for approval.

'If there's a complete antithesis to Gorethrian methods, it must be Forluinish ones! Go on, let's see if it works. I want to know who this boy is.'

The young knight positioned himself so that he was kneeling, facing the vacant-eyed Skord whose boyish face was twisted as if with terror. Estarinel drew a deep breath to calm and ready himself, and fixed his own eyes, unblinking, with a clear and steady gaze, on the boy's.

About ten minutes passed and both figures were quite motionless, quite silent. Medrian and Ashurek watched, conscious of a current between the two, like a radiation passing across a vacuum.

Skord's breathing grew slower and slower. Colour came back to his cheeks but his eyes did not change. A terrible sadness came over the face of Estarinel and his lips parted.

'Skord,' he said. 'Skord.' Again, 'Skord.' Then he began to speak in a low monotone, chanting a ritual which gave Ashurek a strange sensation in the pit of his stomach. There was power in the words, and more to the Forluinish than met the eye.

'That which sealed thy lips is departed. That which stayed thy tongue is departed. That which stilled thy voice is departed. From mine eyes to thine, the key. From thine eyes to thy mouth, the unlocking . . .' on and on. Skord's face hung with an expression of despair; the look that had been on the face of his mother, and Skarred, and the murdered girl, and her mother. '. . . now speak. Speak. Speak.' Estarinel finished the chant. 'Who are you?'

A few seconds passed. Then Skord spoke with a strange accent.

'Schorde,' he said. 'I am Schorde.' It sounded like a different name, rather than a slurring of his own.

'Where do you live?' No response. 'Describe it to me – is it a farm?'

'No . . . a city . . . spires shining in the sun, white and gold, glittering. The sea on one side . . . forests on the other. The sun shines, I play with my friends . . . down through the forests, past the eleven spires, down to the sea we race . . . I am the fastest! Even my friend with his long legs is not swifter than me!' A smile came to his lips but his eyes remained vacant.

157

'Drish! He's a damned Drishian,' Ashurek muttered under his breath.

'Do you come from Drish, Skord – Schorde?' Estarinel asked. At once the boy's face changed, clouding with annoyance.

'Yes, of course.'

'How old are you?'

'Thirteen! Almost . . .'

'And you have always lived in Drish?'

'Of course! Where else would I live?'

'You don't live there now.' Skord frowned and began to turn his head from side to side.

'You're lying. I do, I do . . . I live near the city. Mother and father are with me, yes they are – and my little sister – no! No!'

'What is happening?' Estarinel asked. 'What can you see?'

'They are coming – dark ships on the sea, dark men walking up through the tide . . . black and silver, like demons, dripping with blood. No! We have never done them harm – why do they come? We must fight them, fight, fight . . . father goes. I am holding onto mother and my sister, they are crying – so afraid . . . the dark ones are not human. We wait and wait – but father does not come back! Mother is mad with grief, I cannot calm her. Then our leaders come for us . . . we are herded from our houses to a camp, like prisoners . . . the dark men have taken the city. But our leaders haven't surrendered! There's to be another battle . . . but all those who are not fit to fight are to be sent away to safety. I don't want to go – I want to fight, like father – I argue with mother, she weeps and weeps – I cannot comfort her – then – then something is coming towards us!' Skord was breathing very fast, his face ghastly with horror.

'What is it? What is it?' Estarinel asked.

'Don't know. Can't remember. Very dark – then bright, I can't see. My leg hurts. Mother is screaming, so is my sister – screams all around us. Something slashing at us . . . blood, my little sister covered in blood. No! No! They betrayed us!'

'Who betrayed you, Schorde?'

'The dark men . . . or our leaders. I don't know, I don't understand. They came among us at night and wounded us all. I think they only meant to wound—' his tone became bitter, chilling. 'But in the morning my little sister is dead.'

'Go on,' Estarinel prompted gently, trying to mask the horror in his own voice. Skord gagged with the effort of finding words.

'Forgotten . . . days go by . . . just a nightmare. We think it is over . . . waiting in fear, all of us crowded together, sick, injured rabbits. But no – the dark ones are not satisfied—' The flat tone of his voice escalated towards hysteria as he went on. 'They come again, killing this time – slaughtering, mad – people falling, dying around us – but a few of us escape. I take mother's arm and run, dragging her along – we are beyond the forests, beyond the borders, safe – oh, would that we had died with the others!' He began to rant in the native tongue of Drish, weeping and moaning in terrible distress.

'Skord!' said Estarinel sharply. 'Schorde! Speak the Common Language!'

He fell abruptly silent. Then he went on in a stilted, flat tone.

'It is mother. She cannot forget my father and sister – she is mad with grief, insane. I can't bear it! Nothing, no one can reach her . . . in despair I go off alone, self-pitying . . . as if my grief is worse than her's. When I return she has killed herself. If only I had stayed! Surely my soul is damned – grief and guilt and memories plague me. Surely I am mad myself . . . I want revenge! Yes! The dark ones used demons – I will unleash one against them in return! I explore the old sorceries, find the knowledge . . .' He uttered a moan. 'I call for help – one comes. But oh – it is a creature of hell. It is silver and its mouth is red – I am terrified, my soul is damned. It won't obey me – I am feeble with grief, I long to die. But it – it sends me to Her. She is kind to me. She tells me that if I help Her, She will help me in turn. She takes away my memory . . . I am happy for a time, I am Skord of Belhadra, son of a farmer . . . that is all I know . . . such peace. But then She makes me perform Her work – cast plague – take tribute. That which I called for aid will not leave me. She will not make it go, She torments me with the threat of giving back my memory. I loathe Her, I love Her, I fear Her – I revel in Her power and I despise it . . .' he went on in this vein, growing hysterical again.

'Quiet!' Estarinel ordered. 'Quiet, quiet . . . be still . . . Now Skord, I will wake you.' He held him in trance for five minutes more until Skord's face became calm and his eyes dropped shut. Then, 'Wake,' he said.

He was quite unprepared for what happened next. Skord's eyes flew open; he leapt forward, swung his hand in a blow across Estarinel's face which sent him reeling backwards into the rock wall behind him. The boy staggered to his feet, teeth bared and eyes swivelling like a trapped wild animal.

'Damn you! Damn you! Damn you!' he hissed, overcome with fury and anguish. 'You'll pay! You'll pay for this; all of you! Devil's bastards! Damn you!' He turned and ran through the narrow pass between rocks and rock wall. They made no move to stop him.

Ashurek looked at Medrian and drew a breath through clenched teeth.

Estarinel had been knocked out cold. There was blood oozing from his mouth, and Medrian, lifting his head, felt beneath his black hair a lump where his head had struck the rock.

'Poor Estarinel. I'm sure he did not have this in mind,' she said quietly. Ashurek thought she was showing uncharacteristic tenderness as she made her cloak into a pillow, and then wiped the blood from his cheek.

'I might have known there were demons behind it – I should have seen the signs,' he remarked.

'I won't ask what the Gorethrians did in Drish, Ashurek,' said Medrian tightly.

'Well, it was worse than Alaak,' he said, his voice so rough with self-loathing that she actually looked up at him. 'That's when I turned my back upon Gorethria. Five years ago – yes, Skord would have been about thirteen then.'

'Now we know his past, but we're still no nearer to discovering who "She" is.'

'Other than a powerful and malevolent necromancer.' Ashurek calmed the horses who were upset and restless. 'Ye gods, I feel sorry for the miserable wretch. As if he hadn't suffered enough without falling into the Shana's hands.

'Now, I presume, he will send the nemen to massacre us,' said Medrian without emotion.

'Yes, we seem to have upset him enough . . . but we will give them a fight for their money.' Ashurek's eyes glinted like burning ice. 'Although I thought we were to be delivered to "Her" intact.'

Medrian shuddered.

'Perhaps we are in Her domain already, and this is what she has decided to do with us. If so, my fears were unfounded.'

'You mean you would rather be slain by some mercenary than go to meet Her?' Ashurek asked curiously. She was an enigma – did she really know something, or was she half-mad?

'Yes, that would be preferable,' she said with a self-mocking smile that, for some reason, made him feel less hostile towards her than before. 'But impossible. The path must be pursued by the proper route to the very end, or – well, look at poor Skord. Ah, but he is right; death and forgetfulness would be the best of all.'

They planned to stay hidden until Estarinel regained consciousness, and then perhaps ride to escape, taking the nemen by surprise. But in the end they had no choice in the matter. When dawn came, damp and fresh, Estarinel was still unconscious. Medrian climbed up and looked over the top of the rocks.

Ashurek, kneeling beside Estarinel to see how he was, looked up at the slim, dark figure of the woman.

'Ouch!' he heard her say. 'Some insect. We're still surrounded, but they've not closed in yet. I can't see Skord.' Then she suddenly and wordlessly fell backwards to the ground. Ashurek expected to see an arrow or a knife sticking from her body, but there was no mark on her. She lay still, eyes closed, pale as death. Ashurek looked cautiously over the top of the rocks. The nemen were standing in a semi-circle below their knoll, tall, bronze-limbed, golden-haired. They were very like Silvren in colouring, and he realised that they could easily be of Silvren's race. He saw one of them holding a reed to its mouth and he felt something like an insect sting on his forehead.

It was then that he remembered something else about warrior-nemen: 'They use drugged darts.' The thought came into his mind as it fell away into a cavern of blackness.

Confusion – dizziness – movement. A great mushroom of crystal towering towards the sun which glinted silver and white on its millions of tiny facets. The roar of many waters. Spray. Mist. Damp, cold air. The ice-white walls of a chasm rising to jagged heights, sparkling with great curtains of molten glass and foam. Whispering. Laughter – malicious, joking laughter. And a mass of golden faces, sometimes one standing out clearly – laughing – then retreating into the mass. Estarinel's voice saying, 'I saw them as he saw them – staring, sick faces crowded together.' Day – night – day – night. Blackness and whiteness and disorientation . . .

The next thing Estarinel remembered was crawling on hands and knees down a deserted street. Completely deserted – a vast and choking sense of emptiness, of many fair things that had ceased to exist. He was only half-conscious; a searing pain through his head, his back and his limbs; blood half-blinding him in a warm stream from somewhere on his head; clothes torn; dirt crusted on his hands and face. How long he had crawled he did not know. The blood for some reason stung his eyes like acid and he gasped and sobbed with the pain as he went.

Presently he blundered headlong into a wall. Groping blindly, he found a handhold and agonizingly dragged himself to his feet. He rubbed his eyes vigorously with his hands. The pain in his head spun away with a sinking sense of dizziness, leaving him swaying and heavy-headed but able to see and – eventually – to think.

It was hot, but he shivered convulsively. He saw, as through a red mist, the nature of the city he was in.

It was a city of metal. Gold, platinum, steel, silver, copper. There were tall, round towers of all kinds of metal, all imaginable shapes. Shining tubes of gold and silver stretching towards the sky, twisted, filigreed, inlaid, or with smooth perfect surfaces, all polished like looking glasses, pure and lovely of colour. In each tower one great jewel was set: stones of deep, soft blue, of viridian, purple and crimson, bright as mirrors. Broad, airy streets ran between the towers. They were paved with diamond-shaped slabs of marble, in many-coloured pastel shades, rich with fine, branching veins of purple and gold.

Beautiful it was, but the sun's glare reflecting from the towers, as if from many metal mirrors, pained Estarinel's eyes.

Think. Think.

'Shaell?' he mouthed. Where was his stallion? Memories began to seep back into his mind; there should be two others with him. A battle . . . Skord . . . a vision of Drish, bloodied faces eaten with fear . . . a great mushroom of crystal. He remembered, but his head would not clear and he could not order his thoughts.

'How did I get here?' A piece of logic forced itself into his brain. 'I was unconscious – the nemen must have brought me here and left me.'

He had no idea where to go, but he staggered on down the broad, shining street in search of water. He clung to buildings, his legs too weak to support him. Perhaps the nemen had been brutal with their prisoners, for he was in worse condition now than he had been after the battle. He passed out two or three times as he stumbled slowly on, a whiteness clouding over his eyes, a whiteness like that of Hrannekh Ol, or like snow—

162

'Greetings!' A clear, female voice hailed him from a distance. 'Stay still. I'll help you.'

He looked ahead and saw that the street opened into a square filled with shining fountains, and there was a lady on horseback at the street's end.

Estarinel strained his misty eyes. There was something very strange about her colouring. Thick waves of blue-green hair, like hanks of sea-coloured silk, flowed over her shoulders, caught here and there with a jewel-threaded braid: agate, jade, amethyst. She rode side-saddle on a sea-green horse with golden mane and tail, caparisoned in an ornamental saddle and bridle. Her riding habit was a full dress of blue silken material that shimmered as she moved, deepening to purple on the skirt, tight-waisted with wide sleeves that ended above slender beringed hands. The low cut of the bodice displayed her statuesque shoulders; her face was exquisite, proud-lipped with aquiline nose and large, luminous, turquoise eyes, and with a transparent pallor as if it were carved from white, green-touched onyx. She seemed at once statuesque and fragile, like a figure of marble.

Although Estarinel's mind was in a confused state, his impression of the woman, as she rode towards him, registered sharply on his brain. His head was spinning as she reached him where he was leaning weakly against a curved metal wall. She reined in the green-and-gold horse and bent down towards him. A rich perfume of honeysuckle and musk clung to her. She spoke, but there was a rushing sound in his ears and he could not hear what she said. As from a great distance, he heard his own voice saying, ridiculously, 'I'm all right, really,' as greyness flooded over his eyes and into his mind.

His second wakening was as pleasant as the first had been unwelcome. There was a soft, cool bed beneath him, with sheets of pale gold and a gorgeously-coloured animal skin of green and black fur across it. It had four posts of gold hung with richly-tapestried curtains which, although lovely to look at, portrayed some gory scenes when examined closely.

Estarinel found he had been bathed and his wounds dressed; he was in a sort of loose night-robe, but he saw a new suit of clothes laid out for him. He propped himself up on his elbows to look about the room. His whole body still ached, but not unbearably; he felt fresh and clean.

The room was semicircular, the curved metal wall opposite set

163

with three oval windows of plain glass and hung with four tapestries. The marble floor was strewn with animal skins of various strange colourings: crimson and grey; blue, green and black. Estarinel was unused to such luxury and did not feel at ease in it. Still, he sank back onto the pillows, taking the opportunity to rest and collect his thoughts. His eyes rested on a low, mirror-topped table.

As a mental exercise, he went through all their adventures since leaving the House of Rede. He remembered perfectly up to the battle with the nemen, after which the memories grew vaguer and vaguer. Talking to Medrian behind the rocks; hypnotising Skord, seeing all his previous life in a vision as clearly as if he had experienced it himself. Then – nothing! Like a candle being extinguished. An undefined passage of time, dreams and darkness swirling together; crawling half-dead about a city of gold; a beautiful, statuesque woman with sea-green hair. Then, waking in a luxurious room, feeling almost normal again. He wondered if he had been drugged.

A door opened to the left of the bed and the woman entered with a tray of food. She glided to the bedside and set the tray on his lap, the silk of her dress rustling slightly as she did so. She paused and looked at him, a smile lighting her beautiful pale face.

'I brought you something to eat,' she said. He sat up, embarrassed.

'Er – I have you to thank for nursing me?'

'Yes – I and my maids. I'm afraid you were dragged to the city without dignity by the nemen – I'm sorry. They're not kind folk. They probably drugged you as well.' She sat on the edge of the bed. 'Do you feel any better?'

'Yes, thank you, my lady.'

'What is your name?'

'Estarinel.'

'I am Arlenmia. You must be from Forluin, or Maerna . . .'

'Forluin, my lady.'

'Ah yes.' Her voice was soft, clear and refined, and she spoke the language common to Forluin and most of Tearn, with no trace of an accent, though with her strange colouring she was surely not of that Earth. She had a natural, graceful regality of bearing which accentuated the sculptural quality of her beauty. Yet there was a slight languidity about her movements that seemed abnormal to him; only the faintest hint, as if she were slightly drunk, though she obviously was not.

164

'Lady Arlenmia . . . I had two companions with me who must also have been taken by the nemen. Are they here?'

She took one of his hands between her own slender ones.

'You must have many such questions. Don't worry. I will try to help you. Now, will you please rest and not be anxious? You are more in need of healing and sleep than you realise. If you require anything, ring this bell and a maid will attend to you. I wish to make you feel welcome in my house.' She smiled, rose gracefully and left, leaving a warm exhalation of perfume behind her.

Estarinel lay back on the pillows, bemused. He tried to imagine what impression she would have given him had he not the gravest reasons for suspecting that Arlenmia was She: a warm, charming and gentle woman who had given the best of care to an injured stranger as a matter of course. His instinct to give people the benefit of the doubt had not yet been eroded. Yet she had evaded his question about Medrian and Ashurek; in truth, there was really no doubt about where he must be.

The knowledge of how external powers had manipulated them chilled him suddenly. The Worm had, it seemed, sucked them from the care of the H'tebhmellians and spat them into Skord's lap to be delivered to some unknown and uncontrollable fate. Yet they had escaped the White Plane when the Serpent might have let them die there . . . so were the forces opposing M'gulfn, the supposed 'good' powers, manipulating them also? He had a brief vision of two figures, one light grey, one dark grey, tossing a ball one to the other with blank-eyed impassiveness. He and his companions truly had no allies, no friends; they were nothing, just instruments in a great design.

He sighed. He was too tired to think, so he stopped trying, and ate the good food Arlenmia had brought. It was the first time he had eaten for several days.

Then he rose from the bed and began to dress. Arlenmia was right; he had been more badly injured than he realised. Once out of the comfortable bed he felt stiffness and pain in all his limbs as well as the particular discomfort of each of his injuries. His back and head ached and he felt so exhausted and weak that he knew resuming the Quest would be impossible for several days at least.

The clothes were odd and ornate; breeches and a padded jacket of dull purple silk, embroidered with gold. There was also a lavish, matching robe of the sort that Skord wore. Estarinel did not touch it. He looked at the mirror-topped table and a pallid, battle-scarred face stared back, framed by a tangle of black hair. For a moment he thought he saw a glass ceiling reflected in the mirror, but he looked up and it was only plain gold metal like the walls. He shook off the illusion, and the feeling that there had been another face, the ghost of a face, superimposed on his own in the mirror.

He looked out of each of the windows and found that his room was on the second storey of a house whose walls shone like polished gold. The first window overlooked a private courtyard with an ornamental pool and fountain in the centre; he noticed there were no plants there, nothing except water, marble and metal. The other windows gave panoramic views of the weird city of metal; that certainly had been no fevered dream. The towers of silver and gold shone dazzlingly under the burning sunlight while the huge jewels set into each one glittered with breathtaking colour. He could see no end to the city and could not guess at its size, or what lay beyond it. The brightness of it was beginning to cause a searing pain in his eyes.

He sat on the bed. He did not like to leave the room and wander about the house without permission; indeed, he was really in no fit state to do anything but lie down. He was pondering what to do when the maid entered.

She was a middle-aged, attractive woman with braided brown hair, wearing a long dress of purple trimmed with white, and with a net of blue jewels on her head.

'My lady has sent me to see if you require anything, sir,' she said pleasantly, without any air of servility.

'Yes, you could show me to the rooms of my companions, if you would be so kind,' he said, watching her face. Her pleasant expression did not change.

'My lady has given me instructions that you may go anywhere you wish in Her house and city. She requests also that you may join Her for dinner when you feel well enough.'

'You don't know where my companions are?'

'These are my lady's instructions, sir,' the maid responded, a slight lift to her voice implying surprise that he assumed she knew anything other than what the Lady Arlenmia told her. 'I will call you for dinner.'

'Thank you,' Estarinel sighed, giving up. The maid nodded and left. He had noticed the familiar reverence for the word 'She' (although not the usual bitterness) in the maid's speech.

He felt a growing sense of insecurity. The hideous stories he had

166

heard and the woman he had met did not tally. Yet he remembered Skord's words, '. . . She was kind to me.' The thought of Skord made him shudder. What had happened at the end of the hypnotism – why could he not remember?

Grimly, he realised that anything could have happened in the last few days. Perhaps Medrian and Ashurek were dead – certainly, if they were not here, he stood no chance of finding them.

He decided that his only course was to be exceedingly careful with Arlenmia, to give away as little as possible while trying to discover who or what she really was. Friendly innocence was a good beginning; and a perfectly natural one, as it was his character anyway.

It was a daunting thought to realise that Arlenmia was now his only hope of continuing the Quest.

10

The Glass City

Her house formed a square about the courtyard, with a tall, round tower at each corner. Estarinel sat at the edge of the pond and scanned the gold metal building closely. There was no sign of activity; only the gentle music of the fountain disturbed the silence.

He felt too weak to walk far, and soon returned to his room in one of the circular towers, gained by an oddly twisting staircase. There he lay down on the bed, wondering what had become of their poor horses. His sword and shield had gone too; no doubt the nemen had taken them. But he had also lost the lodestone from Hrannekh Ol, and he could not see how the nemen could have known what it was, or been interested in it.

He fell into a heavy, comfortable sleep without realising it. When he eventually awoke, the long red rays of the setting sun were piercing the windows. A moment later the maid entered, the same innocuous smile on her face.

'My Lady asks if you are well enough to join Her for dinner in half an hour's time, sir.' Estarinel assented, desperately curious to meet the Lady Arlenmia again. The maid went on to say that a nurse would be sent to him to attend to his wounds.

The nurse, an old, harsh-faced, unspeaking woman, rebandaged the great weal on his back, applied herbal creams to his many other cuts and bruises, and left. Yet more clothes had been brought for him: blue breeches and a tunic made from fine linen and embroidered with strange designs in dark blue; a silvery loose-sleeved shirt.

He changed, and the maid came to take him down to another part of the house, by way of many staircases and tapestry-lined corridors. He was shown into a long, large hall, the light of many candles dancing in pools of gold light on the metal walls. The walls were hung with mirrors, tapestries curtained the windows; animal-skin rugs, striped with black, purple, and lilac, carpeted the marble floor. A long mirror-topped table occupied the hall's centre, and several high-backed, ornate chairs stood around it. At one of these the Lady Arlenmia sat, statuesque and beautiful in a dress of deep-green silk, elaborately designed with long folds falling from her marble-like shoulders. Even in the dim, gold-touched atmosphere of the hall, her exquisite and inhuman colouring looked cold.

Seeing Estarinel, she smiled and rose to greet him, a slender hand outstretched. He took it and bowed courteously.

'Do sit down,' she said in her clear, low voice. She sat at the head of the table, Estarinel at her right hand. 'Now,' she went on, 'I am so pleased that you feel well enough to join me. With a few days' rest, you will soon be fit again!' Her large, liquid, blue-green eyes regarded him intently. Some of the colour had come back to his young, attractive face. 'I want you to feel at ease in my home, as if it were your own. I have an extensive library, art galleries and music rooms which you may visit whenever you wish.'

'All of these are within this building?' he asked. She nodded. 'What of the other buildings in the city? Are they all unoccupied?'

'Yes,' she laughed quietly. 'I and my servants have the whole city to ourselves. You may walk about wherever you will, as soon as you feel strong enough. It is a wondrous place, and walking is the surest way to regain your health.'

Did this mean that he was not a prisoner? He longed to ask how long she had lived in the city, why she was there, who she was . . . but the discovery of such information would have to be a subtle and guarded process. He asked a neutral question about the library.

'Yes, it is my own collection – as are the paintings, the musical instruments, and everything else in this house. I love things of beauty!' She continued, talking of art and books with an affection that obviously went far deeper than the mere pleasure of acquisition. He let her lead the conversation, trying to judge which subjects he might approach and which he might not. It was hard to tell. She was so warm and open towards him it seemed he could talk to her about anything.

The pleasant maid and another servant, a dark-haired, unsmiling youth, waited at table. The dinner was good: small rainbow-coloured fish and vegetables something like artichokes; newly baked bread, butter and cheese; fresh fruit; and a sharp, clear-tasting yellow wine. But Arlenmia seemed to eat very little herself.

'I have had your personal belongings sent to your room. There

169

was a sword, a little white stone, a shield, and a knife. Your cloak is intact, but I'm afraid the rest of your clothes were too badly torn to be saved.' She toyed with a crystal goblet of the yellow wine.

'Thank you very much, my lady. It's very kind of you to have taken such care of me.'

'It is nothing. I am pleased to have you as my guest. Tell me, how did you come to be the nemens' prisoner?'

'They were – we came upon them at the Equator. There was a battle. Er – I was knocked out. There were a lot of confusing impressions but I really don't remember anything until I found myself crawling down the street.'

He was trying to be evasive without actually lying. He was afraid she was going to ask him questions – perhaps only friendly ones – and he felt he dared reveal almost nothing.

'You say there were two others with you? Well, Estarinel . . . they may have been killed, you realise. I shall try to find them for you. I can send servants out to the nemen; they fear me—' she smiled a little sadly, '—and will do my bidding. Who were your companions?'

'There was a young woman, dark-haired, and another – a warrior.'

She looked thoughtful. 'Wherever you were journeying, this is an unfortunate delay for you. If I gave you a horse and weapons, would you continue on your own – if your companions weren't found?'

'Yes, I would, my lady.'

'I thought so.' She laughed softly. 'Is this journey very important to you?'

'Yes.' He pretended to be absorbed in his goblet of pale amber wine. 'It is a very good meal.'

'Ah, changing the subject! I'm so sorry – if you don't wish to speak of your journey, I won't pry. I only mean to help you.'

He half-smiled. 'Please don't think me rude. But I'd rather say nothing than lie, my lady.'

'I understand . . .' She went on slowly sipping her glass of wine. She gazed across to a large glass globe with a map of the world engraved on it. It was an exquisitely made object. The pupils of her beautiful hooded eyes dilated widely.

When they had finished the meal, she said to him, 'Come and sit with me by the fire.' She led him to a fireplace, set into one long wall. Two gold chairs, with tapestried seats, stood there, one on either side of the fire, which flickered with gold and blue and green flames, like copper burning. No heat emanated from it.

'It is too hot for a real fire at the minute, but I like the glow that a fire gives – don't you?' She stooped gracefully and passed a hand through the flames. She laughed. 'See! We burn chemicals instead. The flames are cold. More wine?'

Estarinel accepted. He felt relaxed and at ease; perhaps it was the wine's influence, but inwardly this made him more consciously careful not even to hint at their Quest.

'Tell me about your life in Forluin. They say it is such a quiet, pretty place.'

'Yes – yes, it was – is,' he stammered in response to her unexpected question.

'Forluin, Maerna, Ohn; lands of the ten thousand years' peace, they are called. Nothing blights their sweet fields, and the Blue Plane is only a whisper away, so they say.'

'Do they?' Estarinel muttered, inwardly shocked at this turn in the conversation. He stared broodingly into the fire. Arlenmia leaned back in her chair, a touch of languor in the movement; a languor that was not caused by the wine, for she had hardly drunk a whole glassful.

'Estarinel,' she began softly, 'I heard there was an attack on Forluin some months ago. A flying worm came from the North, did it not?'

'Yes,' he replied miserably, both relieved and amazed that she knew.

'Did it take any of your loved ones?'

'Yes, many friends, and left people sick and starving.'

'Might the Worm have come again since you, er – left Forluin?'

'It might have come again. Or once might have been enough . . . I have no news of Forluin,' he said, the old horror and misery re-awakening in him.

'Oh, it is sad that it had to be that way, but Forluin is so isolated,' she murmured.

'What do you mean?' he asked, staring at her and trying desperately to retain a facade of innocuous politeness.

'I mean,' she said gently, her eyes shining so brightly that they might have been full of tears, 'I am sorry about what happened in your country, sorry that it is so far away from the help that Tearn, for example, might have given.'

171

'No one could have helped,' he whispered, believing in her sympathy but wishing she would not continue to speak of it.

There was a long silence and he stared at the fire from which no warmth came. Then she said, 'If you wish . . . there is a way you can see what is happening in Forluin.'

He looked up with a start. 'How?'

'I can show you. If you will be patient for a few days, until you are stronger.'

'How can you do this?'

Her beautiful but unnaturally dilated pupils glistened and a slight flush, the colour of jade, came to her cheeks.

'A gift was given me; to look into reflections and see the truth therein. For mirrors can reflect only the truth; how can they lie when there is no guile within them? Thus, the gift – to turn the mirror's reflection to the knowledge of one's own desiring, to see past truths and future ones, to see into men's minds, to summon and to dismiss. If something is real, the looking glass potentially holds the image, but it is within oneself that the power lies to draw forth the image, to project it and to manipulate it.' She stared intensely at him, eyes shining and lips curved with some suppressed joy.

'Is that how you knew what had happened in my country?' he asked nervously.

'Partly . . . oh, but don't look at me like that! Estarinel, I am no witch, and my only wish is to help you.' She spoke with such ardent sincerity that it was almost impossible to doubt her. Still smiling at him, she turned the conversation to a more normal theme with extraordinary ease. Still unsettled and puzzling over her words, he was not very conversant at first. But gradually he relaxed again, and the part of him that regarded Arlenmia with a detached and suspicious eye began to blur, becoming susceptible to her charms.

Later, he lay in bed staring at the canopy and wondering about her. Delightful she was; intelligent and beautiful and kind. But he could discover nothing definite about her, only vague impressions. She knew more of the geography of the world than he, but had spoken of it like an interested visitor from another earth. And he had the idea that she drew her vitality from strange sources, and that she was motivated by a deep-rooted love of something unknown.

172

Yes, that was it; whoever she was, it was not hatred or vengeance, but love that inspired her.

There was a double full moon that night and their light shining on the mirror-topped table in a silver pool distracted him until he had to cover the table with a rug.

A glistening drop of blue fluid hung from the end of the needle, just before it entered Ashurek's arm. He saw the glass phial empty and felt a coolness enter his vein, spreading through his body.

Arlenmia drew the needle out, then leaned forward and cut the leather straps binding his wrists.

'There,' she said, 'the drug will make you feel better . . .'

Ashurek raised a sardonic eyebrow. 'You mean, safe to be untied?'

'I told you, the nemen tied you up, not I,' she answered sweetly. 'The drug is only to help you to recover from your ordeal, though it may make you feel somewhat – empty.'

He looked up into her luminous turquoise eyes. 'I think I detect a veiled threat.'

'Your imagination, Prince Ashurek. Now, you are free to visit any part of my house and city as it pleases you, and to stay as my guest until you are fully recovered.' He stood up from the bed, flexing his aching hands, and looked out of a window.

'What of my companions, Estarinel and Medrian?'

'Oh, they are here, as you must have guessed,' she smiled coolly at him. 'But existing each in a different reflection, as I will it; so you may search the city and look in every mirror, but you will never see them.' He looked round at her with narrowed, verdant eyes, but she returned the gaze unflinchingly. 'Your Estarinel is lovely, a total innocent. He has not disclosed one word about you, or what you are all doing, thinking he is protecting you; he is a perfect subject for my design. However, I know that you will fight me, and Medrian too – and oh, I wish you would not! What I do is all to the good, in the end.'

The extraordinary sincerity that had come into her voice and face surprised Ashurek – but he could now feel her drug working. Whatever else it was meant to do, it was enhancing that awful sick emptiness that the Egg-Stone had left when he disposed of the thing. He felt he could claw his way from the window, swim oceans and burrow into mountains to recover it. She must know much about him, to be able to practise this subtle torture.

Arlenmia touched his hand with her slender, cool fingers.

'It was a happy day that brought you here, Ashurek.' She made her way to the door. 'I must summon Skord, and reward him.'

'Have you not seen him since we arrived here?' the Gorethrian asked, surprised.

'No; why?' she paused in the doorway.

'Well, I thought he would have come straight to you even before the nemen brought us here.'

'No, he did not. I think he went back to Beldaega-Hal. Ashurek, your words make me think there's a reason I should know where he is.'

'I am more than surprised that you don't.'

She smiled at his sardonic tone. 'Unfortunately, I am not omniscient. However, there's nothing I cannot see if I wish it. I'll locate the boy immediately.'

Grimacing, Ashurek wondered how the lad would fare when she discovered that his arrogance had led to him being captured and hypnotised; and that he had made several attempts – albeit half-hearted ones – to kill them.

Several days passed by. Estarinel spent most of his time sleeping, walking and eating, concentrating, as Arlenmia had sensibly suggested, on regaining his strength. He also spent some time in her library, studying some ancient and fascinating books. He dined with her every evening, although otherwise he never saw her. In fact he never saw anyone apart from the maid, who was ever helpful but impossible to communicate with. No door of the house was kept locked, but there was never even a servant in any room. He found this aloneness in the weird city more eerie with each passing day, so that by the evening he was desperate for Arlenmia's company.

Twice he asked for news of his companions, but there was none. Other than this their conversation was general, friendly, but not touching on personal information on either side. It was frustrating that he still knew nothing about her, but while he was actually talking to her this did not seem to matter. Then he enjoyed her company and ceased to wonder whether she was really the evil tyrant of Belhadra. Sometimes she seemed aware that she was talking a lot while saying nothing, and became desperate to tear aside the pretence and tell him something of great importance. At these times the animation of her eyes and voice in that languid, sculptural form made her the more beautiful. He felt she was waiting and waiting for the right moment to explain herself to him. Perhaps when the moment came he would be able to discover the truth about her at last.

'Is there a boundary to this city?' he asked on the fifth evening. 'I seem to have walked miles, yet not reached the edge.' He realised he was obliquely asking whether the city was impossible to escape, and from her look of amusement, he knew she was aware of this.

'You've probably been in circles,' she smiled. 'It's easily done. Of course it has an edge. You are not a prisoner, you know! To prove it, I'll have two horses readied in the morning and we'll ride out to the countryside. I suppose you will want to be on your way in a few days,' she added rather sadly, 'but I hope you won't leave me yet.'

At this, questions began to plague him again. How could this exquisite and intelligent woman, who had shown him such kindness and understanding, be the same 'goddess' whom the Belhadrians loathed, feared and worshipped? There were three possible answers: that Arlenmia was not She; that her behaviour towards him was a deception; or that the Belhadrians themselves were wrong in blaming Her for their troubles.

He stared down at his plate, wishing desperately that he could broach the subject without the risk of alienating her. Perhaps it was wisest to let the matter be and make an escape as soon as possible. Tomorrow she would show him the way out of the city . . .

'Estarinel, you are poor company this evening,' the Lady said. 'Is something troubling you?' The dim candlelight flickered in the viridian depths of her hair like sparks of sunlight on a woodland river. He made himself reply before doubt stopped him.

'Yes, you are troubling me,' he said with a half-smile.

'You would like to know who I am . . .' she prompted, her eyes glittering like liquid aquamarines.

'Whether you are the one the Belhadrians call, "She To Whom We Pay Tribute",' he said. Her beautiful onyx-carved face betrayed no reaction.

175

'I only wonder that you've taken so long to ask! Yes. Yes I am. You look a little shocked, and draw back from me. I expect you have heard many ill stories of me, is that not so? And you would rather not have known for certain that I am "She".'

'I have not just heard things; I have seen them as well,' he said, challenging her warily.

'So you naturally assume I am evil.' She sighed and a fleeting expression of sadness crossed her face. 'Estarinel, are you able to believe that not everything is as it seems?'

'Yes, of course,' he said, perhaps too willing to hear an explanation that would redeem her.

'Then, dear Estarinel, if you will only be patient till the morning, you shall be told everything.' She touched his cheek then sat back, watching him.

'Yes, I can wait that long,' he replied.

After dinner, when he made his way to his room, he noticed that he felt curiously light-headed, while his limbs dragged like lead. It was certainly not the effect of one glass of wine; but he thought no more of it as he fell into a heavy sleep plagued by repetitious dreams of silvered glass.

Ashurek roamed the shimmering streets of the city without success. He kept coming back to the same place. With a grim smile he silently congratulated Arlenmia on bringing them to such a perfect, inescapable prison. To have created this mirrored trap she must have more power than any demon. Although she worked with them, she showed none of the usual signs of possession. No, she was self-possessed and very powerful. He longed for Silvren's advice; he had never had more need of it. Or the Egg-Stone's power!

Repulsed, he tried to put that thought from his mind. But under the influence of the strange blue drug she had put into his veins, the image returned again and again. He was mentally exhausted by it, his concentration and willpower drastically diminished. Medrian had been right, there did seem to be no escape from Arlenmia.

And 'She' was now biding her time, laughing at him like a rat lost in a maze until he was weak enough to be bent to her will.

'Why should the Serpent waste its time destroying us,' Ashurek thought, 'when it has minions to do that small work for it? Ah, but it will not be satisfied with our destruction; no, we must be tormented and cajoled into working for it. In that way only can it truly win.'

The next morning, the maid woke Estarinel and told him that Arlenmia would be awaiting him in the courtyard after breakfast.

She was already mounted on her blue-green palfrey when he joined her by the fountain. A groom held the reins of a large, light bay mare as he swung into the saddle. He felt a faint sense of disappointment, as though he had half-expected to see Shaell there. Then Arlenmia led the way along the marble streets between the bizarre, shimmering towers of metal until he eventually caught a glimpse of countryside between them.

It was a relief to feel grass beneath the hooves of his horse at last. They were on a flat plain of turf fringed by distant tree-covered hills. As they rode away from the city, he saw that it was in fact quite small, and looked even stranger from without than from within. It was like an extraordinary metal sculpture. A strange idea began to take root in his mind, telling him that it was not a city at all, but had a quite different function . . .

'Come on!' called Arlenmia, urging her horse into a canter. He followed and they circled the gold and silver edifices from the North to the South. Here the hills were closer and only sparsely covered by trees. Arlenmia continued at a gallop to the peak of the nearest.

'There!' she exclaimed, pulling her horse to a ragged, prancing halt, its golden tail streaming like a silk banner. 'From here we have a fine view. Let us dismount for a few minutes and rest the horses.'

The bay mare was blowing hard. Estarinel jumped from her back, glad of a rest himself; he was still not fully fit and felt tired already.

He looked to the South and saw a gleam of white on the horizon, some twenty miles away.

'You can see the white hills and waterfalls at the Equator,' said Arlenmia, coming to stand next to him and pointing with a long, alabaster-smooth finger. 'You see, the nemen did not bring you far. Which way will you go when you recommence your journey?'

'I don't know,' Estarinel began. He was about to explain that he must find a river and sail to Forluin, but stopped himself, feeling

177

disturbed by this sudden loss of caution. He was too much at ease, the memory of Forluin was faint . . . he knew that this was somehow wrong, but at the same time he felt that it did not really matter.

Arlenmia smiled when he paused, and slipped her arm through his. She was only a little less tall than him, and her long jewel-threaded hair spread on his shoulder like turquoise silk.

'You think you're lost, don't you?' she said softly. 'But you're not . . . I've so much to tell you, and to show you. Things of far greater beauty than any painting or tapestry . . .' Her deep blue-green eyes took on an opalescent lustre as she spoke. 'You do not have to leave . . .'

He turned to reply and then he was kissing her, and her arms had travelled in a languorous, snake-like movement to encircle his shoulders. He embraced her tightly and she pressed herself against him, eventually ending the kiss and sighing against his cheek.

'Oh, I knew you would not be as blind as . . .'

'As who?'

'. . . others.' Her smile was more in her eyes than on her lips. 'You will trust me and believe me, I know.'

'Do I have any reason not to?'

'None.' She kissed him again. 'Now, if I was so cruel as to give you a choice of leaving immediately, or coming back to the city with me for good, I wonder what you would say? Ah, but I am not that cruel.'

'Aren't you? You must know I would come back with you,' Estarinel murmured, his arms tightening about her.

'Yes,' she whispered into his ear, her voice passionate and persuasive. 'What happened in Forluin does not matter.'

At this he abruptly disentangled himself from her as if from a serpent, and stared at her with horror.

'If you knew anything about Forluin, you would not say that!' he exclaimed, aghast. A look of regret crossed her face.

'I forgot that I have not yet explained to you . . .'

'Well, I think you had better, and straight away.'

'Yes. We'll go back,' Arlenmia said, lightly mounting her palfrey and arranging her long satin skirts. They began to ride down the hillside, the scintillating metal towers of the city ahead of them. He was sure she had not meant to say what she did, because it had instantly shattered the strange spell she had cast over him. He was not prepared to wait until she was ready to start explaining.

'I've seen a lot of miserable people, stricken by a plague which they blame on you,' he began. 'I've seen a boy, who claimed to be your messenger, commit murder and terrorise his own parents; he also claimed to have shown us a mirror which put us in your power. Belhadra seems full of people who think they are dying of apathy and fear, because of you. Well, is it true? Are you responsible?'

The Lady Arlenmia listened, a warmth of colour coming to her jade-smooth cheek. As he finished, she sighed.

'Estarinel, you look at me as if what happened in Forluin was my fault as well! Well, different things must be achieved in different ways.

'The poor Belhadrians make it so hard for me to help them. I came here some years ago; my work had to begin somewhere, so where better than the vital heart – the Glass City? I came to unite them with the joyous knowledge, but oh, how they fight! I never dreamt it. So I have to make them see through my mirrors and my messengers – it is unfortunate, but the only way to help them. If only they would listen to me I could save them from the plague, from their own foolishness.'

'But what do you want of them? To worship you?'

'Me? No, oh no! I seek eternal life for them – eternal perfection! My work is extending – my messengers work far beyond Belhadra's borders.'

'I don't understand,' Estarinel said. 'What are you trying to do?'

'Oh, it is almost impossible to put into words. I will explain it to you in a different way, in a short while. You see, like so many great works, it will be mistakenly opposed – and this is the greatest work of all.' The wild, deep passion in her voice frightened Estarinel, and he knew she did not speak in madness, but from a true and terrible root of evil. 'Belhadra suffers, but it is only temporary. Forluin and Gorethria will be the hardest, but help is here at last – at my fingertips!' Arlenmia tossed her lovely head back in elation, and her horse danced.

'My companions are here, aren't they?' Estarinel said.

'Yes, of course,' she answered, smiling. 'As you now realise, if Mel Skara's mirror drew you here, it must have drawn them also. You are all here, the three keys: Ashurek, Medrian and yourself.'

They rode from grass onto a marble-paved street.

'Do you mean it was planned we should come here?'

'Do you think you can make a single move of your own volition?' she laughed, and he thought again of the two grey figures. 'But listen, Estarinel. I don't know everything. When a mind is firmly

179

closed against me I cannot see into it. I want us to be friends, to help each other. Open your mind to me; I must see all your thoughts and intentions, so that I may make my own aims known to you. It is fascinating to see innocence become knowledge . . .'

He did not fully understand what she was telling him, but he could feel her charisma begin to enmesh him again. He looked away from her, and tried a specific question.

'What about Skord? He claims to do your work—'

'Ah yes, Skord.' Her face became suddenly livid. 'He was a sick wretch when I found him; I healed him, gave him a new home and peace of mind. I had his adoptive parents believe he was really their son . . . though I think some doubt must have remained on both sides, which would account for the hatred which has developed between them.' Estarinel could not believe the offhand manner in which she spoke, as if manipulating people's memories and the resultant hatred were perfectly natural. 'He was more than happy to work for me in return. Of course, if someone had given back his memory, they would little realise what harm they had done, what torment they had caused him.'

He looked at her, startled. They had arrived at her house, but he was hardly aware of dismounting, or of the groom leading the horses away and out of sight. Arlenmia was glaring at him, her face full of cold rage.

'It may surprise you to learn that I had nothing to do with events in Drish either. I healed Skord. He loved me. But Drish, and Forluin, and Belhadra, at whose names your face becomes grim with outraged horror, don't matter! They don't matter at all!'

She took his elbow in a powerful grip, propelling him inside the house and into the long dining hall. Her face was cold as a winter moon and her eyes two viridian flames of rage. Releasing him, she went to the fire and set a little table between the two chairs. On it she placed a decanter of wine and two crystal goblets, the blue and purple satin of her dress rustling as she moved.

'Please, come and sit down,' she said, her face calm again. She poured two goblets of wine and handed one to him. 'Forgive my temper, Estarinel. I am not really angry at you. It is anger at the Belhadrians, and your companions, and even Skord – all those who will not listen and see the rightness of what I am doing.' The warm and fervent passion began to enter her voice again. Estarinel noticed the unnatural luminosity of her eyes as she continued. 'But perhaps I expect too much. I have not been here long, and this is

180

only the beginning. It is true that the Belhadrians are becoming witless, apathetic and forgetful. It seems a shame, but understand this: in order to replace a dull, poor painting with a glorious work of art, you must first paint the canvas white. This is what I am doing. I send reflected dreams to them; only when their minds are quite clean will they begin to absorb and comprehend glorious colours.'

Her words made Estarinel shudder. He swallowed some wine.

'What of the plague – what use is that?'

'Again, unfortunate – just a simple instrument of fear, to make them aware of my power. But, Estarinel, the victims of the plague do not die – their souls merely wait in limbo until such time as my dream is achieved. So it is not as cruel as it seems.'

'Not cruel? It sounds monstrous,' he whispered, his throat hoarse. He drained the rest of the wine, wishing that he felt able to move, to escape her insane words.

'Does it?' She considered. 'Yes, I suppose it does, from a human point of view.' She put down her untouched goblet and came forward, kneeling with her arms resting on his knees, looking up at him. His instinct was to recoil from her, but her presence held him motionless.

'You think I'm insane, don't you? But, Estarinel, haven't you considered how imperfect human life is? Everything decays and dies and is messy and purposeless. I am seeking a way to eternal life – not just for me but for the whole Earth and everyone on it. Everything will be crystallised into a perfect, ecstatic state. There will be no illness, no death or suffering, no petty human woes and pathetic fleeting joys – only a supreme happiness: that of worshipping perfection, for all time. Naturally the world has to be broken and remade – that is what's happening, in Forluin and everywhere else. But it is only a passing human sorrow – can't you see it doesn't matter?' Her words, in their passion and sincerity, were terribly persuasive. Estarinel bent towards her, beginning to believe that he had misjudged her, that she did have an answer to the world's sorrows. A smile lit her lovely jade-carved face. 'What makes you think humans are of any importance in the great designs of the universe? We are nothing! But I can make us important – make us part of it, for ever!' She grasped his hand. 'Now do you begin to see?'

'A little,' he said.

'Good. You are going to share it with me.' Estarinel felt slightly

181

dizzy, as if his chair was tipping backwards, and he noticed strange whorls of colour creeping across the ceiling.

'Arlenmia, was there something in the wine?' he asked.

'Yes, don't be alarmed. It's so that I can show you my dream in full.'

'Why have you drugged me?' he persisted, as he lost control of his consciousness to the pervading substance.

'Open your mind to me,' she said softly, sitting back on her heels. Just as his contact with reality was completely lost, he stood up and walked past her towards the door.

Every step was like walking against some thick, molten substance; he could see nothing but a soft yellowness, translucent and fluid, in which odd shapes were veiled into greyish silhouettes. He breathed the liquid, it permeated his brain until at last there were only two impressions left in his mind. One was that this was the normal state of the air; the other was that he was not walking at all, that he was still sitting in Arlenmia's hall.

Then the fluid vanished without him noticing and the air was very thin and bright; the street on which he stood was broad and the buildings were tall, round towers piercing the sky. They were made of glass: deep reds, violets, greens and ultramarines. Within each one a hundred faces were pressed to the glass, hanging, pleading, distorted where the flesh was pulled and flattened against the prison wall. Hands clawed and mouths gaped soundlessly and the faces of the prisoners stared at Estarinel as they tried to scratch their way from their glass prisons.

Beneath his feet there were slabs of glass and he felt that they were many hundreds of feet thick, even bottomless; and this gave him the sickening feeling of being poised over a chasm. Then he found he could see for many miles through the glass, and he saw many strange fish encased in the stuff, scaled with odd colours, mouths and eyes wide, as if a moment in the depths of the sea had been frozen.

He felt that all the creatures of the sea were crying out for help; fish, reptiles, birds, mammals – *for we are all creatures of the sea*, he thought. And the vision of all life imprisoned in glass seemed horribly symbolic of something he did not understand, but which Arlenmia would soon explain and instil into his mind.

Afraid, he turned to run, but as he did so, he saw a figure in front of him. In that moment he felt that this place was not a drug-induced vision, but real; that he had stepped into another dimension.

The figure was a young, beautiful woman, not tall, with long hair of deep gold, golden skin and eyes. She was in a simple, pale robe, and he could see through her to the multicoloured, shining towers beyond, as if she were herself made of glass.

'Who are you?' she asked, her voice like crystal in the bright air. 'Are you a friend of Ashurek?'

'Yes,' he replied. 'I am Estarinel of Forluin. And you are Silvren.' She nodded, a smile of relief lighting her face, and stretched out her arms to embrace him. She was real also, but her flesh felt strangely viscid and insubstantial to his touch. He did not feel surprised to see her, only pleased, as if she were an old friend of his.

'I thought—'

'That I was in the Dark Regions? Well, I am. What you see is an astral presence, which I cannot maintain for long. My body is in the Dark Regions and the longer I stay here, the worse it will be when I return to it; it takes so much energy. I am using what little is left of my sorcery to watch over Ashurek, and warn him about Arlenmia. But when I came here, it was all deserted, as I should have realised—'

'But where are we? I was drugged – I thought this place was an hallucination,' Estarinel said. He still held her hands, which seemed to flow through his like liquid.

'No, it is real. This is the old Glass City in its true guise. The city of metal is an illusion created by Arlenmia. But her drug has brought you here in astral form also, thank goodness.' She did not say, though she perhaps thought it, that she wished Ashurek had been drugged instead. 'You must tell me all that has happened, though quickly – we haven't much time.'

He recounted their adventures, in as few words as possible. When he told her of Forluin, tears filled her translucent eyes.

'Oh, curse the damned Worm!' she exclaimed as he finished. 'Nothing is spared – I wonder if it's all worth fighting for. If only I was not bound and powerless, I would be on this horrible Quest with you.'

'I know – I know that you began it.'

'Yes, and now it may not end, because Arlenmia works for the Serpent.'

At these words, Estarinel felt all hope emptying from him.

'I suspected it . . . but how do you know?'

'I know her – she brought another world to ruin before this. She

183

used to be my friend, and it is my fault she came here, though that is another tale.

'The Gorethrian Empire, the Shana, the Egg-Stone – all are the works of the Serpent. The world is falling slowly into its power, and now Arlenmia is continuing its work in the heart of Tearn. The Glass City is beautiful and ancient, a place of power that maintains the tenuous contact with the three Planes; but she has cast an illusion about it so that it seems to be something that reflects rather than something transparent, and its people have fled.'

'And these people?' said Estarinel, indicating the miserable faces staring through the coloured walls of their glass prisons.

'Only an illusion . . . but it is true that the souls of the Belhadrians are imprisoned while their bodies and minds wander hopelessly about their daily lives.

'This is only the start. Her idea and dream is a world that exists in eternal worship of the Worm; and that would mean not only horrors far in excess of those created by any evil agent of Earth. It would mean the destruction of all joy and freedom, the loss of all will to live, but the escape route of death would be closed. No will of your own, but only the eternal singing of the Worm's praises; and the horror of it would be worse than that of the Dark Regions, more terrible than Hell itself.

'The world would become immune to external forces, immune to reality. It would become as a – a bloated sac that can never expel its poison. Estarinel, that is the end the world is coming to; that is what we are fighting against.'

'Oh, gods,' he said, horror enfolding him. 'I never realised it was so . . .'

'Eldor didn't tell you? Perhaps he thought it wouldn't help. Arlenmia can control Tearn, for she has mastered the Glass City, and Gastada is helping her. She will try to get Ashurek in her power, return him to Gorethria and so destroy the Empire. Medrian, I don't know; but she will use her for something.

'The Worm could not gain a hold in Forluin except by attacking it physically. But Arlenmia knows that if she can control you, she can send you back there to instil all the people with the submissive misery that afflicts the Belhadrians. Can you now see why the Worm came to Forluin? It was not a random attack, but part of its plan.

'The House of Rede will be the last to fall, though that will not be safe forever.'

Estarinel listened, speechless with despair and horror, as the sorceress Silvren went on.

'She has no notion that the Worm is good or evil; she only loves it, worships it. Such people are more dangerous than the consciously evil or cruel, such as the Shana or Gastada.' The glass towers that he could see through her shivered, as if seen through warm, rising air. She uttered a sigh. 'She may convince you that what she is doing is good and essential, because she believes it herself. She must have given you the drug to open your mind to her, so whether she can see us together or not I've no idea. When the drug wears off she will try to entrance you. Fight! If you and Ashurek and Medrian use all your intelligence, you may escape. Destroying her is another matter. There is something that her life and vitality depend on . . . I can't discover what it is . . . if you can, you'll have a chance . . .' She sighed again, and this time it was almost a groan, the groan of a hell-tormented creature. 'I can't tell you how important it is that you get to the Blue Plane immediately . . .'

'I know,' he sighed, reaching out to her, but his hands passed through her now. 'Silvren—'

'E'rinel, I am glad that Ashurek has such a good and gentle companion. Perhaps you can talk some sense into him, I never could . . .' Her voice was growing fainter. 'Tell him all I have told you, and that I will watch him whenever I can find strength. Oh, and one last thing, the most awful thing of all.' She fixed him with bottomless eyes of brown-gold, like beautiful lakes in which terrible things were reflected. He loved her and pitied her in that moment, and he knew he was watching the soul of a sorceress being dragged back down to Hell. 'E'rinel – you must know that the Worm also takes a human form . . .'

'Yes,' he replied voicelessly.

'I know Arlenmia,' her voice became half-choked with tears, 'and when she becomes devoted to something, her devotion is total – no half-measures for her. She serves the Serpent with such fanaticism that I believe it wouldn't be beyond her to find a way to become the Serpent's host.'

'Do you believe—'

'I don't know. I hope I'm wrong. I loved her . . . oh, my soul is so weary, sick, I must go back . . . tell Ashurek I love him.'

She was gone, like a grey cat fading into moonlight, though her image still danced before his eyes. There must be some way to follow and rescue her – but as she disappeared, reality vanished with her.

He closed his eyes and his mind, and let the drug take him. It carried him, like spore on a wind, across fantastic landscapes, through blazing lights and infinite snow-tunnels, and it was many nightmarish hours before it left him.

He was still sitting by Arlenmia's heatless fireside when he awoke. It was daylight, well into the following morning. The ceiling had turned to metal once more; he glanced over the marble floor of the hall with its rich animal skins, the silver-and-glass table, the crystal globe of the Earth without really noticing them. His head ached and his mind seemed to have turned in upon itself so that he found it hard to adjust back to the physical world. He was alone. He felt fear pressing on him from all sides and wanted to run, run. But he stood up and walked very slowly, heading for his room where he thought to find some security. Then, he thought, he must find Medrian, must find Ashurek.

The bright corridors with their exquisite tapestries and paintings ran past him in a blur as he walked. At last he gained the door of his room and entered gratefully.

The first thing to greet his eyes was Arlenmia, sitting in stately beauty on a cushion at the little mirror-topped table. Her emerald-coloured hair shimmered with blue lights. One slender hand paused in enclosing a tall, delicately-carved chess piece which was milky-white, translucent as opal, shiny as alabaster. She turned and smiled with such loveliness of nature in her face that he suddenly doubted Silvren's words. There were other pieces on the table, set up as for a game. Half were white, cold and smooth; half were honey-coloured, beautifully carved, tall and highly-polished. Estarinel stared at them and stood motionless at the door.

'Come,' she invited him. 'Come and play a game of chess with me.'

11

Her Mirror

'You are a dark one,' she said, inclining her head to one side and searching his face with her blue-green eyes. 'I have known the mind drug to fail before, but never so totally.'

'In what way?' He sat down facing her across the table, very much on his guard. The drug had left him feeling apprehensive and confused, but he was determined not to let her entrance him again.

'It was to lay your mind open to me – and mine to you. Ah well, it does not always work,' she said softly, smiling. He sensed that she was furious, but in no way did her face or manner betray it. Everything that Silvren had said about Arlenmia was in the forefront of his mind as he watched her smiling at him, her turquoise eyes glowing. Silvren's words contrasted violently with Arlenmia's view, but it was the golden-haired sorceress that he believed.

Had Arlenmia, using the drug and her mirror, been able to see him and Silvren together?

'You must be exhausted, and hungry,' she said when he was silent. 'Let me have the maid bring you something to eat.'

'No, really – I don't want anything,' he replied. His mouth was so dry that he could hardly swallow, let alone eat anything.

'Has the drug made you ill?' She extended a hand as if to touch his forehead. He drew back and she smiled. 'No cramps in your limbs and stomach, or dizziness?' He shook his head.

'Good.' She sounded a little surprised. 'Then you feel well enough to have a game of chess with me. Do you know how to play?'

'Yes – though not without a board,' he murmured through dry lips.

'But there is a board,' she laughed. 'Look!' On the glass, squares were etched out in delicate lines of frost, barely visible. Arlenmia took up a white pawn and slid it forward. 'Your turn. Come, what are you afraid of? I don't play that well!'

Hesitantly, he moved a honey-coloured pawn. As she watched him, she took a sip from a small glass of water.

The game progressed, but Estarinel played badly, unable to concentrate. She must be leading him towards some final trap; he could see no possible escape. If he made any attempt to resist, he knew, she and her servants would bind him effortlessly.

The drug seemed to have fragmented his thoughts. Watching the reflection of the chess pieces in the table's mirror surface, he noticed that although they were opaque, in the mirror they appeared as long droplets of clear glass hanging inverted from a thin film of water. The metal ceiling again looked like glass.

Arlenmia saw him staring at the reflection and paused with one finger resting on the white queen's head.

'It makes everything look different, doesn't it? Appearances can be deceptive, but a mirror cannot lie, or so they say.'

'Then you should take a lesson from your mirrors. What do you want of me, Arlenmia?'

'I only want you to help your own country,' she replied. She moved her piece and captured his queen. 'That was a foolish move; if you had done this instead, you would have won . . .' she slid the pieces to a different position, and as she did so, shapes began to form and swirl in the glass.

'You will let us into Forluin one way or another, eventually. I'm only trying to make it easier for you. I'm asking you to open your mind, invite us in so that we need not force our way in. Save yourself needless suffering. Look at the mirror!'

'Oh no,' he said, averting his eyes, though he could still perceive the colours writhing on the edge of his vision. And he remembered the Serpent's attack on Forluin; '. . . invite us in so that we need not force our way in . . .' His hands were shaking.

'Look,' she said again, this time, more gently. 'I did promise to show you what is happening in Forluin.' She slid the white king forward, and the scene in the mirror grew clearer.

'There', she said. 'It is done. By manoeuvring the pieces I control the image. I can see thoughts, places, events; the past and the future. Look, and I will show you Forluin.'

Estarinel stood up.

'No, I won't look. You've deceived me in every way, with mirrors

188

and drugs. I don't know what you've done with Ashurek and Medrian, but I know you are our enemy.'

She rose to her feet and faced him, her exquisite eyes an irresistible mixture of innocence and fervency.

'Have you not listened to a word I have said to you? Did you not put your arms about me and say you would stay with me forever rather than leave at that moment? And now you refuse this chance to understand and share what I love.' Again her sincerity was swaying him, eroding his judgment. 'I thought you were unlike Ashurek and Medrian, not blind, not stubborn. Now I am not sure; you seem different, and I do not know why . . .'

So she had not seen Silvren, Estarinel realised with a faint thrill of relief.

'You betrayed yourself,' he answered hoarsely. 'You said that Forluin did not matter. You must realise that even if you were right, I could never, never forget that desecration – never stand at your side and worship the evil I've sworn to destroy.'

She stared at him, her passion as awe-inspiring and inescapable as an onrushing tidal wave.

'Now you've betrayed yourself,' she said. 'I knew, of course, but what a long time you've taken to admit it – as if you were safeguarding your precious mission by your silence! I despair of humankind,' she continued, opening her perfect, pale arms in a gesture of exasperation. 'You are all the same; too afraid to see the truth. I will give you one last chance for Forluin's destiny to be delivered in gentleness, not violence. For you can see what happens if you try to resist—' She pointed at the mirror.

Estarinel was nearly caught out, and barely refrained from looking. But from the corner of his eye he saw a flash of an awful colour, a colour which for its terrible associations had burned itself permanently into his brain. It was the colour of the Worm. Then he did look at the mirror, and saw the events of months ago: the Serpent passing over Forluin. His throat tightened to an aching knot of terror and he bit his lip until he tasted blood.

Arlenmia watched the scene too, smiling dispassionately. The mirror cleared and she waited until the fear had subsided in the young knight's face, leaving only bitter misery.

'No wonder you want it destroyed,' she said sadly. 'You would have to kill me, too, before you ever reached it. Could you do that?'

For the first time he wished he lacked Forluinish gentleness and had instead Ashurek's callousness. But he doubted that even Ashurek could contemplate the cold-blooded disposal of this beautiful, misguided woman, especially not after his sister . . . Besides, there was every indication that she had the Serpent's power at her command, or was even its host.

The mirror was alive again.

'Now,' she went on, 'now that you have looked once, you cannot look away, is that right? Estarinel, I abhor violence; I tolerate it only as a "necessary evil", a cleansing process to ready the world for its future. But it need not be necessary.' She gave special emphasis to the last words, giving him a pleading, ardent look that again made it hard to disbelieve her. 'Forluin has two alternative futures. I will show you them both. Then it is in your hands to decide what will be her fate. First!' She shifted a white bishop, a honey-coloured castle and three pawns. In the mirror a long sunlit glade appeared, slumbering quietly under a soft breeze. Two men, a woman, and two girls on horseback were crossing the glade, talking and laughing. As they passed from the mirror's view, a flock of small blue-grey birds spiralled singing into the air. 'Now isn't that Forluin as all your countrymen wish it to remain? But watch her other possible fate.' The picture remained still, but the glade seemed to sicken, its soft greens becoming vulgar, the sunlight becoming harsh. The same five people began to cross again, but all on foot, running, stumbling, crying out in stark terror. A darkness overtook them and there was a glimpse of the Serpent's vile-coloured head, vomiting grey fluid which seared grass and flesh. It swooped and the five were snapped into its maw. Then the Worm flew on and nothing remained of their burned and broken bodies but a few tattered pieces of clothing. No birds rose.

'Which one is real? Which is real?' cried Estarinel.

'The choice is yours. If you return to Forluin to do my bidding, the latter can be avoided.' She rested a slender hand on his shoulder, but he shuddered under her touch. 'We are talking of the great and terrible Serpent M'gulfn. It must have domain over Earth, and it will. Only this foolish struggle is causing you all so much pain. Surrender to it, and all will have eternal life and joy. I will leave you to meditate upon this.' With a rustle of green silk, she left the room.

So Silvren had been right; Arlenmia truly believed that the appalling evil was a supreme good.

The scenes in the tabletop were running wild, filling his mind

. . . Ashurek was a bloodthirsty madman with a gold-haired witch at his side, Medrian a subverter dedicated to destroying the world, and himself an innocent, helping their wicked work with well-intentioned ignorance. Arlenmia's fanaticism was deeply persuasive . . .

This was the final trap, her last resort: the mirror would mesmerise him, instilling his brain with whatever images she chose. Now he realised that ever since he had first come to her, she had been drugging him and practising a slow, tender brainwashing. Perhaps it was a matter of pride for her to feel that he had come to her side more or less of his own free will. She had failed in that, but the mirror could not fail.

He was fighting the Serpent – perhaps even face to face – in a way he could never have foreseen. That thought alone kept his mind coherent as he sank to his knees, leaning over the table as if it was about to swallow him.

Arlenmia could not be right. However deeply she believed that M'gulfn was good, that did not make it true . . .

A terrible projection was swirling in the glass, the beginning of Arlenmia's dream of a world singing eternal worship of the Serpent. Overlaid on it in his own mind was Silvren's view: eternal desecration and misery. He could not bear to see Arlenmia's vision, could not bear to have it distilled into his mind so that he believed it, betraying the land and people he loved for the sake of an horrific, ecstatic fantasy. Slowly he forced his hands towards the chess pieces, felt them cold and heavy beneath his fingers. Reflections spun dizzily as he began to shift them. There must be a danger in this, that the images would race out of control, leaving him insane or mindless.

But as he pushed the pieces to their original positions, the mirror became still.

He took a deep breath and sat back on his heels. He felt sick with dread at the choice she had given him, for he had no doubt of her power. If he did not co-operate, she could cause the Serpent to visit Forluin a second time and complete the devastation.

'They say the Serpent cannot be destroyed,' he thought. 'Maybe this is why . . . it enmeshes all who go near it.' More than ever it seemed possible that Arlenmia could be M'gulfn in human form. 'What the hell am I going to do?' he said out loud.

He closed his eyes and suddenly remembered her words, 'If something is real, the looking glass potentially holds the image;

but it is within oneself that the power lies to draw forth the image . . .'

What made this power particular to Arlenmia? He had managed to still the image she had created to hypnotise him. He wondered if he could also summon the images he wanted into the mirror.

Arlenmia had left her glass on the table. He put it on the floor and began to toy with the chess set. Moving the pieces unleashed a million reflections that danced on the back of his eye, bringing back disorientating fragments of the drug-induced nightmare. For several minutes he persisted, feeling that he was achieving nothing but complete loss of control over the images.

Then at last he began to move the pieces in a somehow instinctive automatic pattern and he realised he had the power to control the mirror.

Immediately he knew: both her visions of Forluin had been false. So what was the truth? A faint image flickered, a grey landscape frozen under topaz glass, grey figures bowed in torment, worshipping the Worm for ever. It was what Silvren had described.

Hurriedly he changed the pattern – better not to know, perhaps. He bent his mind to locating Medrian, Ashurek and Skord, calling into the mirror the knowledge of what had become of them.

Iridescent hues swam and melted in the mercury; then the glass cleared, and he beheld three scenes. They all took place in Arlenmia's dining hall and he felt that he was seeing the recent past, perhaps the previous day. In the first he saw Ashurek, dressed in Gorethrian-style robes of blue, conversing with Arlenmia over the crystal globe. Somehow, in his mind, he could hear what they were saying.

'I hope you are enjoying your stay,' Arlenmia said, smiling.

'No, not really,' the Gorethrian answered. 'Do any of your guests ever leave?'

'What a cynic you are!' she laughed. 'Of course they do – when they have seen my point of view.'

'And are ready to do your work?'

'Don't mock me, Ashurek, and don't underestimate me. I have five countries under my control, not just Belhadra.' Marking the North Pole on the crystal globe was a little jade dragon, which she stroked with a fingertip. 'It was not done with armies, just boys like Skord and a few nemen. But understand this, it is not for myself, or even for some mighty empire, that I do this.'

'I know why you're doing it,' Ashurek replied.

'Yes, but do you understand? Oh Ashurek – you are a mystery to me. You did so much fine work for the Serpent – then threw it all away. What were you thinking of?'

'You call it fine work?' he exclaimed. 'It was madness! It had to stop.'

'And you disposed of the Egg-Stone and suffered the pain of the Serpent's retribution, just for the sake of your independence?'

'Oh no, there was more to it than that,' he answered, cold anger in his face. 'The Egg-Stone caused me to murder my brother and sister. And it seems to me that the Serpent's power began to increase when the Stone was unleashed upon the world.'

'That is true, though it is of little use to anyone, lost in a volcano,' she said. 'You have disrupted our work and left Gorethria in chaos, with revolution and anarchy in the Empire; you and Silvren are a great disappointment to me.'

'Let chaos destroy Gorethria then – it is what she deserves.'

'No! It is not too late to help her. You can return there and reclaim the throne, and the Egg-Stone can be recovered . . . together we can rule the Empire and Tearn, the whole Earth.' She smiled, blue lights shimmering in her hair.

'Are you mad?' Ashurek cried angrily. 'You know much about me, but you do not realise that no offer of power can tempt me. I have had power – and I know that it is sick and evil.'

'Ashurek, be calm. You misunderstand me.' Her smile became cold. 'I am not trying to tempt you with power – I am telling you what you must do.'

Ashurek gave a laugh of grim scepticism.

Arlenmia moved round the globe, nearer to him, and went on, 'I have been very patient with you. I have not tried to drug or hypnotise you to bring you into my power. You've had every chance to join me of your own free will.'

'Not tried – what of that subtle substance which makes me think of the Egg-Stone as I have not thought of it for months?'

'I don't know what you mean; it was only to help you recover from your ordeal. But what you say is very interesting . . .'

'Lying comes to you as easily as breathing, doesn't it?' Ashurek said acidly. 'Well, spare me your deceitful games.'

'Very well, to business,' she said sweetly, unmoved by his attitude. 'As I said, it was my hope that you would join me of your own accord. However, as you resist . . . there is the question of Silvren.'

'What have you to do with her?' he hissed, gripping her shoulders.

'We were friends, once; did she never tell you? But as we went our separate ways, I had to send the demon Diheg-El after her—'

'It was your doing?' He shook her, but he might as well have assaulted a statue of pure diamond, so still did she remain in his grasp.

'Her work was destructive! Better she was out of harm's way – but I can easily have her released. Or, conversely, if you will not agree to help me, things can be made much more unpleasant for her in the Dark Regions.'

Estarinel thought Ashurek would kill Arlenmia then; but he did not. His hands fell from her shoulders, and she watched him with growing triumph.

'You wanted to kill the Serpent so that she'd be released, did you not? Well, if you will help me, she will be freed and you'll be spared your terrible mission,' she added.

Estarinel's heart sank; she had won, then. Ashurek could not refuse her offer. He was silent, eyes brooding.

Then he said, 'Do your damnedest.'

'What?' Arlenmia said, shocked. 'I thought even you could not be that cruel!'

'Think what you like. I am the Worm's sworn enemy. How would Silvren feel, knowing I'd sold my soul to M'gulfn for her freedom? She'd rather spend eternity with the Shana than that. She, at least, has courage.'

Arlenmia stared at him, her face like white onyx.

'Very well. You will do my bidding eventually, do not doubt it; and Silvren will be imprisoned forever.'

Estarinel let the scene fade. He was trembling at what he had witnessed, and dreading what else he might learn.

He began to slide the pieces over the glass again. An image rippled and cleared, and he saw Skord.

He was by Arlenmia's fireside, cowering under the force of her wrath.

'You obey my orders to the letter!' she was declaiming. 'You do not play your own little games with my guests! No matter how bitter you are about your parents or your betrothed, no matter how much you hate Gorethrians or scorn the Forluinish, you act for *me* and not yourself. Oh! By the Serpent, you are a fool!' She paced the room, tossing her hair back.

Skord was crouched on the floor. He muttered something that sounded like, 'You said I'd done well.'

'So I thought you had, but I didn't know the half of it when I praised you. You tried to murder Ashurek! You amaze me! How could you be such an idiot? You let the nemen half-kill them, because *you* were bitter about them. You let them catch you because you couldn't resist lording it over them. And how – how did you manage to let yourself be hypnotised? How could Estarinel break through the double entrancements of Siregh-Ma and myself? By the Serpent – what have you brought me?' In her anger she was like a vibrant tongue of green flame. 'Well. If it has brought back your memory it is a just punishment.' She laughed maliciously. 'How ironic that you, in catching Ashurek, are the envy of all my other messengers. *Her Favourite*, they call you; what a position of power you could have reached. Oh Skord – what did you think you'd gain by being so stupid?' She bent down and stroked his hair, suddenly gentle. He tried to draw away but she entangled her fingers in a clump of hair and held him. 'Ah, but I know. I know that you hate both me and Ashurek. Your thought was to play us off against each other, hoping that one or both would be destroyed. Oh, you foolish scheming wretch!' She dragged him to his feet and cast him bodily back to the floor. 'Most stupid of my messengers! I am not going to give you another chance. I won't take your memory again. I release you from service, and leave you to your demon, Siregh-Ma.'

Then Skord looked up, absolute defeat and terror in his brown fox-like eyes. There was no trace of dignity or even arrogance left in him, he was quite broken. Estarinel felt pity for him then; he was a pathetic sight.

'Please . . . make Siregh-Ma leave me . . .' Ashurek had said, 'The Dark Regions . . . one slip and you will be down there yourself.' Now the boy saw that it was about to come true.

Estarinel shuddered as full realisation came to him; he was responsible for Skord's awful fate. If he had not hypnotised him, the youth would not now be in this doomed and sorry state.

What a dangerous thing was curiosity. With hesitant hands he shifted the mirror's image and sought Medrian. He could not imagine what use Arlenmia would have for her; Alaak was only a small island, and part of the Empire anyway. But there was probably no limit to Arlenmia's ingenuity.

At last the chess pieces brought the mirror into focus, and he beheld a third scene which left him more mystified about Medrian than ever before.

She and Arlenmia were sitting at the dining table. For a moment he did not recognise her; she was wearing a long dress of white silk with her ebony hair falling around her shoulders. Her head was bowed as if she was listening very hard to what Arlenmia was saying.

'The one I could never see, and you arrive on my very doorstep!' Her eyes were warm and luminous as she looked at Medrian. 'Most precious of my guests and helpers – you alone are worth every one of them.'

'You know, then,' Medrian said flatly.

'Of course . . . you are as limpid as crystal to me. So, before you start fighting me, let me explain what I can offer.'

'Please don't; I can do nothing to further your aims, so don't waste your time.'

Arlenmia reached out and took her hands.

'I don't want you to do anything, Medrian; just let yourself be helped.'

'Let me go. You won't change anything,' the Alaakian said coldly.

'There you are wrong. Haven't you ever thought what it would be like to be free?' At this, Medrian looked up at Arlenmia, as if realising that she possessed a precise and terrible power.

'You couldn't!' Medrian exclaimed.

'Oh, but I could. You know it,' answered Arlenmia with warm gentleness. 'Now, if you like – rest your head on my shoulder, and sleep. You will wake free of pain, and you can go home.'

The look in Medrian's dark eyes was one of such misery and longing that Estarinel was startled. Arlenmia held out her arms and Medrian wavered, her body swaying slightly as if pulled by a mesmeric impulse. It was so easy to fall, and so hard to resist.

Her body became still, and she said, 'No.'

'Come, Medrian,' Arlenmia said softly. 'Don't torment yourself.'

'It's too late. My mind was made up, in snow and lead and ice, years ago. I no longer have a choice.'

'You'd condemn yourself to a life without hope?' A touch of frustration crept into Arlenmia's persuasive voice.

'Hope was a small bird of gold guarding an egg in her mountain nest; when the egg was taken, hope fled the world,' Medrian said, her voice bleak as the wind. 'Now I am the world's only hope.'

196

'The alternative is for me to kill you,' said Arlenmia harshly.

'Do what you like. When you finally understand it will be too late.'

The scene turned grey and was lost in the still silver of the mirror. Estarinel sat back from the table, breathless. He felt amazed at his ability to control the mirror; surely Arlenmia had not anticipated it?

He was also aware that the effort had drained much energy from him. He was sweating and shivering at the same time, and suffering the cramp-like pains about which Arlenmia had so solicitously enquired earlier. Even gathering the strength to think was exhausting.

He glanced down and noticed her glass on the floor. He saw that the remaining drops of water had evaporated and left a whitish powder on the inside. Curious, he picked it up and sniffed it. It had a faint but distinctive smell, gingery and very bitter, which was unmistakeable: it was mircam, a drug extracted from the herb called Brownblade, which had anti-narcotic properties. It was never used in Forluinish medicine as it was addictive and affected the personality.

That was the cause of the strange languor she had about her and the unnatural dilation of her eyes; she was addicted to the herb. At last he had discovered, quite unexpectedly, a possible weakness in her. Surprise, followed by a faint ignition of hope, gave him just enough strength to decide what to do.

Somehow he must break through the multiple reflections separating him from Medrian and Ashurek. He would begin by looking into the mirror to see if he could discern their nature. Perhaps that way he would gain a clue as to how to undo her sorcery.

Control of the mirror came more easily than before. He summoned to mind an image of one of the long golden corridors with several doors leading off it. Then he called forth all possible aspects of that view at one particular time – the present. The image moved out of focus, presenting him with several identical reflections that seemed just out of register with each other. His eyes strained to make sense of what he was seeing. Illogical lines of perspective intersected and faded into other lines, all edged with glittering, blurred lights where they reflected sunlight falling through a confused multiplicity of windows.

He knew what to do.

He brought each reflection into equal prominence, disregarding

197

the pains that stabbed through his head with the effort. Then, with nightmarish, slow precision, he began to drag each reflection into line with all the others. Strings of diamond light danced achingly across his vision, sparkling in and out of focus, until at last all slid into register. In the mirror was an image of one sunlit golden corridor.

Two servants, going about their business in different reflections, stopped short with exclamations of surprise when they saw each other.

Estarinel let out a cry of elation. He let the picture shift and began searching swiftly for his companions.

'Ashurek! Ashurek!' he called out loud as he scanned through reflection after reflection, intent on contacting the Gorethrian.

But his strength was exhausted.

He saw into infinite depths of mercury, drawing his mind further and further down. He was fighting, drowning; a small hole broke open in the fluid metal, ripples spreading out from it as it increased in size. Then Estarinel knew that Arlenmia's myriad reflections were broken, but his own mind was lost in the dark hole, and he could not surface. There was a terrible sensation of falling, falling into blueness, and it was as if a laughing, evil power revealed to him terrible phantasms of the future. There was snow and ice, and red glass, and a dark-haired woman – or was it a bird? – crying out for help he could not give.

12

A Welcome Traitor

'I never dreamed it would be so difficult,' Arlenmia said, looking at her reflection in her dressing-table mirror. Behind her the maid combed and threaded jade beads into her blue-green hair. 'I've come to despise them; how can three so foolish and blind give me such a fight?'

'I'm sure it is only a matter of hours before they give in to you, my Lady,' said the maid.

'Hurry up; I must go and see how Estarinel is faring. If he still resists after seeing my mirror, I will have to fetch a demon to deal with him.' She bent forward and rubbed some mist off the glass. 'It's such a perfect opportunity to complete the work . . . I control five countries, Belhadra and her neighbours, yet I cannot control a mere three people!'

'My Lady, they are the gift of the Serpent, after all, and such a gift cannot be taken for granted,' the maid said.

'You and your words of wisdom!' Arlenmia exclaimed. 'Are you really on my side? Perhaps you'll betray me as Skord has.'

'My Lady,' the maid answered, 'everything you have taught me and shown me, I truly believe.'

'Yes,' she sighed, taking the maid's hand. 'I know you do.'

The calm energies that the mircam provided seemed to be waning, as if she needed yet another dose. The drug had been useful once, when she had first come to the world and needed to stay awake for many nights to establish her powers. But now she felt anger at her dependence upon it. The Serpent's energy should be enough.

Ashurek was approaching Arlenmia's courtyard, having spent another wasted hour trying to find a way out of the city. It was like perpetually walking out of one reflection and into another and he felt sure Arlenmia must be watching and laughing at his attempts to escape.

He was certain that she had thwarted him utterly, and wished she would make her final move to enslave him soon; then at least he might have something to fight against. He toyed with the possibility of pretending to co-operate, at least until Silvren was free . . . yet he could not believe Arlenmia would keep her word. He would happily have killed her, had he not feared for Silvren's safety.

As he entered the courtyard he had the sensation that something had changed, just as a place in a dream looks the same but is different. He looked around him and noticed two of Arlenmia's 'messengers' crossing the far side; this was strange, as the city was usually deserted. Then he saw the small dark-haired figure sitting by one of the fountains.

'Medrian!'

For the first time, she actually looked pleased to see him.

'Ashurek – how did you find me?'

'It wasn't deliberate,' he said drily. 'Are you all right?'

'Yes, perfectly.' They regarded each other, each looking for signs that the other had been seduced to Arlenmia's side.

'What do you think of our gracious hostess?'

Medrian's expression was one of distaste.

'She is a very dangerous woman – fanatical but quite sane.'

'A chilling combination,' he agreed. 'Well, how has she treated you?' Medrian did not answer at once, so he went on, 'I have been drugged, lied to, threatened and driven half-mad – though I think that was merely a preliminary. What of you?'

'She's been most kind,' said Medrian. 'At least, until yesterday, when I refused to co-operate with her. Now she wants to kill me.'

'So,' Ashurek concluded with a sour grin, 'we've both observed that she is our enemy, and a powerful servant of the Serpent. But neither of us has yet surrendered.'

'It's understandable that her patience is running out.' Medrian's voice took on a brittle edge as if she was trying to suppress a terrible feeling of dread. 'We're too valuable to her to be lost. Now that a gentle approach has failed, she'll go to any lengths to enslave us.'

'Gentle?' Ashurek exclaimed. 'Subtle, perhaps . . . I wonder if our meeting after a week of deliberate separation is part of her plan?'

'More than likely.' Medrian stood up suddenly. Her long white dress looked incongruous, made him think of Silvren. 'What shall we do?'

'What would she expect us to do?' Ashurek wondered. 'Find Estarinel and try to escape. Predictable, but we seem to have no other choice.'

'You're right . . .' she hesitated as they shared the same thought. 'Perhaps that *is* the trap – perhaps Estarinel has been deceived or forced onto her side.'

'Aye, I fear for him . . . well, whatever happens there must be a confrontation with her and we must be ready to escape. Get some travelling gear on and try to find some horses; I'll seek Estarinel.'

In his room Ashurek swiftly pulled on a high-collared quilted jacket of purple and strapped on his sword. As he turned for the door he noticed something strange about a small looking glass on the wall. It revealed not his own reflection but an infinite silver-green corrdor as if it were facing another mirror. There was a weird sensation in his skull, as if someone was calling his name just out of earshot. Was this the beginning of Arlenmia's last plan?

He hurried from the room and, to his surprise, made his way with an unerring instinct directly to one of the tower rooms. He opened the door and saw Estarinel.

The Forluinishman was slumped across a low mirror-topped table with tall alabaster chess pieces scattered about him. He did not seem to be breathing; Ashurek shook him concernedly, calling his name. After a minute, to his relief, the Forluinishman groaned and slowly came awake. He looked dazedly up at the grim, dark face of the Gorethrian.

'By the heavens,' said Ashurek, 'I thought you were dead.'

'I think I would have been, if you hadn't found me.' He rubbed his forehead and stood up so unsteadily that Ashurek thought it best to guide him to the bed and let him sit down. 'Where's Skord? What happened?' he muttered, confused for a moment and obviously thinking they were still behind the rock barrier with the nemen waiting beyond. Then awareness began to surface and his eyes brightened with excitement. 'Ashurek – it worked!'

'What did?'

'First, tell me how you managed to find me.' Ashurek related his meeting with Medrian and the strange illusion in the looking glass. Estarinel nodded, a grin spreading across his pale and exhausted face. 'Yes, it did work! Arlenmia was trying to entrance me by making scenes appear in the mirror, but I found I could control the images too. I concentrated on shattering her reflections and contacting you.'

Ashurek stared at him, incredulous.

'You're saying that you – you were responsible for—'

'Yes!' Estarinel laughed. 'I don't think you believe me.'

'Well, it is somewhat hard to credit – we thought it was another of Arlenmia's traps.'

'It isn't, I assure you.'

'Can you prove it?' asked the ever-cynical Gorethrian.

'Ah – I suppose I can't. Anyway, there isn't time; Arlenmia may know what has happened already. You must take my word that I am not working for her,' he said, his smile fading.

Ashurek thought that Estarinel probably could not lie even if he wanted to.

'Very well; if what you say is true, it changes everything. Speed is of the essence, if we are to escape. But there's more to it than just walking out of the city. Have you discovered anything that may help us?'

'I don't know. Arlenmia actually took me out of the city yesterday, but I doubt that I could find the way again.'

'She works with demons,' Ashurek said with a sigh, 'and it will go badly for us if she decides to summon any.'

'There is this.' Estarinel leaned forward and picked up Arlenmia's glass from the floor. 'Do you see the white powder crusted on the inside of this glass? It's mircam.'

'I'm no expert on herbs, but that's some kind of drug, isn't it?'

'Yes, a very powerful one. And Arlenmia has taken it continually since we've been here. It's highly addictive, which is why we don't use it in Forluin.'

'Why would she wish to take such a drug?'

'It increases strength and mental alertness and would mean she needed very little sleep. Silvren said she thought her vitality was drawn—'

'What did you say?' Ashurek interrupted sharply. 'What do you know of Silvren?'

Unnerved by the hellish light that had come into Ashurek's eyes, Estarinel began to explain his unexpected meeting with Silvren in

202

astral form. Ashurek seemed to have forgotten how little time they had and Estarinel thought he would never stop questioning him. Eventually Ashurek strode to the window and stared broodingly out at the city, while the Forluinishman went on to describe the scenes he had observed through the mirror.

'So Arlenmia was telling the truth, damn her,' Ashurek said. 'I didn't believe she'd ever known Silvren – how could they have been friends? How?'

'I don't know,' Estarinel replied, made uncomfortable by Ashurek's obvious distress. 'Didn't Silvren ever mention Arlenmia to you?'

'Never. But that was like her; she'd have been so devastated by Arlenmia's betrayal that she would have kept the whole thing to herself. She never would tell me who sent the demon after her, and I did not press the matter. But now I know.' He turned round, his face now menacing with the cold logic that had made his ancestors rulers of half the world. 'The drug, mircam. What could happen if she were suddenly to stop taking it?'

'It would have a terrible effect – she'd be very ill, and possibly die.'

'Good. Then we are going to find a way to deprive her of it. You look strangely regretful at the prospect of doing her any harm; what's the matter?'

'Nothing,' Estarinel sighed. 'It's just that she so nearly fooled me. It's hard to forget some of the things she said.'

'Then remember that she threatened Forluin, caused Silvren to be imprisoned, and seems to have no qualms about murdering Medrian,' Ashurek reminded him sharply. 'She could even be the Serpent's human host – where safer than its own High Priestess?'

'Yes – yes, I know. So what are you planning to do?'

'We need the help of someone who was very close to her. Estarinel, can you look in the mirror again and see where Skord is?'

'No, Ashurek, I can't look again. I'm exhausted. It almost killed me – or my mind, at least. Now I know why Arlenmia needs the mircam.' Ashurek glowered at him, but he went on, 'However, I do know that Skord is in this house somewhere. He's broken . . . he wouldn't have gone far.'

'Then let us find him. There's Medrian in the courtyard. Are you sufficiently recovered? Come on, then.'

Estarinel stood up, trying to ignore the dark spots swimming

203

before his eyes. He donned his cloak and sword and made sure he had the white lodestone, in case it was ever of use again. As they left the room, Ashurek clapped him on the shoulder.

'If we escape this place,' he said, 'it will be thanks to you. I swear I'll never underestimate you again!'

They met Medrian coming in from the courtyard now dressed in breeches, boots and a blue tabard. Estarinel had to restrain himself from hugging her, so glad was he to see her.

'I can't find the horses. I did find my way to the city's edge, but there's a kind of thin glass wall around it.'

'I rode out of the city yesterday and there was no such wall then,' Estarinel said.

'Well, there is now! I shattered a stone trying to break through it.' She looked pale and apprehensive. 'She must be able to see us together by now.'

'Not necessarily – it was Estarinel who broke her "enchantment",' Ashurek said with a grin, and explained briefly what had happened.

'She is bound to know, and she'll be furious,' Medrian persisted, sounding unimpressed. 'You haven't seen the half of her power yet.'

'It's most unlike you to panic, Medrian,' Ashurek said.

'You also might feel a sense of urgency if you knew she'd decided to kill you, and was quite capable of doing so—' she broke off and glanced over her shoulder down the corridor of gold. It was deserted.

Estarinel looked at her, mystified; after witnessing her strange conversation with Arlenmia, she was more of an enigma to him than ever. He began to explain about the mircam, hoping to reassure her, while Ashurek led them along the corridor in the hope of finding Skord.

'So if we can find the herb and keep it from her, she'll collapse without it.'

'Is that so?' The touch of hope in her voice faded quickly. 'Forgive me for doubting, but it sounds impossible. We couldn't even find each other; I can't find the horses; won't she keep her drugs even better hidden?'

They walked on in silence past rows of the paintings and tapestries that Arlenmia loved so much. They turned a corner and something slipped out of sight just ahead of them; at once Ashurek lengthened his stride until he drew level with an alcove.

A figure tried to dart past him, but was cornered by the tall Gorethrian.

'What's this – creeping round the walls like a brown mouse?'

It was Skord, looking as if he had not eaten or slept for days. At the sight of Ashurek there was stark terror in his eyes which showed little more intelligence than a trapped animal. He crumpled forwards to the floor, hiding his face.

'You *have* fallen out of favour, haven't you?'

'Ashurek, don't!' Estarinel exclaimed.

'All right, boy,' the Gorethrian said, almost kindly. 'Get up. We won't harm you.' Skord, after a pause, slowly began to pull himself to his feet until he was leaning against the wall, shoulders stooped and head hanging. 'You're in a sorry state.' The boy made no cutting replies. He had been cast out by Arlenmia and left to the mercy of a demon – a demon which despised him as useless. Still he stayed in the house like a whipped dog trying to regain favour with its master. He had nowhere to go, was terrified to leave, and Arlenmia was still the only one who had the power to redeem him. Estarinel felt sick with himself when he saw him, for however much he disapproved of the boy's past behaviour, he would never have attempted the hypnotism had he known it would bring him to this wretched state.

'You got us into this place,' Ashurek was saying. 'Now you can get us out.' Skord shook his head miserably and muttered something. 'Speak up!'

'She's put – put the barrier round the city. She'll summon them – from the mirrors,' he mumbled, voice stumbling and broken.

'Listen carefully,' Estarinel said. 'You can tell us two things. Do you know where Arlenmia keeps her supply of mircam?' Skord looked confused. 'The drugs she takes – her powders and herbs?'

'Oh – yes.'

'And do you know where our horses are?'

'Yes.'

'Well, will you take us there? The herbs first.' Skord lowered his head apathetically. He seemed in a daze, as if he did not care what he did.

'I can't . . .'

'You're not afraid of turning traitor to Arlenmia? She's released you from service, remember,' said Ashurek.

'No . . .'

205

'Yes; you know it. Now, come on,' Ashurek urged, beginning to guide the boy gently along the corridor. For a moment Skord hesitated, the merest hint of suspicion and hatred entering his face. Then it was gone, and he was shuffling ahead of them with his head bowed.

The maid paused, holding a glass of wine mixed with mircam.

'My Lady, do you think you should take another dose so soon?'

'I have to,' Arlenmia answered, sitting now before a different mirror. 'I feel ill, and I must have the energy to summon all my forces. It is time to finally bind the three—' as she spoke, the looking glass revealed what the three were doing at that moment.

'By the Serpent's eyes—' she hissed. 'Damn them!' She leapt up, knocking the wineglass out of the maid's hand, and flew from the room.

Skord led them to a long, light gallery with doors at either end and a large full-length gold-framed mirror in the centre of one long wall. Here he stopped, sketching signs and strokes across the mirror with one finger, '. . . to bring it to this plane,' he murmured. Absorbed in his task, he took on some of the bearing of the arrogant young 'messenger' again. Presently he pushed the edge of the glass and it slid sideways, revealing a small room stocked with all kinds of herbs. This was where she made her various drugs.

The three entered. There was Brownblade growing in troughs of water, looking rather like mint, but with longer, bronze-coloured leaves; tied in dry bunches; beaten to a white powder. Estarinel pulled off his cloak and they swiftly bundled all the Brownblade and phials of mircam they could find into it.

As they left the room and pulled the 'door' back across, Ashurek impulsively drew his sword and smashed the glass with the hilt. As the ringing shatter died away, they turned to see Medrian staring with horror at one of the doors. She seized Skord's arm.

'Let's find the horses!' she cried and dragged him at a run to the other door, disappearing just as Arlenmia entered.

She stared at the knight and the Gorethrian. Her presence was cold, overpowering.

'Give that to me,' she commanded, pointing to Estarinel's bundled cloak. He took a step back and then, to his amazement, she attacked him. With great strength she pulled him violently to the floor, her face livid. Even as he fell he threw the bundle to Ashurek who caught it and made for the door. She was tremendously strong. Her skin was cold as marble and her nails sank into his arm, drawing blood.

Seeing Ashurek escaping with her precious herb, she struggled to rise, but Estarinel held her down.

'Lock us in!' he shouted after Ashurek, knowing there was a great brass key in the door.

Arlenmia fought free. But by the time she ran down to the door, Ashurek had indeed locked it. She hurried to the other door to find that that too was now locked.

'You have broken the mirror!' she hissed at Estarinel. 'I am no sorceress, I can only work through an unbroken mirror! You have trapped me. I congratulate you, it was beautifully done.' Her face was so full of fury that she seemed likely to tear him apart barehanded. With a visible effort she regained her composure and bit back any more heated words. She paced the length of the gallery, her whole frame so tense that she looked like a marble figure brought to life. Her shimmering blue-green dress was the exact colour of her hair.

'I wish . . . I wish,' she said, pushing at the shards of glass with a silk-slippered foot, 'that I had guessed you had the ability to control the mirror. I should have known, from the ease with which you mesmerised Skord. We have both been foolish in our way, it would seem.' He stood watching her as she walked very slowly towards him. Her large, liquid eyes were shining with suppressed frustration. 'Estarinel, did you listen to nothing I told you? You began to listen, oh you began . . . Now you look at me as if I were not even human. But I am. I don't give my affection easily, it's true, but I loved Silvren. I could have loved you. You could have had Forluin whole and perfect forever, lovelier than you can imagine. But in resisting me you have condemned your land.' She came close to him and put her hands on his shoulders. 'Yes, I could have loved you. But I won't let anything stand between myself and my dream – not anything!'

'That's obvious – I've seen how you treat people you love. Why can't you see the Serpent for the evil it is?' Estarinel exclaimed, raising his hands to hold her wrists. Her look of exasperation made her appear at once more human and more beautiful.

'Did I not explain to you that what seems "evil" on a petty human scale is but a dispassionate act of cleansing on a cosmic one?'

'Yes, you did. And to me that dispassion of great forces is an even greater evil. Do you think the Serpent even cares that you exist? Your vision is false! What happened to Forluin is real – and it is *evil*.'

She stepped backwards as if he had struck her, her hands falling from his shoulders. A look of wretchedness came to her eyes, and he thought for a moment that what he said had reached her.

'I've given you every chance. But I've been too honest with you; I should have told you what you wanted to hear, instead of the truth,' she stated. He stared at her, incredulous at these words. There was no convincing her that she was wrong. She seemed to realise at the same moment as he did that it was futile to continue the argument. All her passion seemed to drain away and she turned and wandered listlessly the length of the gallery.

When she turned towards him again her face was very pale and her graceful hands were shaking slightly. He realised that she was beginning to feel the lack of mircam already.

'So now you are going to stand there and watch me die?' she asked, the touch of humour in her voice far more chilling than outright malice. 'Can you do it? You have the instinct of a healer. I don't believe you can even bear to watch me become ill.'

She half-smiled through her discomfort when she saw that she had hit upon the exact truth. Estarinel turned away, could not bear to look at her. He wished that he had Ashurek's cool nerve.

'Arlenmia, let us go!' he implored. 'You'd have to reduce us to mindless puppets before ever we'd work for you, and then what use would we be?'

'Perhaps you're right. It has been a fair fight,' she said softly. 'Go and ask your friends to unlock the door.'

He hesitated. Then he said, 'No. Not yet.'

'How long can she manage without her drug?' Medrian asked Skord as they crossed a large, fountain-filled square.

'Two – two hours or three,' he muttered.

'What then?' Skord shrugged.

'She might die, I suppose.'

'If you hate her so, why didn't you try to deprive her of her herbs before?'

'I never thought of it . . . it would have been impossible. And if she died . . .' he lifted spiritless eyes to Medrian's face, 'the powers in her mirrors would be unleashed. They'd destroy the Glass City and the connections with the three Planes would be broken.'

'How do you know?'

'She told me,' he said simply. It seemed he had been in such a state of fear that his mind could not cope, and had cut itself off, leaving him apathetic, witless, and easily manipulated.

Medrian was silent with the thought that if Arlenmia died, they would never reach H'tebhmella.

The horses were in an airy, marble-floored stable on the far side of the square. They had obviously been well looked after, though there were no grooms about. They saddled the beasts and started back towards the Lady's house, Medrian leading Vixata and her own black animal, Skord with Shaell.

But as they walked, a knot of darkness formed in the air before them, and from it a figure materialised. It was tall, naked and silver-coloured, its face broad and evilly beautiful. Its red mouth spread in a smile as it looked at Skord.

A demon, summoned once and in possession of a human, could come whenever it pleased. So Siregh-Ma had appeared to tease and torment the youth.

Skord uttered a strangled whimper and dropped to his knees, edging backwards. The brown stallion reared and shied several yards away. Vixata went into a frenzy of remembered fear, and dragged Medrian in circles; luckily her own beast, although she had let it go, stood quietly.

Skord was sobbing convulsively, barely able to breathe, he was so paralysed with fright. But the figure had gone, as quickly as it had appeared.

Medrian regained control of Vixata and picked up the reins of the other two horses.

'It's all right, Skord,' she said. 'It's gone, it's gone. Get up.' But she had to pick up his crumpled body and lay him over Shaell's saddle, for this last fright had so robbed him of his reason that he would not move.

Riding her black horse, leading the other two, Medrian made for the house.

'It's gone,' she repeated. But Skord was mumbling faintly.

'It never goes. It's always there . . .' and Medrian's face became cold as death, as if she was reminded yet again of something she was forever struggling to forget.

'So . . . you can watch me dying, after all?' Arlenmia hissed. She was standing very rigidly as if she might fall if she moved. Her skin was opalescent, almost transparent, and her eyes were glassy with pain. Estarinel could see that her discomfort was real, not feigned, and was increasing by the minute. It was torment to watch her, and only by a painful effort of will could he refrain from hammering on the door for Ashurek to open it. But to do that before Arlenmia was weak enough not to make an escape would be to betray his companions.

That knowledge did not make it any easier to witness Arlenmia's agony, her pallid face now moist with sweat and her convulsively trembling hands. Groaning inwardly, he sat down on a high-backed chair and put his head in his hands.

'I'm very sad to see you suffering as much as I,' Arlenmia continued, her voice hoarse with pain. 'Your concern moves me deeply. I only hope you can judge the precise moment at which you must open the door. But I fear you won't find that easy; I may die very suddenly, and then it will be too late for you.'

'What do you mean?'

'You should have thought more carefully before depriving me of mircam. When I die, Estarinel, your Quest will be lost. You stand in the City of Glass, which maintains the Entrance Points to the Planes. The powers with which I have enmeshed this city will destroy it and you will never reach the Blue Plane – no one will ever reach it again. Do you understand?'

He looked at her, horrified.

'You're trying to trick me—'

'I could be – do you want to take that risk? Naturally I do not want to die, Estarinel. So I am trying to explain how foolish you would be to let me. Don't wait too long!' Her voice was becoming fainter and more strained. She seemed very near to collapse, but she was right in saying it would be impossible to judge the moment to open the door. He stood up, vacillating between the door and

Arlenmia. Then he approached her, determined to see just how weak she was.

At once her hands caught his arms like two steel bands and her eyes locked with his.

'Now you are going to go out and bring me some mircam. I'll tell you what to say to Ashurek.' Her eyes were mesmeric, worse than the mirror. He could not fight. 'Listen to me . . .'

Medrian approached the gallery with some trepidation, but sighed with relief when she saw Ashurek waiting outside the locked door. Beside him were two figures, a dark-haired youth slumped unconscious, and Arlenmia's maid, very much awake but sitting tied up and gagged. When Medrian let go of Skord's arm he slid to the floor next to them, covering his head with his hands as if to ward off his own private terror.

'I locked Arlenmia in the gallery,' the Gorethrian explained. 'Unfortunately Estarinel's in there too. I only hope she's done him no harm. As for those two—' he waved his hand at the servants, 'I had to deal with them before they called for more help, or Arlenmia knew they were here.' The maid's eyes rolled malevolently at him as he spoke. 'What happened to the lad?'

'His demon appeared on the way back and it upset him. It only frightened him then vanished – but it made me wonder why Arlenmia has not yet summoned any demons,' Medrian said.

'She told me that she only summons them through mirrors – that is how she can control them and avoid possession. It's fortunate that I thought to destroy the mirror. The problem is that this damned door is all but soundproof – I've been shouting to Estarinel, but he doesn't reply.'

'But if you open the door Arlenmia may be waiting just behind it . . .'

'Precisely. Did you find the horses?'

'Yes, but listen. We can't just rescue Estarinel and flee, because we need her to remove the barrier round the city. And there's more.' She explained what Skord had told her about the Glass City and the Entrance Points.

'I can believe that,' said Ashurek. 'It tallies with what Silvren told Estarinel.'

'Silvren?'

'I'll explain later.' Then he looked grimly at Medrian and added, 'The Shanin that captured Silvren was sent after her by Arlenmia.'

'Oh. Oh, I see.'

They waited a few minutes more, during which Medrian attempted to ask Skord how weak Arlenmia was likely to have become. But the boy, empty-eyed, did not even seem to understand the question.

'Try the maid,' said Ashurek, standing with his ear to the ornate door and one hand on the key.

Medrian took out a knife and held it against the maid's throat as she untied the piece of material gagging her.

'One sound and I'll slit your throat,' she said matter-of-factly. 'Just how long can Arlenmia be expected to live without the drug?'

'My Lady was already in need of some,' the maid said, her voice a mixture of defiance and panic. 'She didn't take it because of you! Oh, please, please go in – or let me go in with some mircam. If she dies—'

'Calm yourself. You know her; you must tell us exactly how long it will be before she weakens. That's the only way you'll be permitted to save her. Tell us, or she'll die.'

'I believe she'll collapse in about – about ten minutes,' the maid said miserably.

'And how long before she dies?'

'Only – only a few minutes more. She needed a great deal of mircam to sustain her powers.'

'Do you believe her?' Medrian asked Ashurek.

'Yes,' he replied. 'She hasn't the guile to lie. I am going in there to see what's happening. Let me into the room, and lock the door behind me.'

Medrian turned the heavy brass key and cautiously let the door swing open a space. Ashurek sidled in with his sword at the ready, and she quickly closed it behind him. Almost immediately she heard a faint call.

'Medrian! Come in!'

Leaving the maid she entered and saw Estarinel; he was gazing wide-eyed into Arlenmia's face and almost grey with the strain of resisting her will.

'Make them open the door, make them open it,' Arlenmia was whispering, her voice as frail as a frost-encrusted leaf. She was holding onto his arms as if she might fall if she let go. She looked ghastly; sweat was running from her forehead and her lips were the same alabaster white as her face.

As Ashurek and Medrian entered, she turned to glare at them, her eyes glinting with a terrible liquid fire as if the last of her power was concentrated there. As she released Estarinel from her grip he stumbled back against the wall and leaned there with his eyes closed.

She looked at the open door, heard her maid crying, 'My Lady! My Lady!'

Arlenmia turned the hypnotic power of her eyes on to Ashurek.

'Drop your sword. Let me pass.' Wisely, he did not look straight at her. She took a step forward, but then it was too late; her strength failed, and she dropped to the floor.

Medrian had gone to Estarinel's side. He was trembling and breathing very fast, but opened his eyes when she touched his arm.

'Oh, by the Serpent,' he muttered, shaking his head. 'I'm all right, I'll be all right, Medrian.' Arlenmia, lying on the floor and trying to raise herself by levering her hands underneath her, was glaring at them. Her power was gone now; only her anger remained, and that was but a shadow of what it had been. Her weakness made her surrender to panic and the desperate need to survive.

'This battle seems to be yours, I concede,' she whispered. 'Give me my herbs.'

'You can have them,' said Ashurek, 'if you will let us leave the city and be on our way in peace.'

'Yes, anything – my herbs, I am dying!' she gasped.

'Very well,' said Ashurek. He signalled to Medrian who began to help Estarinel forward; then Arlenmia watched in horror as the three went out through the door and re-locked it.

'That was cruel,' Medrian commented. 'What are you doing?'

'Merely being cautious.' Ashurek untied the maid and pulled her to her feet. He reached into the bundled cloak and gave her a phial of powder. 'Now, you are going to mix your mistress a dose of mircam, just strong enough for her to regain a little strength – no more. Do you understand?' The maid nodded mutely. Medrian followed to make sure she did just that, and did not try to alert any other servants.

Meanwhile Estarinel leaned against the wall and sank into a sitting position next to the prostrate Skord. Ashurek began to laugh.

'You're all dropping like flies. What did she do to you?'

'I don't know . . . she was only talking, trying to mesmerise me, but the words . . . it was like having something awful crawling about in my brain, or like being knocked out . . . I feel terrible.' He drew a deep breath. 'If she hadn't stopped just then, I wouldn't have survived much longer.'

His memory returned in a painful jumble of glass splinters. 'Oh – Ashurek, she mustn't die! The Glass City—'

'I know, it's all right,' the Gorethrian reassured him. 'Skord told Medrian. People like her never do die easily, anyway . . .'

The maid returned, holding a glass of water carefully in both hands as if it was some precious elixir. Medrian took charge of the rest of the mircam, tying the cloak into a neat bundle. Ashurek opened the door and ushered the maid in, but at the last moment stayed her hand and took the glass from her.

Arlenmia was lying motionless, but she was not dead. Ashurek took the glass to her. It was all she could do to lift her head and take a sip of the water. Weakly she reached out to grasp the glass, but Ashurek withdrew it, allowing her no more. He was right to suspect that the maid had mixed a very strong dose indeed, and he wanted Arlenmia just able to walk, not restored to her full energy.

From her look of frustration as she began to revive, Arlenmia was well aware of this.

'You're very clever,' she hissed, staggering to her feet and leaning on the maid's shoulder. Then she turned on her servant, 'As for you – what the hell have you been doing—'

'She's not been disloyal,' Ashurek interrupted, 'merely incapacitated. Now, shall we go?'

'I need more mircam.'

'Yes; when you've allowed us to leave.'

'Very well,' she said, her eyes blazing with anger in her opalescent face. 'I'll take you to the city's edge and let you out – but your escape won't be easy. You'll regret what you have done today!' She walked through the door ahead of the maid, not even looking at Medrian, Estarinel, or the unconscious dark-haired servant. But then she noticed Skord and stopped. He looked up at her, blinking through a haze of fear.

'Haven't you betrayed me enough, without this final insult? By the Serpent, it is a miserable day for you—'

'Let him be!' broke in Ashurek unexpectedly. 'He's coming with

214

us.' He did not stop to analyse why he suddenly felt protective towards the wretch.

Arlenmia, Skord, and the three companions reached the city's edge and the recently-conjured glass wall which encased the city like a bubble. The lady was looking stronger and more composed, though she frequently eyed the bundle of precious herbs and powders that Ashurek was guarding. Riding her sea-green and gold palfrey, she seemed a statue of mother-of-pearl and blue jade. Vixata was giving Ashurek some trouble, and even Shaell, carrying Estarinel and the half-conscious Skord, was skittish.

At the glass wall, Arlenmia ordered them to dismount. She did so herself, and stepped forward and touched the hard, transparent shell.

'Leave the herbs just there,' she said, indicating the marble pavement a few yards from her. The air was very still, silent, oppressive under the glass dome. 'I want you to walk from here very slowly, in single file.'

She ran her fingertips over the glass. It became soapy-looking, glistening with ripples of many colours. At last her fingers actually passed through it, as they would through a soap bubble.

Ashurek shook the herbs into a heap on the ground, and returned the cloak to Estarinel.

'Now you may walk through,' she said, smiling, and moving a little towards Medrian as if to make way for them. Ashurek, hesitantly, stepped forward to the wall, which allowed him and Vixata to pass through and then closed elastically behind him.

'You next,' Estarinel said to Medrian. Arlenmia had moved closer to her and was looking over her shoulder; at this Medrian became as tense and poised as a cat with fur on end. She took a step forward, then with one swift movement Arlenmia's arm swept down, and she had sunk a knife into the side of Medrian's neck. Medrian, choking, staggered towards the wall and fell straight through it.

The air above the metal towers shimmered and the glass melted and disappeared completely. Estarinel and Ashurek both started towards Medrian, but stopped in mid-stride.

Although the blade must have passed clean through her throat, she had regained her feet, and, showing no sign of pain, wrenched the knife out. It left only a small, white-lipped mark. Instead it was her sullen black horse who stumbled to its knees, a grey fluid like colourless blood pouring from its jugular vein. It subsided onto its flank and died.

The blood ran to Arlenmia's face, turning her cheeks tourmaline-coloured. Medrian's eyes were black lakes in her ivory-pale face. The two women faced each other across the body of Medrian's protective spirit.

Medrian flung the knife at Arlenmia and it clattered to the ground by the hem of her silken skirts.

'There,' she hissed. 'Try again!'

Estarinel was pulling at the reins of the coloured palfrey.

'Medrian! Take Arlenmia's horse!'

Arlenmia and Medrian looked long at each other, not moving. The jewels in the towers' tops throbbed and pulsed; a low humming filled the air.

'Go! And when you reach your destination with nothing but cold creeping misery to greet you, remember what I offered you!' Arlenmia cried to Medrian. On the plain beyond the city a wind was moving, filled with strange sobbing and booming sounds such as whales make beneath the sea.

'Time we left,' shouted Ashurek. The air was turning thick and brownish, like bromine. Medrian vaulted onto the beautiful turquoise-coloured horse and Estarinel began to trot after Ashurek, but Medrian was still looking at Arlenmia. And the Lady tossed back her heavy skeins of hair and her voice rose clearly above the growing storm.

'You cannot destroy the Serpent, because it is everywhere. Every blow you make to defeat others, it is a little of the Serpent in you. Can you run your sword into the earth, thinking to slay the world? You are M'gulfn's instruments – this world *will* realise my dream, while you go to your deaths!'

Medrian was riding Northwards after the others now. The air above the plain was throbbing with great, slow, sickening pulses of mustard light; Arlenmia, head back, eyes wide, silently invoked the forces of her mirrors, ensuring that the four would be hounded from one trap to another, although she knew it would break her hold on the Glass City.

The booming of the brown air, the slow collective heartbeat of all Arlenmia's forces, throbbed painfully through the heads of the riders. And although an unhealthy current, like that which had sent them into Hrannekh Ol, carried them fast over the plain, the pedestrian rhythm seemed to slow all movement almost to a standstill.

They were galloping – Ashurek on Vixata who was a streak of dull gold, Shaell following at his greyhound gallop with Estarinel not touching the reins but holding Skord's limp body firmly across the front of the saddle. Medrian's new steed, gold mane and tail flying, was catching up.

And now small black shapes darted past them in the sky, and a great heavy wind pushed them on over the turf like a continuous stream of foul breath issuing from some beast's gaping mouth. Arlenmia's forces were driving them, cat after mouse.

The air became full of flying particles against which Estarinel could barely open his eyes, but he could just make out the horizon. On his excursion with Arlenmia he had seen that the plain was quite a small one, fringed by wooded hills, dark and distant. But now, as far as he could see, the plain had no boundaries.

Against the mind-numbing beating of the air, a twittering like a million birds was growing above them. Heads without bodies darted past, grinning. Something like a tiny black ape settled with a thud on Ashurek's shoulder, rubbery and loathsome, digging its tiny blunt paws hard into his neck. Nauseated, he tried to brush it away. It clung like a black leech. It began to lick his face with a slimy, rubber-like tongue, scratching at his skin with sharp teeth. Ashurek dropped the reins – although it meant Vixata began to bolt uncontrollably, bucking – and seized the thing with both hands, but it had a good mouthful out of his cheek before he wrenched it free and flung it in disgust to the ground. But there were more of the foul monkeys descending on them, twittering.

And now a wood sprang up around them – except that the trees, roots trailing, were flying upright in mid-air, slowly overtaking them. Earth and rocks pelted down, but the riders and their mounts were oblivious to the pain.

Like a humming, singing cloud of locusts, the foul monkeys were all around them. With difficulty, Ashurek began to pull up Vixata. She fought, head shaking viciously, sending shards of dull light from her wild mane. At last he hauled her to a standstill and Shaell and the other, new horse cannoned into the back of her. Heads up, facing the wild wind and brown light, the horses stood sweating and trembling.

Ashurek drew sword. The flying apes were pestering, attacking them in an endless swarm.

'Why have you stopped?' yelled Estarinel, beating at them with his arms. Ashurek could not hear his voice, but he lip-read the words.

'We can't get away from these things, we'll have to fight them off.'

But fighting was of little use. A sword blow would send an ape thudding to the ground, only to gain its feet and run chattering to cling to the horses' legs. And unless they moved with the bizarre flying forest, the trees threatened to collide with them.

And then a great brown tidal wave came careering towards them, made now of rock, now water, now glass. Flocks of screaming things came with it. At this the sweating horses, even the staid Shaell, left their riders no choice but took off like a whirlwind through the polluted, pulsing atmosphere.

As they galloped, the trees and the leech-like apes overtook them and vanished. The beats of aching light grew slower and heavier, paining the senses. The tidal wave burst over them with a feeling that was not hot, or cold, but a condition of temperature previously unknown; and when it was gone, the turf had gone with it. The plain was a smooth, flat grey, and they could not see the sky.

All they could see, fleeing ahead of them, was a bird. It was black, its feathers ragged from the buffeting of the Worm-wind; its voice rose faintly above the roaring silence of the plain.

'*Look for me, look for me, I told you where.*'

The horses careered on; and as they ran, a great split bisected the plain, and the two halves slowly tipped in towards the crack until they were vertical walls of greyness; and through the fissure horses and riders were falling.

They were falling far faster than gravity could pull them. Ashurek, leaning forward and grasping Vixata's neck tightly, was aware only of the warmth of her sweat-creamed neck and her mane, like soft wire, pressing into the side of his face. He could not help wondering whether they would be killed when they hit the bottom, or whether they would just fall for ever.

Estarinel, holding his breath, forgot the descent for a minute as half-seen visions or premonitions clouded his brain: a flat expanse of snow; something silver with a dark, shifting heart; doorways, some frightening, some welcoming; a voice he loved saying, kill me, *kill me*.

Below them the bird also fell, spiralling down in an uncontrolled dive; yet she seemed to be leading them on and out of the darkness.

218

'*The world's Hope was I,*' she called distantly. '*Does no one remember?*'

'Yes, I remember,' Ashurek murmured brokenly into Vixata's mane. 'I remember you, Miril.'

Then the bird was gone.

13

Three from the Gorge

The maid watched nervously as Arlenmia walked along the glass slabs from tower to tower, looking despondently at each one and touching them briefly.

Her illusion of metal had gone, ripped away by the unleashing of her powers. The Glass City had returned to its true state; the marble slabs had taken on their translucent greenness, and all the towers and buildings were shining with clear colours – red, amber, emerald, and heliotrope.

Arlenmia was reluctant to return to her house, for all the walls were transparent. All her mirrors had become transparent also, and it made her deeply uncomfortable.

The City's inhabitants were returning, as swiftly and dispassionately as they had left. They were thin, grey, spectral figures who acknowledged her with the merest nod and mocking smile as they floated past. They were not beings in a complete sense, being concerned only with maintaining a balance of energy between the Earth and its three Planes. The balance had only been slightly disrupted by Arlenmia, and it would be easy enough to correct whatever discrepancy she had caused.

When she had first arrived, she had hoped to engage them in her cause – thus putting the Serpent in control of the Planes. But there had been no way of communicating with them or enslaving them. They had put up no fight, but had simply left.

Their return from exile, in some distant domain, showed her that the City was no longer hers, and she must leave. The three enemies of M'gulfn had done this; soon Belhadra and its neighbours would be out of her control as well.

But she felt no anger at all, only a calm joy. She beckoned the maid to her.

'My dear,' she said, 'I want you to call all my servants and messengers together, and tell them that I will no longer need their services. Thank them for all their help, and send them home.'

'Me as well?' the maid gasped.

'You too, dear. You lived in Belhadra, didn't you?'

'Yes, but, my Lady – you can't give up this easily, can you?'

'Oh no, I am not giving up anything! If it were not for those three I would have stayed here for ever. I bear them no ill will. They've made me see what I must do – one great action is all that's needed to complete my work.'

'I don't understand, my Lady—'

'I have to go on a journey.' The Lady smiled.

'Can I not come with you?' Tears glistened in the maid's eyes.

'Look,' Arlenmia pointed down the street and there, to her horror, the maid saw three demons. 'They are coming with me; they are all I need. Would you still want to come?' She shook her head. 'No. Go and do my bidding this last time, and you will receive your reward in a few months' time – the whole world will!'

The maid did not wait to hear what her mistress had to say to the three silver figures, but fled back to the house.

Arlenmia turned to the demons, Siregh-Ma, Diheg-El, and Meheg-Ba, returning their sardonic smiles.

'It is not usual to summon three of the Shana together,' said Meheg-Ba.

'These are not usual times,' she answered. 'I am not afraid to summon three of you, for I can dismiss you as easily. Not that I would . . . we are old friends, are we not?'

'What do you want?' Siregh-Ma asked.

'Something was lost which must be found again, and I believe it is not beyond your abilities to delve in a volcano for something very tiny . . .'

'You speak, of course, of the Egg-Stone,' hissed Meheg-Ba.

'Of course!' Arlenmia answered. 'Would it be easier if I wrote it down?'

'No need for your amusing insults,' Meheg-Ba said. The three demons joined hands. 'We will do it – for the good of the world.' They were too subtle to show their thoughts, that Arlenmia had had a brilliant inspiration to do something which they had not even considered.

'Good. You can go now – I need some time to prepare. I will call when I'm ready to go.' She smiled. 'To Gorethria, of course.'

She returned with slow step to the now eerily transparent house.

221

Along the halls the grey figures went about their obscure tasks with, she thought, insulting disregard for all the paintings and books she had so painstakingly collected over the years in Tearn. But she felt no resentment; there was no more knowledge to be had from them.

In her room, she crushed a herbal root to make a large dose of a tranquillising drug. Having taken it, she lay on her bed to calm and ready herself.

'I must forsake all beautiful things of the Earth in pursuit of eternal beauty,' she thought. 'Material things have been useful to me, but from now on the supernatural will provide all my knowledge and purpose.' Sleep was coming to her. 'Oh Silvren, you little knew what you were starting when you told me about your world, all those years ago . . . if only you'd had the sense to share it with me! And now your beloved Ashurek and his friends are on their way to my loathsome comrade Gastada . . . I wish him joy of them.'

Just as it seemed they would fall for ever, a faint silver light glowed on the edge of their vision. Daylight. Ashurek realised that they were standing motionless on firm ground, and slowly raised his head to look about.

It seemed the Serpent-given powers had allowed their victims a respite. The grey walls had become the plain granite walls of a gorge. They were on the gravelly bank of a small stream trickling over a mica bed. A clean, cold wind blew steadily into their faces, and a few drops of drizzle fell from an overcast – but perfectly normal – sky. All was grey but for the sparks of colour that were the riders.

The horses were trembling with exhaustion and so they dismounted, looking about them, too drained even to speak. Ashurek carried Skord over his shoulder, to give Shaell a rest, and they began to walk along the gorge – in the direction in which they happened to be facing when they found themselves there.

The ground sloped upwards slightly, and the rough granite walls grew lower. The horses' hooves made a companionable crunch on the loose stones. There was something in the air – the touch of it on their skin and in their nostrils – that suggested they were much further North than the Equator. Just how far had they fallen?

They came out of the gorge, and after a scramble up a steep

scree of rock, they reached a thin, paved road curving round the side of a hill. Suddenly the nightmare pursuit by Arlenmia's forces seemed a long way behind them. With the sheer relief of being alive and in one piece, with the freshness of the air, the spirits of Estarinel and Ashurek began to lighten.

'If she meant to send us into another trap, I don't think she's succeeded,' Ashurek said. 'Perhaps her power gave out . . . or perhaps an opposing power took us from her grasp.'

'Can you be sure?' Estarinel asked. 'That we're safe, I mean?'

'Safe? No!' he laughed. 'But the air has an innocent feel to it . . .'

They were walking along the road now; above them the peak of the hill rose in a small knoll of brown earth and granite, while on the other side of the road it fell away in a steep, grassy slope to a wooded fold on their left. Beyond they could see for miles; a vast landscape in tints of misty greens, blues and greys, with the horizon blurred and melting into the sky. It seemed they were quite high, overlooking what was perhaps a vast, flat river valley. But directly ahead of them the road cut straight into a forest of dark green, gnarled trees that shadowed the road and spilled down the hill's flank. As soon as they entered the trees, they cut to the left and started down the hillside, feet crunching on the rich floor of peat and pine needles.

It was only when they had hunted down some small game, made a fire, eaten and rested, that they began to recover. Skord had regained consciousness but refused to eat, and sat apart from the others, miserable and unspeaking.

There was a calm and pleasant atmosphere about the country that took away their fear and sense of urgency. It was this that made them suspect that they were out of Belhadra, that when they had 'fallen' through the plain, they had deliberately been sent miles away from that country, though what Arlenmia had intended for them they could not guess.

They had moved to a place where there was more grass and undergrowth, so that they could graze the horses. Estarinel and Ashurek were looking over the palfrey they had 'borrowed' from Arlenmia, while Medrian added more wood to the fire, apparently uninterested. The horse was about fifteen hands high, a rich turquoise colour with a long mane and tail of glassy gold. It was extremely beautiful with delicate head and perfect, light conformation. It was a stallion, but it was very gentle and friendly.

Ashurek ran a hand down its silky, warm neck.

'In spite of its strange colour, it seems a normal horse. Let's hope it's not some sinister messenger of Arlenmia's!' Estarinel was letting it take some grass from his palm with its soft lips.

'I don't think so,' he said, stroking its fine-boned head. 'Skord! What's this horse's name?'

'She called it "Taery Jasmena",' he muttered in reply.

They went to sit by the fire, watching the darts of white and yellow flame dancing on the logs. There was a new camaraderie between them now that they had worked together to escape Arlenmia. Estarinel no longer felt awed by the idea of who Ashurek was, while the Gorethrian had completely revised his opinion of the courage and capabilities of the Forluinishman. He even seemed markedly less hostile to Medrian. Medrian herself, though still withdrawn and emotionless, was at least slightly more talkative and approachable than she had been.

The conversation inevitably turned to Arlenmia. Estarinel looked across at Skord, but he did not seem to be listening. He wished he knew what to do to ease the boy's wretchedness, and his sorrow for him was made infinitely worse by the guilt he felt.

'It's a shame we had to leave Arlenmia alive,' said Ashurek, somewhat brutally, 'but I think it will be a long time before she regains her powers in full.'

'You don't think the Glass City was damaged in any way?' Estarinel asked.

'No – I think that would only have happened if she'd died.'

Estarinel shuddered. Now that the initial relief of escape was fading, he was beginning to feel more and more troubled. He sensed Medrian looking at him, as though she knew exactly what he was thinking.

'When I think how close I came to betraying Forluin . . .' he murmured.

'You did not,' Ashurek reminded him firmly. 'Something is worrying you, isn't it?'

'Well, we may have escaped, but we have not won. I told you how she threatened me; that if I did not work for her, she could have the Serpent attack Forluin again and destroy it completely. And we left her angry enough to do her worst.'

'Likewise I am very fearful for Silvren,' Ashurek said bitterly. His anxiety was no less painful for being deeply ingrained, something he

224

had suffered day and night for months. 'But there is nothing, nothing we can do.'

'There must have been something I could have done or said!' Estarinel exclaimed, his distress made more acute by exhaustion. 'Now it's too late, and if Forluin is lost it will be my fault. My fault! The very opposite of what I set out to do.' A heavy silence followed his words, compounding his fears. They were all in desperate need of rest, but even that would not erase their anxieties. Estarinel was right to be worried. Ashurek felt there was nothing to be said.

Then Medrian spoke. She sounded very tired, like one who has just surfaced with difficulty from a deep sleep.

'There is no possibility of the Serpent attacking Forluin again.'

'What – are you sure?' Estarinel said, startled.

'Yes, I am.' In her distant way, she sounded quite adamant. 'Arlenmia could never persuade M'gulfn to do so, even if she was – in communication with it. It would not have the energy for a second attack.'

'How do you know?' Ashurek demanded.

'I just know,' she stated, apparently unaffected by the fierce intensity of his visage. She abruptly got to her feet and went over to the horses, obviously to avoid any further questioning. Ashurek decided to let her be and poked aimlessly at the fire, sending bitter whorls of smoke into the crisp air. But Estarinel stood up and followed her.

'I believe you,' he said softly. 'I don't know why, but I do. You've helped set my mind at rest – thank you.'

She busied herself checking the palfrey's feet, and said nothing.

'Medrian . . . when Arlenmia was trying to entrance me with her mirror, I saw a scene in which you had a conversation with her which I didn't understand.'

'You saw—' she straightened up and faced him. She looked very grim, as if she was fighting an inward battle which she was only winning through a supreme effort of self-will. 'It's as well you didn't understand.'

'Why did she try to kill you?' he asked, hoping she would finally communicate the cause of her unhappiness to him. 'And the horse—'

'Estarinel, will you do as I ask and stop questioning me?' she said with a hint of desperation. 'It matters – believe me.'

'If that's what you wish . . . I respect that,' he said softly. 'But you cannot hide the despair you are in, for all you try so hard.

What makes you so certain that no one can help? Can you not trust even me?' She met his eyes, and her own dark ones widened for a brief moment with tenuous hope. But then the look transformed into one of stark anger and pain, while her face became as bleak as an ice-carved mask. And she turned on him, her voice very quiet but echoing with a suppressed rage that shook him.

'Are all your race like this, or is it just you? I've watched you agonising over Skord's parents, and over Skord as if his misfortunes were entirely your fault, sympathising with Ashurek despite the terrible things he has done, even feeling sorrow for Arlenmia, hating to watch her suffer without her drug. That almost killed you, didn't it, as if nothing she did would ever be evil enough to make you truly hate her. After what happened to Forluin and all your friends, how can you possibly care about anything else? Why should you, anyway?' He stared at her, stunned. 'And you even care about me, as if – as if—' she faltered, distinct self-loathing in her voice. 'I've warned you already, but still you persist in caring about me. No one has ever – I don't understand you. No one can have that much compassion or love to spare!'

She looked down, wanting to avoid the questions in his gentle brown eyes. But she did not walk away.

'Medrian,' he said, 'you misunderstand the nature of love. Why should it have a limit of one friend, or five, or twenty? It is a blessing, something to be glad of, not to question. Yes, we are like this in Forluin. It's not a philosophy; it's just the way we are.'

She continued to gaze at nothing in particular, but her expression changed from harsh to merely cold and a little sad.

'And this is the way I am,' she said.

'I think you dislike yourself.' He took her hand and tried to warm it in his own. 'I don't know why. There is nothing unlovable about you, but I'm sure there's a very real reason for your despair . . .'

'Stop,' she told him quietly. 'I know you think you can help me, but . . . I cannot bear warmth. I can only live in the cold. Don't trust me, or confide in me . . . or give me love. I can't return it. You may be most cruelly betrayed.'

In spite of her words – or because of them – he suddenly realised how strong his feelings for her were. Some strange, dark, indefinable quality about her had drawn him since he first met her, transforming his natural compassion for any creature in pain or sorrow into an affection that went far deeper than simple friendship. Yes, he loved her, but there was no point in telling her. The realisation was painful.

'Medrian,' he said suddenly, 'don't you have a home and family to return to when the Quest is over?'

'Something to make me seem more human?' she said, her face bleak. 'Once . . . long ago . . . but there's nothing left. Still, when choice is gone and the last journey is ahead, that has a kind of comfort of its own, doesn't it?'

And she gave a smile so chilling that he almost recoiled from her. He thought of her sinister black horse, dying as she pulled a knife from her own unharmed throat. And he suddenly saw her as a fiend hurtling towards him across a void, all black, flapping shadows; a dual thing of sorrow and evil, an unwilling child of the Serpent.

But at the same time, he wished he could hold her until all the coldness and sadness had left her.

That night they mounted no watch, but all slept. The cloud cleared and two half-moons gleamed coldly down at them amid the myriad points of light. Ashurek felt he could almost see the movement of inconceivably vast, distant powers as they ebbed and flowed about the universe, heartlessly dangling the three on puppet-strings.

'For when we started upon this path to destroy the power, we instantly became its victims,' he thought. 'What if the Serpent is not only a channel for evil, but for the life-force itself? Still, I care not if the world is destroyed . . . it must die.'

He realised more strongly than ever that reaching the Blue Plane H'tebhmella was their only chance of finding the means to complete the Quest. Tomorrow they must find a river, and sail for Forluin.

Before dawn they were suddenly awoken by the sound of Skord screaming. Ashurek leapt to his feet to see a silver figure standing before the cowering boy, casting a silver aura into the black forest. He felt anger rise in him.

'Get you gone!' he shrieked at the demon, and now he had his hands on the boy's shoulders, pulling him to his feet. The demon gave Ashurek a very strange look and folded its arms.

Behind the figure, a darkness flickered, a doorway to the Dark Regions. Something seemed to float through; both Estarinel and Ashurek recognised it instantly. It was a young woman, insubstantial as a phantom, with long, dark gold hair. She stared at Ashurek and he left Skord and made to run towards her.

But he found he could not move. The demon slowly turned to Silvren and placed its hands on her shoulders. Her face fell in dismay, and both figures began to elongate into two vast, albescent shapes. They mingled into one monstrous, ghost-like form rising above the trees, while the air was torn by a black-and-blue wind which seemed filled with the chattering and droning of a million demons. Against this hellish commotion both screams and laughter were heard.

Then the shape was gone. The rift in the air's fabric was healing. Ashurek uttered a cry of torment and looked wildly about him. 'Curse them – damn them—'

Estarinel was bending over Skord who had collapsed. Trembling and white-faced himself, he said, 'That was his demon – Siregh-Ma . . . I never dreamed they were so . . .'

'Unpleasant? Frightening? Yes, and worse . . .' Ashurek was untethering Vixata. 'And they hold Silvren, for her courage to challenge M'gulfn's rule.'

The Forluinishman shuddered.

'Come on,' Ashurek said, 'we'll get no more rest in this place. Let's be on our way.'

They stamped out and scattered the fire, and Estarinel lifted the witless Skord across Shaell's saddle. Then they rode on, Ashurek leading; he cantered recklessly through the trees, head down, teeth clenched to bite back the re-awakening of bitter, bitter misery.

They travelled North for three days, cutting down through the tree-flanked hills towards the river valley. They hoped the river opened into the Western sea, so that they could find a ship and sail for Forluin. They had not seen any sign of habitation; but once they heard two horse-drawn carts passing each other on one of the thin roads through the forests, and a cheery 'Good day' called between the two. Later they saw a small band of horsemen. It seemed likely they would come upon a village or town soon.

Although they were reluctant to have any contact with unknown people, after what had happened when they went to Skord's farm, they had to find a safe place for the boy to stay. Since the last visit of Siregh-Ma, Skord had been growing weaker and weaker. He refused to eat or drink; his formerly healthy, rosy face was sallow and skull-like, with great, dark hollows round his eyes; he had a fever which would not abate, and he hardly spoke or slept, but spent the hours staring witless out of his fear-eaten eyes.

They could not abandon him to die, or to be taken by the demon. They met and followed a road, hoping it would lead them to a village of some sort.

On the fourth day they were jog-trotting down the road, which now cut through low pasturelands, when they saw an outcrop of rock ahead. As they followed the road round it, a neman jumped into their path, brandishing sword, axe, spear, and a shield emblazoned with a strange four-limbed symbol.

'Halt,' the creature cried. They reined in sharply, causing the horses to snort and stamp. The tall, bronze-skinned figure stared at them. Its eyes alighted on Ashurek and showed first fear, then curiosity, then surprise.

'You're alive!' it exclaimed to Ashurek.

'Yes,' said Ashurek sarcastically, 'it certainly looks that way.'

'Well, who are you?' the neman demanded.

'Three travellers,' Ashurek answered curtly. At this, the neman gave an explosive laugh of disbelief.

'You're mad! Travellers? You'd better come with me . . .' It beckoned offhandedly.

'Why?' Ashurek enquired.

'Because if you carry on along this road, you will be massacred in a small battle that happens to be raging less than a mile away. Either follow me or clear off back the way you came.'

Estarinel looked at Ashurek, and said, 'We have a very sick boy with us, he'll die if he isn't attended to.'

The neman looked at Skord, sighed, and rubbed its chin.

'I know,' it said. 'I'll take you to the village. Setrel will take care of you.' They were not sure what 'take care of you' meant, but they followed the neman; it didn't seem to offer them any danger.

'I can't wait to tell them this,' the neman said as they walked. 'No one travels into Excarith at the minute. Unbelievable!'

Ashurek knew Excarith was a large country North of Belhadra; they must have been transported many miles to reach it.

'Are you at war with Gorethria, then?' he asked. He felt incautious and did not much care what he said.

'Gorethria!' the neman almost laughed. 'Have you been living as hermits till now? They're all pulling out of Tearn now – the Empire's a complete mess. No offence meant, of course!'

'No offence taken,' Ashurek responded quietly.

'Well, if you were a little further East you'd be massacred as soon as show your face . . . but I must say I never thought I'd see

229

the day when I'd be happier to see a live Gorethrian than a dead one!'

'And why should that be?'

'You really don't know, do you?' said the neman curiously. 'It'll be very difficult explaining what we are at war with . . . still, we may have a practical demonstration on the way down.'

'You don't sound particularly concerned about your war,' Ashurek observed.

'Why should I? This is my job, fighting other folks' battles. I'm one of Sphraina's merry outcasts.'

They took the left track of a fork in the road as it climbed the side of a tree-cloaked hill. As soon as they entered the trees they noticed an unearthly silence within the juniper-green depths of the forest. No birds were singing. The branches joined above the road to form a leaf-patterned roof, which made the clop of the horses' hooves sound muffled on the flint track. A few grass tufts straggled down the road's centre.

In the distance a horn sounded. The neman listened intently, as if divining some message from it, then placed a hand on its sword hilt.

There was a faint noise in the trees above them.

A few minutes later, three nemen, bearing swords and axes, loped up the road towards them at a long-legged run. They stopped and saluted their comrade.

'Ho, Benra! We're under attack on both sides of this ridge, only about a mile down. Where are you going?'

'I'm taking these four to see Setrel,' replied the neman.

'What! The only way to the village is to cut straight through the battle unless you want to make a mad dash across the top of the ridge and straight through the marsh – or go down and jump the Boundary Wall,' one of the nemen said scornfully.

'I know – more fun than keeping watch on a miserable deserted road, eh?'

'Who are they?'

'I don't know and I don't really care. Setrel can sort that out. They've been very co-operative,' the neman Benra answered.

The three nemen were staring at Ashurek.

'A live Gorethrian – co-operative? Wonders will never cease,' one said. 'Perhaps we'll see you for a skin of wine later – if we survive this battle.' The bronze-skinned warriors strode down among the trees and were soon out of sight. The notes of a horn were heard, carrying a message back to the encampment. Presently the reply came, high and distant. The neman listened.

'Well,' said Ashurek, 'I'm as eager to reach this village as you are. Which do you prefer—' he addressed Medrian and Estarinel, '—the wall or the marsh?'

'Shaell can jump anything,' said Estarinel, and Medrian shrugged.

'The wall then,' said Ashurek.

'This way,' Benra said, a smile touching its long and sombre features.

It jumped a small ditch in the grass verge and started running through the trees where the hill sloped up to their left. The riders followed, finding that Benra ran so fast that they had to canter to keep up.

The first part of the hill was steep and difficult to climb, overgrown with rhododendrons with large, waxy green leaves and great white and mauve blossoms; clumps of green-fronded bracken; carpeted by a soft floor of trailing bushes, twigs, and fallen branches on a rich, dark earth. The trees were tall, rough-trunked, with arching branches and very dark leaves, but they were widely spaced.

The neman had drawn all its weapons; it went swiftly through the undergrowth, strong and lithe as a mountain cat. The horses picked a way through, jumping fallen logs and pressing through tangles of undergrowth. As they climbed, the hill began to flatten, and although it was still steep, it became easier to climb.

Still no birds sang, but now and then came a horn cry, or a faint, half-heard sound of voices raised in battle.

'The Boundary Wall,' the neman was saying, 'was built hundreds of years ago when this country was divided into two. The gateway through it is on the far side of this hill – unfortunately on the bare hillside where the battle is. As for the wall, it's falling into ruin – you may get across it if your horses are enchanted; it's safer than the marsh.'

They crossed a large, grassy clearing and then forged up through the trees again. At last they pressed their way to the peak of the ridge, but the trees and undergrowth were too thick for them to see any sign of the battle, or hear anything but faint sounds. Two nemen passed well below them, running. More horn calls were heard. They began to descend, and masses of young leaves and twigs brushed against the horses' flanks.

'Don't they have their own army in this country?' Ashurek asked.

'Oh, indeed. They're camped on the far side of the village. This is only a small battle, a preliminary raid,' Benra replied.

Presently, about half-way down the hill, they heard a scuffling some way below them and to their right. The ring of sword blows, the thud of sword dropping on shield, was carried up to them.

They began to trot down through the trees. There was a scream from below them, then silence.

'Oh no,' cursed Benra, quickening its pace. They came upon a thin, muddy track through the forest, running across their path. To the right, about a hundred yards away, it branched into two. Here Benra halted, looking up and down the path. They could see nothing unusual.

They were about to move on when a figure appeared, walking from the trees at the fork.

'We'd better run. It may not notice us,' Benra said. But the riders stared at it, fascinated.

It was a Gorethrian, Ashurek noticed with a jolt. But its clothes were so tattered and muddy they were unrecognisable, and the figure walked with a zombie-like, unfaltering gait. As it drew closer they saw with a shock that its flesh – bared in many places – was covered with great gashes and weals, which did not bleed and which seemed to give it no pain. It stared out of unseeing, unblinking eyes. And half the flesh on its face had rotted and fallen away.

'By the Worm,' gasped Ashurek, 'if I didn't see it walking I'd swear it was dead . . .'

'It *is* dead,' said Benra, preparing to fight it. 'That is our enemy.'

Ashurek seized Benra's shoulder.

'Who has done this – abused the corpses of my countrymen?' he hissed.

'Never mind – get back into the trees,' Benra said, but Ashurek had already spurred Vixata into a gallop towards the figure.

He had no great love left for his country, but the hideous sorcery which had been practised upon the Gorethrian was to him the ultimate, appalling blasphemy. A tearing scream of horror and anguish issued from his mouth as he bore down upon the thing. And as he wielded his sword, the blade shone with a leaden light, as if instilled with the hell-driven rage of its bearer.

The creature swung a mighty sabre, but Ashurek dodged; then his own blade cleaved the air and the creature's head was severed, hitting the ground with a dull thud. Vixata galloped on, a streak of dull gold, but as Ashurek pulled her round he saw with horror that the corpse still walked.

Benra faced it as it advanced and hacked off its sword arm; then Ashurek approached it from behind and with a series of violent blows to its legs and trunk, finally felled it. Estarinel and Medrian watched with horrified fascination.

'This is our problem,' Benra said. 'You can't just kill them; each one must be hacked into pieces to stop it fighting. Always go for the arms, and legs too if you have the chance.' On the ground, the mutilated corpse still jerked and writhed. Ashurek glared down at it, shaking, his eyes blazing with a baleful green fire.

'Whoever is responsible for this is going to die,' he said quietly.

14

The Village Elder

They continued down through the trees. The bracken grew more prolific, the trees younger, until it seemed the end of the wood was perhaps only half a mile further on.

There were rustles in the trees to their right. The neman blew three short blasts on its horn but there was no reply.

'They aren't our soldiers,' the neman said.

Now they could hear two or three people running towards them.

'Let me take the boy,' Benra suggested to Estarinel, and cast Skord across its shoulder. 'It'll be easier for him and for you.' As they cantered on, they caught a glimpse of three more of the corpses, just to the front and side of them, running through the trees with a fast, clockwork-like gait. One limped, for it had a foot missing; another's arm was half hanging off. Two were Gorethrian; the other was a dead nemale warrior.

The riders sent their horses into a gallop. The corpses burst from the trees in front of them. The horses swerved and darted past their swinging blades unscathed, and flew on downhill, while the corpse-soldiers sped after them like automatons.

They ran unnaturally fast; as fast, it seemed, as Vixata could gallop. Ashurek found one gaining on him; he swung his shield with a thud into its face, sending it off balance, and spurred Vixata on. Racing her fastest she managed to outrun them.

The young trees gave way to a sea of bracken which spilled onto a slope of sparse grass and shale. At the bottom of the slope was the Boundary Wall. They could not let the horses career straight down the slope and so veered left, dodging the dead warriors who seemed slow to gain a sense of their direction. They circled up the hill and saw Benra hurling itself headlong into the bracken to avoid a sword blow, then swinging its axe, hacking at the Gorethrian's legs until it toppled over. It leapt up and ran on.

'Come on! You'll have to jump straight over the wall. Look out!'

Medrian's horse squealed and leapt forward as a dead neman's sword swung but only tangled in its tail, pulling a few strands out. Medrian made the animal prop sideways, then swing down the hill at a canter. Shaell and Vixata were just ahead of her, with Benra running its fastest towards the wall.

The stony scree sloped down almost to the base of the wall, separated from it by a wide ditch. The wall itself was built of ancient, crumbling stone, completely covered in silvery lichen and soft green moss. It was close on six feet high and about ten wide, and what was on the landing side – perhaps a thorn-choked drop, or heap of tumbled rocks – they would not know until it was too late.

They collected their horses until they were cantering almost on the spot. The two dead warriors, the Gorethrian and the neman, set upon Ashurek but, with Vixata's skill, he was able to keep them at bay. She kicked, struck and lunged at them, dodging sword blows like a feather.

They saw Benra negotiate the wall – with Skord on its shoulder – as easily as a cat. Its long, well-muscled legs flexed and it leapt the ditch, found a hand-hold on the wall, and in one clean movement sprang to the top and hauled itself onto it.

'It's all right. You can bank it!' it yelled, making to climb down the far side.

The third warrior was on its feet again and lumbering down the hill, limping.

With a parting kick at the corpses, Vixata was on her way towards the wall. It seemed to grow higher and higher as she continued downhill, and Ashurek knew that when her momentum was carrying her downwards, it would be difficult to gain height in the jump. They were reaching the ditch; he made her take off and with a rush of air she made a vast leap and landed on top of the wall; gathered herself; leapt off the other side and landed on good ground well out over a second, small ditch.

'Your courage will make up for my lack of it,' Estarinel told Shaell, running a hand down his great, powerful neck. The warriors were just behind him as he cantered at the wall, then Shaell leapt, skidded slightly on the mossy top of the wall, regained balance, and made a stomach-sinking leap to the ground below.

Behind him he heard Medrian – as always more cheerful in a crisis – shout, 'In case this horse can't jump I'll close my eyes!'

A dead Gorethrian was at the palfrey's flank; twisting, she

hacked off its arm, but it would not drop back. She made the horse dodge, and upset, he began to canter, much too fast, towards the wall. And she did close her eyes, but felt him take off; and the others, in amazement, saw the palfrey, like an eagle of pearly blue-green and gold, come soaring over the wall in one great leap. The horse landed like a feather.

They all, even the neman – its kind were noted for their dislike of horses – stared at the animal in astonished admiration.

'It seems worth returning to Arlenmia to ask where we can get a few more of those beasts!' suggested Ashurek.

They continued from the wall, forded a deep stream fringed with bulrushes, and then turned and followed it along its course. It ran almost parallel to the wall for some distance; about two miles further on they saw the wide gap in the wall where once a gate had been, and now they could quite clearly hear the sounds of battle – shouts, steel ringing on steel.

'One of our many disadvantages,' said Benra, 'is that whenever one of our soldiers is killed, it automatically joins the other side.'

'But corpses don't just walk from their graves and wage war on countries,' Ashurek stated. 'Whose army is it?'

'Oh, they are the pets of a certain Northern nobleman who's decided to conquer this country – I gather re-animating corpses is one of his favourite hobbies. Setrel will tell you.'

Ashurek did not ask who the nobleman was, for he already knew, and did not wish to hear the loathed name spoken.

They followed the stream across flat, marshy meads until they came to a cart road which ran between fields and copses. At last they came to a village, with a sign planted in the road, 'Hamlet of Morthemcote, Retherny Valley'.

A few wisps of mist clung round the village. They rode down the track which now ran between two rows of cottages. Each one was a small, round building of granite, rich silvery grey and tinted with pinks and fawns. They had pointed thatched roofs, low oak doorways and small leaded windows. Many of the cottages consisted of several of the round buildings fused together. A wide grass verge ran on each side of the road, the grass bright with white and yellow flowers. The road bent slightly to the right, and to the left, beyond the village, were grey wooded hills.

The village was quiet, the silence broken often by birdsong, a dog barking, a cow lowing; some children shouting; a cart rattling down the road out of their sight.

At last Benra led them to a cottage which had five of the round stone sections fused together, a moss of age crusting the delicately tinted granite walls. A spiral of smoke floated from a chimney. The neman motioned them to dismount and knocked at the plain oak door. On it was a small sign saying, 'The House of Setrel; Village Elder by appointment to the Long Table at Mardrathern'.

The door opened and a rosy-faced girl of about fourteen looked out. She was wearing a long, sleeveless dress of purple velvet with a belt of heavy silver, and a silver circlet set on her long, fine brown hair.

'Is your father in?' the neman asked.

'Yes, come in, Benra,' she said, smiling.

The interior of the cottage was a round room with floor of beaten earth, fine oak furniture, and a stone fireplace opposite the door; three more doors led into further rooms.

By the fireplace sat a boy of twelve, very similar to his sister, whittling a piece of wood. And poring over many parchment documents at a table was Setrel himself, the village Elder. He stood up as the five entered.

'Greetings!' he said. He was not a tall man, but he was somehow imposing. His face was bony and noble and his black hair and beard were streaked with grey. He was dressed in a plain black robe. 'What's this, have you found some strangers?'

The nemale warrior saluted him.

'Sorry to disturb you, sir, but I detained them up on the road, heading straight for the battle area. I guided them round the danger . . . more or less. They've got a very sick boy with them, so I thought I'd better bring them to you. Also, I thought you'd like to check their identity.'

'Yes, thank you, Benra, you've done well. Have they got horses?'

'Yes, sir.'

'Very well—' he motioned the two children to the door and both rushed outside eagerly. 'Atrel and Seytra will look after the animals. Now will you get back up to the battle, Benra, and bring me a full report?'

The neman grinned, saluted, and strode out.

'Now . . . bring the lad through here.' Setrel led them through one of the doors into a round bedroom and Ashurek laid Skord on the bed.

The boy lay on his back, staring at the ceiling, breathing very fast. His skin was like wax and felt cold and moist to the touch.

237

Setrel took Skord's chin in his fingers, turning the boy's head from side to side while looking intently into his eyes.

'I don't know who you are, or what you're doing wandering about in Excarith,' said Setrel as he examined the boy. 'I thought we'd warned everyone away . . .' He struck Estarinel as a kindly and wise man who was distracted by many troubles.

'We are three travellers on a personal errand,' Ashurek began. 'We were transported to this country by supernatural means from Belhadra, and found ourselves in a rocky gorge, not knowing where we were. We know nothing of your war, except what Benra told us.'

'Supernatural means?' said Setrel, pausing in his examination and looking hard at Ashurek.

'I am only telling you this much about us because we need your help,' the Gorethrian said.

'It seems to me you haven't told me anything at all,' Setrel said shortly.

'More than you realise. But I think there can be trust between us, because your terrible enemy is also mine: Gastada.'

At this Setrel looked with sober surprise round the faces of the three.

'I wonder who you are,' he said as if to himself. 'What is the help you need?'

'A safe place for the boy to stay, so we may continue our journey – aboard a ship if possible.'

'The boy will be safe enough here – but I cannot see what is wrong with him. He seems to be in deep shock.'

Estarinel explained as best he could what had happened to Skord.

'I think he's killing himself through terror,' the Forluinishman finished. 'He's lost the will to live.'

'A wasting disease,' Setrel agreed, looking down at the pallid, blank-eyed youth. 'I will do what I can; first I'll give him a herbal mixture to make him sleep. He needs rest, and then food. I hope you'll stay with us for supper, so that we may talk . . .'

The village Elder's two rosy-faced children had fed and settled the horses, and gone to bed. Darkness was falling as his wife Ayla, a stout, cheerful woman with curly brown hair, made them a meal of meat stew with bread. They had heard Setrel talking to her outside, as she returned from an errand.

'We have guests – there is a Gorethrian inside.' His wife's

response was a startled, 'Oh!' but he continued, 'However, don't fear them – I believe them to be friends, they may help us. And listen – they said they came up out of the gorge.'

To this Ayla had replied laughingly, 'Oh, you and that wretched poem!'

Now, as they sat round the wooden table, Estarinel noticed that Medrian was eating very little, and she had been silent all evening. She listened with head bowed as Setrel spoke to them.

'I know you are not spies, if you had wondered, because our enemy is of a quite different nature. As you said, it is Gastada we are fighting. We've heard many stories over the years of the terrible things he has done in his own country, but only in the past year has he launched this attack against us.'

He stroked his long, silky beard and gazed round at them, his eyes reflecting sparks of light from the fire. The room, in semi-darkness, was very warm and homely, a complete and welcome contrast to the cold, metallic beauty of Arlenmia's house.

'Countries invade other countries,' Setrel continued. 'It is no rare thing. But Gastada, the Duke of Guldarktal, is no conventional enemy. His army is one of walking corpses, as you saw! They say he summons demons for his power . . . and in battle, any soldier of ours that dies immediately joins his dead army; can you see what that means?'

'It means his army is invincible,' said Ashurek.

'Yes,' Setrel shuddered. 'And he is just playing with us. He sent a message outlining his intention to invade Excarith. What cool arrogance! Well, we haven't much of an army, so the Long Table decided we should employ nemen mercenaries. They are good, but we haven't yet won a battle. There's been skirmish after skirmish, and each one, like today's, has been ended only by the Dead Army withdrawing! You understand,' his face was calm but his hands gripped the chair arms whitely, 'he can finish us whenever he chooses.

'We are an optimistic people – stoical, you might say. But we can see no way out of this horror. Gastada said he would send three black crows over as a sign when the final battle is nigh – so, we wait for the sign. We laugh, and dance, and polish our weapons, and live our normal lives – and wait for our doom.'

'Our optimism is wearing thin,' Ayla put in. 'I fear most for the children. But my husband, bless him, still thinks a miracle will save us.'

Setrel laughed.

'It's true, if foolish. But I don't let such speculation interfere with the practical work that must be done.'

'So,' Ashurek said after a pause, 'Gastada will graciously let you know when he decides to destroy you – much in character.'

'You speak as if you know him.'

'I do. He held me prisoner in his castle only a few years since.'

'You are Prince Ashurek of Gorethria . . . are you not?' Setrel said, his eyes narrowed in speculation.

'Your guess is correct,' the Prince replied evenly.

'By the gods . . . of all the strange things that have happened, this is the most unbelievable. You, appearing on my very doorstep! You must know that you have become a legend of the worst kind in Tearn. However, I hold that the reality behind any myth is always something quite unexpected, so I am not about to sit in judgment on you or flee for my life.'

'I am gratified,' said Ashurek with a wry grin.

'Tell me, how did you escape from Gastada? If we could only find some vulnerability, some weakness in him—'

'He has none, as far as I know. As you say, demons and fell creatures of the Serpent provide his power. I escaped only by a sorcerous raid made on the place.' He explained Silvren's bright enchanted rescue of him, but was unprepared for Setrel's reaction to the account.

The man leapt to his feet, eyes shining and his black robe flapping.

'It's true then! Ayla – did you hear?' Estarinel and Medrian stared at him, but his wife just smiled and nodded in her down-to-earth way. 'Sorcery exists! I knew! All my life – every moment of my spare time has been devoted to proving that there is a power other than the Serpent in the world. There is magic!'

'Setrel, don't raise your hopes. Silvren was a sorceress, the world's first and its only one. Her power was foreign to this world, and to use it was great pain to her. And now the Serpent's creatures have imprisoned her, afraid of her magic,' Ashurek said with acute sadness. 'Perhaps you have made a few small spells work.'

'Yes I have, in my workshop – that's just it,' Setrel said with slightly less enthusiasm.

'But there can be no more sorcery on this Earth unless the Serpent should perish – until then demon-summoning is the only force, and no one in his right mind would resort to that.'

Setrel sat down and said, 'But my discoveries were not wrong. Sorcery can exist – if the Serpent were to die.'

'If the Serpent were to die, Gastada would trouble you no longer either. And talking of that, in spite of your own problems, we would appreciate assistance in continuing our journey . . .'

Setrel looked intently at the three. And he saw not, as others had, three very unlikely travelling companions, but three people of single-minded, sound purpose. Excitement and hope glowed warmly within him, though his noble, calm face did not betray it. Perhaps there was a way from the path of blood and death and darkness that threatened them.

He took a long draught of beer and stood up to replenish the fire with wood.

'Well, as supper is finished, let us go in and see how the boy is.'

In the bedroom the Elder woke Skord very gently. He came round slowly, seeming dazed. Estarinel propped him up and Setrel fed him a bowl of broth mixed with healing herbs. To their surprise he drank it all without protest. It must have been the first time he had eaten in over a week. He coughed a little, and after a few minutes fell asleep again, breathing slowly now. For the first time in days he seemed to be at peace. They stood about the oak bed, a single candle casting their shadows on the wall of the circular room.

'We'll let him sleep until he wakes of his own accord,' Setrel said. 'As I said, he'll be safe here for now – though what will happen with the war, I don't know.'

'Ashurek,' said Estarinel, 'isn't there something we should tell Setrel?'

'Tell him then,' the Gorethrian replied shortly.

'It's that—' he began hesitantly. 'Skord's demon can appear to him at any time. I don't think it's fair that you should have such a thing in your house . . .'

But Setrel smiled at this.

'Ah, there you are wrong. No demon will cross my threshold. You poured scorn, Ashurek, upon my few small spells, but I have taught myself enough to keep a demon at bay.'

'I do not scorn the power. I know it could be strong. But nothing can come of it until the path is cleared.'

'Do you believe in fate – precognition?' the village Elder asked suddenly. 'Follow me.'

He led the three into the central room of the cottage, his

workshop. There was a fireplace, but no windows; it was an almost sinister place, with vast experiments set up on two long tables, and papers and scrolls and great books scattered everywhere.

'There is so much knowledge to be had of this world,' Setrel began. 'I believe everything that is to be known has been written down – history, everything about the Planes and their inhabitants, even all that is known of the Serpent – everything. Yet the ignorance of people amazes me. They know nothing, only superstition and hearsay. They never bother to search for knowledge, or read. Many do not even believe the Serpent exists – I did not myself, thinking it only a symbol of evil that was used as a scapegoat for inexcusable acts.

'But, many years ago now, I visited Eldor. He taught me that not only must I learn all I can from books, but that I must make discoveries of my own – so all my spare time is spent researching, and everything I find out, or think I've found out, I write down.'

'How can you do it all?' Medrian said, her first words that evening. 'Learn and discover everything, and fight a war at the same time?'

'Because I believe in fate,' the man answered with a smile. 'Everything falls into place. And my theory is proved by your arrival here – I believe you three are part of the greatest, vastest design the Earth has seen since its creation.'

Estarinel shook his head in denial of this awful thought, but Setrel continued, eyes glittering with an anxious enthusiasm.

'Look – I am going to show you a prophecy. Think me an old fool if you will—' he was rummaging now among piles of books on table and floor. At last he found the one he sought; it was handwritten and hand-bound in brown leather, worn with much use. He opened it at a certain page and set it on the table before them, so they could read the sprawling calligraphy:

> When the three come from the gorge
> Respite from evil shall there be;
> The dead shall not walk in torment
> But find peace in the cold ground.
> Darkness for darkness shall be bargained
> And a half-year's light issue therefrom.
> They shall come from the gorge
> And by dark birds be taken.

'Who wrote it?' Ashurek asked.

242

'My grandfather,' Setrel replied. 'He was a mystic, and a poet. His family thought he was half-mad, though we loved him dearly. But this poem of his has always preyed on my mind, ever since I was a child, and especially since our present troubles began.'

'What do you think it means?' Estarinel asked, with the sinking feeling that it was true.

'Well, you say you came from a gorge . . . and though there were four of you, I don't believe Skord is truly one of your party. And corpses do walk about, bringing us evil. I think the poem is saying that you can find a way to help us.' He stroked his long beard, looking at the faces of the three.

'But what about the rest of it – what's the "half-year's light"?' Estarinel said. Medrian answered, her voice cold and quiet.

'It means that if we do save Excarith from Gastada, there is still only six months left before the Serpent has full power over Earth.' Setrel himself looked shocked at this.

'I, ah – er, never followed the line about the dark birds, either . . .'

Medrian was silent.

'Setrel, do not delude yourself,' Ashurek said, the firelight catching green glints in his eyes. 'It's only a poem. A miracle will not save you; only your own bravery can. We cannot stay to help, we have to leave as soon as possible, for our journey becomes ever more urgent.'

Setrel sighed and sat down, his face lined with worry and premature age.

'I have to go to the Long Table at Mardrathern tomorrow. I am supposed to report everything, but I won't mention you . . . oh Ashurek, what's to be done? You know that the Dead Army consists in the main of Gorethrians, killed in the battles across in E'Sel-Hadra.' He drew a weary breath. 'It was a terrible thing you did when you invaded Tearn – terrible. How are you ever going to make amends?'

Someone else had once said that to Ashurek, five years before, and he could not forget the tragedy that had preceded the words. It had been in Drish, that forest-covered country on Tearn's East coast. The Gorethrian army had invaded from Elegar and from the sea, pouring over the hills in their bronze and black and gold hordes, eyes burning like emeralds and teeth gleaming in cool smiles as they cut down the Drishian soldiers before them. Led by Ashurek, they seemed infected by the electric force that moved him.

So they came down through Drish, taking its only city, the City of the Eleven Spires, as it was named. It did have eleven spires which gleamed pale gold and white in the sun, and it was beautiful, as if the Drishians had put all their art and imagination into building this one city.

And now Gorethrians walked its streets, and the hillside below was infested with their bizarre hide tents, like many poisonous beetles lying in wait.

The Drishian army, with its tall, swarthy soldiers, had withdrawn. But they were waiting, Ashurek knew, and there would be at least one more battle to subdue them.

He sat in his tent, writing swiftly upon parchment. A lamp shone with hazy luminescence upon the rugs and furs which, as always, were provided for the Commander.

He felt no pleasure or pride in the conquest; but around his neck, in a small leather pouch on a chain, hung a tiny blue stone. This motivated him, so that he could form plans and perfect strategies without thinking; any attempt to resist the Egg-Stone's whims caused him agony.

He finished the letter and rolled it up, sealing it with wax. He handed it to the thin Gorethrian at his side, saying, 'Get a messenger to deliver this up to Battalion XII in Elegar. It just tells the present situation . . .' General Karadrek, his second-in-command, obeyed the order. When he returned, there was a look of irritated amusement on his thin, hawk-like face.

'Sir, there's a Drishian outside. He says he wants to speak to you. Shall I have him killed?' Karadrek asked.

'No,' said Ashurek, not even looking up. 'Send him in.'

The man entered. He was tall, stockily built, with tangled brown hair and beard. His face was weather-darkened, and he wore a knee-length brown tunic belted at the waist, and sandals laced up his shins. He seemed very nervous but his head was held high.

'Sir—' he began, but the General pushed him to his knees.

'Address the High Commander as Your Highness,' Karadrek said softly.

'Your Highness,' the man tried again. 'I come to throw myself upon your mercy.'

Ashurek looked hard at him.

'I have little. What do you want?'

'There – there will be a battle soon. We most humbly request that all children, with their mothers, and all those lame and crippled may seek refuge over the hills in Dasheb.'

'Very well. I have been called child-slayer, but it is not true. Be ready to move your refugees out at dawn, and come to me with their numbers and details,' Ashurek answered without hesitating.

'My thanks, Your Highness,' the man gasped in relief. He had expected to be dead by now; certainly he had not expected the request to be granted. The soldier led him out and sent him back to his own camp.

Ashurek continued looking over maps. But at his shoulder the thin General cleared his throat and said in a tone of soft amusement, 'Forgive me, sir, but you obviously do not know your Drishian history.'

'Why, what of it, Karadrek?'

'Three centuries ago, Drish was invaded by Elegar. They made a similar request, and it was agreed that all the sick and crippled should go into Dasheb. The next morning, every single Drishian had maimed or injured himself, and every single one of the cowards limped over the hills into Dasheb.

'Elegar was left with a deserted country, made complete fools. So they dithered a while, then followed the Drishians, and were massacred by a large force mustered in Dasheb. For Dasheb, as you should know, has always been Drish's ally.'

'You talk like a fool, Karadrek. They'll not dishonour the agreement,' was all Ashurek had to say. The General looked sourly at his Commander, then stooped under the tent flap, and left.

Later, in the night, he returned. Ashurek was sleeping soundly, for Karadrek had made sure something had been put in his wine. Trembling only slightly, he reached down to Ashurek's neck and felt for the tiny leather pouch on its chain.

Loosening the top of the pouch, he peeped inside and saw the little blue stone, egg-shaped, smooth and gleaming. It felt almost gelatinous – and then he felt its power.

His veins were filled with molten lead and a spasm shook his body. His head dropped down to rest on Ashurek's chest, while one arm stretched out rigid into the air behind him, the flesh bleached to snow in the lamplight.

'How can he carry this thing?' he thought. And as he knelt there, shaken with horror, he forgot the words he was going to say. But in spite of this, as if drawn by the rhythm of Ashurek's heartbeats, a demon appeared.

Meheg-Ba stood smiling down on the sleeping Prince, the second figure crouched over him like a vampire.

'Karadrek,' it said. 'You called me, through the power of the Egg-Stone and in Meshurek's name. A clever move, as it means I cannot possess you. What do you want?'

'I do this for Meshurek,' he gasped, paralysed in the position. 'I fear Ashurek will make a fool of himself and of the Gorethrian army.' He explained the agreement with the Drishian.

'I see,' said Meheg-Ba, uttering a hissing laugh. 'Then let us ensure that only Ashurek is made a fool of, eh?'

Then Karadrek shakily stood up, and he and the silver demon went into the Drishian camp and wreaked their terrible work.

The Drishian man was brought before Ashurek in the city's shining main street the next day. He stood as proudly as before, but he rested on crutches and his face was drawn with pain, and one foot had been replaced by a bandaged, bloody stump.

'Your Highness, all the Drishians are lame, or crippled, or blinded.'

Ashurek heard Karadrek, at his side, draw in a soft, smug breath. Anger flowed through him.

'What miserable cowards you have proved yourselves – to betray an agreement and maim yourselves sooner than fight? Was not a simple surrender easy enough, or would you have Dasheb do your fighting for you? Get you all gone over the hills – the wretched cowardice of Drish won't be forgotten.' He made to turn away, but the man stopped him.

'Wait, Your Highness – we did not betray the agreement, and we did not maim ourselves.' Red tears of anger and sorrow flowed from his eyes as he spoke. 'A demon came among us – there was nothing we could do – a demon and that man there—' he pointed a shaking hand at Karadrek. The General was quick with a convincing denial, but not quick enough, for Ashurek had glimpsed the brief unguarded guilt on the thin face of his second-in-command.

'Get back to the camp,' Ashurek said to the Drishian.

'Yes, Your Highness, and we will not leave, for there can be no battle now. But how – how are you ever going to make amends for Gorethria's evil work?' He turned and limped away.

'Well, I did warn you,' Karadrek said.

But Ashurek summoned two soldiers and said, 'General Karadrek is under arrest. Have him taken to my tent.'

'Prince Ashurek, I don't understand you,' Karadrek said, smiling although he was now chained by one wrist to the central tentpole. 'It was my responsibility, I now admit it, but I was only trying to save you from making Gorethria look foolish.'

'So Gorethria may look evil, bloodthirsty, cruel, anything but foolish?' Ashurek said, fury smouldering in his eyes.

'Sir, I think you are becoming handicapped by compassion. I was doing the best thing—'

'Compassion, eh? So pity has become such a dangerous thing that you must meddle, summon a demon to remove the risk? Of all the appalling things the Egg-Stone has caused, this maiming and torture of people has got to be the worst. By the Serpent, Karadrek, I'll show you compassion.'

Horrified, Karadrek watched as his Commander picked a sword from the weapon rack.

'Sir – I only did what the demon told me to—'

'I know, I know. And I know the grudge you bear me for not stealing the throne from Meshurek. How shall I maim you, Karadrek? How do you maim a power-seeker? Shall it be your foot, like the Drishian . . .' he slashed at the General's ankle, and he danced like a monkey around the tentpole. 'Or your eyes . . . or your tongue . . .' the blade danced dangerously close to his face, and a sweat of fear ran off his forehead.

'None of those. I'll set you free.' Karadrek wilted with relief, and then the sword came down and severed his chained hand.

'It has got to stop,' Ashurek told himself tormentedly, alone in the tent. The Egg-Stone was before him on the table; and then he found himself pounding it with the flat of his sword, again and again and again, crushing it to powder.

But when he stopped it still lay there, seeming to mock him. Groaning, he replaced it in its pouch.

'It has got to stop. It will stop, now,' he thought. 'The senseless, bestial cruelty of the Serpent.'

And the invasion of Drish was Ashurek's last act perpetrated for the Empire, because the next day he left the encampment, and the events which culminated in the murder of his sister and his flight to Tearn took place. But worse was still to come.

He had left Karadrek under arrest, but with the demon's help he escaped and took command of the battalion. And then, in one of Gorethria's most notorious and despised acts, he had the crippled Drishians slaughtered.

Ashurek would have sought revenge; but after this Karadrek disappeared. Some said the demon had taken him, others that even his own men thought he was mad, and had murdered him.

'How can I make amends?' Ashurek thought to himself. It was the following day, and he was leaning on the paddock fence behind Setrel's cottage, watching Estarinel giving Atrel a ride on Shaell. Medrian had wandered off alone, more morose than ever. 'Gorethria should burn, be swallowed into hell . . .' At least the Empire was weakening, for the royal family had disintegrated, and there was a struggle for leadership. But Ashurek was no longer concerned with what happened to his country. Now his only purpose was to fulfil Silvren's Quest and slay that scourge of the world – the Worm M'gulfn. 'But perhaps I've already done too much on its behalf . . . I brought the Egg-Stone into the world, and banished the Earth's hope – Miril. Perhaps it's too late, because of what I've done . . .'

He felt a gentle tugging at his sleeve, and roused himself from his thoughts to see Setrel's daughter, Seytra, looking shyly up at him.

'Is it true,' she said, 'are you really Prince Ashurek?'

'Yes I am,' he replied. 'And do you spend much time listening at doors when you should be asleep?'

She lowered her head, cheeks reddening.

'I heard everything you and my father said. It's all right, we know all about the war anyway. We learnt about Gorethria at school. Is the Empire really like they said, with lots of mysterious countries, and people with blue and black skins, and strange animals?'

'Yes,' he answered gravely. 'It is a weird and colourful continent, far more so than Tearn.'

'And what about the fierce barbaric warriors bravely struggling against the dark Gorethrian forces?' She swallowed. 'That's what the history book said anyway. I think Tearnians are pathetic, compared to that.'

'Seytra, Tearnians are not "pathetic", as you say, only different.

There was fighting all the time in the Empire, but there was nothing romantic or exciting in it – just senseless bloodshed. Do you understand?'

'I don't know,' she said hesitantly. 'You're different to how I expected . . .'

'What did you expect?'

'Well,' Seytra was almost whispering now. 'They made you sound like a sort of – invincible monster. But you seem – er – more heroic.'

'Perhaps I seem as you want me to seem,' Ashurek said, but she did not really understand what he meant.

'I heard all about demons, and sorcery, and that you loved a golden-haired sorceress—' she glanced up at him, eyes shining. 'I want to be a sorceress too, but – I'm afraid I'll never be able to. Can I tell you something that I've never told anyone?'

'Yes,' Ashurek sighed.

'Well, when my parents are there, my brother and I dance and sing and pretend nothing is happening. But I keep having nightmares – corpses walk down into the village and kill my parents and us, and then we all go walking, killing other people—' she started to tremble, struggling not to cry. 'I'm frightened. Please, can't you help us?'

The plea burst from her, and her eyes were a well of hope and desperation. Sadly he placed a hand on her thin shoulder.

'Seytra, I don't think anything can be done.'

'Everyone here seems so helpless, but you seem stronger. Oh please, there must be something you can do?'

Yes, there must be something, Ashurek thought. He said, 'Look, don't worry. Go across and talk to Estarinel, you'll find him a more cheery companion than me.'

'All right,' she said, hanging her head. But she was still determined to make a show of bravery. 'My brother rides like a sack of turnips. I'll show him.'

Later that day, Setrel returned from his Long Table council, seeming depressed. At the meeting had been army leaders and officials from all over the country – the people who formed Excarith's government.

'We haven't got long,' he said to the three and his wife. 'They've received another message in Mardrathern – that's our capital, you know. It said, "Expect the crows soon. When you see them, you

249

will have two days to prepare. Fight or surrender or hide, it will make no difference. You will all be slain, and you will all become my slaves." '

Ayla gave a gasp and Setrel said, 'Sorry, my dear,' as if it was his own fault. 'They've only been able to get twenty more nemen soldiers. Twenty! They've heard what's happening here and won't come . . .'

'Come and have some food. We'll need the strength,' Ayla said with comforting, if somewhat banal, practicality.

'Yes, and afterwards,' Setrel said, 'I would like the three of you to ride down to the river with me. There's something I wish to show you.'

After eating they rode through some pleasant country. The sun threw down cloud-softened shafts of light, and the trees covered the hills in a green and gold mist. They rode through the encampment of the country's own army; a vast maze of tents of hide and canvas. The air was filled with the bitter smoke and flying carbon particles of many fires; the sound of voices, shouting and laughing, the clangour of a steel-smith at work. The only animals were pack-horses; they did not use horses in battle.

On the look-out peak of the encampment, they could see for miles Northwards. The landscape was streaked with layers of mist, touched with lilac, blue and rose from the sun. The river that curled across the valley floor was a still, shining grey like mercury.

They continued the ride down into the valley, and about two hours after setting out they came to a cluster of cottages and inns that was a small port. There was no harbour. The natural flat bank of the river served well enough for a quay, for there was not much river traffic except for a small fishing trade.

Setrel reined in his chestnut roan cob at the water's edge.

'You told me that you needed to reach Forluin. This river leads out into the Western Ocean, and it is a broad and good waterway.'

He led them at a brisk canter round a bend in the river, to a small bay where two fishing boats and a ship were moored in front of a shipyard that was set back on the bank.

'See that little ship?' They looked. It was a beautiful vessel indeed, larger than *The Star of Filmoriel*, trim and light and strongly built, and richly gilded in designs of red, gold, and blue. 'If you can find a way, any way, to help us, she is yours, and a crew to sail her, and anything else you ask. I'm afraid this may sound like a bribe, but I mean to show you that you will be repaid. And if the prophesy is hollow, well . . . you might as well take the ship anyway, who am I to deny you that?' Setrel sighed, sounding deeply sad. 'The odds are against us, but we will not surrender. With our own army and the army of nemen we'll stand till the last of us is felled.'

Ashurek stared at the ship as if looking straight through it. Then he looked round at the Elder.

'I know Gastada and I know the Shana, and there is one plan only which may defeat your enemy. It is something that I swore I would never do again; but necromancy is the only force of this Earth by which we may achieve impossible things.' Setrel felt his own optimistic bravery turning to cold fear as Ashurek went on. 'It is a dark and terrible plan, but I will do it so that my dead countrymen may lie in peace, and not walk down and murder your children in their beds.'

He spoke shortly, as if bitterly regretting what he said, and when he finished he did not look at them but turned his eyes to the broken grey-and-cream sky.

As he watched, three great black crows sailed over against the clouds.

15

'I can see no escape'

Skord was sitting up in bed the next morning, his face very drawn and pale. Thanks to Setrel's care his wits had returned, although he was by no means himself yet.

'Are you feeling better?' Estarinel asked as he entered the circular bedroom.

'Yes, thank you,' Skord responded automatically. Then he frowned. 'Why – why did you save me after all the harm I've done you? You should have left me to die.'

'Nonsense,' he replied, smiling in an attempt to cheer the boy. 'You're dispirited, I know, but rest and food can work wonders.'

'A girl comes to talk to me – what is her name, Seytra? She reminds me of my sister. She would have been like that, if she'd grown up . . . I wonder where she is? And my parents . . . my father had the Plague – my fault – no, his fault – he should have died bravely in battle . . . but he did, didn't he? And my mother . . . I deserted her. Left her alone at the farm. Oh, I must go back – I must go back now, she'll kill herself!' The boy's eyes were full of confusion and fear, and Estarinel realised that the memories of his lives in Drish and Belhadra were hopelessly muddled.

'No, Skord, calm down,' he said, pushing the boy back against the pillows. 'It's all right . . .' but he knew nothing was all right, and anything that sounded comforting would be a lie.

'There was a girl I was betrothed to . . . we were to be married when we were twenty-one – what happened to her? Ye gods – I killed her! You saw me – you watched, you didn't try to stop me!' Skord's face hung with horror and he leaned back, squeezing his eyes shut. 'I've lived two separate lives and now I can't tell them apart – I don't know who I am,' he added weakly.

Estarinel could almost have wept to see him. It had been easy to despise the boy when he had been the arrogant and callous

252

messenger of the Serpent. Now Estarinel felt he had transformed him into its tragic victim.

'You must not blame yourself,' Setrel had said the night before when he had explained Skord's troubles in more depth. 'Perhaps Skord can never come to terms with his past – but without his memory he was no better off. The price of his freedom from pain was to be without conscience . . . forever trying to take revenge for a wrong he could not remember and did not understand. Perhaps, in the end, you will have helped him.'

At this, Ashurek had suddenly stood up and walked out of the room. Estarinel had stared after him, then remembered Gorethria's involvement in Drish. He had been so preoccupied that he had, unbelievably, put it completely from his mind.

'Ashurek feels a far deeper guilt than you,' Setrel had continued quietly. 'Yet I sense that he won't even admit it to himself. He thinks he has no conscience. But I believe he has a very high sense of responsibility, so acute that it torments him continually . . .'

Now, sitting with Skord, Estarinel reflected that the boy's best chance would be to stay with Setrel. Surely the Elder's gentle and wise counsel would eventually untangle his diverse miseries – if only Gastada did not win the war.

'Listen, Skord,' he said, 'you've been very ill, and you're bound to feel confused. But you're alive and here now, with an opportunity to start a new life. Are you going to use it?'

'What's the point? That thing waits outside to take me . . . and if she . . . oh, I've forgotten her name. Arlenmia – if she has her way, the Serpent will rule everything. Oh, I don't want to remember who I am – it's unbearable.' But after a minute he reopened his eyes and said, 'That's better – that's the best. When I was in the forests with all my friends, racing, climbing trees . . .'

Estarinel sighed to himself. Perhaps Skord could find a way to cope, by filtering out only good memories, but would he ever be really well again?

Ashurek entered and looked at Skord and Estarinel.

'Here's a cheerful company!' he said. 'We'll be leaving tomorrow, after the start of the battle, to carry out the insane scheme. It has to be done in a dark place, well away from human habitation.'

'I haven't got to come with you, have I?' Skord said, his eyes flying open.

'I'm afraid you have, lad,' Ashurek answered gently.

'I can't! I won't set foot outside the door,' he protested, eyes full of fear. 'It's waiting for me out there—'

'Perhaps it is. But it is part of the plan to save both this country and you, so if you won't come we'll tie you up and drag you out,' Ashurek said, a dangerous light in his eyes.

'Ashurek, can't you see how frightened he is? Let him be – he's suffered enough,' Estarinel said.

'I should have stayed with Arlenmia,' Skord shuddered. 'I betrayed her to you . . . I didn't care what I was doing. I loved her, though I always behaved as though I loathed her. I'd follow her anywhere if she only asked me . . . Everything I love I behave as though I hate – why do I destroy everything I love?'

Estarinel put his arm round the boy's thin shoulders and shook him gently.

'Listen, you're destroying yourself with self-pity. Things are bad for all of us – try to find some courage.'

'I daren't leave the cottage,' was all Skord would say.

That afternoon, to their surprise, the entire village launched itself into a festivity, as if there were to be no dreadful battle the next day.

'It's just tradition,' Setrel informed them. 'Whenever something bad happens we dance and sing, so it can always be said we faced our fate in joy, not sorrow.'

The sun touched the delicate grey tints of the village and glowed behind the dancing village maidens. Seytra stood out among them, a moth of white and silver. There was a large throng around the village green; women in long, full-skirted tunics of wine, grey, crimson or cream velvet, with neck and arm ornaments of silver; men in war gear of leather and bronze; village officials in robes of state. Children shouted and sang. The festivities lasted into dark, when fires were lit and whole oxen roasted.

The next day the preparation for the coming battle was in full swing, all festivity forgotten. Ashurek had outlined his plan to Medrian and Estarinel, and although they all had misgivings about it, it seemed the only course of action that might work.

The fighting did not begin that afternoon, as they had expected, but at dawn the next morning. The waiting, as Gastada must have known, increased their tension and fear one hundredfold. The three saw that beneath the armoury of calm stoicism, the people of Excarith were in deep terror of the darkness they could see descending upon them.

For Ashurek's plan to be effective the three could not set off until the Dead Army came forth. The night seemed endless, full of movement and voices as soldiers prepared anxiously to fight. Medrian, Estarinel and Ashurek caparisoned themselves as for war, and Setrel made them gifts of leather shields and breastplates, and heavy axes. He also gave them a glass phial filled with a pale gold powder.

'This was one of my most important discoveries,' the noble-faced Elder told them. 'A powder that can hold some sorcerous energies within it. If in peril you scatter it about you, and it will repel evil creatures. This is how I have protected the cottage against Skord's demon.'

'Our thanks, Setrel,' Ashurek said. 'And if your cottage is so protected, your wife and children should remain inside, and lock and bar the doors.'

'Oh no,' Seytra broke in. 'We can't do that. We're all going up to the army camp, to help the wounded men.'

'She's right, we have to do what we can, not cower inside,' Ayla said with a smile.

Skord appeared, also dressed and armed, looking very white.

'You won't have to tie me up and drag me after all,' he said. 'I have rallied. Are you surprised?' There was a hint of his old mockery in the words, but not in the tone of his voice which was flat and characterless.

'No, very pleased,' said Estarinel. 'Setrel has kindly said he'll lend you a cob to ride out with us.'

Skord did not ask where they were going. Perhaps wisely, he preferred not to know.

Estarinel must have checked Shaell over ten times, feeling down the strong, sinewy legs of the stallion, lifting his feet, checking girth and buckles over and over again. Ashurek seemed filled with an impatient fiery energy, though Medrian was as emotionless as ever.

At last, as a silver net of light broke over the village, Setrel came to them and said, 'The Dead Army is advancing. Are you ready?'

They took their leave of Ayla and the two children who watched them ride away with quiet courage in their faces. Seytra held her younger brother's hand, inwardly hoping that Ashurek had taken note of her plea.

Setrel rode with them to the army encampment. As they trotted between the smoking embers of camp fires on one side and tents on the other, they saw a wounded soldier being carried to a tent.

255

'When the battle is over,' he was sobbing, 'we have to go out and hack all the dead to pieces – hack our dead friends and brothers to pieces to stop them standing up and fighting the next day . . .' he was carried out of sight under the tent flap.

'I'll leave you here,' Setrel said. 'I have much business to attend to. I must thank you for coming to me and for agreeing to help, and apologise for involving you in our sad affairs.' He pulled at his long, silky beard. 'I wish you every success in your mission. Of course, I hope to see you again tonight, and we will give Skord a home while you continue your journey. And I must thank you for allowing me to record the details of your Quest.' The previous day, they had told him who they were, and all that had befallen them. 'Though it is not complete, it means the world shall remember what truly happened, and not create foolish myths. Yesterday I buried the document, and all my other books, so that they won't be destroyed by Gastada. Tonight I hope I'll be able to unearth my own books, but your record shall remain secret, until the Quest is over, for good or ill.'

His face was grave, but a smile sparkled in his grey eyes. 'Again, my warmest thanks, and fare you well.'

They all shook hands with him and parted, saluting.

At the lookout peak, the four riders studied the vast, flat, softly-coloured valley. They looked at the river Retherny and thought of the small ship that perhaps that very evening would be carrying them towards the sea.

About two miles North of the encampment, over several square miles of field and wood, armies manœuvred and forayed. The fighting was patchy, and laborious and violent, due to the necessity of cutting each enemy to pieces. Over the past year the armies of men and nemen had been so pressed and disciplined by fighting against the Dead Army that against a normal army they would have been invincible.

Ashurek unfurled and studied the map Setrel had given him. Then they began the ride down to the yew forests that Ashurek had chosen for his plan, cutting through copses, fording streams and keeping to small, sheltered valleys. They managed to avoid the battle completely for some time.

After they had cantered steadily for about half an hour, they heard the ringing of weapons and battle cries burst suddenly from a clump of trees near them.

'That sounded close!' Ashurek said. Vixata began to pace,

nostrils flaring. They drew their battle axes from their belts and rode cautiously on, heading for trees ahead. For a few minutes the air quivered, soft and still, and the only sound was the thud of the horses' hooves on grass. Then the battle sounds broke out again, further away but ahead of them now.

Immediately, at this threat of danger, Medrian seemed to relax out of the cold tension that gripped her, and began to exchange a few words with Ashurek. But Estarinel was quiet, brooding on the realisation that had come to him, slowly, over the past few weeks. Forluin had suffered a dreadful attack, but other countries were suffering too, in different but equally terrible ways. And perhaps it was not just Belhadra and Excarith, but every country in Tearn, and the Empire too. A half-year's light only, before the Serpent swallows the world.

They trotted into the trees, following paths through the brown and green tangle of bushes and sun-dappled trunks. There was movement ahead and, suddenly, behind them and to one side of them. They had ridden straight into a corner of the battle.

A few yards ahead they saw a dead Gorethrian plunge a sword through a neman's belly. The neman collapsed, choking. Three more warriors came scouting through the trees, set upon the Gorethrian, and felled it; in turn more of the walking corpses came through the trees and engaged them in battle.

From the riders' right, a group of about ten men and corpses moved across, fighting furiously. The battle seemed to be moving into the trees, and as the riders took off for a gap in the foray, they became caught up in it.

Vixata gave such a sudden leap that it almost caught Ashurek off balance. She shot out her hind legs at a corpse just behind her, then twisted as he regained control of her. Facing the corpse, he dodged it and took its sword blows on his shield until he managed to hack its arms off. He saw Estarinel turn in his saddle to hack at two of the corpses; by manœuvring Shaell to push at them, he felled one, but the other dealt him a deep cut on the arm. Blood welled from it.

Ashurek tried to get nearer to Skord, who luckily had not been seriously assailed. The boy, still weak and ill, had never been trained as a soldier and would have no chance in such a fight.

Another corpse came at Ashurek; a huge bearded man followed it and with a mighty axe blow, severed it clean through the trunk. Ashurek reached Skord, turned Vixata to strike at one corpse, and

257

hacked the arms from another. There was no joy in this battle; he felt only loathing at the fight.

'Chop their hands off!' he yelled at Skord. It seemed useless to try and give a fighting lesson in the heat of battle, but the boy seemed to hear and began to make an attempt to defend himself.

Medrian was having a hard time with the palfrey. Although it was an exceptional steed, it was no war-horse. It took her all her time to control the nervous and untrained animal, besides using a weapon to which she was unused. She much preferred the sword, yet axes were of more use against the Dead.

Now they were pressed on all sides by fiercely struggling warriors. Noise and confusion reigned. Ashurek felt anger blaze in him, and gathering his strength he began to cut a path through the Dead Army. Skord followed him, so close on Vixata's heels that the cob was kicked several times.

Meanwhile, Estarinel had become entangled in a mass of fighting soldiers. Shaell sidestepped suddenly as a sword nicked his flank; he put a hind foot into a tangle of creeper, and was suddenly pushed completely off balance. He fell to the ground with a crash that winded Estarinel and knocked him out for a second. His leg was trapped under Shaell's great bulk, but the stallion got up immediately, unharmed. Estarinel, blinking away the red and black stars from his eyes, dragged himself to his hands and knees and managed to crawl through the bushes until he found a clear spot to stand and force his way back to Shaell.

Medrian saw Ashurek, eyes blazing, teeth bared, blood running down his face from a sword cut on his forehead, forcing his way through the battle. It was beginning to thin in places. She saw her opportunity. There was a small clearing across which she made the palfrey gallop; then she jumped clean over the heads of a clump of warriors. Estarinel, breathing hard from being winded, followed her. The live warriors scattered before the powerful, snorting stallion, and the dead ones, staring from rotting, blind eyes, were unceremoniously knocked out of the way.

Ashurek turned in the saddle. The battle was moving further down below the trees. Corpses littered the wood, lying still – for the time being. He saw that the other three were following him. They were making good progress, leaving the battle well behind them. As soon as they were clear of it he slowed down to wait for the others. Skord could not stop the rather hard-mouthed cob and it cannoned into Vixata's hocks. She jumped forward irritably.

Ashurek turned her round, and panting like a wolf, with blood streaming down his face, he looked ready to tear Skord apart. But all he said was, 'Let the horses cool down. An hour's steady riding and we'll be in the yew forest.'

Well clear of the battle now, they walked the horses on a loose rein until they were cool and rested, then they cantered on across fields and past villages. All of them were wounded, but none seriously; they were able to ignore the wounds for the time being.

With no further misadventures they reached the old yew forest. It was a gloomy place of gnarled, low trees forming a thick roof of dark green and black. The floor was clear of undergrowth. It was a dark, stuffy, claustrophobic wood; the branches of the trees, hung with dark leaves and poisonous, cup-shaped red berries, drooped low over the paths.

They went a long way into the oppressive place as Ashurek fastidiously sought the most suitable place for his dark work. At last he chose a large space with a roof of tangled branches and they dismounted. He was trembling; he would not admit it, but he was afraid.

'Now,' he said, his voice level, 'we begin.'

'What are we going to do?' asked Skord in a fearful tone verging on hysteria.

'You'd better tie him to a tree,' sighed Ashurek with grim humour. 'We're going to release you from your demon.'

'But you'll have to summon it!'

'Look – I'll not have this plan set awry by you panicking. Go and stand with Medrian and Estarinel. Put your arms round Shaell's neck; there's nothing like a horse to comfort you if you're afraid.' Ashurek spoke distantly and his eyes looked strange. Skord fell back to where the others were, rather fearful of the Gorethrian. 'When the demon appears, don't look at it or listen to it; ignore it, think of something else. It can possess an unguarded mind in an instant.' To himself he whispered, 'In your name and for your sake, Silvren, I pray this plan will work.'

He began the incantation. Words of an old, long-dead language fell from his lips. Too fast, they tumbled over each other as if someone else was speaking them. As when the storm had dragged them into the White Plane, and when Arlenmia's forces had carried them to the gorge, he had the feeling of being dragged into a fell darkness.

The others watched him, a thin, dark figure standing motionless, his back to them, speaking in a low monotone alien words, words that should never have to be spoken. At first it seemed nothing was going to happen. The forest seemed very stuffy and dim, as if all air and light were being sucked from it. Skord was huddled against a tree trunk, very alone and shaking with dread.

Suddenly the wood became quite black. The darkness clung round their faces like cobwebs, or old, rotting velvet. For a moment Estarinel thought he was not in a forest, but in a place of cold, wet stone that was always lightless, and there was something in that darkness, begging, begging to die. But now a silver figure appeared in front of Ashurek, slipping through the dark gate as an egg slips from its shell. It was not a lovely silver but more the colour of a blazing acid flame, and its face was broad and leering.

It was worse than Estarinel had remembered. He thought he had never seen anything at once so beautiful and so hideous. Beside him Skord crawled forward a yard, as if unable to stop himself.

The demon ignored Ashurek and moved towards the boy. But Ashurek stepped between them.

'Siregh-Ma!' he said. The demon ignored him still and, floating as if it was not on that plane, moved round him to reach Skord.

'Siregh-Ma!' Ashurek cried again, keeping himself in front of the boy, who, paralysed and trembling with fear, was prostrate on the forest floor. 'Siregh-Ma! At the third invocation you must answer your summoner!' Ashurek shrieked.

The demon stared at Ashurek. It opened its mouth which gleamed wetly as if full of fresh blood.

'Ah . . .' it began sibilantly, 'I know you. You are the one that Meheg-Ba wants.'

'I am your summoner,' said Ashurek through clenched teeth. The summoning was worse than he recalled; he felt the lobes of his brain being pulled apart, probed by spidery fingers.

'Why have you summoned me – me, in particular? Still, as you have, I might as well take the boy . . .'

'Forget the boy and listen to me. I offer a bargain.' He cringed inwardly as he said the words, words he had sworn he would never say.

'How very interesting,' the demon hissed, and its voice seemed to echo as if from a vast abyss. 'Nothing, I hope, to do with the little witch Silvren—'

'Be silent!' Ashurek commanded, and the demon stopped in mid-sentence. Skord began to look up, amazed. How could Ashurek have such courage as to give orders to a demon? 'The Shana have mocked me and tormented me for the last time. We'll do our business and you can go.'

'You were never renowned for your manners,' smiled Siregh-Ma. 'What do you want?'

'Release the boy and leave him free.'

'Him! What do you want that wretch for?' the demon exclaimed. 'What can you pay me?'

'An army of the dead that have invaded this country. You may take them all in exchange.'

The demon grinned.

'Oh come, Ashurek. Do you think the Shana had nothing to do with their existence? To offer them to me is a ridiculous bluff.'

Ashurek thought quickly.

'But they are Gorethrian soldiers – I was their High Commander, therefore they are mine to offer.'

'Ah, nicely said. It seems to me, though, that *I'd* be doing *you* a double favour . . .' Their hearts sank. It seemed that the demon had seen through the bargain.

However, Ashurek knew something of the primitive psychology of demons, and said, 'Think of it. The energy of the fighting corpses, created by many Shana, all pouring into you alone. You'd gain power by it. Or is your love and loyalty to Gastada such that you wouldn't betray him?'

'I loathe Gastada,' Siregh-Ma answered with feeling. 'You have a point . . . the boy is useless to me, and it would be a grand joke to foil Gastada's plans.' All creatures of the Worm loathe each other, Ashurek thought sourly. 'What Gastada is doing,' the demon continued, 'is ineffective anyway, compared to what Arlenmia has undertaken . . .'

Ashurek did not reveal his curiosity at this statement, for to do so would lay himself open to possession.

'So – the bargain is made,' he said sharply.

'Yes,' said the demon. 'Why not? It matters little. Though Gastada will be furious, unfortunately for you!' It began to float slowly about the murky forest, bestowing Skord with a taunting smile.

Ashurek began the words to dismiss it, but it seemed oblivious of him. It looked at Medrian, and to his surprise, she looked fearlessly back, standing still and quiet as stone. The silver figure

261

stared at her, hesitated, and then retreated, now floating before Estarinel.

'The bargain is made. Go!' Ashurek cried. The demon's intention to possess the Forluinishman was obvious.

'How sad for Forluin . . .' it hissed, and Estarinel sensed the appalling magnetic power of it. He had been so careful to look down at the forest floor, yet now he was staring directly into its terrible argent eyes, seeing ghastly forms and patterns in them. The eyes seemed to fill his whole field of vision, the atmosphere became a dark silver-rust membrane shot with iridescent veins of dull green. And the membrane vibrated, softly, like an eardrum. He could hear screams, not realising that they were his own.

Ashurek knew then that the summoning, as he had feared, had gone terrifyingly wrong. All the strength left his body and he crumpled onto the ground, the words of dismissal refusing to leave his lips.

Then Medrian began to walk towards the demon. The others did not see her, but her hands were outstretched like white claws and she seemed engaged in a painful, intimate struggle with herself. She put herself between Estarinel and Siregh-Ma and looked into the demon's terrible eyes.

'You are disobedient, you are breaking the bargain,' she uttered in a strained yet commanding voice. 'Get you gone!' Her blanched skin reflected the demonic glow as if the awful pale light was streaming from her own face.

The demon's mocking smile was gone; for an instant it actually looked frightened. Then it was sucked into the knot of shadow behind it. The ground heaved and the wind like a roaring beast tore through the trees. A moment later the forest grew light again.

Ashurek stood up and saw Estarinel helping Skord to his feet, although the Forluinishman's face was drained and his hands were shaking visibly. Medrian was leaning against a tree, her hair falling across her face, breathing hard as if she had been running.

He stared at her with both intense relief and suspicion; how had she dismissed the thing?

He went to fetch the horses who were shying nervously away through the trees. Estarinel took the palfrey from him and led the animal over to Medrian.

'Are you all right?' Estarinel asked, placing a hand on her shoulder. She turned to him like a terrified child seeking comfort, and he held her, stroking her hair. Trembling convulsively, she hid her face against his shoulder, knowing she had done something for which she would pay dearly later.

'You saved me from that thing,' he said with awe and gratitude. 'Did it harm you – is anything wrong?'

Abruptly she pulled away from him and took the palfrey's reins. She swept her hair back from her face with a hand that was now perfectly steady.

'No, nothing, nothing at all,' she said, her voice very cold. 'And you, are you all right?'

'Yes. I don't really remember what happened.'

'Just as well,' Ashurek said. 'It seems I must thank you, Medrian . . .'

'No, forget it,' she replied curtly.

Skord seemed dazed as Ashurek helped him onto the roan cob, muttering, 'It's gone, it's left me . . .'

'Yes lad, even a demon must keep a bargain,' the Gorethrian said. 'So, Setrel will have his miracle . . . but at what cost? Come, let us not brood on this event. We'll ride back to Morthemcote and see how things are.'

As they rode back through the yew trees, there was a hoarse croaking as of crows flying above the forest. The trees seemed to close in around them, and they felt no light-heartedness at the success of their mission, only an increasing depression and fear.

'We always have Setrel's phial, if anything attacks us that cannot be fought by sword,' Estarinel said.

'If it works,' replied Ashurek. They suddenly noticed that Medrian had pulled her fairy-like horse to a standstill. 'Why have you stopped?'

She did not answer. She had turned the horse to face the way they had come and was looking intently into the trees. They saw that she was looking at a horse; a black, long-bodied, plain horse, standing riderless in the forest. It stared at her with baleful eyes. It looked distinctly similar to her protective familiar, 'Nameless'.

She began to trot towards it as if to chase it away.

'Go!' she shouted at it. 'I don't need your services now.' It did not move.

'Good grief, where's she going?' said Ashurek. The black horse turned and cantered away, and Medrian chased it. In only a few seconds she was out of sight in the trees. 'I'd better bring her back,' Ashurek said, and cantered after her.

263

'Wait!' Estarinel shouted, but his companions had disappeared into the darkness of the yew forest. He waited fruitlessly for them to reappear, overcome by a terrible sense of foreboding and an irrefusable urge to follow them. He looked at Skord. 'I've got to go after them. But I think it's safest for you if you carry on straight back to Setrel's house. Will you do that?' Skord looked rather blank, but did not argue. 'Here, take the map. Be careful, won't you? I expect we'll catch you up in a few minutes, but if not, we'll see you later.'

'All right,' said Skord dully. He opened his mouth as if there was something more he needed to say, but all that emerged, ominously, was, 'Goodbye.' He turned the cob and trotted away through the trees.

Estarinel pushed Shaell into a gallop, ducking to avoid the low, dark branches. His sense of dread was now verging on panic, which he only controlled by telling himself it was the natural aftermath of the summoning and therefore quite unfounded. But it was with great relief that he eventually saw Ashurek ahead. Vixata was dancing from side to side as he slowed her down. Estarinel caught him up and saw Medrian, ahead of them in the trees, still chasing the black horse. Patches of light showed through ahead, where the wood ended.

'Go! I'll have no more of your sort!' she was shouting at the horse.

'Come on,' said Ashurek. 'If we can chase that horse off, perhaps she'll come to her senses.'

The black horse led her out of the trees, and vanished.

Ashurek and Estarinel rode from the trees onto a bare hillside and Medrian came trotting to meet them, hair and cloak streaming behind her.

'It's gone,' she said. 'Thank goodness.' There was a cawing of crows above them. 'You needn't have come after me. Did you think I'd gone mad?' Her voice was very quiet and her eyes looked bleak and miserable. Estarinel suddenly remembered her words, 'Don't trust me . . .' and the feeling of dread was growing ever more intense. Whether it was the doing of Arlenmia, or Siregh-Ma, or Medrian herself, the Serpent's inevitable, inescapable trap was about to close on them.

Against the vast grey arch of the sky, three huge crows swooped down so fast that there was not even time to draw sword. They were gigantic and they were monstrous; their wings were vast soot-black cloaks of barbed metal, and on their heads black spines bristled. They had huge saw-edged beaks the colour of rusted iron, and their eyes shone cornflower blue.

The horses began to gallop and the crows swept down on them. Ashurek heard great, heavy wingbeats behind him, and suddenly the bird's claws closed around his body, lifting him from the saddle. The crow's talons, like steel blades, pierced clean through his leather breastplate and into his stomach and chest. The pain was agonising and inescapable. He tried to draw breath and sharp pains shot through his body. He could not breathe. With the blood pounding through his head and exploding across his eyes, he fell unconscious.

The crows were gaining height with their three prisoners, wings beating, claws swinging beneath them, the air currents ruffling the black thorny blades of their feathers.

Tiny as flies, the horses galloped on below them. Unseen by the three captives, the pale apparition of a beautiful woman with dark golden hair hovered in the trees, staring at the sky with despairing eyes. She flickered and vanished.

That evening Setrel sat by his fireside, listening gravely as the neman, Benra, gave him a full report of the day's events. The fighting had gone on until mid-morning, when all the corpses had fallen to the ground as one, becoming truly dead again.

'You should have heard us cheer!' the neman said, and Setrel nodded, smiling. Around him sat Ayla and the children, Atrel and Seytra, eyes shining. There was another figure in the room, huddled by the fire, unsmiling but seeming at peace.

'Skord,' Setrel said to him. 'You say they rode off North, but they did say they were coming back?'

'Yes, sir,' Skord answered.

'I can't understand where they've got to. They should be back by now.' He turned a book over and over in his hands, his head bowed.

After a few minutes his son, Atrel, said, 'Dad, you're crying. What's the matter?'

'Oh – nothing. Just relief – we never could admit how much danger we were really in, and how frightened we were. But now we are safe again—' he sighed and rubbed his eyes, 'I keep thinking of the three who saved us, and the prophecy: "They shall come from the gorge/And by dark birds be taken." '

'They've got to come back, dad,' Seytra said. 'Because of the

265

ship, remember?' But her father only shook his head, grasping his grandfather's book.

Eventually he said, 'Benra, I want you to go on a long errand for me. The pay will be good.'

'Of course, sir,' the neman answered.

'I want you to journey down through Tearn to Morrenland, and there take ship to the House of Rede. I want you to tell Eldor every single thing that has happened here, and everything you see on your way as well.'

'I'll do it, of course, but can I ask why?'

'I just think he ought to know. Perhaps he knows already, but I want to make sure.'

The crows flew for hours over the landscape that was now tiny and far below them. A grey, desolate night swept the daylight away, and two crescent moons, like half-closed eyes, stared through the clouds; and the crows flew on.

Pain roused Ashurek to consciousness suddenly, and he saw an estate of stone and ash, corpse-grey in the dull night, passing below them. There was a huddle of buildings – a farmhouse, perhaps?

Arlenmia had never meant them to arrive in the gorge and help Setrel; only a failure and misdirection of her power had allowed that. But now they were once more on their way to her intended destination. And it was, short of the Dark Regions, the most unpleasant place Ashurek knew: the castle of Gastada.

16

A Certain Northern Nobleman

The castle was set on a shapeless plug of obsidian, like the broken stump of a tooth. The crows circled steadily down towards it, cruising on the sluggish wind currents.

Their three prisoners were too dazed with pain to know or care what was happening. But more than their breastplates stopped them from being gored to death by the crows' talons. Gastada wanted his guests alive.

The castle was of bleak aspect, its jagged, decaying surface broken only by one door. It was a tall, triangular door, black and smooth but for two discs, one above the other, near its pointed arch. The discs were large and circular, and from each spewed a continual river of a viscous yellow fluid.

Ashurek was not aware of entering the door, only of the crow releasing him; for the pain as it withdrew its claws from his body was so severe that he was aware of little else. Within the castle they were carried through a network of hot, dark corridors and small rooms without windows. There was movement around them – guards were carrying them into the heart of the castle.

'Careful with them,' a harsh voice shouted, 'we don't want them to bleed to death before they get there.'

The atmosphere alternated between stifling humidity and cold clamminess and there was a thick stench like musk, but sickly sweet and nauseating. All was as Ashurek remembered it from when he had been prisoner here before. Impressions drifted through his dimmed awareness: the motion of being carried; dark corridors closing around him; the sickening smell. All blended into a nightmarish dream such as haunts the twilight between sleeping and waking.

What he became aware of next was half-lying on a damp stone floor. He and his companions were in a small, crookedly-built room, wet and filthy, with no furniture but one table and one chair.

A candle guttered on the table. There were two doorways, both triangular, each without a door so that a clammy subterranean gale was let through. This was no cell, but one of Gastada's own living rooms. He cared nothing for luxury.

Estarinel and Medrian were both unconscious, great holes gouged through their breastplates and their clothes torn. Blood poured from their sides. Ashurek could not understand what it was that kept them – and him – alive. He was weak from lack of blood and it was agony to breathe, yet he had formed a great resistance to pain over the years of battle and torture, and so was able to stay conscious.

Ashurek – who had thought he cared about no one except Silvren – found that he was deeply concerned about his companions. He had come to like and respect Estarinel, who had shown uncomplaining courage and remarkable abilities throughout the journey. As for Medrian . . . he still did not know what to make of her. She had dismissed that demon, then she had appeared to lead them deliberately into the crows' claws. She was a perpetual contradiction, and there was something sinister about her. Nevertheless he saw her as a comrade, and at times he had shared a fellow-feeling with her that verged on understanding.

The three of them, so unalike and at first so uneasy and distrustful of each other, had become firm companions. We could have been a powerful force, Ashurek thought, if we had not met our end here—

He was roused suddenly from his thoughts. There were voices approaching. He tried to stand up, but could not move.

It was actually not this pain, or torture, or the castle's dark powers that he dreaded – just Gastada's mockery and jubilation when he found Ashurek recaptured.

'Here they are, your lordship – as you requested,' a guard's voice said.

'Await orders outside!' commanded another voice, thick and soft as mouldering flesh. It was Gastada.

Ashurek closed his eyes as the man entered, delaying a first sight of him, then reopened them reluctantly.

'My present from Lady Arlenmia,' the voice intoned. 'You're late.'

Gastada was a short man but he carried his insect-thin frame with great arrogance. His head was small and round, almost bald but crusted with a little lichen-like hair; his features also were round, puffy, sneering and corrupt, with cruel lines about mouth and eyes that were ingrained with dirt. His eyes were terrible. The whites showed above them always and the irises were a sickly, opaque pink with glaring white pupils. He looked blind but was not. He wore thin robes of some grimy, overdecorated stuff. His appearance made even Ashurek, who had met him before, feel physically sick.

'I am so pleased you've returned,' Gastada said in his thick, whispering voice. He bent down towards Ashurek and began to laugh. 'But you are late, late – Arlenmia can be so incompetent.' In fact he was extremely jealous of her. 'Never mind. We have all the time we want. Are you not going to reply? How rude.'

Ashurek glared at him, unspeaking.

'You are a fine fish for anyone to catch,' Gastada went on. 'Arlenmia could not hold you, nor could the Dark Regions, nor could I – but I have learnt by my mistakes. There'll be no little fair-haired sorceress to rescue you this time, will there?

'Who are these friends you bring with you?' He walked, quick as an insect, to look at Medrian. 'A lady? She's bleeding a lot. She is not very pretty – not as pretty as my wife.' Then he went to Estarinel. 'Oh – Forluinish. I do not like the Forluinish.' He lifted the hem of his robe and pushed Estarinel onto his side with his foot, deliberately digging it into one of the talon wounds. Estarinel groaned faintly as he came round.

'Leave him alone!' Ashurek tried to say, but it was agony to speak and it came out as a whisper.

'What? Why, have you changed your ways? Prince Ashurek, I am very distressed at your misjudgment of me. I am a kind and merciful man. For example, I will now let you all rest while I decide on your entertainment . . .' Gastada's awful voice whispered on, punctuated by thick chuckles, for what seemed to be hours. It was like him to let them lie there in the dark, small room, collapsed with loss of blood and pain, for as long as he cared to; Ashurek had expected nothing different.

He did not listen to the Duke's monologue, but let himself drift into unconsciousness again. Once he thought he saw Estarinel drag himself to his feet and lean doubled up against the wall, blood spilling over his fingers; some time later, he half-awoke again and Estarinel was lying on the floor once more.

At last he awoke fully and he was alone in the claustrophobic room. The candle had melted to a stump and cast cold, black shadows into the corners of the ceiling. He crawled to the table and used it to haul himself to his feet. The talon-wounds had stopped bleeding and his side was aching and so stiff that he could barely move. Each time he drew breath there was a stabbing pain through his chest.

A sinking despair flooded him as he realised that Medrian and Estarinel had been taken to the lower levels of the castle where prisoners were held and tortured. He did not understand why he had not been taken down there himself; perhaps Gastada had some even more inventive punishment for him.

His sword and axe had been taken, and crippled by pain as he was, he could see no way of helping his companions. He leaned against the slimy wall, trying to gather strength.

Gastada was the Duke of Guldarktal, a country which had once been a wild, cold, beautiful land. Gastada himself had once been a normal young man who had inherited the Dukedom from his father. But his power was tenuous, and the country was wracked by civil war. Determined to end the struggle and safeguard his authority, Gastada summoned a demon.

Soon he was in full control of the country, but intoxicated with success, he summoned more demons to fulfil his various desires. The sacrifices they demanded in return grew ever greater, and he quickly became insane. First, all the enemies who had opposed his rule disappeared into his dungeons. Then other citizens began to disappear. At first there were plausible excuses, that he needed servants or soldiers, but later he gave up the pretence. The people lived in fear; the demons gave him terrible creatures which he sent out across the land, burning forests and towns, devouring men and women.

The Shana, delighted at having found this willing tool, encouraged him to ever greater excesses. His insanity grew until, possessed by a monstrous hatred of all living things, he had destroyed every human and animal in his country.

Guldarktal was laid waste, and became a taboo subject for its neighbouring countries. They never spoke of it, lest it happen to them.

It was said that when a man had lived by necromancy for so long that he had nothing left with which to pay the Shana, they would work for him for no reward. So it was with Gastada, for he had proved himself a true and faithful servant of the Serpent.

Ashurek left the fetid room and began to make his slow and painful way down a corridor. Before he had gone a few yards, Gastada came from a doorway and stopped him.

'Ah, you have revived at last. Where are you going?' he asked, leering.

'It's such a nice day, I thought I'd go for a walk,' Ashurek gasped.

'Are you in pain?' Gastada asked, seeing him half-doubled up, clutching his wounds.

'Yes, thank you,' he said through clenched teeth.

'You still have a morbid sense of humour, I see. Come with me.' Gastada beckoned with a stick-like finger and led him down low-roofed, damp corridors. Even if he had had the strength, there would have been little point in jumping Gastada and strangling him. It would not help them escape. And how – how could he ever have revenge on this evil little man for his abuse of the dead Gorethrian soldiers?

'Why aren't I downstairs in the cells, with the others?' he asked.

'I have nothing left with which to entertain you! Still, I know that just to spend the rest of your life with me will give you the utmost delight,' he cackled. 'It's very lonely here, except for my wife.'

'I didn't know you were married,' said Ashurek, wondering what poor girl he was keeping prisoner.

'Did I not introduce you last time? I'll take you to meet her. But there's no hurry – you'll be here a long time, after all . . .' Gastada began to chuckle and wheeze.

Ashurek knew there was no way to escape now. Last time, Silvren's sorcery had opened doors and disposed of guards and shaken the castle to its decaying foundations; but without sorcery, even should he kill Gastada and every guard in the castle, escape was impossible. The only exit was that triangular black door, and it was deep in dark powers. Only Gastada could open it; not even a demon or the Serpent itself could do so.

Yet Silvren had opened it. Small wonder the Shana so feared her.

'Do make yourself at home here!' Gastada choked through his

271

laughter. 'I grant you the freedom of my castle.' Granting a captive the freedom of his prison! It was the kind of contradiction that Gastada loved. Ashurek refused to be goaded, and remained silent.

They walked on down the narrow, stench-filled corridors, thick with darkness. The castle was airless and the only light came from a few sickly, faint torches.

'Darkness is there – I can see no escape,' Medrian had said, and at last Ashurek believed her. This was what she had foreseen – not Arlenmia's domain.

'I am expecting good news soon – it is taking a long time to arrive, but it will be soon . . . I will have a new country to add to my estate.' At this Ashurek grinned maliciously, but Gastada appeared not to notice. Obviously the demons had chosen not to tell him the unfortunate news about his Dead Army as yet. What would Gastada do to the three when he eventually found out?

He led Ashurek on through dim rooms and corridors, muttering incessantly. Ashurek did not listen to his insane ramblings, and only took notice when he stopped to speak to a guard, saying that Ashurek was to be attended to and obeyed as an honoured guest.

He had forgotten, but now he remembered. The guards were not human. Though they stood upright and were clad in leather and metal, they walked in a shambling way, like apes. They were large and strong, heads and hands covered in a brownish, bristling hair. Some had long, hairy tails trailing behind them, but the most inhuman thing about them was their faces. The skin was red and looked somehow raw and naked; a long nose fused into a cleft, pendulous upper lip. Their small, pale eyes were too close together, almost touching. The main thing that he remembered, however, was that they were all grossly stupid.

At last Gastada took Ashurek to a room in which there was an ageing four-poster bed, heavy with dust-covered, decaying hangings.

The Gorethrian looked with longing at the bed, for he could hardly walk.

'Do you want to lie down?' Gastada asked, face twisted.

'Not if you'd rather chain me to the wall,' he gasped, leaning against the doorway. 'But there's already someone lying there.'

'Ah yes – now you may meet my wife.' Gastada bent over the slight figure on the bed and kissed her face. Ashurek stumbled over to the bed and hung onto one of the posts of soft, rotting wood.

'No one will ever lie on this bed beside her except me, and that not until I am dead,' Gastada said, looking at Ashurek with his awful pink-and-white eyes. 'Isn't she pretty?'

Perhaps she had been once, but now her eyes stared unseeing at the ceiling, her jaw hung open, and the flesh was falling away from her long-dead face.

Ashurek saw then the most ironic tragedy of all, that even the Serpent's agents were its victims. Along with all the things Gastada loathed, the one thing that had been precious to him had perished also.

The guards had dragged Estarinel along a labyrinth of corridors, down steep, perilous stairs, to a small, damp cell lit by a dying torch. For a while he thought that, out of the sight of their master, they were going to show him mercy. They let him sit down and gave him water to drink. But as soon as he had finished it, they seized him, roaring with mocking laughter.

'Let us see what fevers that swamp-bilge will give you!'

They twisted wires around his wrists and tied him to rings on the wall. They extinguished the torch, and ignoring his entreaties to know where Medrian was, left him in the cold, suffocating darkness.

He was slumped against the wall but with his arms bound painfully above his head, and he could not move. He swallowed against the tightness of his throat, thinking, 'I've never before wept out of fear, only for my country. How do I find courage now?' But he felt he had no courage at all, and that if he had known the Quest was going to end in darkness and sickness and dread, he would never have set out. Despair and dark, negative thoughts possessed him, not only for his own situation, and the impossibility of helping Medrian and Ashurek, but for the whole world. It was all swamped in sickness and evil; attempting to destroy the evil ended in pain and death. He thought of his mother's sorrow if she could see him now. And he thought of his beloved sisters, Arlena and Lothwyn, and of Falin and Lilithea, and all the others he so loved. Forluin seemed like a dream now, a perfect green jewel that could never have existed.

A persistent faint scratching penetrated the feverish twilight in which he drifted; he shuddered and recoiled, for it sounded like a rat's claws on the flagstones. Or was it some worse creature, some thing of the Serpent? Yet it also, ridiculously, sounded like a bird hopping about . . .

'It's all right, it's all right, it's all right,' a ghost of a voice lilted in birdsong. *'You've forgotten again, haven't you?'*

Then Estarinel's feverish dream continued, but his body became numb of pain and his thoughts clear as crystal. Forluin was real, and other lovely things were too . . . the Blue Plane was real.

'Where are you, oh Lady of H'tebhmella?' he cried, though it emerged as a whisper. 'You said you would help us!'

At last, the demon Siregh-Ma itself appeared to Gastada, alone in one of his cave-dank rooms. It laughed as it told him the news.

'Your three prisoners made a bargain with me, to de-animate your corpses. So I did, and you have lost Excarith!'

Gastada became as a man demented. His round, ugly head swayed on its insect-thin neck and his eyes were wild. The demon had betrayed him; it had delayed the information, and it had the cheek to bring the news itself. And worse, now probably Arlenmia would send her own messengers there and control Excarith, the filthy witch. Dancing with murderous anger, Gastada threw everything he could lay his hands on at the demon, but the silver figure simply shook with mirth as the missiles passed through it.

When Gastada's fury had exhausted itself, Siregh-Ma said, 'However, to make up in some way for my appalling behaviour, I bear some information concerning the loathsome woman Medrian . . .' The demon explained in careful detail as Gastada listened, his face twisting with various emotions.

Then the demon left, saying as it departed, 'Don't fear that Arlenmia will take over Excarith. She is putting a far greater design into motion!'

'What—' Gastada spluttered, but the silver creature had gone. He was trembling with fury still, but now it was all focused into one ghastly purpose.

He had lost interest in Ashurek; he had never had any in Estarinel. But Medrian, now, held endless possibilities for venting his rage and malice.

Many miles away, in the House of Rede at the South Pole, Eldor put his head in his hands. The great frame of the sage shook with exhaustion, and his wife, Dritha, watched him sadly. She looked equally tired, her silver-grey hair dishevelled.

'I'm going to have to start turning them away,' Eldor said sadly. 'How can I? We call this a House where anyone can come for any reason, but it isn't true . . . there just isn't room for everyone!'

'The other Guardians would say they told us so,' Dritha said. 'They never approved of this House, after all.'

'Well it's too late for them to say anything! We are involved in human affairs too deeply to desert the world now.'

Over the past few weeks, refugees had been pouring into the Southern continent from Tearn and the Empire, with tales of fierce fighting, and wild animals, and weird happenings of nature.

'It seems to me the Earth has fallen through a hole in space and landed in Hell,' said one dark-skinned man of the Empire. 'Everything is falling apart! We always cursed Ashurek and his armies, but things are worse since he vanished – the Gorethrians have gone mad and so have the rest of us – it's anarchy. And as for the volcano . . .'

A shipload of fearful people had come from the Empire, saying that they had seen 'a golden bird in flames, falling from the sky'. One old woman still babbled that she had seen the death of hope and the end of the world. Others had come, saying that the ocean had frozen down to the North coast of the Empire, and that evil creatures of the Arctic stalked the lands, devouring people. And in Tearn, equally terrible things were taking place: senseless fighting, roving bands of savage wolves or bears, appearances of demons, illness and countless other afflictions.

The people who had come to Eldor were only those few who had had the presence of mind to remember him and had managed to find ships to take them to the House of Rede. Even so, there were hundreds, filling the house and camping all over the cold hills round the valley. And they were afraid; he saw and felt their fear every day, and it was an ever-increasing, terrible burden. There was so little he could say.

'It is the doing of the Serpent M'gulfn,' he would try to explain. 'Three people have gone to try to kill it. That's all I can tell you.'

'What if they fail?' said one person.

'I thought you were a sage,' said someone else.

But usually they listened in silence, taking what comfort they could from his presence, and putting their burden of fear onto him.

Alone, he told Dritha, 'I'm very worried. I've thought and

thought, but I can divine no news of them. It's as if they have left our shore and passed into a void.'

'They never reached the Blue Plane, I know,' she said grimly. 'We cannot have sent them to their deaths – there cannot be so little hope, can there?'

'No,' he tried to reassure her. 'Dritha, the Guardians have summoned us. Even without knowledge of the three, we must still ready ourselves to go and perform our task.'

'Yes, blindfold,' she stated with irony. 'Although the other Guardians treat us as outcasts, and will not tell us what the great design is that they have set in motion, still they need us to help them!'

'We are still Guardians,' he reminded her gently, 'and you know that while we are on the same Earth as the Serpent, even we cannot be allowed to know their plan, lest it find out.'

'I know,' she sighed. 'Beloved Eldor, I am not going.' He started to protest but she silenced him. 'Once you have that knowledge you will not be allowed back on Earth – at least until the Worm is dead. Someone has to stay with the people at this House. I am only a Grey One, not even human – but I care.' Eldor knew that once Dritha had made a decision she would not be swayed.

'So be it,' he said gravely. 'I will go alone – but not totally without hope.' They regarded each other sadly. For only a few evenings more would they sit together by the fireside. Eldor's gaze moved to the tapestry of the bird; these days he looked at it more and more often.

'Ah, always the blackbird,' Dritha murmured. 'The lost bird and the forgotten song.'

There were two figures in the low-ceilinged, mausoleum-like hall. One was bound by hands and ankles to a purpose-built stone post, a small, slender, upright figure who stood motionless, like wind-carved ice. The other was thin, grotesque, manically active.

'I know all about you, little Medrian, and your foolish, wicked activities,' Gastada whispered, his voice soft as mould.

'I think you know nothing at all,' she answered icily.

'Wretched woman! I am now going to teach you something very important: justice.' Sickly torchlight flickered on his sneering face and terrible eyes. 'I would not torture Ashurek, for just for him to know he can never escape again is perfect justice. And the

Forluinishman, for him to find that life is not all joy as he ends his days in darkness, that is perfect justice. But Medrian, what is perfect justice for you?'

He grasped a needle with a fine wire thread and held them up so they caught the faint light. Medrian thought, there is no escape, I am afraid; here it all ends, in darkness, as I knew it would.

'Justice,' Gastada whispered on. 'I am going to close your mouth so that you may never speak of who you are, or ask for help in your wicked, evil intentions. You shall be silent and invisible, as you were meant to be.' He sneered in triumph, but Medrian was smiling.

'You laugh!' he exclaimed thickly. 'You have something to say, perhaps? Speak! It is your last chance!' That she had made him suddenly uneasy was obvious. Her eyes were dark and fathomless in her frost-pale face, and her hair was a black flame. The sight of her, her cold, humourless laughter, filled him with disproportionate fury; he was trembling.

'You are a damned fool,' was all she said.

Then she closed her eyes and rested her head back against the post, waiting for the torture to commence.

Ashurek knew Gastada had lost interest in him when he felt the demonic force that had kept him alive waning. His wounds were not healing, and he was weak with loss of blood and hunger.

Alone in a black, stinking corridor, he tried to analyse coolly how long he had to live.

'Gastada's power has kept me alive for – what? Three or four days? Time does not pass here. I have no infection. If I can find water, I might last two days . . .'

It seemed Medrian had foreseen this from the time in Beldaega-Hal; they had truly come to a dead end in their journey. They were doomed to rot away with the great black walls of the castle closing ever in on them.

Was there anyone, anything out there to fight the Serpent now that the Quest had failed? He thought of Silvren; her terrible sorrow for the world's fate. For a moment she seemed to be hovering before him, her hands stretching out to him in despair, her mouth open in a silent cry. And he thought, 'I am not dead yet! Much can be done in two days . . .' Stiffly he stood up, and began to limp along the corridor.

He decided to find his way down to the cells where Estarinel and Medrian were held. Then he remembered the confusing network of lightless corridors that led there. He might never find his way through, but die in that black web; still, what did it matter?

He found his way down to the lower levels, seeing only one guard on his way. The creature sneered as he passed but did not stop him.

Then before him was a small black archway. He did not hesitate, but plunged into the claustrophobic maze. He felt the slimy, rough stone of the walls, rank with some dark-loving algae. And he made his way blindly forward; but as he took the first few steps, there seemed to be a faint green light glowing ahead. Was it his imagination, or was there really a hazy patch of luminescence on the wall, showing him the way?

Then he remembered.

'Silvren, even when you are not with me, you help me!' he thought. For there had been clumps of luminous green fungus growing in the wall, and when she had rescued him she had used it to mark the way through the labyrinth so that they could find their way out again.

He reached the patch and touched it, wondering if it still held some of her sorcery. And he could see the next glowing marker, leading him surely through Gastada's hellish maze.

There were two guards at the entrance to the dungeons. Behind them was a corridor lit by guttering torches, with many black iron doors leading off it.

Ashurek approached them and said, 'I wish to visit my two companions.'

'Very funny!' one guard spluttered. 'Get lost, before I stick this sword in your belly.'

'Gastada would not be pleased at that. I am his guest; you are supposed to obey and honour me, remember?'

They looked at him, a thin, dark figure with very bright, cruel eyes and long, tangled hair. He looked as wild as a wolf about to attack as he glared at them.

'That's stupid talk – go away, you've no business here,' retorted the guard with less certainty.

But the second one said, 'I don't see why he shouldn't come in.' The words were guttural and distorted, for their mouths were not suited to human speech. 'The woman's not here anyway, he took her to the Great Hall. And the other one's dead – as good as.'

The ape-like guards stood aside, laughing and giving a mocking salute as he passed. Then one followed him and unlocked an iron door, letting him through with sneering politeness.

In the cell the young knight was lying on the floor against the wall, but wires twisted round his wrists suggested that he had been strung up on the wall for some time. The wires had bitten into the flesh, which was bruised and bloodied. His face was pale and hollow and drawn, moist with a fevered sweat, and his eyes were sunken and red. The only sign that he was alive was his rapid and shallow breathing. The talon wounds in his side were festering and he was obviously very ill.

Ashurek slowly unwound the wire from his wrists and raised him into a sitting position.

'Estarinel, it's me; are you awake?' His eyes flickered but it was hard to tell whether he was aware of Ashurek's presence. We're both dying, he thought; the Worm wins. On the edge of his vision, he seemed to see a flash of blue light, through the open cell door. He dismissed it, but Estarinel stirred and said, 'Did she hear me?'

Ashurek supported him, realising he was delirious. But there followed a commotion in the corridor; a clash of swords, the guards uttering shouts and then deep, throat-tearing screams. There was a sound of running feet.

Ashurek lay Estarinel back against the wall and got to his feet, looking out into the corridor. There was only one guard there, silhouetted against flickering torchlight.

Ashurek approached him, calling, 'Is something wrong?'

The guard turned, holding his sword threateningly. It was the one who had let him in.

'Get back!' His pale eyes were wild with terror. 'There's been a terrible attack. *They* are in the castle!'

'Where's your comrade?' Ashurek asked coolly.

'Gone to raise the alarm – fight them!'

'Hadn't you better go too?'

'I have to stand by my post,' the guard stammered in fear.

'Very brave. Very commendable. But look, you go; I will take your sword and stand guard in your place.'

The red-faced guard, confused, and made even more stupid by fear, handed his sword in relief to the Gorethrian. Immediately Ashurek gathered his waning strength and plunged the blade into the creature's stomach; he collapsed, coughing blood, and died.

Ashurek staggered back against the wall, fighting exhaustion and the sharp, aching pain of his unhealing wounds. Then he returned to Estarinel and helped him to his feet.

'Something's happening,' he said. 'We must go; try to walk.'

Estarinel was barely conscious, but supported by Ashurek, they progressed slowly down the corridor. The Gorethrian did not know what they could do; it could take hours to find Medrian, and there would still be no way they could escape. But now curiosity drove him on. Something was in the castle, and although it was probably just a trick the demons were playing on Gastada, there might be some hope in it.

It was a long, arduous trek through the web of passageways. At last they reached broader corridors, but when they eventually gained the stairs leading to the upper level, Estarinel collapsed completely and could not go on.

'Come on,' Ashurek urged him. 'A few more steps—' he broke off. There was someone coming towards them. It was the figure of a woman, tall and extremely beautiful; she had very long hair and it seemed she was dressed in white, but a soft and shining blue light glowed from her. She seemed to glide rather than walk. She passed very close to them, so close that she brushed against Estarinel, yet she did not seem to notice them. She left sparkling trails of the lovely blue light behind her; she seemed not of that plane.

As soon as she had passed, Estarinel got straight to his feet as if suddenly recovered.

'Tell me I'm dreaming!' he exclaimed, beginning to smile. 'I just saw a H'tebhmellian!'

'Do you feel better?'

'Yes – yes, I can walk alone now . . . I thought I had died . . . what's happening?'

'You tell me,' said Ashurek cryptically.

'If H'tebhmellians have come into the castle, they must be able to leave again – there must be an Entrance Point to the Blue Plane on orbit through the castle,' Estarinel said. Ashurek looked at him with amazement and growing hope.

'Would it be visible?'

'Yes, they say so – like a cloud of blue light.'

'Then let us seek it!'

'You go – I must find Medrian.'

'Very well, though don't let us raise our hopes too high. Can

280

you manage alone?' Estarinel was swaying on his feet and looked very feverish, though Ashurek looked no better.

'I can now,' he said. He could still taste that soft blue light like fresh, lovely air, and felt suddenly light-hearted and clear-headed.

'The guard said she was in the Great Hall. That's where Gastada prefers to torture – I'm sorry, Estarinel, she may be in a mess when you find her.' Ashurek explained, as best he could remember, where the Great Hall was. Sighing, he turned to make his way to the higher levels of the castle.

'Wait,' said Estarinel, fumbling with numb fingers in a pouch on his belt. He drew out the lodestone from Hrannekh Ol; and they saw it was now glowing pale blue. He pressed it into Ashurek's hand. 'It might help. I don't know.'

Estarinel, stumbling along and supporting himself with one hand against the wall, managed to follow Ashurek's directions. At last he found Medrian in the long, damp stone hall.

She was no longer chained up. By the guttering, sickly flame of the torches he saw her, crumpled in a dark heap on the flagstones. There were no guards in sight. He went up to her and gently touched her shoulder.

She was conscious; she jumped violently.

'Medrian,' he whispered, 'it's Estarinel. We must try to escape.'

She raised her white, dirt-streaked face and looked at him with desperation. She half sat up, wincing as if with pain, and keeping one hand pressed to her ribs. Her mouth was torn and bloodied and tightly closed. The look on her reddened eyes was so hopeless and agonised that he could not meet it.

'Medrian; what has he done to you?' She shook her head slightly, not opening her mouth.

'Can you not speak?' he asked anxiously. Again she made a slight painful movement of her head. He caught a tiny gleam of black thread at the corner of her lips and he realised what was wrong. Gastada had sewn her lips together. He looked more closely at her mouth and saw a criss-cross of many tiny black wire stitches, plastered with crusted blood, with many white tears where she had tried to open her mouth to scream.

Estarinel felt anger grow in him. He supported Medrian with an arm about her shoulders.

'I'm going to undo the stitches. Don't worry,' he said, as gently as he could. She shook her head again, almost frantically, and stared down in misery. 'I won't cause you any more pain; I have herbs to make you sleep. Wait.' He laid her gently down on the flagstones and cast a nervous eye round the doorways.

Setrel had given him a good supply of herbs, including the ones from which he could make a sleeping vapour. Luckily Gastada had not taken them away. He found a discarded goblet and began to fill it with herbs from his pouch, crushing the leaves between his fingers until sap came from them. His hands were bluish-white and numb – the effect of the wire round his wrists. At last he had crushed the herbs to a liquid pulp in the bottom of the goblet. He hoped they would work.

Estarinel set the goblet down on the floor and sought Gastada's instruments of torture. They were lying on an oak table like a maiden's embroidery set: rolls of various wires and threads; a selection of steel needles; and the object of his search – a small pair of scissors.

He returned to the goblet and took three leaves from his pouch, bruising them between his fingers. He dropped them into the juice, and after a few seconds, wisps of vapour began to drift from the goblet.

Taking it to Medrian, he lifted her up and made her breathe the vapour. She moaned as he did so. After a few seconds her sore eyelids dropped shut and she went limp in his arms. He lowered her tenderly to the floor, leaving the goblet beside her head.

He set to work with the scissors, inserting the point under the first thread and snipping it as delicately as if he were clipping the wing of a moth. There were many tight stitches of wire through her lips, and some he could barely cut without ripping her mouth. Blood ran from the scraps of torn flesh round her bruised lips. It took what seemed hours, though it was only a few terrible minutes. Medrian sighed through torn lips in her sleep. His fingers became soaked with her blood, and as he worked, he wept.

At last he drew the last fragment of wire from her tortured flesh; and when it was finished he sat back on his heels and with a damp hand pushed his plastered hair back from his forehead. His throat ached.

He wished he had water to bathe her wounds.

It would have been better to have let her sleep on, but they could not stay in the Hall. He took the goblet away from her head and shook her gently. After a minute she began to stir. Then her eyes flew open and she sat bolt upright as if awakening suddenly from a nightmare. She let out several long, shuddering sighs and stared past Estarinel with dark, pain-dazed eyes.

He held her in his arms until she had recovered enough to move. Leaning on him, she pulled herself to her feet, keeping a hand close-pressed to her side over her unhealing talon wounds. He stood up with her, supporting her, just as Ashurek entered.

'Thank goodness you've found her,' he said, wielding a flickering torch that he had pulled from its wall-bracket. 'I've seen the Entrance Point, as you said. It's moving slowly but there's a commotion, I don't know if we will reach it. By the way – the lodestone works.'

Need gave them energy and, with Estarinel helping Medrian, they stumbled after Ashurek as he led them down a dim passage-way. And as they struggled on in pain through the evil-smelling darkness, an extraordinary sight met their eyes.

There were Gastada's guards, some twenty of the inhuman creatures, their red-raw faces deformed with Serpent-sent fury. A pale sickly light streamed from their eyes and their swords glowed with supernatural electricity. They were enmeshed in a blue cloud, and two H'tebhmellian women stood before them, repelling their sword blows with shafts of azure light. The battle was unspeakably weird, unworldly, bathed in the light of another Plane, and ringing with strange sounds, hideous and beautiful.

The three watched, spellbound, as one by one the guards fell to the ground, stunned or perhaps just overcome by fear. When the last of them fell, the H'tebhmellians vanished, but the blue light drifted slowly on.

'That's it!' Ashurek cried hoarsely. 'We must reach it, before it leaves the castle.'

They started forward again, Ashurek realising vaguely that they were outside the room where the body of Gastada's unfortunate wife lay. And they had only gone a few paces before Gastada himself stepped out in front of them.

There was an expression of extreme disgust and annoyance on his small, ugly features.

'Where are you going?' he intoned thickly. 'Those damned people of the Blue Plane – how dare they come here? It's your doing, I know – curse Arlenmia! Where are my guards, where are my demons?'

'They have deserted you, as all creatures of the Worm desert each other,' Ashurek hissed, and vengefully plunged his sword through the little man's belly. Gastada staggered backwards and sank to the floor, his pink eyes glaring insanely at them.

'That was most unfair!' he gasped in his thick voice.

'Yes, unfair!' Ashurek shouted. 'You should have taken a week to die!' He twisted the sword cruelly and wrenched it out.

'I – I cannot die,' Gastada moaned in fear. 'The demons said I couldn't . . .' but he did, and his grotesque body was still.

'Would that that blow had been mine,' said Estarinel. Ashurek was staring with revulsion at the body as if he had just trodden on some particularly loathsome insect.

'Would that it had,' he said bitterly. 'I will perform one kindness for the vile creature . . .' and Ashurek lifted Gastada's thin frame and took him into the room. There he laid him on the bed beside his long-dead wife, and placed the sword between them.

They went on their way, Ashurek holding the torch and the lodestone to guide them along the warren-like passages. Medrian was coughing with pain as they hurried along and Estarinel, supporting her, felt his eyes were bleeding with the effort of looking out for the elusive light.

The lodestone did not misguide them. At last they had the Entrance Point in sight again; but soaring on its orbit, it was heading for the outer walls of the castle. Stumbling, weak and desperate, they followed along a corridor and under a low arch.

But they were not fast enough. Ashurek felt the torch knocked from his hand as it caught on the arch, and suddenly they were surrounded by black, wet stone and pitch darkness. The Entrance Point had vanished.

'Oh ye gods,' Ashurek said, 'is it the Black Plane?' He stretched out a hand and touched a wall. 'We're still in the castle. It's a dead end. We've missed the Entrance Point.'

He stepped forward and struck at the wall with both hands in despair. Estarinel and Medrian came up beside him and touched the slimy stone, wretched with misery and disbelief; and in the same moment the wall became viscid and gave way beneath them. They fell forward onto their hands and knees.

There was light; gentle, soft blue light. They were on the shore of a tranquil lake that shone under an airy sky of bluish-mauve. Far across the lake was a beautiful rock formation with a broad, flat top and a thin stem, luminous and sapphire-coloured. A delicate bridge arched from it, its far end obscured by small pinnacles of stone flowering from the water near the shore. Little bridges and spirals of rock led to the pinnacles, and lilies floated about their roots. The air was cool and sweet. They were kneeling on sparkling blue-green moss, and as they looked out over the lake, all their weariness and pain and illness fell from them.

The exquisite beauty of that lake, its calmness and gentility, were overwhelming. Estarinel, gazing across the scene, could have wept for joy.

'The Blue Plane,' he whispered. 'I never, never dared hope I would see it . . .'

They had completed the first stage of their journey, and now they had no wish and no need to move. They rested on that calm, sweet shore, trailing their hands in the crystal-blue water and drinking deeply of the sweet, cool liquid. The blue light touched them; they tasted it and breathed it. The Blue Plane washed away their weariness as months of rest could not have done.

Beauty and joy suffused them, even Ashurek and Medrian, for H'tebhmella had a power that no darkness could resist.

17

H'tebhmella

The Blue Plane H'tebhmella was a place of infinite tranquillity and beauty; and because reaching the Planes was never easy, it had become as mythical and sought-after on Earth as paradise.

It was very different to the White and Black Planes, seeming multi-dimensional whereas the other two seemed one-dimensional. The Lady of H'tebhmella would have explained the difference by saying that the Earth was as an equilateral triangle. The White and Black Planes were at each corner of the base and the Blue Plane at the apex; the life-energies generated on Earth flowed upwards and out through the apex. So H'tebhmella was transformed by strange electrical forces to the wondrous place it was, and it was also a channel through which other worlds could be reached.

The Planes had been created by rifts in the vast cosmic energies when the Earth itself was born. Each was inhabited by immortal beings; Hrannekh Ol by men, Hrunnesh by nemen, H'tebhmella by women. But their sexes were extraneous, for they were not human. Originally it was designed that they should help Earth, but although the inhabitants of each Plane were concerned with Earth's affairs, they had become too greatly distanced from her to be fully involved. The Peradnians of Hrannekh Ol had worked out the world's history and fate in mathematics; the Hrunneshians concerned themselves with philosophy. But their sciences were so pure and sufficient unto themselves that they were incomprehensible to the people of Earth. It was difficult to find Entrance Points and the two Planes could not support human life for long anyway; so none but a few scholars had deliberate contact with the White and Black Planes.

But the women of H'tebhmella were different. They were deeply concerned with the affairs of Earth, and their sadness was that they had little power to help her. But their exquisite Plane, invigorated by flowing energies, could support life, and so they did whatever they could for the world.

And because the people of Earth loved them and sought after them, the Serpent and its minions loathed and feared them; especially as H'tebhmella was the one place over which it had no power.

'You are here at last,' said a voice that was clear, melodic, and full of relief. The three turned and saw a woman who must have approached in total silence, so unaware had they been of her presence. A sense of awe propelled them all hurriedly to their feet. She was one of the H'tebhmellians who had battled with Gastada's guards. 'We thought you had missed the Entrance Point!'

She stretched her arms out to them; then Estarinel realised that she was *the* Lady, the one who had no name. She was tall, almost of Ashurek's height, at once stately and ethereal. Her hair was long and silk-brown, and her face was exquisitely beautiful, with eyes grey as rain and filled with tranquillity and gentleness. She wore a white robe and an indigo-coloured cloak, and a soft blue light glowed from her and radiated in shafts from her hands.

A few yards away was the other woman of the battle, standing by a small boat at the shore. She was less tall but as beautiful, with darker hair and eyes of clear blue. Estarinel immediately knew she was Filitha, the one who had first come to Forluin after the Serpent's attack.

The Lady embraced each of them in turn, kissing them on the forehead with obvious joy and relief; her hands were cool as crystal and full of the Plane's healing power.

'I can't tell you how relieved I am that you are here,' she told the three. 'We could divine no news of you, and thought you lost to the Serpent; then we heard E'rinel calling, and were able to divert an Entrance Point through the castle, using your lodestone as a guide.'

'So – you've saved us again!' Ashurek exclaimed to Estarinel.

'Oh no, not I,' he said, looking at the Lady and feeling shame fill him as he remembered *The Star of Filmoriel*, stranded on the White Plane. 'I'm sorry, my Lady; you entrusted me with the *Star* and I lost her. I don't know how I can make up for it.'

'E'rinel, on the contrary, we have failed you. When the *Star* was swept into the White Plane you should have stayed with her. We never told you that you should stay aboard through all adversities, because we didn't think anything would happen to you. She came

287

home without you and we thought you lost.' She smiled. 'Don't look so dismayed! Considering what we are fighting, let us bless the hour that brought you here at all.' A smile touched her lips as she added, 'You may be interested to hear that there were a number of Tearnian sailors aboard her. We have returned them safely to Earth . . .' Estarinel saw the surprise on his companions' faces and found himself at once half-laughing and half-crying. 'Now, whatever lies ahead, this is no time for you to be down-hearted. The first part of your journey is over and you are here; Estarinel of Forluin, Ashurek of Gorethria, and—'

'Medrian of Alaak,' said Medrian. Her face betrayed no particular emotion as usual, but Estarinel noticed that her eyes were very clear, almost violet, as though reflecting the colours of H'tebhmella. Her torn mouth had already been healed by the Plane's power.

The Lady gave her a long, searching and compassionate look.

'Yes,' was all she said, but the word seemed full of enigmatic meaning.

'I remain silent and invisible,' Medrian added with a touch of irony. 'But nothing can turn me aside from this path – not even the release of the Blue Plane.'

'You have great strength,' the Lady said softly, and Estarinel thought he saw tears in her eyes. 'Come; we'll sail across the lake and you may rest and refresh yourselves. There is much to talk about, and the Blue Plane heals all woes.'

There was a small boat of pale wood, pulled by a silver-grey sea-horse, moored by the shore. With Filitha they stepped aboard and, on a word from the Lady, the horse began to pull them across the lake.

'It was a timely rescue,' said Ashurek as they drifted through the translucent water. 'Gastada himself is no more; I made an end of him on one of his own swords.'

'Your adventures have left you very bitter,' the Lady murmured. 'But his evil work is at an end, which is good.'

'I thought I saw a third H'tebhmellian in the castle – it was only her passing that gave us the strength to escape,' said Estarinel.

'That was Neyrwin. I sent her to find your horses, for you will need them again – but don't fear for her, she can travel swiftly and find an Entrance Point whenever she needs to.' The light, blue water broke in shimmering waves on either side of the boat as it passed through the lake. The Lady continued, 'Does one of you feel fit enough to tell us about your journey? We are eager to know.'

Ashurek seemed in a buoyant mood and Estarinel, feeling tired and peaceful, was content to let him do all the talking.

Medrian was staring blankly across the lovely stretch of water. She had relaxed out of the grim coldness that was her usual demeanour, but she now seemed empty and drained of everything. Estarinel put an arm round her shoulders. She did not draw away but rested on him, and he could sense her profound physical and spiritual exhaustion. Presently she looked at him and said quietly, so that only he could hear, 'I warned you not to trust me. I stranded us on the White Plane; I made us easy prey for Gastada's crows.'

He remembered how strangely she had behaved at those times; was it possible that something had compelled her, against her own will, to try to sabotage the Quest? He did not want to believe it.

'Medrian, you can't blame yourself for those events,' he said gently. 'Anyway, we've reached the Blue Plane now in spite of you!'

'It is not something I speak of lightly,' she reprimanded him, an undertone of wretchedness in her voice. The hope that she was about to confide the cause of her unhappiness leapt in him. 'I've been very unfair to you and Ashurek . . . expecting you to tolerate me with no explanations of any kind.'

'It's all right. I always felt you would tell us eventually, when you were ready. And I don't find it necessary to "tolerate" you; to me you're a trusted companion and friend.'

She looked at him, hearing the warmth in his voice.

'I beg of you, don't put too much faith in me. I try to my utmost limit, but sometimes I am not strong enough.' Her voice could only be so characterless if she was trying desperately to suppress tears, he thought. 'Estarinel, you are right. You will know about me one day, but that time is not yet. All I can say is this: half of me wants the Serpent destroyed, but half of me is in its power. Do you understand?'

He felt somehow shocked by these words; a sensation as if he had unthinkingly rested his hand on a piece of ice, then realised too late that the cold was burning him.

'We're all in its power to some extent,' he said.

'Yes, that's true,' she said ironically. 'You do understand. This is as much as I can say for now. Please don't feel tempted to ask me any more questions – not for any reason, ever.'

'Then I won't – not if it distresses you.'

'It does,' she said decisively, still looking at him with her unreadable dark grey eyes.

'But there's a paradox. I have to have faith in you, Medrian, in order to agree to trust your silence.'

At this her expression became one of amusement, and for the first time her laughter was untainted by its usual grim, sinister quality. Still laughing, she turned to gaze across the lake again, her head resting on his shoulder.

He thought about her – how she bled and suffered in battle or under torture, and yet when an actual attempt to kill her had been made, her horse had died in her place. It was as if something toyed with her, played cruel mocking tricks with her life. And what could do that, except M'gulfn? He held her closer as if to protect her. Everything about her that had frightened him had faded; there was only her enigmatic sorrow, her emptiness and her resolute strength of character left.

Ashurek finished the account of their adventures as they reached the roots of the rock formation that they had seen from the shore. Other boats floated there and several sea-horses swam and dived loose in the still water. The Lady called them and they swam around the boat, raising their noses to be petted.

The travellers climbed from the boat onto the rock and the H'tebhmellian women led them over the bridge. It arched high above the shining water and they had to cross it in single file, yet they had no fear of falling. The bridge glowed like sapphire with a heart of deep blue crystal.

The castle of Gastada seemed years in the past and with every breath they took they grew stronger, as if they had never been gored by crows' talons or trapped for days in that disease-infested darkness. A cool, sweet breeze blew across the shining stretch of water below them and the clear, high sky cast gentle light over the Plane. All shades of blue gleamed in the islands and pinnacles and mushrooms of rock; pale blues, tints of silver and grey, blue jade, turquoise, indigo, ultramarine, blues verging on purple and violet, soft, pure blues, and light, transparent blues.

Estarinel felt infinitely moved by the beauty of the Plane and its inhabitants; he could hardly believe he was in the place which he had heard spoken of, all his life, with such awe and love. He had thought he would have many questions to ask about its existence, but they seemed unimportant now.

The far end of the bridge fused into a shore growing thickly with soft blue-green moss and lovely trailing flowers. They walked for several miles without noticing the distance. The ground rose and fell gently and here and there were tall, graceful trees with indigo trunks and showers of blue and silver leaves. Presently they came beside a spring rushing between banks of moss-covered rock. A few deer were grazing in a gap between some trees; beyond, they could see a shore and the quiet lake. Nowhere in H'tebhmella was far from water.

'Do you sit and rest here. We'll return soon,' the Lady said, and she and Filitha walked away through the trees, shafts of silver-blue light following them.

Ashurek and Medrian sat down on the bank and the three looked at each other.

'It's not all going the Serpent's way after all, is it?' Estarinel said.

'No, by the gods, you're right,' said Ashurek, grinning. Then his green eyes became moody. 'If only Silvren could be here, instead of where she is . . .'

'But she'd be more than glad to know that you've reached H'tebhmella,' Estarinel said quietly.

'Aye, my friend, you are right in that.' The bitterness faded from his face; for a time, at least, all three felt less haunted by their troubles. There was an unspoken comradeship between them and they felt no need to discuss what lay behind or ahead of them. 'This is truly a place of beauty, Estarinel,' Ashurek sighed.

'I wish I could go to sleep here, and never wake up,' Medrian said with feeling, stretching out on the moss.

They all slept, wrapped in a deep blue radiance through which light shone, pure as diamond and soft as moonlight. Around them there were the faint, soothing noises of air moving in the trees, deer grazing, water lapping as sea-horses swam through it.

When they awoke, now feeling calm and refreshed, the H'tebhmellians had returned. As well as the Lady and Filitha there were many others, all tall and graceful with beautiful, grave faces and shining hair of all colours. They had come to meet the three, and hear what the Lady was going to say to them. They noticed a human among the unearthly beings, a tall woman with long red-brown hair.

'Now you are here at last,' the Lady began gravely. 'And it is as it should be; three of you met, each for different reasons, at the House of Rede, and you have come to H'tebhmella.'

'Forgive me, my Lady,' Ashurek broke in, 'but you speak blithely of our Quest as if we had trod lightly through some preordained ritual. We have felt more like three floats, tossed by a child into a raging torrent to see how we fare. Can you tell us the truth – are we just playthings to be fought over by the Serpent and its enemies?'

'I'd tell you the truth if I could,' the Lady sighed, 'but I don't know what it is. I can only tell you what I know and believe.'

'Tell us then. It's why Silvren sent me here,' Ashurek said shortly.

'You have all set out to kill the Serpent for personal reasons, but it also must be killed for the sake of the Earth and Planes, and even our universe. Did Eldor tell you anything of this?'

'No. Silvren seems to know more than Eldor,' Estarinel said.

'That is not so, but I can see his reasons for not saying anything; he did not want to discourage you.' A light shone from her lovely face as she spoke. 'I will tell you a history of the Earth which may help to explain what is happening. Many billions of years ago there was a great whirling of energies in the cosmos, and out of it was spun the world with two lifeless moons. The energy was not "good" or "evil" – it was just an energy, but part of it spun outwards and part inwards, so creating a balance. They say as the two spinning parts touched each other, creating immeasurable fields of force, the three Planes came into being – each flat, infinite, populated for eternity by static life-forms, and existing in its own dimension.

'As the part of the power we are now pleased to consider "evil" spun inwards, it became ever more concentrated in the centre of the Earth. At last, as fires fell into the oceans, a living creature was born of that infinitely concentrated energy.

'It was borne up in the water until the seas of the Arctic froze beneath it, and it was left lying in snow at the North Pole.

'Later, when men came to the world and saw the shape of it, they called it a Serpent. But in those days it simply was, and it was all-powerful.

'It had three eyes with which it could see everything, control the elements and even manipulate the creatures that would one day inhabit the world. In effect, the eyes made it omniscient. It was in such complete control of the Earth that it almost *was* the Earth. And it lay there, toying with the land masses of the world and waiting for life to evolve so that it might feed on the energy that would be produced.

'Then the Guardians, as they are called, began to notice what was happening on this newly-born Earth. They are neutral beings who try to regulate a balance in the energies of the universe; so they looked at the world and knew they must bring some order to it.

'To the life-forms of the Planes they brought shape and thought, and they made a mechanism which is now called the Glass City, to create and maintain Entrance Points. This was so that the Planes could assist Earth and be a true part of her; but their work was not perfect, of course.

'There was little they could do about the negative energy that had become the Worm. They mounted a dangerous mission and took its third eye from it, so it would never hold full sway over the world. This was a drastic reduction of its power.

'What we must understand is that the Worm is composed of a vast negative energy that is spinning inwards, whereas the positive energy that is its opposite, is spinning outwards and dispersing. But the Guardians were able to take a small part of it and create a second creature, a bird. Then the Serpent's third eye was placed under the bird's protection, so that M'gulfn should never regain it.'

Ashurek became very still and tense as he heard this. The Lady went on.

'At this the Serpent grew afraid and began to create its own creatures out of its abundant energies. The most notable of these were the Shana, the demons; but the Guardians placed limitations on them, so they were confined to their own Region.

'Then the Guardians thought they had done all they could and left Earth, though a few stayed to watch what would happen.

'Life evolved at last; plants and animals and finally men. Of all the lands, the island of Forluin was the only one that the Worm had overlooked, and so the only place where people lived free of its influence.

'Everywhere else it had laid the basis of its work, and soon found willing agents. It made a refuge for its mind within a human, so that it would survive if attacked. And though attempts have been made to kill it, all have failed miserably, and its power grows.

'You have all seen evidence of its work, in Gastada and Arlenmia, Gorethria and the demons; I do not have to tell you

293

what appalling evil and suffering it has caused. But there is more, and worse.

'Energy does not stop moving. The negative energy is still spinning inwards, the positive outwards. And now, after all these billions of years it is reaching the summit of its powers, while the "good" power has almost dispersed entirely.'

'Silvren said that when that happens,' Estarinel broke in, 'the Earth would be unable to evolve but would become – how did she put it? "A bloated sac that can never expel its poison".'

'Yes, she is exactly right. The Serpent should die, not only because of that, but because energies all across the universe will displace and cause untold chaos.'

'You have answered my question,' Ashurek said grimly. 'Now I know what I suspected is true; we are just the puppets of benign figures, trying to put their precious universe to rights. I'd be inclined to say, let the Serpent rule and chaos take them!'

'Thank goodness no one else shares that opinion!' A voice called; it was the red-haired woman. She grinned cheerily at Ashurek as he looked at her. He continued, speaking again to the Lady.

'If I understand you . . . the "Egg-Stone" I took from Miril is the Serpent's third eye?'

'It is so,' she said without condemnation. 'Can you remember what she said when you took it?'

'Yes, every word. She said that it had been given into her keeping so that the Earth was protected from it . . . but she would not stop me from taking it, because the Worm's time had come. And she said that she is the world's Hope, but unless I find her again, the world will be doomed . . .' he trailed off, lost in acute, sad memories of Miril.

'She was the world's Hope,' the Lady said, sighing gently, 'for she was a piece of that elusive positive energy that is deserting the world. You, Ashurek, unleashed that Third Eye upon the world, and that was when the Serpent's power began its terrible acceleration.'

'I know that now,' he said.

'But you didn't then. At least the Serpent didn't regain the Eye, thanks to the selfish ambitions of the Shana who want their own power. You can imagine its anger, and especially at poor Forluin, over which it still had no influence . . .'

Estarinel bowed his head, painful memories returning now they were no longer driven out by danger.

'There is yet more,' the Lady went on, an incandescent azure light glowing round her head. 'It is painful to admit a selfish reason for wanting the Serpent killed, but I have to. H'tebhmella also has her own motive in wanting its death. As you know, all the Planes have two sides. This side faces down, as it were, to Earth, whereas the other side faces out to the universe, to infinity and eternity—' She fell silent as if too sad to speak.

'What is on the other side?' Estarinel asked quietly.

'Paradise,' the Lady answered. 'That is one name for it. But a clot of darkness is preventing access to it – not only for us but for all living beings. A terrible, evil trick was played on us, the darkness put there without our knowledge, and it must be cleansed.' Estarinel and Medrian stared at her, and Ashurek's face fell in horror as she finished. 'The Dark Regions are there.'

In Forluin, within a small stone cottage, a young woman looked through her window across a valley. Her small, sweet face was set in a pale mask of sorrow and her thick bronze-brown hair hung in an uncombed tangle to her waist.

The valley had once been green, full of animals, clad in hedges and trees. Now it was a sick, desolate grey, covered in ash and soaked with the Worm's poison. The girl gazed steadily upon the crumbled ruins of a house, where only a few days earlier they had greeted Arlena and Falin home from their sea voyage. The ruins looked so still and sad, like a small animal that had died of fear.

Behind her a young man with long brown hair entered the room.

'Lilithea,' he said, 'you've been sitting there for hours. It won't help.' His own face was white and his eyes reddened with tears. She reached out and took his hand.

'I can't see how it could've happened, Falin,' she said. 'Can that creature kill even when it isn't here? First his father died of the fever . . . then this . . .' The Serpent's poison had spread and, as if it had soaked into the mortar, the farmhouse had collapsed without warning upon its inhabitants: Estarinel's mother and two sisters. And I have lost Arlena, was Falin's continual, inconsolable thought.

'I can't believe it,' he half-sobbed. 'Oh Lili, how are we ever going to tell E'rinel when he comes home?'

'Perhaps he won't come home,' she said, her throat tight. 'The creature won't rest until we are all dead. How can he do anything to stop it, just him? At least he wouldn't ever know what's happened to his mother and sisters.'

'Or see that although the Worm only came once, things are getting worse and worse. I still hope he comes back, though,' he said, his voice full of grief.

'Falin, I can't stay here any longer,' Lilithea said. 'Too many memories. It's too much.'

'Where are you going?'

'South . . . where my parents live. Do you want to come?'

'No, I'll stay in the village, in case E'rinel does come back. There's a lot to do as well, for all it's worth . . . You'll take care, won't you, Lili?'

She nodded, unable to force a smile. 'Yes, I'll take care, for all it's worth,' she thought. And when Estarinel comes back, as I know he will, I wonder if I'll have the strength to bear his grief as well as mine, and to hold him and bury my hands in his hair, and love him until he forgets. Would I even try?

On the Plane, a flat crystal that was as delicate and lovely as blue glass, the meeting continued. The Lady listened gravely as Estarinel spoke, his voice full of doubt.

'You've explained clearly enough why M'gulfn should be slain, but it sounds even more difficult than I'd thought. We've already been told it's impossible, and I thought that was because it was merely powerful . . . but how can we even think of destroying something made of a vast, evil energy?'

'Certainly nothing exists on Earth with which you could destroy it,' the Lady said gently. 'But this is precisely why you had to come to the Blue Plane; because information that the Serpent must not know can only be kept here. Soon there will be a way.'

For a moment he wished that the Lady had said, 'There is no way; why not give up and go home? It is not your responsibility.' But there could be no thought of turning back; what they had taken upon themselves they must fulfil.

'If I say the only thing that can destroy the negative energy is the positive energy, you will understand the logic of it,' she went on, light from the spring dancing over her grave and lovely face. 'I said the positive energy is dispersing, so that sounds impossible as well. But the Guardians are working upon a great project based on a tenuous theory.

'The energy spins in a huge ever-increasing circle, but it must soon enter a domain where it is only a comparatively small ring of power. There they hope to capture and contain it within an ancient supernatural weapon: the Silver Staff.

'Then you must set forth on a perilous journey to fetch the weapon. It will be dangerous and perhaps unlikely to succeed; but I tell you this is our only hope.'

'It's little enough, but no less than I expected,' said Ashurek drily. 'But there are other obstacles. What of the Worm's human host? Surely it will survive if the host isn't killed as well, and all our effort will have been wasted.'

'You are right; but I believe that that problem will eventually be resolved through the Silver Staff.'

'And what of Miril?' he persisted, looking grim. Estarinel seemed equally depressed.

'I do not know,' the Lady said frankly. 'If she must be found again, you will have to find her in your own way. All I know for certain is that the Silver Staff will be your greatest, and only, weapon.

'We'll help you in what other ways we can: a warrior, Calorn, will help you find the Staff—' she indicated the tall red-haired woman, 'and we will give you all you need to go into the Arctic snows.'

Suddenly the prospect of actually setting out to face M'gulfn struck a cold blow to Estarinel's soul; momentarily his view was blotted by a vision of lights burning on snow; someone turning this way and that, crying out as if pitifully lost; red glass and shadowy figures that looked straight through him; and the cold, cold, cold . . . the vision passed and the coldness subsided, but for some reason he could not look at Medrian.

They waited for the Lady to go on, but she fell silent.

Then Medrian spoke, so softly that some of the H'tebhmellians leaned forward to hear her.

'There is one small thing in our favour,' she said. 'No one has thought of it, but it may be important. The Serpent quests for world domination, but it is old and tired. It has been there for billions of years; perhaps it does not regard the idea of eternal life as favourably as we think. That is all.'

Estarinel took her hand and kissed her, feeling suddenly grateful for her words of encouragement.

'You may have a point,' Ashurek grinned. 'We certainly must

set out with hope and determination, or we might as well not go at all.'

'I am glad to hear you say so. There may be needs for sorrow, but never despair,' the Lady said, her grey eyes full of the light of hope. 'There is more that must be said of the Silver Staff and the journey to fetch it, but that will keep for now. Listen; your world is going through an evil age in which all the Earth seems sad and at a loss. It is on your shoulders to turn her face to the morning. Now I am not saying that once the Serpent is dead, all the Earth will become sweet and fair for eternity; on the contrary, new evils may spring up in its place. There will be a wild, wild age in which sorcery, a bright magic and a dark one, will hold sway; an age of vigour as opposed to this age of lethargy and decay. The change must take place or your world is doomed to Arlenmia's vision. Silvren knew this from the start, for her power is of the future.'

Silvren. Ashurek stood, hands on hips, staring moodily at the crystal-blue rock beneath his feet. Could it be true, that horrific revelation that the Dark Regions were on the other side of the Blue Plane? He remembered the vision of her, when she had said, 'The Dark Regions are not black at all – they're blue . . . like the egg of a small bird, washed by the rain and left to rot in a deserted nest . . .' Yes, it was true. So there must be a way to go through and seize her from the demons . . .

He remembered Arlenmia, and wondered what she would do now in her fanatical devotion to the Serpent. How had Silvren known her, and been friends with such a one?

He sighed and walked on beside the sweet, clear lake towards Estarinel and Medrian. Now they were waiting for news of whether or not the Guardian's project was successful; only then could they go to fetch the Silver Staff. It was a time of peace, but still anxieties surfaced to make them all frequently uneasy. Setting forth on a journey was always easier than waiting and waiting; especially now that the first stage of their Quest was over and the dread business of setting out to slay the Serpent was before them.

'You are quiet,' Medrian said. 'What are you thinking about?'

'Well . . . if the H'tebhmellians would permit it,' Estarinel replied slowly, 'I would like to visit Forluin briefly before we go.'

Medrian stood still and gave him a look of astonishment.

'I don't think that's a good idea,' she said sharply. 'What if things

298

are worse there – or better – and you lose heart to continue the Quest?'

'I won't – not having come so far.'

'It's a chance I'd rather not take!'

'Medrian – I have to go. It might be the last time I ever see my country, don't you see?'

'You've said your farewells. Why repeat the agony?' She sounded angry, but then her face changed, became thoughtful. 'Nothing I say will stop you, will it?'

'Not if the Lady will let me go.'

'Would you let me come with you?' she asked unexpectedly.

'Of course. I would love you to,' he answered, surprised and pleased. 'Why the change of heart?'

She turned away from him, looking out across the tranquil lake to the formations of crystal beyond. A breeze stirred her long, ebony-coloured hair. There was a diamond-like clearness of purpose in her face, contradicted by the confusion and bitter longing in her dark eyes.

'I don't know,' she said, half-smiling as she began to walk on alone. 'I don't know.'

Interlude

A dream hung in the dark void like a jewel. Glittering like a rare canary diamond, it seemed self-sufficient, as though it needed no dreamer to conjure it, but had created itself. Approaching the glittering yellow orb, in the slow curving drift of a space traveller drawing close to a strange planet, the dreamer could see that the gem was a living thing. A network of shining capillaries enmeshed it, pulsing with the joyful passage of some glistening alien blood. They throbbed to the rhythm of a vast, unseen heart and each pulse was a leap of joy, a graceful continual tribute to the supreme beauty of the heart.

Now in orbit around the vast topaz, the dreamer's breath was stopped by its splendour. The dream-jewel was singing. The capillaries sang; the blood within them sang; the gold crystal fabric of the gem sang. *We are on our way to the Heart. We are of the Heart. We are the Heart.*

Now, cresting the rim of the orb, a Pole came in view and the Heart could be seen at last. It was of purest blue crystal, a fadeless amaranth sapphire that filled vision and soul with sudden infinite joy. The dreamer's ecstasy was indescribable. Perhaps it could not be experienced by a human spirit except that insanity was bound to follow.

The Heart did not sing, yet it called. It bestowed blue radiance around it, entreating all life to come to it, to receive the blessing of its infinite joy and grace. Through the radiance it could be seen that each corpuscle of the blood was in itself a jewel, jostling its neighbours in its quest for the Heart's fulfilment until all became a coruscating river of worship of the sapphire godhead.

And when they neared the Heart, its azure touched their rich yellow and they shone emerald as if the very colour was fulfilment made visible.

And did any ever enter the Heart? No; all their joy was in

yearning, for surely to enter that perfect eternal crystal would destroy them. And their stasis, their eternal, pulsing worship, was a paean to infinity. In the eyes of the dreamer it was supreme perfection.

And the dreamer held that jewel in her hand. Through long meditation and certain drugs, she achieved at last her ambition: mental commune with the Serpent. Within her mind she stood before it, stretching her arms wide in jubilation as she spoke.

'Behold, M'gulfn, your servant. Tell me what you want me to do!'

Bring me the eye, the Serpent replied. Its voice startled her; it was thunderous, tremulous, yearning, confused. Almost human. *I must have my eye. This way only can the dream be achieved.*

'Then it shall be done!' she exclaimed, her purpose becoming a fanatical, religious ecstasy. 'Only wait for me, M'gulfn – I am on my way, and the dream shall be fulfilled.'

There was a knock at the door of Setrel's cottage. He answered and stared with shock at the tall woman on the threshold.

'Good grief!' he exclaimed, recognising her at once from the description given him.

'I've come for the boy, Skord,' she said.

'You most certainly have not!' Setrel stated, his whole frame tensing with protective anger. He began to shut the door against her. 'Get you gone from here! I know who you are, and there is no question—'

As if she was not even listening, the woman pushed Setrel aside with such force that he was slammed to the floor, cracking his skull. He saw her step into the room and he saw Skord in another doorway, staring at her . . . Then he lost consciousness.

The boy stood transfixed at the sight of the woman of extraordinary beauty with a cascade of aquamarine hair. In one breath he was back in the phantasm of ecstasy and terror that he thought he had woken from for good. He began to tremble; colour came to his cheeks and his mouth half-opened. A distant part of him saw Setrel lying injured and knew he should go to his aid. But it did not seem to matter. Revulsion and loathing flooded him and he raised his arms as if to ward off the spectre of Arlenmia.

'I've come to take you with me, Skord,' she said, smiling, her voice as warm and reassuring as a mother's.

'No,' he protested weakly. 'I'm staying here . . .'

'I have made mistakes in the past; I have been blind,' she continued. 'But that is over now. I hope you can forgive me. I have seen the truth and I understand what I must do. And this is thanks in part to you, most devoted of my messengers; I want to share it with you. I need you to help me, Skord. Come, let me show you the beauty I have found. You will have your reward. Come.'

She held out a pale hand that seemed to have been exquisitely sculpted from marble. His will was no longer his own. Loathing became inextricably merged with adoration, his mind splintered by visions of gold and blue and green crystal, layer upon layer of pain and beauty. Weeping, overwhelmed, witless, he stumbled past the prostrate form of his forgotten protector and followed Arlenmia.

End of Book 1. *A Blackbird in Silver* will be continued in Book 2. *A Blackbird in Darkness*